Novels by
C. S. Friedman
available from DAW Books:

*Coming soon from DAW Books

C. S. FRIEDMAN

DREAMSEEKER

Book Two of
The Dreamwalker Chronicles

DAW BOOKS, INC.
DONALD A. WOLLHEIM, FOUNDER
375 Hudson Street, New York, NY 10014

ELIZABETH R. WOLLHEIM
SHEILA E. GILBERT
PUBLISHERS
www.dawbooks.com

First Paperback Printing, August 2016
1 2 3 4 5 6 7 8 9

DAW TRADEMARK REGISTERED
U.S. PAT. AND TM. OFF. AND FOREIGN COUNTRIES
—MARCA REGISTRADA
HECHO EN U.S.A.

PRINTED IN THE U.S.A.

FOR TANITH LEE
WHO TAUGHT US ALL HOW EXQUISITE
THE MARRIAGE OF BEAUTY AND DARKNESS
COULD BE

Acknowledgments

Thanks once more to my beta team for all their moral support and creative input: David Walddon, Zsuzsy Sanford, Carl Cipra, and Jennifer Hina. Also to Kim Dobson and Larry Friedman, whose story suggestions led to some delightfully evil plot twists. Bradley Beaulieu gave me some timely and very insightful feedback, for which I am also grateful. (His newest book is amazing, btw, and you all should read it.)

Thanks to Brandon Lovell for his help with Farsi. 'Cause undead Persian necromancers don't just name themselves.

Last, but not least—never least!—special thanks to my agent, Russ Galen, and my editor-goddess, Betsy Wollheim. Betsy's creative input was invaluable, as always; I couldn't imagine writing books without her.

PROLOGUE

VICTORIA FOREST
VIRGINIA PRIME

SEBASTIAN HAYES

Backlit by a blazing orange sunset, the floating rabbit was an eerie sight. The dappled forest shadows made the snare almost invisible, so that it looked as if the small body was levitating of its own accord, and as it swayed back and forth in the breeze it appeared more ghostly than real.

With a quick and practiced motion, the wanderer known as the Green Man freed the dead rabbit and tucked it into his game pouch. Then he reset his snare.

It was Sebastian's third catch of the night. All had been young animals, without much meat on their bones, but that was to be expected this time of year. Summer's offspring were so busy exulting in their new existence that they rarely saw the snare's fine line strung across their path. The older ones tended to be more circumspect.

With a sigh he settled the strap of the game pouch on

his shoulder, ready to return home. The pressure of the thick leather band across his chest conjured an unexpected sensory memory, from a time when the pouch at his hip had contained not freshly killed meat, but black powder cartridges arranged in neat rows. He remembered how their newsprint wrappings had tasted as he used his teeth to tear them open, spitting out bits of blackened paper as he fed explosive powder into the mouth of his musket. A ravenous beast, that weapon. Always wanting more.

Memories from another world, another time.

The hike back to his new base camp was a long one, and by the time he reached it the sunlight was nearly gone.

I should have gone to Shadowcrest with them, he thought.

Not a night passed that he didn't think about the three young people from his homeworld, or regret that he had sent them to face the Shadows alone. Yes, it had seemed the logical choice to make at the time—the only rational choice, one might argue—but that didn't make it any easier to accept. Once, long ago, he had failed to protect his own child, and she had died as a result. Now these young people had needed him, and he had abandoned them.

I was a prisoner in Shadowcrest once, he reminded himself. *There are wards all over the place that no doubt are still attuned to my presence. Had I remained with Jessica and her friends, I would have triggered those alarms. The only chance they had to sneak past the Shadows' security was to go in without me.*

Such a thing might indeed be true. But guilt was a visceral torment, not so easily banished.

What happened to the teens from Terra Colonna after he had parted company with them? He knew that the Blue Ridge Gate had been destroyed—even the

Shadows couldn't keep something that big a secret—but his informants had been unable to bring him any specifics on the matter. Had Jessica and her friends made it back to their own world, or remained trapped in this one? Or worse yet, had they become lost in that place between the worlds that all sane men feared? He might have been trapped in that nightmare realm himself, had he tried to cross over with them.

As he approached his camp the trees began to thin out, and the dirt beneath his feet gave way to patches of naked stone, windswept and lifeless. From here he could see the opening of the crevice he now called home, a deep black gash in the mountainside. The cave that he'd located halfway up one of its walls wasn't the most luxurious shelter, but these days caution trumped comfort. He didn't think the Colonnans would tell anyone about him, but the local boy they'd been travelling with was a wild card. And if Jessica and her friends were taken prisoner, their willingness to talk would cease to be a significant factor. Both the Seers and the Domitors had the means of squeezing secrets from a human mind, and if the Shadows decided to question the teens, their methods did not bear thinking about.

He had almost been at the receiving end of those methods, once.

Almost.

What was the name of the local boy who'd been travelling with them? Isaac? So pale, that one. So haunted. The edge in the boy's voice when he'd asked Sebastian about a murdered Shadowlord had been unmistakable, but what exactly was Isaac's connection to that secretive Guild? Clearly he was not a Shadow himself: no one born to that Guild would have been allowed to wander the world without supervision as he was doing. But his family might have business ties to a Shadowlord, or perhaps some sort of political alliance, that gave Isaac a vested interest in the undead. So did he seek out the Shadows after he left Sebastian, and tell them what he'd learned about the Green Man? Did he tell them that the possible murderer of a Shadowlord was hiding out in Victoria Forest, and might be located by following the trail of dead vegetation he left in his wake?

It wasn't the truth, exactly. But Sebastian doubted that would matter to the Shadowlords.

I should have killed the boy when I had the chance, he thought. But even in the midst of war he'd had no stomach for killing innocents, and the boy had done nothing to harm him. Not to mention Isaac had helped the three Colonnans escape from the Warrens, so that Sebastian could meet them. That deserved a better answer than death.

I saved his life as well as theirs, he reminded himself. *Hopefully that will earn his silence.*

There were just too many variables in play. Even for a man who thrived on mysteries, it was an uncomfortable situation. So he had broken camp after they left and moved to a place that was naturally barren, where his curse would not give him away. It was a desolate, unpleasant location, but its inherent lifelessness would mask his presence.

Maybe I should leave this forest altogether.

How long had he been here, anyway? Ten years? More? True, Victoria Forest was only a base of operations—his endless search for information kept him constantly on the move—but there was danger in remaining anywhere too long. Maybe it was time to move on.

Suddenly he saw something on the ground ahead of him, a mark imprinted in a narrow strip of soil. The fading sunlight made it hard to see, so he had to squat down low to be able to make out its details.

A paw print. Wolf sign.

Larger than any natural paw print should be.

He drew out his knife and quickly rose to his feet—but it was already too late. Something massive burst from the forest with unnatural speed and barreled into him from behind, sending him crashing to the ground. Only by thrusting both hands out in front of him could he keep from smashing his head into bare rock, but in doing that he lost hold of his knife. Now he had only his hands, his wits, and a thick leather coat to protect him from the beast's assault.

He could feel the great wolf's jaws closing around his neck, trying to crush his windpipe, and he barely managed to evade them; dagger-like teeth pierced the heavy collar of his coat, coming within a hair's breadth of tearing out a chunk of his neck. The beast jerked back with a growl of rage, ready to try again. But this time Sebastian was ready. He twisted around and elbowed it on the side of its head, hard enough to stun it for a second, then managed to reach out and grab his knife: long and sharp and tempered in the blood of bears and mountain lions and men, it had never failed him.

Now they both were armed.

The wolf lunged for his throat again but he twisted lithely out of its way, and all it got this time was a mouthful of coat lapel. It jerked its head back and forth wildly, tearing at the garment as if it was raw flesh. Sebastian's fettered brooches broke loose and flew in every direction while he thrust at the creature, aiming for its gut, but the wolf's wild movements skewed his aim, and he sliced into its shoulder instead. As the beast's hot blood splattered everywhere Sebastian yanked his blade free, bracing himself for the next attack.

Then he looked into the wolf's eyes, sensed the cold human intelligence behind them, and he knew that this was more than a simple attack.

He stabbed at the animal again, but instead of renewing its attack the wolf backed away, leaving Sebastian's blade to slice through empty air. He had misjudged the thing: it didn't want to kill him, only force him to the ground and scatter his protective fetters beyond reach. Dark figures rushed in from all sides—four? six? eight?—and though they were human in shape they were bestial in their ferocity. Sebastian struggled to get to his feet before they had a chance to engage him, but there was no time. No time. The fetters that might have helped him escape glittered on the ground surrounding them, reflecting the last of the sunlight in tiny points of fire. Even the nearest ones were hopelessly out of reach.

The ambush had been well planned.

Ingrained reflexes took over as the shadowy figures fell upon him. He moved automatically, channeling combat instinct from his soldiering days, kicking out sideways to sweep the legs of the first man out from under him. Then another assailant moved in and Sebastian rolled deftly away from him, grabbing the arm of a third who was swinging a weapon at his head. He used that man's own momentum to yank him off his feet and send him sprawling to the ground. He tried to send him straight into one of the other attackers, but he wasn't as agile as he had been in his youth—nor as strong—and the maneuver fell short. Then some kind of impact weapon struck him from behind, between his shoulder blades, and for a moment the whole world was awash in crimson. Half blinded from pain, he kicked out wildly in the direction the blow had come from, hoping to drive his attacker back just long enough for him to recover his bearings.

But there were just too many of them, and now that they had him surrounded even a soldier in his prime would have been hard pressed to prevail against such numbers. And he was not that, by a long shot. Usually he had fetters to bolster his strength or sharpen his reflexes, but they were out of reach, and though he fought with the ferocity of a cornered animal, he knew that a single hunting knife was not enough to save him.

He was going to die tonight. After so many years of tempting fate, of walking a tightrope between treacherous patrons and powerful enemies, his time had finally come. A terrible sadness filled his heart, but also determination. Very well. If these were the men who would remove the Green Man from Terra Prime, he'd give them scars to remember him by. Maybe even take one or two of them out before he died.

But then something struck him on the side of the head with numbing force, and the world began to spin wildly about him. Vomit surged into his throat and he swallowed it back with effort, knowing that surrendering to sickness meant surrendering to death. And he wasn't ready to die yet.

Blackness was closing in from the corners of his vision, and a terrible keening sound filled his ears, drowning out the ruckus of combat. He shook his head to clear it, and instantly regretted the move. Spears of pain shot through his skull. The world was growing darker each second.

Drawing in one final breath, he braced himself for the death blow that was sure to come.

But then hands grabbed him by the upper arms and hauled him to his feet. Someone jerked his knife from his hand, and he was helpless to stop them. Spears of agony lanced through his shoulders as his arms were pulled roughly behind his back, but the pain was a strangely distant thing, as if it belonged to someone else. His wrists were being bound behind his back. A stranger's wrists.

These men hadn't come to kill him. Whoever had sent them here wanted the Green Man taken alive.

It was his last thought as darkness claimed him.

||||||||||||||

Light. Too much light. It made his eyes hurt.

But pain was good. Pain meant that he was still alive.

He squinted, trying to bring the world into focus. His head throbbed, as did his neck, his chest, and every other part of his body. But it wasn't the kind of sharp pain one would expect from shattered bones and torn flesh. That pain was gone; this was only its memory.

Someone must have healed him.

Slowly his surroundings came into focus. He was in a small room, dimly lit by a single glow lamp; once his eyes adjusted he found it a comfortable illumination. He was lying on some kind of bed or couch, and there were two people standing over him, armed men dressed in uniforms he didn't recognize. Had they been among those who attacked him in the woods? He tried to move, and discovered to his relief that he wasn't bound. As he sat up, the guards made no effort to restrain him.

He discovered he'd been lying on an opulent couch, deep crimson velvet with coordinated brocade pillows. The room looked like some kind of study, with bookcases and a desk of dark wood, polished to a glassy shine. He was hardly ungrateful to find himself in such benign surroundings, but where in God's name was he? Who would assault him in the woods like that, then heal him and bring him here? It made no sense.

A door at the far end of the room suddenly opened. The woman who entered was dressed entirely in white; in the dim room she seemed to give off a light of her own.

"Leave us," she said to the soldiers.

They seemed surprised by the command, and one began to protest, "But your Ladyship—"

"*Leave us.*"

Her tone allowed for no argument. They bowed in unison and left without a word.

The woman in white looked at Sebastian. "Do you know who I am?"

He could guess her identity from descriptions he'd heard, though he'd never seen her in person. "Lady Alia Morgana, Guildmistress of Seers." It was rumored she was more than that—much more—but even hinting at such knowledge was likely to get him killed. There were secrets he was sure she would kill to protect.

She nodded. "And you are Sebastian Hayes, who served as a private in the Ninth Virginia Regiment during the Colonial Insurrection." A cold, dry smile curled her lips. "Do I have it right?"

He couldn't remember a time when he'd shared that much of his background with anyone. The Shadows knew, of course, as they knew every other detail of his history. But Sebastian understood enough about how the Guilds functioned to know that any cooperation between the Shadows and the Seers was strictly superficial; at best they were fierce rivals to one another, and at worst, something much darker. He couldn't think of any reason why the Shadows would share his personal information with Morgana.

Which meant she'd discovered it on her own.

Impressive.

"We called it the War of Independence, but otherwise you have it right." America had never won its independence in this world.

"Do you know why you're here, Private Hayes?"

"I presume you ordered your men to bring me in."

Her pale eyes glittered. They were mostly grey, he noted, the color of fog, smoky crystal, the sky before a storm. Subtle blues and greens played in their depths as she moved. "Ah, but those were not my men who attacked you."

"Whose, then?"

"Think, Private Hayes. Whose authority have you

repeatedly defied? Who might have reason to suspect that you played a part in the death of one of their leaders?"

There was no safe way to respond to that, so he said nothing.

"Apparently the Shadows heard rumor that you assassinated one of their own. It's easier for them to interrogate a bound spirit than a living man, so no doubt that's what Lord Virilian intended. However, you're of more use to *me* alive than dead—for now—so I'm forced to disappoint him." She paused "You understand, it's no small thing for me to frustrate the plans of such a powerful man. I would expect my efforts to be ... appreciated."

For a moment Sebastian said nothing. She was asking him to serve as her agent. And perhaps much more. He'd heard whispers about a secret consortium that sought to gain through conspiracy the kind of power that could not be obtained otherwise. Morgana was rumored to be a member of it. Which meant that if he became indebted to her, he would effectively become a pawn of that group.

Their agenda was unknown. For all his sources, he had been unable to verify their membership.

"Or I could just deliver you to Lord Virilian," she said affably. "I'm sure he would be generous in his gratitude, after I stepped in to capture you when his own men failed."

I have no choice, he thought. Some debts could not be denied. "I owe you my life," he said quietly.

"Excellent!" The pale eyes glittered; something in their depths made him shudder. "Then we do understand each other. I'm sure we're going to have a most productive relationship."

She withdrew a handful of items from a pocket of her silk slacks and held them out to him. He hesitated, then put his own hand out beneath hers, palm open. Slowly she dropped his fetters into his hand, one by one. All except the last. She held that one up to the light, so she could see it better.

"Fetters from the Guild of Obfuscates are very rare," she mused. "It's almost unheard of for a Grey to share his Gift with an outsider." She looked at him. "You must have done something quite remarkable to earn this one."

He shrugged stiffly. The motion hurt. "Simply a trade of information, your Grace. In this case regarding an assassination plot against a high ranking Master of the Greys. He was grateful for my warning."

He continued to hold his hand out. After a moment she dropped the last fetter into it. "I have sufficient influence to turn the Shadow's attention away from you," she said. "For now."

"I would be most grateful if you did that."

"You would be well advised to keep a low profile for a while."

"I understand."

His heart skipped a beat. *Low profile* suggested he would not be kept a prisoner here, that he would be allowed to go about his own business again. At least until she needed him. His hand closed around the Grey fetter. All he needed was a moment when she wasn't looking directly at him and he could use it to escape from this place.

He nodded. "I believe I can manage that."

"Good. I may have a task for you soon. In the meantime, I trust that if you come across any information that would be of interest to me . . ."

He bowed his head ever so slightly. "It would be my honor to share it with you."

"Excellent. Rest here for as long as you like, then. My people will bring you whatever refreshment you require, and will see you out when you're ready to leave."

"Thank you, Your Grace."

She walked toward the door, the fine white silk of her garments rippling like water. But at the threshold she paused, then turned back to look at him. "Did you really kill Guildmaster Durand?"

The words were more than a question, he knew. They were a test of his commitment, and perhaps of his value. He chose his own words carefully. "Durand was killed by a rival Shadow, who slit his throat with a sacrificial knife. There were so many death-impressions on the blade already that no one could draw forth from it any useful information. Hence the killer remained undetected. Rather clever, actually." He paused. "Of course, I have no idea what sort of information Durand's rival might have come across, that convinced him such drastic action was necessary."

For a long moment she just looked at him. One corner of her mouth twitched slightly; he could not tell whether it indicated disapproval or amusement. Perhaps both.

Without further word, she left him to his thoughts.

1

BERKELEY SPRINGS
WEST VIRGINIA

JESSE

THE BLACK PLAIN feels unsteady tonight.
Normally I have better control over my dreams than this. Normally I can force the energy under my feet to take whatever shape I want it to. It's only an illusion, after all. The space that lies between the worlds is a realm of utter chaos, with no real physical substance; it's hardly the sort of thing one can walk on. But in my dreams I can make it take whatever form I want. If I want the primal chaos that separates the worlds to look like a sheet of black glass, a field of obsidian gravel, or even a dusty linoleum floor, that's my choice.

It's always black, though. I've tried a thousand times to give it color, but I can't.

Tonight the dreamscape seems unsteady. Energy shivers beneath my bare feet as I walk, squelching up between my toes like mud on a beach. Is there some special meaning to that? Should I worry about it? Or is the dreamscape just harder to control some nights than others? I look behind me and see my path marked in thin lines of golden fire on the plain, as always. And as always, I take a moment to memorize its pattern, in case I need that information in the future.

I'm only now beginning to learn the rules of the place. And of my own abilities.

The doors scattered across the black plain look like cavern entrances tonight. Not naturally shaped caverns, but gaping, surreal mouths with crystal teeth jutting inward, like something out of a grade B horror movie. Waiting to swallow me whole. That's what the Gate in Mystic Caverns looked like, before we destroyed it. Now it's what all my dream doors look like, every night. Apparently that image has been burned into my brain, and no conscious effort can banish it.

But tonight the openings seem different, somehow. I can't put my finger on how, but it makes me uneasy.

I pass the nearest doors without looking inside. I already know what's behind them. Each archway allows me to gaze into a parallel world, and the closest ones will be similar to my own. Maybe a universe where my brother got an A in History instead of a C-, or Mom decorated the living room a little differently, or *Star Wars* bombed on opening night. Little changes. Such worlds have nothing to teach me, and peering into them, I have learned, is a waste of time.

I still don't know if those worlds are real or not. Oh, parallel worlds do exist—I've still got a nasty scar across my belly from the last one I visited—but whether my dreams give me access to the real thing or just show me the kinds of worlds that might exist, is something I haven't figured out yet.

As I walk along the black plain, crystal maws gaping on all sides of me, I suddenly feel a chill. Something is wrong, very wrong. I sense the wrongness without know-ing its cause, and I feel the sudden urge to run.

But no. The world of the black plain is mine, I tell myself. My dream, under my control. Nothing can hurt me here, because nothing can exist here without my consent. So I have no need to flee.

That calms me a bit, and I start to look around, seek-ing the source of my unease. When I find it at last, the shock is so great that for a moment I can hardly think, much less absorb what I'm seeing.

She's standing maybe ten yards away from me, a slen-der young girl with wind-mussed hair and enormous eyes. Or maybe it's a boy; the lean body offers no clear sign of gender. Complex geometric patterns flow across her body, sketched in golden light, and they change when I try to look directly at them. It's as if my brain can't decide exactly what the patterns are supposed to be, so it keeps trying different ones.

A stranger. In my dream!

I can sense the otherness in her, and I know instinc-tively that she senses it in me. This isn't just some image my mind has created, but an alien presence invading the landscape of my sleeping mind. An intruder, where no intruder should be.

I open my mouth to speak, but words never have a chance to get out.

She turns.

She runs.

I hesitate for a moment, then begin to run after her. But her legs are longer than mine, and she seems to know the twists and turns of the dreamscape better than I do; I'm hard pressed not to lose her. Several times she makes a sharp turn to pass behind one of the crystal arches, and I have to slow down to keep from impaling myself.

What will I do if I catch her? Block her path? Tackle her to the ground?

"Hey!" I call out. "Stop! I just want to talk to you!"

She glances back at me for a second but doesn't stop running. Now we're approaching a place where the spiked arches are clustered together so tightly that it's hard to make out any space between them, but she's not slowing down at all. I can't see how she's going to make it through that tight maze, so I brace myself for whatever evasive maneuver she's about to come up with. But instead of avoiding the arches, she heads straight toward one of them. Then into it.

And she's gone, swallowed by the darkness of another world.

I skid to a stop in front of that arch, and for a moment I just stand there, struggling to absorb what I've just seen. I've been dreaming about these doors for years—though I didn't understand what they represented until recently—but never, ever, have I been able to pass through one of them. Yet beyond this arch I can see the misty shadows of another world, and I know that the girl I've been chasing is out there now, somewhere on the other side of the gate.

Holy crap.

Slowly, warily, I reach out a hand, trying to extend it through the arch. Always before, such efforts have failed.

It fails this time as well.

Standing in the middle of the black plain, I experience a kind of fear I never felt before. This dreamscape is my territory. MINE. How can someone else enter it? Why would this invader be able to enter a doorway that was conjured by my dreaming mind, while I, its creator, am stuck at the threshold?

It matters. I know that instinctively. This is more than just a dream.

But I don't have a clue how to make sense of it.

||||||||||||

When I first woke up, it took me a moment to remember where I was. The ceiling overhead was unfamiliar, with thick crown molding where none should have been, and an antique lamp of painted glass hanging from its center, now dark. The furniture was weathered pine with dark brass fittings, wholly unfamiliar. The cotton quilt I had thrown off while tossing and turning was country calico, not something I would ever have chosen for myself.

Then I remembered.

I shut my eyes for a moment, trying to come to terms with the recent changes in my life. Mom, Tommy, and I were living in Berkeley Springs now, in the home of Rose and Julian Bergen, distant relatives who we'd been told to call Aunt and Uncle. They'd generously taken Mom in after our house had burned down, and when Tommy and I returned to this world we'd joined her there. Their house was a rambling, century-old creation with period gingerbread details adorning its wrap-around porch, and plenty of guest rooms for visitors. It was packed to the brim with antiques, and original works by local artists hung on every wall. A museum curator would have been envious. Normally it was the kind of house I would have enjoyed visiting, and I could have spent many days exploring its nooks and crannies, but given the circumstances that had brought us here, it was hard to take pleasure in anything.

I reached out to the nightstand and took up the sketchpad I kept next to it. I knew from experience that I had to record my dream as soon as I woke up or the details would fade from mind. Each time I returned from the black plain I recorded the path I had walked through the dreamscape, along with notes about any doors I had opened. Their patterns reminded me of the glowing lines that had appeared inside the Shadows' Gate just before we crossed through it, as well as the codex that I'd activated later to get us home. They were all maps, I understood now, only they charted metaphysical currents instead of roads. Maybe if I studied enough of them I could learn how to read them—or even design them—and then I could—

Do what? Travel between the worlds again?

The mere thought of it made me shiver.

"Jesse!" Aunt Rose's voice resounded up the staircase and through my bedroom door. "Breakfast!"

I glanced at the window. There was light seeping in around the edges of the heavy shade. I'd slept longer than usual.

"Jesse?"

"I hear you!" I yelled. "I'll be right down."

I tried to do a quick sketch of the girl (boy?) I had seen in my dream, but my drawing came out looking like a cartoon. Try as I might to capture the patterns that had flowed across her body, they were already fading from memory, angles and lines slithering from my mental grasp before I could commit them to paper.

Start without me, I wanted to yell down to her, but I knew that she would never do that. Food was more than physical nourishment to Aunt Rose, it was a vehicle of emotional bonding. Which meant that family meals had existential significance, and she wouldn't start this one until all of us were present.

With a sigh I finally closed the sketchbook, slipped on a robe, and turned the lamp off. Then, with the pad tucked under my arm, I headed downstairs to join my family.

〰〰〰〰〰

Coming home.

It should feel good, shouldn't it? Especially after spending time in a parallel universe as terrifying as the one called Terra Prime, being hunted by shapechangers and angry undead. Home was familiar. Home was safe.

Home was the one place where you could relax and be yourself.

That was the theory, anyway.

But the home that I'd known all my life was gone. The house I'd grown up in was ash. A lifetime of art-work, into which I'd poured my very soul, ash. My jour-nal, my computer, my schoolbooks, my jewelry, the dolls that I'd kept since childhood because they brought back special memories ... all of it gone forever. You didn't appreciate how much those things kept you grounded until you lost them all.

Tommy was still around, and in some ways we were closer than ever, but he wasn't the same kid he'd been before. We both slept with kitchen knives under our pil-lows now, and I knew he wouldn't hesitate to use his if he had to. Granted, some of the nasty things that might come calling were not flesh and blood, but at least we'd be prepared to face those that were.

He told me that late at night he sometimes heard voices. As if people were whispering by his bedside, too softly for him to make out the words. He said they sounded like the ghosts in Shadowcrest, so these were probably ghosts as well. But were they local spirits, drawn to the strange boy who could sense their pres-ence, or something more ominous? Shadowlord spies, perhaps. Spirits of the dead who had followed Tommy home from his prison cell in Shadowcrest.

Neither of us sleep much these days.

As for Mom, she was alive, but her spirit was sorely wounded. The night our house burned down she'd man-aged to escape the flames, but not before inhaling more smoke than human lungs were meant to contain. She'd stopped breathing altogether on the way to the hospital (the EMTs told us later) and though they managed to bring her back to life, apparently something in her brain had gotten damaged in the process.

Don't be discouraged, the doctors told us. *She may get better over time.* But it was clear from the way they talked to us that they didn't really believe that.

Some days weren't too bad. Some days she seemed almost normal. Other days she might not remember who we were staying with, or the names of her own children. It was heartbreaking to witness, and I couldn't help but feel that I was responsible. I was the one with the forbidden Gift, who had drawn the Shadows' attention to us. I was the one whose dreams had caused the Greys to kidnap my brother, thinking he might be a Dreamwalker, and burn our house to hide the evidence of their visit. If I'd just been a normal kid, with normal dreams, none of this ever would have happened.

And then there was Rita. I still didn't know if my former traveling companion was dead, or a prisoner on Terra Prime, or trapped between the worlds. If not for me, she would still be safe at home.

Breakfast that morning was pretty stressful. Not because the food was bad. Aunt Rose made killer french toast, and the mere sight of it made my mouth water. And not because the company was lacking. She and her husband Julian were genuinely warm people, hospitable to an extreme. They'd taken in our whole family when we were homeless, hadn't they? And they were both pleasantly quirky. Rose was an accomplished ceramics artist, and her husband . . . well, hunting wasn't my thing, but Julian had taken me out target shooting once and taught me how to clean, load, and shoot a variety of guns, which might be a useful skill someday.

No, everything about breakfast was just fine, except that my brain was still buzzing with details of my strange dream, and what I really wanted was to show Tommy my drawings and see what he thought about them. Sometimes he had insights that a person more firmly rooted in reality might not. But first the ritual of breakfast had to be satisfied, so I put my sketchbook beside my plate, and after a moment's homage to the pile of luscious french toast in the middle of the table, went to the pantry to fetch my second favorite breakfast, toaster strudel. I didn't want to risk having all that syrup around my drawings.

Of course, as soon as Rose saw the sketchpad she asked what I was working on. I said I was drawing a character for Tommy, an illustration for one of his games. Of course she asked to see it. So I opened the pad to my drawing of the dream visitor and showed her that. My brother played along, leaning over to look at my work and murmuring, "Yeah. Yeah. That's it!" I could sense how curious he was, but he didn't ask me any questions.

We'd become well practiced at hiding the truth from family.

Then Rose reminded me about her booth at a local art gallery, and how I really should display some of my work there. We had that conversation pretty much every morning. Berkeley Springs was a haven for local artists, and there was a converted mill on the outskirts of town where people could rent booths and sell their work. Rose had a table for her pottery, and she kept trying to convince me to display some of my drawings there. She seemed to think it would help with my emotional healing, though she never said that directly. Truth was, under normal circumstances I would have jumped at the chance to display my artwork in a real gallery setting. But all my pieces had burned in the house fire, so I had nothing to display. Unfazed, Rose pointed out (again) that I could always paint something new, and she offered (again) to buy me any supplies I needed.

Art heals, right?

Finally breakfast wound down and it was possible to take my leave of the family. As I left the room I heard

Tommy follow suit. He walked behind me in silence through the house, holding back any questions he had until we could find a place to talk privately.

As we passed by the front parlor I saw Uncle Julian's gun cabinet, which had been adapted from a 1930s wardrobe. It now had shatterproof glass in the front and a modern lock on the bottom drawer. He'd told me it was a compromise between his desire to have a gun rack on the wall and his wife's demand that weapons be stored under lock and key. Of course he explained to me during my shooting lesson that you would never fire a rifle in the house, for fear of the bullet going through a wall and killing someone in the next room. I didn't bother to argue that if the servants of the undead came for you in the middle of the night, you might deem it worth the risk. I just studied the cabinet when he wasn't around, noted that the back of it wasn't as solidly constructed as the front, and stashed a crowbar behind the cushions of a nearby couch, just in case.

Past the parlor was the front door. As we left the house I looked around the porch to make sure that no one else was outside, then sat down in one of several squeaky metal chairs and handed Tommy the sketch pad. He settled onto a nearby wooden bench and whistled softly under his breath as he flipped through my latest drawings. He stopped when he got to my picture of the girl. "This is from a dream?"

"Someone I saw in a dream. I think she came from outside it."

He looked up at me, eyes wide. "No shit?"

I nodded solemnly. "No shit."

I told him the whole story. I tried not to sound too anxious, but once I started putting the experience into words, I realized just how truly bizarre—and threatening—the situation really was.

Tommy looked over my drawings while I talked, and

when I was done he turned back to my portrait of the intruder. "This looks like anime."

Startled, I realized that he was right. I wasn't a big fan of Japanese animation, but Tommy was, and I'd caught sight of enough brief snatches while he was watching to recognize the general artistic style. And yes, the over-sized eyes, wildly spiked hair, and other subtle details of disproportion did indeed suggest that genre. Did that mean my dream invader was some kind of Japanese cartoon character? From a style of media I didn't even watch? What kind of sense did that make?

"Could be an avatar," Tommy mused.

"An avatar?"

"You know. Like in a computer game. It's an image that you use to represent yourself in a fantasy universe."

"I know what an avatar is," I said sharply. "What makes you think this is one?"

He shrugged. "Young androgynous figure with strange magical effects floating around it . . . pretty common design elements, really. The anime crowd loves that kind of thing."

I was silent for a moment, trying to wrap my brain around this new concept. "So . . . you think the avatar's owner wasn't really in my dream? He or she was just projecting a fantasy image into it?"

"*You* weren't in your dream either," he reminded me. "It's like when you play a computer game. You create a fictional identity that allows you to interact with it, and its image is visible, walking around inside the game universe like a real person, but you're not really *there* in any physical sense." He paused. "Maybe someone did the same kind of thing with your dream. Treating your brain like a multi-player platform."

"If that was the case, wouldn't I have had complete control over the programming?"

"You'd think," he agreed.

But what if I was just imagining the whole thing? Dreamwalkers were supposed to go insane over time. Maybe an early symptom was that you thought strangers were invading your dreams.

It was an unnerving concept.

Just then my phone vibrated. Pulling it out of my pocket, I saw that I had a text message from Devon. I continued talking as I went to read it. "If so, then the next question is—"

I stopped. And stared at the phone. I could feel all the color drain from my face.

"Jesse?" Tommy was immediately on high alert. "What is it?"

Slowly I turned the phone so he could see it. The message was only two words, but as he read it I saw his eyes go wide in astonishment.

"Holy crap," he muttered.

Rita's back, it said.

2

SHADOWCREST
VIRGINIA PRIME

ISAAC

THE ELEVATOR'S CAGE carried Isaac smoothly down into the earth, its lamp revealing rough-hewn rock walls pressing in on every side. Two years ago Isaac might have found the closeness unsettling, but compared to the dank, lightless tunnels of the Warrens, he now found it downright inviting.

Besides, he had bigger things to worry about.

He practiced breathing steadily as the elevator passed through level after level of Shadowcrest's underground complex, offering fleeting glimpses of the floors where the Guild's most secretive business took place. He tried not to fidget. Real Shadows didn't fidget. They didn't shift their weight nervously from foot to foot, or pace from one side of the steel cage to the other, working off their nervous energy. They certainly didn't crush a letter from their father in sweaty hands until it looked more like a crumpled wad of toilet paper than a meaningful communication.

Swallowing dryly, Isaac unwadded the short note and read it one last time. It offered no more insight into his father's intentions than the last ten readings.

Well of Souls
Midnight
Lord Leonid Antonin, Umbra Maja

He hadn't even known that his father was back in Virginia Prime until that note arrived. The elder Antonin had been attending to business in another sphere for the last few weeks—some kind of probability survey in the Sauran Cluster—and Isaac had been stuck in limbo, waiting for his judgment. Oh, his mother had welcomed him home right away, and had championed his cause among the other Antonin elders, encouraging them to accept him back into the fold despite the fact that he'd run away for two years. But she was still alive, an *umbra mina,* so her influence among the Shadows was limited. Not until his father returned would Isaac's fate be decided.

And now there was this note. With no explanation.

Isaac had no clue what to expect from his father. The days when human affection might have impacted the Shadowlord's actions were long past, and whatever undead emotions coursed through his heart now were shadowy and mysterious things, beyond the understanding of a mere teenager. Leonid Antonin had accepted First Communion—the transformative Shadow ritual—soon after Isaac's birth, so his son had no memory of him that didn't involve moaning soul shards and eerie whispers from other worlds. Not exactly the kind of father it was easy to bond with.

And then of course there were all the other souls that

gazed out at him from his father's eyes. One never got used to that.

With a sigh Isaac shoved the crumpled note back into his pocket and wiped his sweaty palms on his jeans to dry them. At least he was alone in the elevator. Displaying this much agitation in front of an *umbrá maja* would have reflected poorly on his entire family and probably doomed any chance of earning his father's approval. Assuming that was still possible.

The Well of Souls was a level of Shadowcrest that apprentices usually didn't enter, so Isaac had no clue why his father wanted to meet him there. It was where the darkest and most secretive rituals of the Guild were performed and, normally neophytes were not privy to such things. If he'd been just a little more paranoid, or a little more ignorant, he might have feared that his father intended to force him to submit to First Communion. But any schoolchild knew that one had to submit willingly to the transformation for there to be any hope of success.

Isaac drew in a deep breath as the elevator finally slowed and stopped; a section of steel grate moved aside to reveal a large, dimly lit chamber. As he stepped out, he saw that everything in the place was black. Black floor, black walls, black pillars supporting a black vaulted ceiling. The only hints of color were polished gold sconces affixed to the pillars, with tiny glow lamps inside, though what little light they exuded was sucked in and devoured as soon as it hit one of those merciless black surfaces. In such little light Isaac could neither see any details of the chamber, nor even be sure how large it was.

There were spirits present, of course, whispering indecipherable secrets into the darkness. Any place the Shadowlords frequented drew the dead to it like flies to rotting meat. Many of the spirits here were probably just soul shards, fragments of identity incapable of independent thought or motive, but there might be a few bound souls as well, serving as guardians of this place. Isaac had heard rumors about the ritual used to create such servants, and even by the dark standards of his Guild they sounded unusually gruesome.

Then the tenor of the whispering changed. New voices were approaching, whose cadences were familiar to Isaac; these were the spirits that were bound to serve his father. Drawing in a deep breath for courage, he turned to face their master.

Leonid Antonin was a tall man, stoic and dignified, and the long formal robes of an *umbra maja* fell from his shoulders in crisp, precise folds. He seemed more solid than most of his kind, with only the outermost edges of his form fading out into darkness, but for some reason that made his presence even more disturbing. Black, hollow eyes fixed on Isaac, cold and dispassionate; it was impossible to meet that gaze without shivering.

This is what they want me to become, Isaac thought, suddenly remembering why he'd run away from home in the first place. "Father," he said, bowing his head respectfully.

For a moment his father studied him in silence. Isaac dared not meet his eyes, for fear of the condemnation he might find there.

"Come," the Shadowlord commanded at last. He turned away and began to walk. Isaac followed, jogging slightly to keep up with his father's longer stride. Across the chamber and through a narrow archway they went, moving quickly, into a long corridor dressed entirely in black marble. Glow lamps in the ceiling sparked to life as they approached, illuminating white veins in the polished stone; the lamps extinguished after they passed, creating the illusion of an island of light that moved down the hallway with them. Isaac caught sight of doors marked with mysterious symbols to either side, but his father was leading him forward too quickly for him to get a good look at anything. One door was open, and there was just enough light for him to make out the shape of a vaulted chamber beyond it, with some kind of large table in the center. He thought he saw shackles lying on top of it.

He shuddered.

At the end of the long hallway they came to a pair of ornately carved doors, twice as high as a man. They reminded Isaac of the ones at the entrance to Lord Virilian's audience chamber, but these were grander in scale, and the carvings were much more complex. Images of men, beasts, skeletons, and demons had been rendered with such depth of detail that they seemed about to burst from the door's black lacquered surface. Subtle gilt highlights only increased the illusion. The artwork was beautiful but morbid, and Isaac could feel his skin crawl as he studied it.

"Images from the Lost Worlds," his father said. "Meant to remind us of the burden of responsibility that we bear, in our duty as Shadows."

The Lost Worlds. Those were human civilizations that had been destroyed by the coming of the Shadows. Some had been unable to handle the sudden influx of alien germs and parasites that outworlders brought with them, some had been raided so often by slave traders that their gene pool fell below the threshold required for species survival, and some simply could not face the revelation that they were no longer masters of their own fate, and died a slow spiritual death.

And then there were those rare worlds that needed to be Cleansed, because the Shadows decided they were a threat to interworld commerce. That might mean destroying the underpinnings of local technology, so that society collapsed into barbarism, or taking actions more directly destructive.

Now Isaac understood why the doors here were black. Why this whole place was black. The path to a Shadow's duty was paved in death: this was their reminder of it.

He watched as his father took hold of the ornate lever that served as a door handle and turned it to the right. Nothing happened. Then a prickling at the back of Isaac's neck alerted him to the approach of a new spirit, whose presence was far more powerful than that of the others. He could sense it approaching the door, perhaps touching it—and then the lock snicked open.

Of course, he thought. Since no one but an *umbra maja* could command spirits, any lock that required the touch of both the living and the dead would be impassable to other Guild members. It was a simple but effective security.

"Come," his father repeated as the great doors swung open—seemingly of their own accord—and Isaac followed him into a vast, shadowy chamber with tiny golden lights hanging in mid-air as far as the eye could see. Like stars in a night sky. As his eyes adjusted he could see that each light was in fact set atop a marble pedestal, and that there were walkways running around the chamber at several heights, each with its own row of pedestals, evenly spaced.

His father gestured toward one of the nearest pedestals, indicating he should approach it.

There was just enough light for Isaac to make out the shape of a golden sphere with symbols inscribed in it, protected by a glass dome. He recognized the mark of the Weavers on the glass; there were others he didn't recognize.

"We call these soul fetters," his father said, coming up behind him, "but they're not really that, you understand. Simply recording devices that store the memories of former Guild members."

Suddenly Isaac realized what he was looking at, and a wave of nausea came over him, fear so thick in his throat he could hardly breathe. This *thing* was the source of Communion, the mechanism used to pour the soul of one Shadow into another. He had to fight the urge not to back away from it, and though he managed to keep his expression calm, his heart was beating so wildly it made his chest shake. Had he been wrong about his father's intentions? Had the Shadowlord discovered a way to initiate an unwilling candidate into the ranks of the undead? Why else would he have brought Isaac down here?

But his father made no move toward him, and after a few seconds Isaac found himself able to breathe again. Turning his attention to the pedestal itself, he saw a column of small brass memorial plaques with names and dates on them. Three dates each. There was also a narrow shelf with a thick leather-bound journal on it, and as his father reached out to remove the book, his arm brushed against his son's, sucking all the heat from his flesh. Isaac tried not to flinch.

"The names on the plaques are those who contributed their memories to this particular fetter," the Shadowlord explained. "Some of the earliest date all the way back to the Dream Wars. Most are more recent. Communion didn't become common practice until centuries after that." He placed the book on the pedestal in front of Isaac and opened it. "These are the histories contained in this fetter."

Isaac looked up at him. "I thought Communion only transferred a single set of memories."

"In a technical sense, yes. But each man's input includes the memory of his own Communion. So when you accept the memories of one Shadowlord, you inherit echoes of all the others."

Good God, Isaac thought. That meant that a Shadow

who accepted Communion one time would absorb the memories of what, dozens of other men, hundreds? How could anyone maintain his sense of identity in the face of all that?

Not everyone succeeds, he reminded himself. Though it had been a long time since any Antonin had been driven insane by First Communion, the lesser bloodlines lost people regularly. Initiation into the ranks of the *umbra maja* was a high-risk enterprise, and only the strongest survived. "It sounds . . . chaotic."

"The memories of a Shadowlord fade in clarity over the centuries. A few generations down the line, only the most intense fragments remain," his father said. "But, yes." A faint, cold smile was briefly visible. "The experience can be quite disconcerting."

Isaac reached out to the book and slowly turned the pages. The paper felt ancient beneath his fingertips, and the pages made a soft rustling noise as they moved. There were handwritten notes in a variety of scripts, some of them noting major historical events, others more personal details. Every few pages he saw a new name and a set of three dates: Birth, undeath, and true death.

"These are the histories of the Shadowlords whose memories are contained in this particular fetter," his father told him. "The elders try to match each candidate to an appropriate fetter. Compatible Shadows stand a much better chance of successful Communion."

Isaac looked up at him. "So . . . you get to choose whose memories you absorb?" That certainly wasn't something they'd taught him in school.

But his father shook his head. "The living don't know enough to make an informed choice. So that decision must be made for them. But our family is ancient and highly respected, and rest assured, I would allow no outsider to dictate who *my son* was to bond with."

There was pride in his words, but also admonishment;

the combination brought a lump to Isaac's throat. He looked back at the book, unwilling to meet his father's gaze.

"So," his father said softly. "Is this what you feared so desperately? Enough to compromise your family's honor by fleeing the Guild like a frightened colt?"

The words left his mouth before he could stop them. "Shouldn't I be afraid?"

For a moment there was silence. Then: "Yes. This is a place worthy of fear."

Isaac hesitated. Normally he would never ask his father a personal question, but this was hardly a normal moment. The Shadowlord clearly wanted Isaac to understand how Communion worked; wasn't the man's own experience part of that picture?

"Were you afraid?" he asked. "When they handed you your first fetter, when you had to open your mind to the memories of so many Shadowlords? Didn't that frighten you?"

"I was terrified," his father admitted. "And any Shadowlord who claims that he wasn't, is lying. But I understood that my family's honor was at stake, which was far more important to me than my own fleeting pleasure."

Isaac said nothing.

"There is beauty in the change," his father told him. The ghosts around him had grown strangely quiet; perhaps they, too, were listening. "The pleasures of the living world are but pale shadows of it. To step beyond the boundaries of one's birth world and plunge into the chaos that lies *between,* to feel one's soul resonate with the music of the spheres, to know with utter certainty that any world which can exist, does exist, and that we — and *we alone* — have the power of free passage between them . . . What earthly pursuit can rival that?"

Isaac had never heard his father talk that way before. He had never heard any Shadowlord talk that way before.

For a moment he was at a loss for words. "Aren't we supposed to not feel passion?" he stammered. "For anything? I mean, that's what they keep telling me."

His father chuckled; it was a disconcertingly human sound. "The passions of the living are forbidden to us, my son. As are the passions of the dead—though those are so bizarre that few men are tempted by them. To cling to either world too closely threatens the balance of spirit that we need to survive. But there are passions unique to our kind, more intense than anything you can imagine. There is a kind of beauty that only the *umbrae majae* can see, senses that a man gains access to only when he is willing to leave his life behind forever. And of course there are the memories—centuries of knowledge and experience that attend one's every thought." He paused. "Shadows may fear their First Communion, but none regret it afterward."

Isaac looked back at the fetter. "Is there one of these that contains your memories? Or don't they make one of those until after you die?"

"I have a soul fetter, though it's not stored here. Right now it's functioning as a recording device. Nothing more. Not until I die will my memories be available to someone else." A corner of his mouth twitched. "It would be quite confusing otherwise."

"But if all a soul fetter does is give you knowledge, how does it transform you?"

A faint smile ghosted across his father's face; he seemed pleased by the question. "It doesn't. Communion simply grants a man knowledge of how to join the ranks of the *umbra majae*. He must embrace the change on his own."

"So . . . you could undergo First Communion without becoming a Shadowlord?"

For a moment, there was silence. "No man who has gained such knowledge has ever chosen that course."

"But you *could*," Isaac persisted. "In theory, at least. Right? You could absorb all those memories, all that knowledge, and remain a living man. Couldn't you?"

His father's gaze was solemn. "In theory. But the memories you absorb come from men who chose to walk the line between life and death. Your mind would contain all the reasons they did so, the force of their commitment, their satisfaction with the results. Resisting such influence would be like swimming against a rip tide. And what would the point be? Higher knowledge is wasted on the *umbrae minae*. Only by embracing the change can one map the currents of the universe."

"What is it you want from me?" Isaac asked suddenly. "Why did you bring me here?"

If his bluntness displeased his father, the Shadowlord showed no sign of it. "I simply wish to advise you to keep your options open. If you resume your training to be an *umbra maja*, all paths will remain open to you. But if you surrender that honor, and commit to a more lowly rank instead, doors will be shut in your face. Your education will be restricted to the things that living men are allowed to learn. And your status in the Guild will be severely constrained. All for what purpose? So you can make a public show of rejecting an Antonin's duty? What will it gain you?"

Isaac said nothing. No words were safe.

"You can undergo the training of an *umbra maja* without setting a date for your First Communion. Perhaps in twenty or thirty years you will feel differently than you do now. Perhaps you will hunger to join your father in exploring unknown worlds, to bring honor to your family. There is no need to close that door forever, Isaac."

He said nothing.

"Do not shame the family name unless there is need for it," his father said quietly. There was an edge of harshness to his tone now, but delicately sheathed, like a knife in a velvet scabbard.

So that's it then, Isaac thought bitterly. *I'm free to follow another path, so long as no one finds out about it. And what if I don't play along? Will you cast me out of the family? Or is this just a test, to see how much I really want to come back?*

But he couldn't deny that his father's suggestion had appeal. As a Shadowlord in training Isaac would have access to documents and artifacts that no *umbra mina* would ever be allowed to see. He would study the true history of the Guild, taught by men who had witnessed those events. Or rather, men who had absorbed the memories of others who had witnessed them.

But he would be living a lie. Pretending to be something he was not.

For his family's sake.

Isaac observed how the edges of his father's body faded out into the darkness. He felt the unearthly chill that enveloped the man like a shroud. He heard the whispering of the dead souls who never left his father's side; invisible harpies who never fell silent. Maybe in twenty years Isaac might be willing to transform into a creature like that, but it didn't seem likely. Still, all his father was asking was for him to keep his options open. To pretend there was a chance that someday he would change his mind. Couldn't he manage that, if it was the price of acceptance?

Isaac looked back down at the book, now open to the first page. *Twice-decorated Grand Crusader in the Final War between the Shadows and the Dreamwalkers,* it said. Hell, Isaac hadn't even known there *was* a war between Shadowlords and Dreamwalkers. All he'd been told was that the Guilds had banded together to hunt the dreamers down, to save the human worlds from destruction.

This fleeting reference hinted at centuries of history he knew nothing about.

Jesse had asked about the dreaming Gift, he remembered suddenly. Had she done that because her brother was suspected of dreamwalking, or for some more personal reason? These records might hold answers for both of them.

"I see no reason to choose my path now." He formed his words carefully, trying to echo his father's formal tone. "There'll be time enough later, when I understand the situation better. I acted rashly when I fled, for which I humbly seek your forgiveness and the forgiveness of my family. I will resume my former course of study immediately, if the Guildmaster sanctions it."

A cold hand fell upon his shoulder. He tried to ignore the icy burning sensation where it touched him, to focus on the warmth that the gesture was meant to communicate. Or maybe it was just meant to be cold approval. Who knew what a Shadowlord was feeling?

"I accept your apology," his father said, "and I am sure His Grace will approve your petition." For the first time since Isaac's return there was pride in the man's voice. "Welcome back, my son."

3

BERKELEY SPRINGS
WEST VIRGINIA

JESSE

BY THE NEXT MORNING I was so brimming with nervous energy that I felt like I was about to explode. There was no way to give it safe outlet indoors, so I went outside and started pacing the length of the porch. Back and forth, back and forth . . . It helped a little, but it also left my mind free to worry. Tommy came out and sat down on one of the metal chairs to watch me. He had as much invested in this as I did, and I could tell he was equally nervous.

Devon had been disturbingly uncommunicative since Rita's return. Normally he texted me as often and as casually as most people breathed, but after his first mind-blowing announcement of her arrival he'd sent only a few sparse messages, maddeningly uninformative.

Time dilation maybe, he'd texted. *Will drive up 2morrow we can talk.*

How did u find her? I asked.

Later. Will leave here after breakfast. Promise.

After that there was only silence.

"You think he'll be here soon?" my brother asked.

"It's a two-hour trip," I pointed out. Suddenly I realized I didn't know if Devon was a morning person or not. What time did he eat breakfast? We could be waiting for a while.

Tommy asked, "You think he showed his dad the fetter?"

"I don't know," I said. It was frustrating to have no answers for him. "We'll find out when he gets here."

Devon had wanted to tell his Dad the truth about what happened to us in the other world, so I'd given him the glow lamp. The alien tech with its thought-sensitive light would at least bear witness to the fact that he wasn't making the whole story up, though what Dr. Tilford would deduce beyond that was anyone's guess. What if he decided that Devon's story was just too crazy to believe, tech or no tech? What if he became concerned about his son's mental stability, and thought that maybe my influence had caused him to start raving about shapechangers and world gates and undead necromancers? If so, he might never let me see Devon again.

I couldn't handle that. Devon and Tommy had become vital psychological anchors for me, my only two confidants in a world gone mad. Who else could I confide in, when I feared that my Gift was unhinging my mind? Mom had always served as my rock—and I hungered to tell her the truth about Terra Prime now—but I knew she wasn't strong enough to handle this stuff. She was having a difficult enough time dealing with one world, without my throwing parallel universes at her.

I needed Devon.

He's coming up here, I told myself as I paced. *Which*

means his father gave him the car. So he's okay with Devon seeing me. That's a good sign, right?

I looked at my watch for the hundredth time. The small hand hadn't moved significantly since my last check.

I'd dreamed about Rita the night before. I dreamed about her every night, guilt-drenched nightmares from which I woke up sweating and trembling. But this last dream wasn't a regular nightmare. Nor was it a symbolic dream full of mystical doors and arcane symbols, and a sense that the universe was a puzzle I must solve immediately or terrible things would happen to me. This one was simply a memory, like a movie playing out in my brain.

I witnessed our flight from Shadowcrest and our descent to the crystal Gate that controlled passage between the worlds. I relived the moment when the Greys jumped us and all hell broke loose. I felt blood splattering my face as I stabbed a Grey in the neck with a ball point pen, to free my brother. I saw how we ran back to the Gate, grabbing hold of each other as we dove into the unknown darkness between the worlds. Rita had gripped my arm so tightly that her fingernails dug into my flesh; I still had the marks. So what had gone wrong? How did we get separated? Even in my dream I couldn't identify the moment it happened. One minute she was hanging on to me for dear life, and the next minute I was immersed in the chaos between the worlds. Then Devon, Tommy and I arrived in Mystic Caverns without her. Had she lagged a split-second behind the rest of us, and been trapped in Terra Prime when the Gate collapsed? Or had she entered the archway with us, but lost her grip on me afterward, and gotten lost in that terrible place? Try as I might, I couldn't remember.

At least I knew now that she wasn't dead. That eased the burden of guilt a little. And time dilation could ex-

plain why she'd arrived here a week later than the rest
of us, though it still didn't answer the question of why
that phenomenon had affected her, and not Devon or
Tommy or me. But soon she would be here. Then I
would learn what had happened to her.

ıııııııııııı

Shortly before noon, Dr. Tilford's Lexus drove up the
gravel road leading to the house. The sight of the car
stirred such powerful memories that for a moment I
flashed back to the night we had abandoned it in the
woods—that awful night which began in one universe
and ended in another. By the time it pulled into the
driveway and stopped, my heart was pounding.

The motor shut off. Three doors opened.

Three?

The first to get out was Devon's dad. I guess I
shouldn't have been surprised that he came along, all
things considered. Devon must have told him *something*. But was he here to support his son, or to confront
the bad influences that were misleading him? Then
Devon disembarked from the passenger side. I wanted
to run to him, to throw my arms around him and hug
him until his ribs hurt . . . but with his father there, such
a display was out of the question. So I just stood at the
head of the stairs, waving and smiling, my heart pounding, waiting for him to come to me at his own pace.

Then Rita got out, and when I saw the condition she
was in my stomach tightened and the joy I'd felt a moment before vanished in an instant. She moved with the
stiffness of someone injured, her face was cut in several
places, and there was an angry purple bruise covering
most of one cheek. Tommy and I had looked pretty bad
when we first came home, but a week's time had muted
our bruises to dull gold and our bodily aches to memory; her damage looked much more recent, and the

bright purple hue of her wounds made my own fading bruises throb in sympathy. She was wearing long sleeves, I noted, and given how hot the day was, that suggested there were marks on her arms as well. I wondered if Dr. Tilford had seen them.

"Well, hello!" Aunt Rose's sudden voice exploding behind my shoulder made me jump. "You must be Jesse's friends!"

The greeting was so mundane under the circumstances that it seemed almost surreal, but Dr. Tilford just took it in stride, smiling and coming up the stairs to shake her hand as if this was a normal, everyday visit. And then my uncle came out and was introduced, and Rose asked Dr. Tilford how his trip was, and he said that it had been lovely, thank you, this part of the country was lovely, and by the way, so was her house. She beamed. The banal irrelevance of their chatter made my head spin, but there wasn't much I could do about it. I knew my aunt well enough by now to recognize that she wasn't going to leave us alone to talk about anything substantial until basic social amenities had been taken care of.

She had lunch ready and waiting for the newcomers, of course. Mom joined us there, and she offered her hand to Dr. Tilford as he entered, as if greeting a stranger. "So nice to meet you. I'm Jesse and Tommy's mom." I felt my heart sink, and I could see a shadow of concern in Dr. Tilford's eyes, but he responded graciously and shook her hand like nothing was wrong. They'd met before, of course. He was the one who had brought us back to Manassas after we'd escaped from the Shadows' prison, and driven Tommy and me home to meet my mother. So this moment was a painful reminder of how much memory she had lost.

Rose began to chatter as she set out chicken salad sandwiches and lemonade, filling what could otherwise have been an uncomfortable silence. The Fourth of July celebrations were this weekend, with a big cookout during the day and fireworks at night, so it was a pity our visitors wouldn't be here for that. Of course if they wanted to stay for it, they were welcome to, though someone might have to sleep on a couch. And the local gallery was open on the weekend, so if they wanted to stay that long, she could show them her work there. Speaking of which, she was really hoping that I would display something at her booth. Maybe the newcomers would help talk me into it?

I caught Julian looking at Rita, and sometimes Rose's eyes fixed on her a bit longer than they should have; clearly they were wondering about her bruises. But no one asked any questions about them, at least during lunch.

One small thing to be grateful for.

Not until all the food was eaten, and the social chit-chat had gone on for so long I was ready to scream, were we finally able to get away from the adults. Devon, Rita, Tommy and I headed up to Tommy's room in the attic to talk. It was a narrow room that ran the length of the house, and we figured it would offer us decent privacy. A small cot and chest of drawers had been fitted into one tight corner, and there were boxes everywhere, many with a film of dust on them. Makeshift accommodations at best, but as soon as Tommy saw the space he declared this was where he wanted to sleep, and I totally understood why. With two dormer windows offering direct access to the roof, he had a quick and easy escape route should aliens come calling.

As soon as we were alone, I turned and hugged Rita like the world was about to end. I'd spent a week thinking she was dead—or worse—and blaming myself. Now she was here, in the flesh, and not only was I glad to see her, but the guilt that had been my constant companion since our return was finally easing its death grip on my soul.

"Hey, girl. I do need to breathe." She chuckled as I let her go, but I saw the glimmer of tears in her eyes, and there were some in mine as well. It was a pretty overwhelming moment.

"What the hell happened?" I asked her. "How did you get separated from us?"

She shook her head. "No clue. One moment I was right there next to you, then next . . . well, everything was gone. I mean, *everything*. The Gate, the cave, all of you guys, even the world we had just come from, completely gone. I was so terrified. I just couldn't move, couldn't breathe. I couldn't even think. Then suddenly I felt myself falling, and I landed on something hard. It was totally dark. I yelled for you guys, but no one answered. I didn't know if you'd been lost between the worlds, or killed back at the arch, or . . . or what. I didn't even know where I was, but when I felt around all I could find was rubble. Oh God, Jesse, I was so scared."

I reached out and rubbed her shoulder. It seemed to steady her a bit.

"I fumbled for my flashlight, then realized it had been taken by the Shadows. I had no light. It was so dark." She shivered. "The place smelled damp, like a cave, so I guessed I was back in Mystic Caverns. But the room the Gate was in had been enormous, and this place . . . When I called out your names the echo didn't sound right for that. So I reached out over my head and I . . ." Her voice broke for a moment. I saw her tremble as she fought to pull herself together. "There was rock only a few feet above me. It was like I was sealed in a tomb."

"Shhh," Devon said. He put a hand on her other shoulder and squeezed gently. "You're here now, okay? You're safe."

"I just lay there," she whispered. "Overwhelmed. I knew that I needed to do *something*, not just lay there and wait to die. But what? I didn't even know which way was out, and crawling randomly in the dark wasn't going to get me anywhere. I never felt so helpless in my life.

"But then as my eyes started to adjust to the darkness, I realized that there was a faint light off to one side. Really faint, barely enough to see by, but at least it was something." She drew in a deep, shaky breath. "I can't even tell you what that moment was like. Like something inside me was coming back to life, and it wanted to live. It wanted desperately to live. So I began to scrabble toward the light, mostly by feel. It seemed hopeless, there were mounds of rubble in my way, and I had no idea where I was going, but I just kept crawling toward the light."

God. I couldn't even imagine what that must have been like. When Devon and Tommy and I had arrived back home Mystic Caverns was in the process of collapsing, and it was hard to believe any of the chambers had survived intact. If Rita arrived after we did, which was what it sounded like, it was a miracle she'd found any space big enough to crawl through.

"Slowly the light grew brighter," Rita continued "and eventually I got to a place where there was an opening overhead, and I could see stars through it. And that's . . ." her voice broke for a moment, "that's when I lost it," she whispered. "Just laid there and cried like a baby."

Suddenly it hit me how recent all this was for her. Devon and Tommy and I'd had a week to recover from our ordeal in Shadowcrest—and to heal our wounds—but if Rita had just arrived, then for her all that had happened yesterday. I reached out and hugged her again, oh so tightly, and she just held me, while Devon rubbed her shoulder sympathetically and even Tommy offered her a fleeting touch of reassurance. "I must have arrived pretty close to the surface," she whispered. "I don't know how that happened. Maybe without its Gate, a portal can't stay anchored right. And we destroyed the Gate that controlled this one." She laughed weakly. "Maybe I owe my life to a malfunction."

"Whatever the reason," Devon said, "you're damn lucky. The lower levels are a wreck. Police couldn't get down there at all."

Rita shut her eyes and sighed heavily. "When I finally climbed out, that's when I saw the scraps of yellow police tape all over the place. The wind had torn it loose in a few places, so I figured it had been put up a while ago. That was when I realized that you guys must have arrived before I did. That you might be safe." She opened her eyes again. "I managed to find my way to a nearby house, slipped in an open window, ate some food, and borrowed some clean clothes. They had a landline phone, so I used it to call Devon, to see if he'd gotten home safely. His dad answered." She looked at Devon. "He didn't have a clue who I was."

"We couldn't tell anyone about you," he said. "If you never came back . . ."

She nodded. "People would keep looking for me, even after you guys came home, and there would have been more media attention. Don't worry, I get it."

Devon looked at me. "Since our cover story was that we'd been kidnapped, I told Dad that someone we'd met in our captivity had turned up, but was hurt. He didn't ask any questions, just drove us out there to pick Rita up. I texted you on the way, but when you started asking questions, I didn't have any other information to give you . . . I'm so sorry, Jesse."

" 'It's okay," I said softly. "I understand."

"Once we got back, and Rita was all cleaned up, Dad gave her something to help her relax." He drew in a deep breath. "I told him about Terra Prime, and what really happened to us. Maybe it wasn't the best time for that conversation, but with Rita back, I couldn't put it off any more."

"How'd it go?" Tommy asked.

Devon hesitated. "He didn't accuse me of being crazy, or of getting into his drug cabinet or anything. So I guess you could say it went well. I had given him the glow lamp a few days earlier, figuring if he looked it over before we talked that might help. But he didn't say anything about it. Just listened to me without saying a word, and then said we needed to come up here together, so all of us could talk."

I opened my mouth to say something, but a call from downstairs came first.

"Jessica!" It was Julian. "Tommy!"

We looked at each other, then Tommy yelled back, "What is it?"

"Dr. Tilford wants to talk to the four of you. Can you all come down to the parlor, please?"

I looked at Devon. His face was ashen.

"It'll be all right," I told him. "He's seen the glow lamp. He'll come to the right conclusions."

I could see how much effort it took for him to force a smile to his face. "Yeah. And the fact that he knows from those earlier tests that our DNA doesn't match, so I'm not really his son . . . it won't affect his reaction at all, right?"

There was nothing I could say to that, so we headed downstairs to talk to Dr. Tilford.

|||||||||||||

The glow lamp on the coffee table appeared as bland and uninteresting as an object could possibly be. If you looked closely enough you could make out the Weaver's etched sigil etched into the small fetter, but it was subtle—like a watermark—and easy to miss. Other than that, the thing was featureless. A child who was shopping for a glass marble would probably pass it by in favor of something more interesting.

Dr. Tilford gestured for us to take seats around the table, which we did. He was a handsome man, with skin the color of dark chocolate and the long, lean features of East Africa. Given that Devon wasn't really his son, the resemblance between them was remarkable. But his expression was that of a statue right now, rigid and unreadable. Even his eyes, as he looked us over one by one, revealed nothing of his thoughts. At least with the other adults gone we could talk freely.

"You understand," he said, once we were all seated, "I was limited in what tests I could run. I didn't want to show this item to anyone else, lest word get back to the government that there was an object of unknown tech in the neighborhood. Trust me when I tell you, that wouldn't be good."

Devon nodded solemnly. I got the impression his father was referencing a specific past incident and Devon knew what it was.

"The object appears to be made of quartz crystal," Dr. Tilford continued, "albeit a more perfect specimen than we usually see in nature. I could detect no structural or chemical variation of any kind, which suggests there isn't a physical mechanism. Regarding electromagnetic energy, there's nothing detectable when the item is dormant, but there's a brief spike when it's activated. The lamp appears to require the electromagnetic charge of human skin to activate it. I was able to trigger it with my bare finger and with a conductive stylus, but not with an insulating object." He stared at it for a moment, his eyes narrowing slightly. "The necessity of *intent* defies all my analysis. How one's desire to have the lamp activate figures into the trigger mechanism, I still don't know, but given my other findings, my guess is that it's some sort of electromagnetic signal." His lips tightened. "That's all my tests could tell me—enough to raise new questions, but not enough to answer the one that matters most."

He reached out to the lamp and touched it. There was a strange hesitancy to the gesture, almost a sense of awe. The light flickered on briefly, then off again. The blue glow was dimmer than before. Whatever energy source powered the thing was clearly starting to run out.

"No one has published any articles hinting at this kind of tech," he said quietly. "Not even speculating that something of this nature could be produced. I suppose it's possible someone has been working on a completely new type of technology, and not a whisper of it has gotten out . . . but secrets on that scale are hard to keep." He shook his head, clearly frustrated by his inability to solve this puzzle.

Devon leaned forward slightly. "So you believe it could be from another world?" Another question, unvoiced, hung in the air, edged with silent desperation: *You believe what I told you about our experiences?*

For a long moment Dr. Tilford stared at the marble. I found I was holding my breath. "Are you familiar with Clarke's Law?" he said at last.

Tommy spoke up first. "Any technology sufficiently advanced is indistinguishable from magic." When I looked at him in surprise, he said, "What? I read science fiction."

A faint smile flickered across Dr. Tilford's lips. "Our army has developed a pain ray for crowd control. Point it at a target and he or she will feel pain, without actually being harmed. Just like in science fiction. Scientists have isolated the force required for a functional tractor beam, so we may see that in our lifetimes. A 3D printer has been used to replicate pizza. The speed of light has been altered in a laboratory." He shook his head. "So many things done today that would have been considered impossible a mere decade ago. Ten years from now the world will be so far advanced that aspects of it would seem magical to us today ... but the seeds of that future technology are all around us. No unearthly source is required to explain them." With a deep sadness in his eyes, he looked at his son. "I'm sorry, Devon. What you're asking me to believe ... this artifact alone isn't proof of it."

The crestfallen look in Devon's eyes made my heart ache. "I understand," he whispered.

Dr. Tilford looked around at all of us. "The four of you were held prisoner for a week, isolated from the world. God alone knows what you experienced. Your captors appear to have drugged you with something in the Rohypnol class, which makes all memories suspect." He looked back at his son. "So, I'm sorry, Devon. I do think you genuinely believe what you told me, but that doesn't mean it really happened."

Devon lowered his head. All he had to do was indicate he wanted help, and Rita and Tommy and I would back him up. If the four of us reported the same events, wouldn't that be convincing? Rohypnol didn't cause *mass* hallucinations, did it? But Devon just sighed and shook his head. He knew his father better than we did, and maybe he sensed that whatever story we told, Dr. Tilford would just explain it away like he had done with the glow lamp. And if his explanation cast the rest of us in a bad light, he might forbid Devon from seeing us.

Dr. Tilford turned to me, and the look in his eyes became gentle. "Devon told me what happened to your mother. I'm so sorry."

I looked down at my hands. I was grateful for a change of subject, but wished he'd chosen something else to talk about. "The doctors say there's not much hope."

"The brain is a remarkably resilient organ. When one part of it ceases to function, another sometimes take over its duties. Usually that involves vital processes: speech, physical movement, things a person needs to function. But medical science is full of surprises. Don't give up hope yet, Jesse."

I blinked away tears that were coming to my eyes. "Thanks," I whispered. Why did a cool, rational guy like him offering sympathy affect me so deeply?

Dr. Tilford looked back to Devon. "Could I keep the lamp, to study it further?" His tone was quiet, even casual, but you could sense the intense hunger behind it. He was a scientist. The lamp was a mystery. He wanted it.

Devon hesitated. "It was given to all of us. So everyone would have to agree."

My first impulse was to say yes. The lamp was clearly running out of power, and soon wouldn't be useful to anyone. Why not let him study it further? But it wasn't that easy to give up an alien artifact, especially when it was the only proof you had been to another world. "Could we maybe have some time to talk about it?"

"Of course." He nodded. "Let me leave you to that, then." As he stood up to take his leave, his eyes never left the fetter; you could tell how much he wanted to pick it up and take it with him. He walked around the table, heading toward the door, then paused beside his son. He looked down at Devon for a moment, then put his hand on his shoulder. Briefly. Silently. Just a fleeting touch, but it spoke volumes.

Then he was gone.

Devon fell back in his chair with a weary sigh. He reached up a hand to rub the bridge of his nose, as if the spot pained him.

"Could have been worse," Rita said gently. "He could have thought you were crazy."

"He may still think that," Devon said. "Granted, I

hadn't really expected him to believe me, but damn it, I'd hoped . . ." He shook his head as his words trailed off into silence.

"Sorry about the Rohypnol," Tommy muttered.

I blinked. "Say what?"

"It was my idea to add that to our cover story, so that we didn't have to explain too much about our disappearance. Only now, Devon's dad won't believe him because of it."

"That's not the only reason," Devon assured him. "And if you hadn't come up with that idea, we'd still be in the police station answering questions about what happened to us the week we were gone. Sooner or later one of us would have gotten the story wrong, and then all hell would have broken loose. So don't you *ever* regret that suggestion. Ever."

Tommy bit his lip and whispered, " 'Kay."

Rita turned to me. "I'm really sorry about your mom, Jesse. Didn't get a chance to say that before."

I sighed. "Yeah. Not much hope on that front, though Dr. Tilford was nice to pretend that there was."

She hesitated. "Jesse . . . you know . . . there might be Healers who could help."

I stiffened. "You mean from Terra Prime?"

Eyes wide, she nodded.

I leaned back in my chair and shut my eyes for a moment. Yes, there were Healers in the other world. Sebastian had used a fetter to heal my leg, and fetters were created by binding someone's Gift to an object, which meant that there were Healers in Terra Prime, probably a whole Guild full of them. Could someone with that kind of Gift help my mother? Possibly. But w*ould* one of them help her? That was a much bigger question, and one that Tommy and Devon and I had been debating all week.

The mere thought of dealing with someone from that

world filled me with dread. It would be best for all of us if Terra Prime just forgot we existed. But if there was someone who could help Mom? I sighed. "Even if a Healer was able to help, why would she? It's pretty clear that Guilds don't give two squats about outworlders. And how would I even find one to ask? It's not like a Google search will turn up 'Healers from Terra Prime.'"

Rita shrugged. "No clue how to find them, but once we do, the rest isn't a big mystery. They sell their Gifts, remember? There were fetters for sale all over the place in the other Luray. All we would need is money."

"I've got some savings," I mused. "But who's to say that would be enough?"

"I'll chip in," Devon offered.

"I'll throw in what little I've got," Tommy agreed.

Rita snorted lightly. "I think you can guess the state of my finances. If I had anything, you know I'd offer it."

I was so moved by their generosity that it took me a moment to find my voice. "Even if that added up to enough, we're still left with the problem of finding someone. I can't just go the Greys and ask for help in hiring a Healer, not after what we did to their Gate. They don't strike me as the forgiving type. And they work for the Shadows, who we *really* need to avoid."

"Well," Rita said, "forgive me if you've already discussed this—I'm playing catch-up here—but what about Miriam Seyer?" She raised a hand to forestall my objection. "Yeah, I know you don't trust her. I don't either. But all you need is someone to set up a meeting, right? Can't you use her for that?"

For a long time I said nothing. In my mind's eye I could see my house burning, that black-haired Seer standing across the street and watching it. Just watching it. What had brought Seyer to my home, just in time to witness the fire? It couldn't have been coincidence. Later, when I overheard her talking to Morgana in the

Seers' garden, it sounded like the two of them wanted me to be safe. But they also talked about controlling my movements, and my being part of some mysterious project they were running. Games within games within games. Every instinct in my soul warned me to keep away from her—far, far away—but Rita's suggestion had merit, there was no denying that. Seyer was one link between the worlds that did not involve Greys or Shadows. Perhaps the only one.

"Why would she help?" I asked at last. "She doesn't give a damn what happens to Mom. And her Guild seemed pretty affluent; I doubt the kind of money we could offer would tempt her."

"But you have something else she wants," Tommy said. "Your paintings, remember? She wanted to buy one. Well, now all your art is gone, so there's nothing she can buy from you, or even steal, unless you paint something new."

The thought of giving one of my paintings to Seyer made my skin crawl; it bothered me that I didn't know why. *Easy, girl. It's just a painting. Not like you're selling her your soul.* "Even if I did that, how would she find out about it? She saw my work the first time because it was in a show at the school."

Rita said, "What about the gallery your aunt was talking about? Could you put something on display there?"

"Yeah, but what are the chances Seyer would wander through on the day it happened to be there? I just don't see that happening."

"Maybe if there was some kind of publicity?" Devon suggested.

Tommy pulled out his cell phone and start scrolling through web pages. I couldn't read the text from where I was sitting, but I saw a picture of Berkeley Springs Castle flash by. Then: "Bingo!" he announced, and he turned the phone to face us. The text was too small to read, so I took it from him, read what he'd found, and then passed it on to the others. The web page was *www.bsoldmillgal lery.com.*

Vendor list for the Independence Day Show, it said. Aunt Rose's name was on it. So were dozens of others.

"Of course," Tommy said, "Getting on that list would only help if Seyer was still keeping tabs on you online."

A chill crept up my spine. "You think she's doing that?"

"Don't you?" he asked.

I wanted to say no. I wanted to believe that when we left Terra Prime, that was the end of our involvement with that dreadful world. But Alia Morgana had referred to me as her *project*, which meant she probably had people keeping tabs on me. And since we knew that there were Greys who used the internet for surveillance— that's how they'd found out about Tommy's alleged dreams—we'd be fools not to expect the same level of expertise from Morgana's people.

She was watching me. The thought of it made my skin crawl, but I knew in my gut it was true. "Only three days away," I muttered. "Not a lot of time to paint a masterpiece."

"It doesn't have to be a masterpiece," Devon said reasonably. "Just good enough to pique her interest."

I shut my eyes for a moment. I could see Seyer standing in front of me, her eyes glowing yellow, like a serpent's, reflecting the flames from my house. Like a demon from Dante's Inferno.

It's for Mom, I told myself. Gritting my teeth, I forced the ominous image out of my mind. *Do it for Mom.*

"All right," I muttered. "I'll talk to Aunt Rose about painting something for the show." I shook my head. "She'll be ecstatic about that, anyway." I handed Tommy back his phone. "Let's see if we can't draw the serpent out of her den."

4

Berkeley Springs
Virginia

Jesse

'M NOT ALONE.

I look around, but no one else is visible in the black dreamscape. I listen as carefully as I can, but I hear nothing out of the ordinary.

No, that's not quite accurate. There's music surrounding me, a ghostly orchestral hum like you sometimes hear in the middle of the night, conjured by the vibrations of the air conditioner. Maybe real music, maybe imagined. Almost subliminal.

That's new. And on another night I might have paid more attention to it, perhaps even tried to trace it to its source. But tonight I have bigger things to worry about. The sense of someone watching me is so strong that it gives me goosebumps. Is it the avatar girl again? The mere thought that a stranger might enter my dream is so unnerving that my spirit wavers briefly, and for a mo-

ment I'm tempted to wake myself up, to flee the dreamscape. But my hunger for knowledge is greater than my
fear. I need to understand how other people can enter a
world that my mind created, and what they can do to it
once they're here. Not to mention the sheer stubborn-
ness factor: I'm damned if I'm about to be driven out of
my own dream.

Slowly I begin to walk, but my attention is less on the
doors this time, and more on the darkness surrounding
them. As I come to each door the ghostly music seems
to get a bit louder, then it fades again. The melody is
changing each time, very subtly. Like each door has its
own musical theme. Weird.

Suddenly I see a flash of movement off to one side. I
turn toward it and see the avatar girl standing there,
watching me. Why didn't I see her before, when I looked
in this direction?

As soon as my eyes meet hers she turns away and
starts walking.

"Wait!" I cry out. "Just for a minute! I want to talk to
you."

She shows no sign of having heard me. She's walking
quickly, speeding up bit by bit but not running outright,
moving off into the darkness. I follow her, mirroring her
pace, not wanting to close the distance between us (because what would I do next, tackle her to the ground?)
but hoping that if she realizes I'm not a threat to her
she'll slow down and talk to me. I have questions that
only she can answer, and I'm not going to let her out of
my sight before I get a chance to ask them.

The music seems louder, now that I'm focused on her.
Maybe that's just an illusion. Or maybe it's easier to hear
such things when you're not paying attention to them.
The arches are changing shape as she passes them, too.
Crystal spines vanish in a puff of glittering smoke. Stone
arches stretch upward, sides thinning out, rounded tops

transforming into a graceful point. The new shapes, tall and peaked, remind me of an Arabian palace.

It's a shape that has meaning to her, rather than to me.

The implications are chilling, but I continue on. The only thing worse than having a stranger mess with your dream, is having that happen and not knowing how they did it. Or why.

As we approach a dense cluster of archways she breaks into a run. With a start I realize that the pattern of these arches is familiar: this is the cluster where she lost me the last time, when I couldn't follow her through an arch. I can see from the way her body is tensing for one last burst of speed that she's about to try the same trick again.

Not on my watch.

Her final dash is sudden, but I'm right behind her, and I'm ready for it. As she enters the arch I launch myself at her, closing the gap between us with all the reckless ferocity of a baseball player sliding into home plate, grabbing hold of her so that she can no longer pass through the arch alone. The force of my momentum knocks us both off our feet—and then suddenly we're falling through the archway together, and we hit the ground on the far side with enough force to drive the breath from my body.

Fear and elation flood my soul: I made it!

But to where?

Thick grey fog surrounds us, so I can't see much of anything. While I struggle to get my bearings the girl breaks away from me and gets to her feet. I see a flash of fear in her eyes; clearly she didn't think I could follow her here. Then she's running again, full speed this time, and by the time I can get to my feet the fog has swallowed her whole.

I look up at the shadows looming over me, tall and

thin, their crowns spreading into a dark mass overhead. Trees? Am I in some kind of forest? There are long black streamers trailing down from unseen branches, and I fervently hope they're just some kind of hanging moss. The ground beneath me is soft and damp, and it takes impressions well; I realize that I can see her footprints clearly.

I start to follow her. The fog changes as I do, shifting in color from bluish gray to a dull green, then to brownish mauve. It's still thick enough to hide her from my sight, so I'm forced to run blind. The trees are also changing, shrinking in both girth and height, and there is less and less of the black stuff hanging from their branches. All in all the place doesn't look as threatening as before, but I'm not reassured. I'm chasing a girl who invaded my dreams. The rest of this is just window dressing.

Finally the fog thins out, and I see that the last of the trees are gone. There's an open plain ahead, and my quarry is visible in the distance. She must sense my approach, because she glances back nervously over her shoulder to see where I am. Too close for her comfort, apparently. She starts running even faster, and I sense desperation in the effort. This time I'm hard-pressed to keep up. But all of that only increases my determination: I'm not going to let this strange creature get away from me until I find out how—and why—she's invaded my dreamscape.

Now the entire world is changing around me, far more dramatically than before. First I'm running on a field of plain dirt, then it's a field of grass, then it's poppies stretching out as far as the eye can see. Overhead the sun is yellow, then white, then red and swollen, filling half the sky. Then yellow again. Whatever dream world we've entered, it appears to be totally unstable.

There's a wide hill ahead of us, and she's starting up

its slope. It's not very high, but once she goes over the top I won't be able to see her any more. I try to run even faster, but I'm already going at top speed, and my legs are starting to get tired. How long have I been chasing her? I thought it was only a few minutes, but now it feels like an eternity. Dream time.

But if this is a dream, then I can control it, right? Thus far I've been too busy running to think about strategy, but surely I can leverage that to my advantage. As I continue running I try to detach my mind from the pounding rhythm of the chase, focusing my attention on the hill itself, trying to unmake it. God knows, this dream is volatile enough that doing so should be easy, but to my surprise the alien landscape rejects my efforts. I try to make other changes, but nothing responds to me. I can't make a single poppy wilt or a butterfly leave its perch, much less flatten a multi-ton mound of soil.

She's nearing the summit now. I'm getting tired. Any minute now I'll lose sight of her, perhaps for good. And all the answers she might provide will be lost.

I can't let that happen.

I try again to alter the dreamscape, drawing upon the force of my frustration as a kind of fuel. And after what seems like an eternity the dreamscape finally responds. I see a tiny bit of soil come loose from the top of the hill and roll down the slope, breaking up as it does so, and I know that I caused that. But it's all I can do. Part of me is elated to have managed even that much, but part of me wants to scream in frustration, because I can't seem to do anything useful. This unstable world shows amazing tenacity when I'm the one who wants to change it.

I focus all my attention back on running, not wanting to lose her. But by the time I reach the base of the hill she's already at the top. The slope turns out to be much steeper than I expected, and covered with loose rocks that shift underfoot, forcing me to concentrate on each step. Progress is agonizingly slow. By the time I reach the top she's long out of sight, and I just pray that from that vantage point I can spot her again.

I pause for a moment at the top to catch my breath and take stock of the situation.

The view on the other side of the hill looks like it's from a completely different dream. There's a vast lake stretching out to the horizon in all directions, its water so still that the surface is like a mirror. The sun (still yellow) reflects from it with such painful intensity that I'm forced to squint to see things clearly. I can make out a narrow tongue of land extending into the lake, from the base of the hill, but it's not made of regular earth, rather some kind of black sand. I can see the girl's footprints in it, though not as clearly as in the forest soil. Her trail leads down the hillside, along the length of the peninsula, then out into the lake itself.

Or rather, onto the lake.

She's running on top of it.

At first I figure maybe there are stepping stones right under the surface—the mirrored water could hide anything—but her feet aren't splashing when they hit the lake, as they would if that were the case. Anyway, there's no reason dream-water can't support a human being, if the dreamer wants it to.

In the distance an island of black rock juts up from the lake; stark and jagged, it's her obvious destination. There's a tall building perched on its peak, and at first glance it looks like a castle of some kind. But then I blink and it looks more like a cathedral. Another blink turns it into a ziggurat, only with lines of windows instead of ledges running around the outside in a spiral. It's like the building itself can't decide what it wants to be. The only thing that remains constant through all the transformations is the shape of the windows: narrow and peaked, just like the new arches that appeared in my black plain. Through them I can see flickering movement, but though I'm too far away to make out details, I get the sense that no two windows look in on the same interior.

The avatar girl is halfway to the island.

With renewed energy I start down the hill after her, half running, half stumbling. The sight of the strange island has energized me, and even if she manages to lose me now, I might be able to find some answers there. Soon I'm racing down the length of the narrow peninsula, bracing myself to step out onto the lake's surface, just like she did. Because the same rules should hold for both of us, yes?

No such luck.

My first step splashes down into ice-cold water and I land on something loose and slippery. I lose my balance and go flying forward, landing face first in the frigid stuff with a force that sends up gouts of white spray in all directions. Ripples spread out from me like the concentric circles of a great target. When I surface, coughing, it takes me a few seconds to find a section of the lake bed stable enough to stand on. The stones underwater are slick, and like glass marbles they shift beneath my feet with every movement.

Jesus. How am I supposed to follow the girl now? This water is too cold for me to even contemplate swimming, and there's no way I can walk any distance on such unstable ground. I look up, and the sight of her walking so easily across the surface of the lake fills me with frustration and anger. Why can she control this dreamscape so easily, while I have to strain to dislodge a single clump of earth? It shouldn't be that way. A stranger shouldn't be able to control my own dream better than I can.

Unless, I think suddenly, it isn't my dream at all.

The mere thought sends a shiver down my spine, but there's no denying that all the evidence points to that. If I were the true invader here, someone who burst into her world—her mindscape—without invitation, then control of this setting would come naturally to her, and I would be powerless to change things. Which seems to be exactly what's happening.

No, I remind myself. I'm not completely powerless. I did change this landscape, albeit minimally. And maybe now that I understand the rules of the place I'll be able to do more.

Reaching down into the water with all the force of my mind, I attempt to reshape the lake bed. It would be foolish to try to make the water itself support me, like she's doing; one moment's inattention might get me dumped back into the frigid lake. But moving dirt from one place to another offers a more permanent solution. So, gritting my teeth from the strain of the effort, I try to mold this dream as I would one of my own, superimposing my preferred reality over the current one. The task should require no more than a concentrated thought, but even though I strain my utmost, there's no response. Then, just as I'm about to give up in frustration, a thin strip of earth begins to rise up from underneath the lake. Water falls back from its flanks as it breaches the surface, and a narrow land bridge takes shape. It's only a foot wide and a few yards in length, and it's so close to the water's surface that ripples lap over the edge of it, but as I climb up onto it I feel confident I can extend it all the way to the black island, and once I do that, it should stay in place even if I get distracted.

Finally I'm standing on it, swaying slightly on its wet, uneven surface, ready to get moving again. I look up to see if my quarry is still visible. She is.

She's watching me.

She's almost at the island, but she's not running any

more. She's just standing on the water's surface, her eyes, narrow and dark, fixed on me. The message in them is clear: *how DARE you try to take control of my dream!* Slowly she raises both her hands, like a conductor signaling an orchestra to start, and I know in my gut that something very bad is about to happen. Is she going to try to unmake my land bridge? I prepare to defend it (however on earth you'd do that), but to my surprise, the dream-construct remains steady beneath my feet. That's not her target. The water surrounding me is beginning to move, however, and slowly it draws back from the shoreline, revealing the lake bottom. Fish are flopping helplessly in tiny pools as the receding tide leaves them stranded—

Oh, shit. I've seen too many disaster movies to not know what's happening. Or, more precisely, what's about to happen.

Desperately I look around for high ground. Or something I can climb. Or even something to hang on to, before the great wave that she's summoning hits me like a giant flyswatter. But there's only the one low hill behind me, and even a small tsunami would sweep right over that.

No trees in sight.

No protection anywhere.

The water in the center of the lake is starting to rise up now, and a foam-capped ridge is taking shape that stretches from horizon to horizon, blocking the girl from my sight. I can't be sure of its position, but I can measure its rise as window after window of the strange citadel is hidden from my sight. The ground beneath my feet has started to tremble, and a cold wind gusts across my face. It's coming fast.

For one brief, crazy instant I want to stand my ground. I want her to see that her dream can't scare me off, no matter how scary she makes it. Maybe she'd respect such an effort and tell me what's going on.

Yeah. Right.

I need to wake myself up. Now.

Turning my attention inward, I reach out with my mind, trying to reconnect to the reality of my sleeping body. Waking up should be easy once that's done. But even as I begin to concentrate, the wave starts to transform. Color bleeds from it, the stormy blue water becomes a dull grey. The foam turns to white mist, then to smoke, then it's carried away on the wind. The wave itself starts to collapse, and row after row of windows become visible again as it falls back into the lake that spawned it.

Stunned, I hesitate.

I can see the girl now, and her expression is one of pure horror. She's staring at a point directly above the collapsed wave, where a wraith-like shadow has suddenly appeared. It's darker than any natural shadow would be, and its presence is so cold that even from where I stand I feel its chill. I sense that it has no substance in the normal meaning of the word, but rather is a void, a gaping wound in the dreamscape into which all reality is draining.

It's heading straight toward her.

With a cry of terror, the girl begins to run to the island. She's hasn't got far to go, but the shadow-wraith is moving quickly, and in its wake the entire dream world seems to be dissolving. Beams of sunlight fade as if the wraith passes through them, the shining surface of the water grows dull beneath it, color bleeds from the sky and the clouds overhead, and even the sun dims as the wraith passes in front of it, its bright golden surface dulled to a muddy brown, its brilliant light all but extinguished.

I need to leave this nightmare now, before the horrific thing notices me. But hard as I try, I can't seem to wake myself up. That's really frightening. Ever since my visit to the other world I've been able to end my dreams at will, just by shifting my awareness to my sleeping body. The fact that I can't do so now suggests that the rules I've come to take for granted don't operate here.

I turn back the way I came and start running. Hopefully if I can get closer to the arch—closer to my own dreamscape—I'll be able to escape this nightmare.

But as I turn, it seems to notice me. And in that instant, as it pauses in mid-air deciding who to go after, I can sense the full scope of its horrific nature.

It is Death. It is Pain.

And it is hungry.

I flee from the terrible thing as an animal would flee, blind in my panic. All thoughts of exhaustion are gone now, all muscular weakness forgotten. I will run till the last ounce of strength leaves my body and I collapse, rather than let this thing touch me.

It's following me now. I know that because the world is transforming around me, reflecting its horrific nature. I run through a field of poppies, but all the flowers are dead, motionless insects strewn like black snow across their browning petals. I run through an open meadow, but the grass has been eaten away to stumps, and corpses of fallen birds litter the ground as far as the eye can see. I run into a forest, but the ground is buried in fallen branches and rotting leaves, and the place is so putrid with the stench of decay that I can barely breathe.

The arch must be here somewhere. It must be! I have to find it before that thing catches up with me.

Suddenly my foot catches on something underneath the dead leaves. I'm falling—falling!—and I cry out in fear as I hit the ground. Color is draining out of the whole world now, leaving only shades of murky gray, which means the creature is close, very close. I roll over onto my back so that I can defend myself—but how does one defend against an incarnation of Death?

It's closer than I'd imagined, and though I can see nothing but shadow when I look directly at it, I can sense vast black wings spreading over me, blotting out the last vestiges of sunlight. Instinctively I raise up my arm to guard my eyes, and something sharp and cold rakes across it. The pain is like nothing I have ever felt before. I hear myself crying out in terror, and I try again to wake myself up. No luck. I'm trapped here.

A ghostly voice cries out my name in the distance. My mind is so paralyzed by fear that at first the sound doesn't register. The death-wraith is lunging at me again, and I roll to one side. The frigid claws pass so close to my face my cheek feels numb. What will happen to my waking mind if this thing kills me here? Will I ever wake up again?

Jesse!

This time I recognize the voice, and I feel a spark of hope. I focus myself body and soul on my brother's voice, using it as a lifeline to connect me to the world of living things. Even as the death-wraith attacks me again I reach out for Tommy with all the strength that is left in my soul, trying to absorb his perspective into myself as he stands over my sleeping body—

||||||||||||||

"Jesse!"

I awoke gasping. My body was shaking violently, and I was sick from terror. But I was also home again, and that meant the creature was gone. Thank God.

My brother was kneeling on the bed, his hands on my shoulders. He'd been shaking me, trying to wake me up, and not until my eyes were fully open did he stop. "Are you okay?"

For a moment I had no words. I just lay there, drinking in reality. "Yeah," I rasped at last. "I think so."

"You were moaning in your sleep. I figured whatever dream was causing that, you'd want to wake up."

I whispered, "Good instinct." Then I asked, "Did anyone else hear me?"

He shook his head. "They're all asleep. I wasn't." He paused. "It wasn't that loud, just ... damn scary-sounding."

"Damn right," I muttered. "Thanks."

What would have happened to me if my brother hadn't tried to wake me up? Would I have been trapped in that dream forever? I remembered the death-wraith, and I shuddered. At least it lacked the power to follow me here. The waking world was my refuge.

I tried to lever myself up to a sitting position. My muscles were sore, like I'd really been running for hours, and the upper part of my left arm stung fiercely. I winced and used my other arm to push myself upright. The sensations were just echoes of my dream, I knew, and they should fade soon.

"So what scared you so badly?" Tommy asked. "Can you talk about it?"

I sighed. I didn't feel up to telling the whole story right then, but he deserved at least the bare bones of it. He might well have saved my life. "I ran into the avatar again. This time I followed her through a door, which led me into another dream, not one of mine ... I think maybe it was her dream. Then a death-wraith appeared and the whole dream fell apart. It was attacking me when you woke me up." I put my hand on my arm where the claws had torn my flesh—

And I froze.

"Jesse?"

There was pain in that spot. Way too much pain for a mere dream memory. The sleeve of my sleep shirt was warm and wet.

It was a dream, I told myself. *Just a dream. I probably banged my arm against a bedpost while I was trying to wake up. Or something.*

Slowly I pushed my sleeve up my arm, not wanting to see what was under it, but knowing I had to. The source of the blood turned out to be a jagged slash that ran diagonally across my arm. It wasn't deep, but blood was oozing out of it, and the surrounding flesh was red and swollen.

I think I was more afraid in that moment than I had been while the wraith was actually attacking me. Because however frightening that had been, it was just a dream. This . . . this was *real*.

It was my brother who found his voice first, and with it the perfect words for that moment.

"Holy crap," he muttered.

5

JESSE

RITA ACCEPTED MY AUNT'S INVITATION to stay with us a few days, and I was grateful for the company. She and I might come from different backgrounds, and have few interests in common, but once you faced death together those things didn't matter as much. And it was good to have another confidant in the house, who could look at my wound and hear the tale of how I got it, and reassure me that somehow everything would be okay. Yeah, Tommy was doing that, but it helped to hear it in stereo. Devon wasn't able to stay, but we convinced Dr. Tilford that the two of them should come back up for the show, in part by telling him we wouldn't be able to give him the glow lamp until then. Then Aunt Rose talked Dr. Tilford into staying the night, so that we could all watch the fireworks together without his having to drive for hours afterward.

So for a brief time, the world-travelers were reunited.

Rose's gallery was at the north end of town, in a converted 18th century mill. It had a waterwheel on one side, a millstone and grinding mechanism in the center of two open floors, and a vast expanse of parkland outside. According to the tourist pamphlets, the mill had been grinding wheat back when George Washington came to soak in the town's famous hot springs, and I saw no reason to doubt that. These days there was no grain being processed, of course, but a different kind of harvest was being celebrated, that of local artists and craftsmen. Every weekend they displayed their work in small open spaces which were (for reasons that were a mystery to me) called "booths." This weekend the place would be packed, every inch of it filled with paintings and pottery and hand-dyed silks and wood carvings . . . and my new painting.

Of course we had argued about who would be in Rose's booth with me, while we waited to see if Seyer would show up. Rita and Devon both wanted to be there for our meeting, and truth be told, it would have steadied my nerves to have them there. But I was afraid that too much of a crowd might scare Seyer off, and I didn't want to take any chances. In the end they had to settle for wandering around the old mill, perusing art displays with poorly feigned interest as they tried to look like legitimate tourists. Probably they wouldn't fool anyone, but at least it gave me room to breathe. As for Tommy, his coming to the show simply wasn't an option. If he really was hearing ghosts, I told him, the last thing he needed was to be in the presence of a Seer, whose job it was to identify kids with interesting powers and kidnap them for Terra Prime. He sulked a bit, but he didn't argue the point. He knew I was right.

My aunt was actually a talented potter, and her impressive work was displayed on wooden bookshelves six feet high, arranged to mark out the periphery of her booth on the second floor. She moved one bookshelf back a bit to make room for my display easel, but it was still a pretty tight fit. I hoped that when Seyer showed up we would be able to talk without Rose listening in on us.

If Seyer showed up.

What was I going to say to her if she did? I'd tried to anticipate every possible avenue of conversation, as a mental exercise, but things like this never went the way you expected. I was just going to have to wing it.

The mill didn't have central air conditioning, so the exhibit space got warm pretty fast. I'd worn a long sleeved shirt to hide my dream-wound from Rose and Julian, so I was pretty damned uncomfortable. But at least the wound was healing normally. Despite Tommy's fears that I had become infected with death-wraith essence, and would slowly transform into a creature of darkness, that didn't seem to be happening. I joked with him about it—"This isn't *Lord of the Rings*, you know"—but in truth, I was pretty damned relieved.

Then Seyer arrived.

It was noon, and the place was a madhouse; I almost missed her. Devon spotted her first, and he signaled me from across the floor to draw my attention to her. She was dressed in her usual goth black, which was so out of place amidst the frothy summer crowd that once you noticed, she stood out like a sore thumb. My heart pounded as I watched her approach Rose's booth, but she was apparently in no hurry. At every booth she would stop to peruse its offerings, handling every glass necklace and walnut tissue box and raku vase as if it were a precious museum piece, whose every detail had to be studied before she could put it down. It was maddening, and no doubt quite deliberate. She was sending me a message: *Don't think that because I answered your summons, you are the one in control here.* What could I do? I tried to breathe deeply and pretend I didn't care if she came to Rose's booth or not. Let that be my message to her: *You can play whatever games you want, it's not going to shake me.*

Finally she arrived at Rose's booth, and of course she studied every piece of pottery before coming to look at my painting. For a while she just stood there, gazing at the dark loops and whorls, and the temptation for me to say something was overwhelming. But I just waited. Let her make the first move.

My painting had two round shapes, one smaller than the other, that were woven together into a single mandala-like composition. Tentacle-like rays splayed out from the larger one, that divided again and again until the whole canvas was filled with tiny curling lines. At first glance the painting appeared more chaotic than my usual work—no neat fractals in this one—but if you relaxed while viewing it, and didn't try to impose an artificial order upon it, you could sense a greater pattern underlying the chaos. You realized that the dual figure was reaching outward to surround all the other elements on the canvas, as if trying to ensnare them. Disturbingly, the ends of some of the tentacles were unclear, so that you couldn't be sure exactly where they ended, or whether or not they had made contact. A deadly net.

It was a fate portrait of Alia Morgana.

At last Seyer spoke. "It's darker than your previous work."

I shrugged stiffly. "I've been into some dark stuff lately."

She looked around the edges of the canvas. "I don't see a price tag. Or a 'not for sale' notice." She looked at me. "Does that mean you aren't sure if you want to sell it?"

"For the right buyer, I'd consider it."

She glanced over at Rose, probably to assess how

much privacy we had. But my aunt was busy with her customers at the moment, explaining the intricacies of raku pottery to a pair of tourists in Hawaiian shirts and Bermuda shorts. No one within ten feet was paying any attention to us.

Seyer turned back to me. As always, her thick black eyeliner and Cleopatra-style haircut lent her gaze an Egyptian flavor, like something you would see painted on the wall of a Pharaoh's tomb. "I'm guessing it's not money you're after." She spoke very quietly.

I nodded. "Good guess."

"Name your price, then."

I could feel my hands trembling, and I put them behind my back where she couldn't see them. *Everything rides on this moment,* I thought. From across the room Rita and Devon were watching, having abandoned their pretense of being interested in art. I wondered if Seyer was aware of them.

Finally I said quietly, but with strength: "I want a Healer for my mother."

Her eyes narrowed slightly. "For the damage she suffered from the fire?"

I kept my voice steady. "Yes."

She sighed deeply. "I'm afraid you're asking for something I can't give you, Jessica."

My heart sank. "Why not? I'm sure you have the connections needed to find a Healer. There are probably some on your Guild's payroll. Are you telling me— what?—that they won't Heal someone from my world? Is that it?"

I saw my aunt glance in our direction, and realized that my voice was rising in volume. I nodded reassuringly at her and drew in a deep breath, willing myself to be calm.

"It's not that simple," Seyer said softly.

"Then explain it to me."

She glanced at Rose again, then nodded toward the staircase. "Come. Walk outside with me."

I hesitated, then told Rose I was going to leave for a few minutes to buy some apple fritters from a food truck outdoors. She asked me to bring her back a lemonade, and gave me money for both orders. Then she turned back to regale her customers with glorious tales about raku glazing, and we headed toward the stairs.

"Your mother isn't sick," Seyer said as we walked. "She's *damaged*. There's a difference. A Healer works in harmony with the body, prompting it to do what it does naturally, only better. Their Gift can make bones knit faster, stimulate bone marrow to produce more blood, or even prompt the immune system to attack a cancerous tumor. Anything that a body has the natural capacity to do, a Healer can improve on. But your mother's brain has been damaged, Jessica. Neurons have died. That kind of cell doesn't regenerate naturally, which means that a Healer can't prompt it to do so." As we reached the bottom of the staircase she stopped walking and looked at me; there was sympathy in her eyes. "I'm sorry."

I felt like I'd been struck in the face. "You're lying," I whispered.

"What reason would I have to do that? You have something that I want to purchase—something *her Grace* wants to purchase. I could bring in a Healer for you, and take your painting home with me in return, and leave you to discover the truth after I was gone. Consider it a sign of respect that I'm being honest." There was pity in her eyes now, and I hated her for it. "I'm really sorry, Jessica."

We were heading outside now, to the area where the food vendors were hawking their wares. The smells of greasy meat, popcorn, and fritters breezed across the lawn. "So what now?" I had to fight to keep my voice steady. "Are you telling me there's no hope? That there's a whole universe full of people with fancy mental Gifts, and not one of them can help my mother?"

"Ah. I didn't say that. In fact there is one Guild that might be able to help you. But they're reclusive, pricey, and don't generally travel to other worlds doing favors for people."

"Who?"

"We call them Potters. Fleshcrafters. Unlike Healers, they can force living flesh to do things it wouldn't do naturally. Sometimes that allows them to repair things that can't be healed."

My breath caught in my throat. "They can cure my Mom?"

"*That* I can't promise. Few outside their Guild know exactly how their Gift works, or what its limits are. But I've heard about them taking on cases like this, so let's say . . . it might be possible."

"Okay." I nodded. "Okay. Then let's call that my price."

"For the painting?" She smiled slightly.

"That's right."

"You do value your work rather highly."

"No, I don't. But *you* do, or you wouldn't be here." When she didn't respond I pressed, "Am I wrong?"

She looked at me in silence, taking my measure. I tried to meet her gaze confidently, even though deep inside I felt the opposite of confident. Finally she said, "The Potters don't just hire out for odd jobs, Jessica. And there's nothing you possess that they would value in barter. You would need someone with enough personal influence to call in a favor from them, on your behalf. And given that you're talking about one of them travelling offworld, which they don't like to do, it would be a significant favor." She shook her head. "I just don't have that kind of influence. I'm sorry."

I felt my heart sinking. No. No. I refused to give up. To be so close to an answer and yet have no way to make it happen . . . I refused to accept that. There had to be a way.

Suddenly I realized who could help me. Not that she *would* help me, necessarily. Or that I wanted to ask her for help. In fact, the mere thought of dealing with her made my blood run cold.

Alia Morgana.

She was the one who had ordered Seyer to spy on me. And had put Tommy's life in danger by lying to the Greys about him, telling them he was the Dreamwalker they were looking for. She was the type of person one should do everything possible to avoid. But what if she had the kind influence Seyer was talking about? What if she could help me hire a Fleshcrafter?

It took effort to force out the words. "What about Morgana?"

Seyer raised an eyebrow. "An intriguing suggestion. She's the one who's interested in your art, you know; I'm just her purchasing agent. And I suppose if anyone had enough sway with the Potters to do what you want, she does. But that would have its own price, you know. Apart from your painting." She nodded back toward the building. "And she's not going to come to Terra Colonna just so you can bargain with her. You would need to go to her."

Go back to Terra Prime. A wave of vertigo came over me, like I was standing on the edge of an abyss, gazing down into a bottomless darkness, while the dirt beneath my feet crumbled away. But was the idea truly untenable? Seyer had once referred to me as Morgana's *project,* which suggested that the Guildmistress wanted something from me. I didn't know what it was yet, but maybe if I was face to face with her I could figure it out. Maybe I could leverage it for the favor I needed. Maybe I could do that and get home safely again.

Maybe.

"So," I said slowly, "if in return for my painting I wanted passage to and from your Guild headquarters—*safe* passage, door to door, with all the proper documents and clearances—and an audience with your Guildmistress . . . would that be a reasonable price?"

She smiled slightly. "I believe that would be within my budget."

"And if I wanted to bring someone with me?"

Her expression darkened slightly. "I'll cover expenses for the ones who were with you before. No one else."

We took a few minutes to buy fritters and lemonade and then started back. As we headed up the stairs, Seyer opened her purse and took out a business card, which she handed to me. "I'll be leaving tomorrow morning for Terra Prime. You can travel with me if you want. Give me a call tonight, and we'll discuss the details. You can deliver the painting yourself when you arrive." As we neared the pottery booth she instructed, "Introduce me to your aunt as an old family friend, so we can arrange for the proper cover story. The fact that your mother doesn't really know me won't be an issue, given the current state of her memory. No doubt she has forgotten a lot of other friends."

My heart clenched at the callous reminder of my mom's incapacity, but as we delivered Rose's lemonade, I did as Seyer had suggested, and marveled at how easily she slipped into a new role, playing the part of an old family friend to perfection. Truly, she was a social chameleon of impressive skill. I listened as she told Rose about a cabin she had in the mountains, and how she would love to invite me out there for a week. It would be restful, she said. Good for my soul. Rose said she wasn't sure this was a good time for me to part from my family, given recent events, but Seyer said she'd stop by in the morning to discuss it with Mom, and that was good enough for now.

"Pack for overnight," she said in a low voice, as Rose turned her attention to her customers. "And leave your electronics behind. I don't want trouble with Customs."

"But Mom hasn't agreed yet—"

She put a finger to her lips, cautioning me to silence. "She will. I promise. So will everyone else. Trust me."

When she left I was far too agitated to hang out with Rose, and besides, I needed to fill my friends in on what had happened. So I said goodbye to my aunt, and gestured for Devon and Rita to follow me outside the building. There, at least, people wouldn't be breathing down our necks as we talked about aliens and mind-readers.

As we descended the worn wooden stairs of the mill, I wondered if I had just done something very clever, or very stupid.

〰〰〰〰〰

"You're *what?*" Rita's tone left no room for doubt about what she thought of my bargain with Seyer.

"I'm going back to Terra Prime." I tried to say it casually, like you might talk about taking a train to visit Philadelphia. Maybe if I could keep myself sounding calm, the fear swirling in my stomach would settle down. "Round trip tickets compliments of Ms. Seyer."

"You *trust* her?" Devon asked sharply.

"No," I said, equally sharply, "and I trust Morgana even less. But what else am I supposed to do, Devon? Sit home and watch Mom fade away little by little, knowing there are people in that world who could help her?" *It's my fault she's sick,* I wanted to say. *So it's my responsibility to heal her.*

Rita was silent for a moment, just staring at me. Finally she muttered, "You shouldn't do this alone, you know that. I'll go with you."

I'd been praying she would say that—hence the

relevant clause in my bargain with Seyer—but I couldn't accept it without challenge. "You just got back from there. You've still got bruises—"

"And you shouldn't be alone with those people. Least of all in a place where if something happened to you, no one back home would know about it." She raised up a hand to silence me. "Don't even argue with me, Jesse. I'm coming."

Relief washed over me. "I would like the company," I admitted.

"Provided Seyer makes proper arrangements for us to cross over, of course. And protects us from the Shadows while we're there. Assuming she—or anyone—can do that." How quickly and easily Rita committed herself to that other world again! I remembered what she told me, the last time we talked about going through a Gate. *I've got nowhere better to go.* With no family or home she cared about, Rita could pick up and leave at will. And while I'd never asked about the intimate details of her upbringing, I knew she came from a challenging environment, and wasn't the kind of person who expected life to be easy or safe on a normal day.

The thought that I would have her by my side in Terra Prime did a lot to steady my nerves.

Devon shook his head, clearly frustrated. "I wish I could say the same, but it's not as easy to walk away when you've got a parent watching you like a hawk. My dad was pretty shaken by our 'kidnapping,' and he's determined not to let me out of his sight for a while. Just in case any of our assailants survived. I'm so sorry, Jesse. I'd go with you otherwise."

"Seyer said she could convince my family to let me go. She sounded pretty confident that she could deal with all their objections. Maybe she could do the same with your Dad as well."

God, it would be good to have him with me. Good to

have both of them with me. The mere thought of us going to Terra Prime all together bolstered my spirit considerably.

Hopefully we would all come home together.

▐▌▐▌▐▌▐▌▐▌▐▌▐▌

Filling Tommy in on my plans didn't go quite as smoothly as I'd hoped.

"I'm going with you," he said, folding his arms defiantly over his chest.

I shook my head. "You can't, Tommy."

"Why? Do you think I can't handle myself there? I tricked the Shadows into keeping me alive," he reminded me. "I kept them thinking that I was the one they were interested in, so they wouldn't go after you. I even fooled one of them into making their ghost guards leave me alone. Isn't that enough to prove I can take care of myself?" He threw up his hands in exasperation. "What more do you want?"

I sighed. *You're my 13-year-old brother. The 'brother' part of that means I'm supposed to protect you, not drag you into danger. And the 13-year-old part matters. I'm sorry, but it does.* Yes, Tommy was a hellishly resourceful kid, and with his background in fantasy gaming he was probably more qualified to explore an alien world than the rest of us put together. But we weren't going there to explore. We were going to negotiate with dangerous and powerful people, and having Tommy play fly-on-the-wall would only complicate that meeting.

None of which would matter to the kid standing in front of me, of course. All he would hear if I said that was that his sister was going to visit an alien world and not allowing him to come. "I have as much right to go there as you do," he said between gritted teeth.

But he didn't. That was the key point. I'd been born in Terra Prime, Devon and Rita also. Discovering that our DNA didn't match that of our parents had been the first step in that discovery. Tommy was a child of this world, and though that might not matter to us, it mattered a hell of a lot to the people we would be bargaining with. And they were the ones responsible for our safety. I'd already seen how they treated children from their own world, and I didn't want to think about how they would treat Tommy, who had no intrinsic right to be in their territory.

With a sigh I took him by the arms and drew him near to where I was sitting on my bed. I held him like that for a moment, just gazing into his eyes, wishing I had some words to offer that would make this easier. "What about Mom?" I asked gently. "What if I don't make it back — or at least, don't make it back in the right time frame? Because you know that's a possibility, no matter how well we plan. Losing one kid would be hard enough on her. How would she take it if both of us disappeared, and she never found out what happened to us?" I paused. "It would kill her, Tommy."

He stared at me for a moment. "Aw, crap," he muttered. He jerked out of my grip. "Crap!"

"You know I'm right," I pressed.

He turned from me and stomped melodramatically out of the room, slamming the door shut behind him. I shut my eyes and sighed deeply. It was not the way I'd wanted to end this conversation, but at least he seemed to accept the inevitable. One hurdle down.

The rest would be dealt with in the morning.

░░░░░░░░░░

We watched the fireworks from the roof of the house that night, Devon and Rita and Tommy and I, four world-travelers strung out in a line along the gritty shingles, while a backyard full of adults with beer cans in their hands watched from the property below. The night was misty and warm and the park was near enough to the house that, as each rocket exploded, it blossomed overhead, lighting up the sky from horizon to horizon. It was an amazing sight, invigorating to watch.

But it was also saddening. I couldn't help but think about Sebastian, who'd fought in the war we were now celebrating. I wished there was some way to bring him home to Terra Colonna, so that he could see the whole country lit up like a field of stars, honoring his victory.

Devon caught sight of a tear forming in my eye and put his hand over mine. We stayed that way until the last of the lights were gone from the sky, and the mist faded into darkness. Then we climbed back in through the attic window to go join the others.

6

SEER GUILDHOUSE IN LURAY
VIRGINIA PRIME

ALIA MORGANA

THE SAFETY LAMPS CAME ON as Morgana entered the underground chamber, providing just enough light for her to make her way to the large circular table at its center. A dozen velvet-upholstered chairs were visible surrounding it, but the rest of the chamber was shrouded in shadow.

Fewer distractions that way.

Morgana walked to the table and put down the two things she was carrying: a golden mask with a length of striped cloth attached, and an elaborately carved box. The mask was in the style of ancient Egypt, regal and elegant, the kind one would expect to find in the tomb of a queen. The box, when opened, revealed a large quartz crystal cut neatly into slices, nested in folds of velvet. Morgana lifted out one of the slices, looked at the Guild sign etched into its polished surface, and then put it back. Not the one she wanted. She inspected other slices, one by one, placing the ones she needed on the table as she found them. Elemental, Fleshcrafter, Obfuscate, Domitor, Healer, Soulrider, Weaver, and of course Seer. Eight Guild sigils in all.

"Brighter," she commanded, and the fetter lamps obediently increased their illumination. Now patterns etched into the table's surface were visible, a series of stars radiating out from its center, each with a different number of points. The resulting design was somewhat chaotic, and it took her a moment to isolate the star she wanted. Eight points. Using it as a guideline, she placed her crystal slices at the ends of the rays, so that they were perfectly spaced around the edge of the table. Then she sat down in front of the Seer sigil and checked the time. There were still a few minutes left to go.

It was rare these days that she experienced quiet. Rare for her to be so far away from other people that the incessant buzz of their thoughts and emotions was dulled to a murmur, little more than soft background music. She'd built this chamber far beneath the Guildhouse so that the earth would provide her with privacy—as much as was possible for a master Seer—and now, as she waited for her meeting to begin, she drank in the silence with relish.

A few minutes later her fetter watch vibrated gently. She took up the golden mask and fitted it to her face, smoothing the striped cloth back over her head until her hair was completely covered. Then she reached out and placed her hand on the Seers' crystal. As soon as she did, ghostly figures began to take shape around the table. Each one was masked, and like her, had its hand upon the crystal fetter corresponding to its Guild.

The first to appear was a Healer, a man wearing a mask of polished silver with a jeweled eye set in the center of the forehead. Right after that a Domitor appeared, a short and stocky man whose fierce red-and-black mask reminded Morgana of a Kabuki demon. Next came an Elemental, whose mask appeared to be carved from ice and crowned in flickering fire. Though the flames danced realistically about her head they brought no heat to the room, and the light they cast did not extend more than a few feet past her fetter. Next, an Obfuscate and a Weaver appeared simultaneously. The Grey was a small man whose mask had a mirrored surface; as he looked around at each of the others, their own faces were reflected back at them, distorted as if by a funhouse mirror. It was more than a little disturbing. The Weaver's mask was an intricate tapestry with arcane symbols woven into it and more designs embroidered on top of that; despite her exhaustive knowledge of symbology, Morgana didn't recognize all of them. Next a Soulrider arrived, a tall, lanky man in a wolf mask, and right behind him came a Fleshcrafter. The latter's mask was colorful, a bright carnival design that was elegantly human on the right side and twisted and bestial on the left. Morgana wondered which side better represented her true nature.

They all knew each other, of course, but given that their consortium sometimes acted against the interests of the Shadows, it was best to make sure that any spirits who might spy on them wouldn't recognize the participants. "I'm glad to see everyone could make it," Morgana said. "Master Grey, would you be so good as to update us on the situation with Luray's Gate?"

The Grey's mask hid his expression, but from his posture Morgana guessed that he was surprised to be the first one addressed. He was relatively new to the group, and of lower Guild rank than the rest of them; it was possible he felt a bit intimidated in this company. If so, that was something he would have to get used to. He was too valuable to the group to be cast out for simple social awkwardness.

He cleared his throat. "Things are moving at a good pace, but we've still got tons of rubble to move before we can allow access to the main chamber. The Lord Governor has crews working day and night on it, and the Elementals have provided terramancers, but it's still a monumental task. I estimate another week before we can send someone down to evaluate the condition of the portal. If we find that it's collapsed or become so unstable it's beyond practical use ..." he hesitated. "Then there's no point in clearing out any more rocks, is there?"

The Weaver spoke quietly. "The Luray portal existed for centuries before the Gate was built to stabilize it. It's hard to believe a simple explosion would damage it."

"That explosion took place on the Gate's threshold," the Grey reminded her, "and thus did far more damage than an explosion in the chamber would have. We already know that it resonated in other spheres; we can't ignore the possibility that the portal itself has been damaged."

The Domitor shook his head. "Bad news for Luray if the Gate is gone for good." He was one of the few members of the group who didn't live in or near the city, but he sounded like he would take a perverse pleasure in Luray's being humbled. Morgana made a mental note of it. "What's this I hear about lawsuits on the horizon?"

Morgana answered him. "Every day the Gate remains nonfunctional means our merchants have to route their goods and people through distant cities. That costs time and money. People will expect compensation for it: it's human nature. And Luray is a hub of interworld commerce, so the compensation will be sizeable."

"Who are they planning to sue? Or, to put it in plainer English: Who's getting blamed for all this?"

The Grey reached up nervously to rub his forehead and seemed startled when his fingers encountered the mask. Such disguises were a necessary precaution, but it took time to get used to wearing one. "Lord Virilian has informed the governor that my Guild was responsible for the Gate's security, hence this was our failing. Which is bullshit," he muttered. "We're facilitators for his Guild, nothing more. Don't they keep telling us that? The ultimate responsibility for this mess lies with them. But who wants to drag a Shadowlord into court? It's much easier to target us."

"This will go all the way to the top," the Healer mused. "And if it turns out the portal can't be made functional, someone big is going to go down for it. Possibly even a Guildmaster."

"Let's hope it's Virilian," the Weaver offered, "and not the Grey's Garret."

The Grey turned to glare at her. Even through his mask one could sense the intensity of his gaze. "Lady, I spent ten years in a hellhole in the Sauran Cluster because of one spoiled aristo brat who suffered a week's time displacement and missed a final exam. When his family demanded that someone be punished for that, Guildmaster Garret decided that I was the ideal scapegoat. Do you know what it's like to milk a six-foot centipede for venom? No? Because I do. It's not fun. It's even less fun when you have to do it for eight years straight. So either Virilian or Guildmaster Garret can go to hell for all I care."

"Easy, brother." Morgana's tone was sympathetic but firm. "You're among friends now."

The Domitor nodded. "The fall of your Guildmaster, pleasing though it might be, won't help us achieve our goals. We need to make sure this incident serves our greater purpose."

The Grey lowered his eyes and said nothing more. Like a child being admonished, Morgana thought. Such a gesture of submission wasn't necessary in this company—or appropriate—but the Grey wasn't a political player by nature, and he didn't yet understand all the fine points of the game he had been dragged into.

We'll have to keep an eye on him, Morgana thought. *See that he makes no mistakes while he's learning.*

Normally they would never have invited someone so inexperienced to join their conspiracy, but it was hard to find any Grey who was willing to act against his undead masters, and the opportunity could not be wasted. Never mind that this one had just returned from exile and had neither influence nor authority among his fellow Greys. For Morgana and her allies to have eyes and ears inside the Guild of Obfuscates had value in its own right.

He needs training, she thought. *Someone to take him under wing and see that he becomes what we need him to be.*

"Virilian isn't the most stable of Shadowlords on a good day," the Fleshcrafter noted. "If he gets hit with the blame for this, things could get interesting. And not in a good way."

The Elemental snorted, "I'm not sure 'stable' is an adjective one can apply to any Shadowlord."

"They're all pretty crazy," the Healer agreed.

"But some more than most," the Grey warned them.

All eyes turned to him.

Startled to have suddenly become the focus of attention, the Grey needed a few seconds to find his voice. "There are dark souls in our Guild. Monsters who should have been left in their graves, but whose spirits were preserved for future Shadowlords to Commune with. Only the strongest ones can take them in without going insane ... or so I'm told, anyway. But as the Lady Elemental pointed out, how many of the undead are sane to start with?"

The Domitor breathed in sharply. "Are you telling us that Virilian is host to one of these—what did you call them—dark souls?"

The Grey hesitated. "It's rumored that he is. No one knows for sure."

"So the psychopathic Guildmaster may be host to an even bigger psychopath?" The Weaver shook her head in exasperation. "That's just great."

"It won't change our plans if he is," Morgana said evenly. She bowed her head respectfully to the Grey. "Thank you for that information." *Which no one but a Grey could have provided,* she thought with satisfaction. *You are as close as we will ever come to having a spy among the Shadows.*

The Healer looked at Morgana. "You said you had a tool that might prove useful to us, something you were testing. Can you give us an update on that?"

"I wish I could," Morgana answered, her voice tinged with regret. Fortunately she was the only one in the room who could sense when a person was lying. "But at this point I need to keep the details quiet, so my testing environment won't be compromised. When I have results worth talking about, you'll all know it. I promise."

The Domitor stared at her for a moment in obvious displeasure, then snorted. "Well then, there's not much point in going on with this meeting, is there? Because we can't discuss future plans without knowing the status of the portal. And some people clearly aren't willing to talk about their existing plans." He glared at Morgana.

"There's no reason for you to share in the risk of my work until I've confirmed its value," she said steadily.

Before the Domitor could respond the Healer clapped his hands, putting an end to the exchange. "All right. What say we close this meeting now and reconvene next week for an update? I'm sure there will be more to report then." He looked pointedly at Morgana.

"I second that," the Weaver said.

"Any objections?"

There were none.

The Elemental was the first to remove her hand from her fetter; the minute she did so her image vanished. One by one the others followed suit, until the Soulrider's image was the only one left in the room.

Before the wolf-masked figure could break the connection, Morgana gestured for him to wait.

"A moment, Hunter."

The Soulrider looked at her.

"I need a favor from you. And I'm afraid it's a somewhat challenging one."

"Challenges temper the soul, Lady Seer. What is it?"

"Four changelings from Terra Colonna crossed into our world a short while ago. They're back on their adoptive world now, but I expect some of them to return here. When they do, I need time to observe them ... without interference."

It took the Soulrider a minute to realize what she was driving at; when he did, he breathed in sharply. "You think one of my Guild will be tasked with hunting them down?"

"They angered Virilian. He's a notoriously vengeful creature. If he learns they're back on Terra Prime, there's a good chance he'll go after them, if only for personal satisfaction. And his Soulrider already knows their scent."

He nodded. "Rhegar is a skilled tracker, and he's fiercely loyal to Virilian. I doubt he would refuse to hunt someone if the Guildmaster asked him to."

"He doesn't have to refuse the request," she said quietly. "He just has to fail at it."

For a moment the Hunter stared at her in silence. Then he shook his head. "You weren't kidding about the *challenging* part, were you? Rhegar's as proud—and as stubborn—as his undead master. Asking him to feign a hunt would be like asking a champion prizefighter to throw a match."

"But sometimes prizefighters do that, when the price is right. So the issue is not *whether* it can be done but *how*." When the Hunter said nothing she pressed, "Can you arrange it?"

He considered for a moment before answering. "My Guildmaster trusts my counsel. I could probably convince him to give the right orders. But I'd have to come up with a damn good reason for him to comply. Our Guild is less involved with the Shadows than yours is, but defying the will of a Shadowlord is still no small thing. Especially that particular Shadowlord." He cocked his head to one side, a move that was oddly canine. "So are you going to give me a story to offer him? Or do I need to come up with something on my own?"

She spread her hands. "I don't know the inner workings of your Guild well enough to know what would convince him. So I'm afraid I would need to leave that in your hands."

"And is this part of your secret experiment?"

A practiced wave of Morgana's hand casually dismissed the thought. "If you must know the truth, my Guild assessed the potential of these changelings when they were born, and sent them into exile on Terra Colonna. Now they're back. When's the last time you heard about a changeling finding his way home like that? It's a once in a lifetime opportunity for us to see what these children are capable of, when isolated from Gifted influence."

"Do you think they may be Gifted themselves?"

"I've seen no signs of that yet," she lied easily. "But if it turns out that one of them is, that would mean a Seer failed in his duty when he evaluated them. . . . so you understand why it's something I would need to investigate. Discreetly."

The Hunter sighed. "I understand, Lady. I'll do the best I can to keep Rhegar off their tail."

"Thank you, my friend."

The ghostly figure lifted his hand from his fetter and then he, too, was gone.

For a few minutes Morgana sat alone in the dimly lit room, wondering if she had told the Hunter too much. Or perhaps too little? She didn't dare let the others know why she was really watching Jessica, but she had to tell them something. Which meant that the closer her plan came to fruition, the more dangerous it would become.

I've risked everything for this experiment, she thought. *Let's hope the girl proves worth it.*

7

JESSE

THE SOUND OF GLASS SHATTERING woke me up.

For a moment I lay there in the darkness, not sure if it was something I'd dreamed or something real. Then I heard a heavy thud downstairs, like a body hitting the floor. Reflexively I reached under my pillow for my knife, just in case trouble came calling. These days it was reflex.

As I got up and moved toward the bedroom door I could hear people stirring in the hall outside; it sounded like the noise had awakened everyone in the house. I opened my door and saw my aunt and uncle rushing down the stairs, Rita and Tommy behind them. My brother had his knife in hand, which was probably why he was keeping to the rear of the pack: there was less chance of someone noticing that way.

I followed the flood of people down the stairs.

The ruckus was apparently coming from the kitchen. Dr. Tilford was already there. Devon was crouched on the floor, his back against a cabinet, wrapped in a trembling ball with his arms around his knees and his head down. Fragments of glass and pottery were scattered all around him, as well as pieces of what had once been a sandwich. He must have come down here to make himself a midnight snack.

As Rose and Julian rushed to his side, I looked around the room for anyone or anything that might have hurt him—perhaps oddities in the room that the others might not notice—but the only people there were known to me, and no objects looked out of place save for the mess on the floor. That didn't necessarily mean there was no one else present; I'd learned the hard way that there were aliens who were skilled at going unseen. But for now, at least, this seemed to be a mundane accident.

Devon's father knelt by his side, and as we all pressed in close to see what was going on he looked up and said, "Give him room, please." I could sense fear coming off Devon in waves, like heat off the summer pavement. Dr. Tilford seemed calm and collected on the outside, but I guessed that was just a facade. A good doctor knew how to keep his patient from sensing how worried he was.

"I'll call an ambulance," Uncle Julian said.

"Already did," Dr. Tilford told him. Then he turned back to his son. "You'll be fine. Try to take deep, slow breaths."

Devon didn't respond to him. His breathing was rapid and shallow, like a dog's panting, and his body vibrated with tremors every few seconds.

Aunt Rose asked, "What happened?"

"He's having trouble with his balance," Dr. Tilford said without looking up. "No idea why, yet."

"Is there anything we can do?"

Lips tight, he shook his head. "Not at the moment."

My aunt crouched down and started to clean up the pieces of shattered crockery. It wasn't what I would have worried about at a time like this, but maybe she needed the distraction.

Devon whispered hoarsely, "It's worse when I move my head."

"I know," his father said. "Just sit still for now. Help is on the way."

I could hear sirens now, moving toward us at a fast clip. That was one benefit of living in a small town; there were no traffic snarls to slow down an ambulance.

Devon looked up at me for an instant . . . or tried to. One of his eyes was twitching wildly back and forth, and I got the impression he couldn't see anything clearly. Then he shut his eyes again, leaned his head back against the wall, and shuddered. I was so terribly afraid for him, and also frustrated. There's nothing worse than seeing a friend in pain and not being able to help. I looked at Rita and Tommy and saw similar emotions in their eyes. None of us knew what to do, or even what to think.

When the ambulance finally arrived Rose met the paramedics at the door and led them to the kitchen. Dr. Tilford identified himself and gave them a quick rundown on Devon's condition. Mostly medical jargon, but some phrases were recognizable. *Sudden loss of balance. Disorientation. Severe nausea.* He displayed such an air of medical authority that I felt somewhat reassured; clearly he was on top of this.

With his hand on Devon's shoulder he asked, "Can you move?"

"I'm not sure." His son's voice was barely audible, and he winced when he spoke, as if even the slight movement of his jaw made him feel sicker.

Then the paramedics took him by his arms and helped him get to his feet. He was swaying like a drunk, and at one point it looked like he was about to throw up. Two more paramedics had brought in a stretcher, and they helped ease him onto it while Dr. Tilford watched in obvious torment. I could taste how much he wanted to step in and help, but that wasn't the protocol, and he knew it.

When Devon was finally lying down he shut his eyes, sighing deeply as they strapped him in, as if relieved that he would not have to move for a while. His color was ghastly. The paramedics wheeled him out with Dr. Tilford close behind; the rest of us followed in their wake, down the hallway, through the entrance foyer, and out onto the front porch. From there we huddled together and watched as they slid the stretcher into the back of the ambulance. Dr. Tilford exchanged a few words with the head paramedic, then the two of them climbed inside the back, and the heavy doors swung shut behind them.

Suddenly I realized that we weren't alone. Neighbors had come out onto their porches to see what all the commotion was about, and a few people in robes and pajamas were standing in the roadway across from our house. For one sickening moment I had a flashback to the pajama-clad crowd that had surrounded my house when it burned down. I tried to shut them out of my head as I looked back at the ambulance.

Someone grabbed my hand and squeezed it briefly. Rose? Tommy? I didn't want look away long enough to find out.

Finally the ambulance began to move out. Sirens pierced the night as brightly colored lights began to strobe from its roof. I felt tears start to gather in the corner of one eye, born of fear and frustration. I felt helpless not being able to help the friend who had been such comfort to me in my own need.

"C'mon." Uncle Julian's strong hand gripped my shoulder. "Get some clothes on, we'll take the SUV."

||||||||||||||

The emergency room was sleek and clean and mostly empty. In one corner was a middle-aged woman who was knitting nervously; every few minutes she would glance at the double doors that led to the hospital's interior, a look of concern on her face, then she would turn back to her yarn and knit even more furiously. Other than her, we were the only non-nurses there.

A woman in scrubs showed up to tell us that Devon was being cared for and that for now he seemed to be okay, but she wouldn't give us any more details. We weren't family.

Eventually Dr. Tilford came out. His normally stoic façade was clearly being strained to the breaking point.

"Devon is suffering from an acute attack of vertigo," he told us. "They don't know the cause yet, but they've ruled out some major concerns. He seems stable for now." He turned back toward the double doors. "I'll let you know if anything changes."

Before he could leave I asked, "Is he going to be okay?"

He hesitated. "We're doing everything we can to make sure of it."

He didn't wait around for any more questions, so I pulled out my phone and looked up vertigo. *Extreme dizziness*, Wikipedia said. *Sometimes comes on without warning*.

Not a big help.

Time crept by after that with agonizing slowness. Tommy had stayed at the house to monitor the internet channels, searching for any sign that other changelings were getting sick. It wasn't so long ago that someone had been killing them off one by one, and if that was starting up again, we needed to know. But he said he hadn't found anything to suggest that was the case. One bit of good news, anyway.

Finally Rita and I were allowed to see Devon.

He was sitting in a hospital bed, in a small enclosure with curtains for walls. He seemed to be aware of us when we entered the room, but he didn't open his eyes.

"Hey," I said.

"Hey," he whispered weakly.

"You okay?"

"If I don't move. Or try to look at anything." He paused. "Or breathe too hard."

He barely moved as he spoke to us. His hands were gripping the rails of the bed as if he was afraid of falling out of it. I placed my hand gently on top of one of them. His skin was clammy, and I felt him trembling.

Dr. Tilford came into the enclosure. "Tests all negative so far," he told Devon.

"Is that good?" I asked.

"Well, it doesn't tell us what's wrong, but some rather serious possibilities have been ruled out, so that's good. Sometimes this kind of thing just comes out of the blue. We may never know the cause."

A nurse entered the enclosure, took Devon's blood pressure, and gave him some medication. Then Dr. Tilford left for a minute to go talk to the doctors. And the three of us were alone together.

Devon whispered, "Do you think *they* did this?"

Neither Rita nor I had to ask what he meant. Was it possible that people from Terra Prime were responsible for his sudden illness? I couldn't recall a case where any changelings had been struck down exactly like this, but that didn't mean much. There were probably dozens of changeling deaths we didn't know anything about. Tommy's online research suggested that none of the others were being assaulted, but the three of us might be a special case. We were the only changelings who knew the truth about where we were from. The only ones who had crossed into the world of our birth and destroyed a major transportation hub on our way out. The Shadows might want revenge for that. The Greys might want revenge for that. Hell, a dozen other Guilds whose Gifts we'd never heard of might want revenge for that.

But they could have killed Devon if they'd wanted to, I reminded myself. *This was just a warning shot.* "They have people who can heal. I suppose they have people who can un-heal." I spoke softly, so no one outside the curtain would hear me. "Maybe they're trying to scare us off."

"To keep us from going back to Terra Prime?" Rita asked.

I nodded.

She folded her arms over her chest, a gesture that managed to be both defensive and aggressive at the same time. "So what, then? Are we supposed to give up, just like that? What about your mom?"

I looked down at Devon. His coffee-colored skin was filmed in sweat. "We can wait a few days, until Devon gets better. I can talk to Seyer—"

"No," Devon rasped. "No. You two have to go. Now. Don't wait for me."

"Why?" I asked.

"Because if you're right, and they're trying to scare us off, what will happen when they figure out you're just delaying the trip, not cancelling it? They might do something worse than this, to drive the message home. Maybe go after Rita next time . . . or even you. But once you cross over, there'll be no point in threats anymore; they'll have lost that battle."

"Shit," Rita muttered. "He's right."

"And second . . ." He sighed. "I'm sorry, Seyer's Gift may be terrifying and powerful and utterly beyond my comprehension, but nothing short of a direct message from God Himself is likely to convince my father I should go with you. I mean, it was nice to dream, but. . . ." His words trailed off into a pained silence.

For a moment no one said anything. I wondered if Dr. Tilford was rethinking his response to the story Devon had told him. No one on our world could cause sickness like this, but Devon had described a world where people could. Was Dr. Tilford wondering now if he'd dismissed his son's tale too quickly? Was he wondering if the maker of our alien artifact might want to hurt his son? Or was he ascribing the timing of this to mere coincidence?

"I don't want to go without you," I murmured.

He sighed. "Yeah, and I don't want to lie in a hospital bed worrying about whether you're both safe or not. But we don't always get what we want." He attempted to shake his head, but winced as soon as the motion began. "I wish I could go with you too, Jesse."

Something about the way he said my name made my heart lurch in my chest. I leaned down and kissed him gently on the forehead. His skin was cool and salty against my lips. At least he had no fever. That was good, right?

He opened his eyes and looked at me. His left eye was twitching less than it had in Rose's kitchen. "Come home in the right time frame," he whispered. "Even if you have to stay there a while to figure out how to do it right. Don't end up like Sebastian, coming home after everyone you love is long dead." *Including me,* his eyes pleaded.

"We will," I told him, and Rita said, "We promise."

Dr. Tilford came back then, so I let go of Devon's hand. The doctor told us he was going to spend the night by Devon's side, and promised to text us if anything changed. So we left them both there. What else could we do? Whoever had struck Devon down had played his hand well.

One third of our team was lying helpless in a hospital bed, we hadn't even left home yet.

As omens went, it was a pretty lousy one.

8

BERKELEY SPRINGS
WEST VIRGINIA

JESSE

SEYER SHOWED UP IN THE MORNING, right on schedule. My mother hadn't been all that happy about our plans, when we'd discussed them the night before, and with Devon's midnight emergency having shaken us all pretty badly, she was even less happy about them now. Despite our assurances that Seyer had once been "an old family friend," Mom said she didn't know her *now*, and that was what mattered. As Seyer drove up she stood on the porch with her arms folded across her chest, and it looked like we weren't going to be traveling anywhere.

Seyer had brought a young girl with her, a thin waif in a flowered sundress, who she introduced as Samantha. The girl stuck by Miriam's side, her wide blue eyes taking in the scene as Seyer explained to my mother how good it would be for me to get away for a while. A kind of vacation. It all sounded pretty lame to me (vacation from what?) but within minutes Mom was nodding and smiling, and saying yes, yes, it might be good for me to get away, and she was glad that Seyer was giving me the opportunity to do so. She agreed that while it would be nice if Seyer's mountain retreat had good cell phone reception, so she could keep in touch with us, of course in the mountains of West Virginia, service might be spotty and she understood that. Ten minutes later I had her permission to go, and even Rose—who had been more wary of the trip than Mom was—beamed as she gave us a tin of chocolate chip cookies to take with us. So Rita and I fetched the bags we'd packed for the trip, including a large black portfolio with the painting in it, and she climbed into the car while I said goodbye to Mom.

As we hugged I pressed my cheek against hers, drinking in her scent, her warmth, and her affection, trembling as I tried not to think about all the things that might keep me from returning to her. True, I was only going to Terra Prime to talk to someone, and Miriam Seyer had promised to bring us home right after that, but neither Rita nor I was so naïve as to think that it would all go off exactly as planned. The universe just didn't work like that. Terra Prime was a frightening and unpredictable world, and we barely knew a fraction of its rules. When we left our own world behind, we had to accept that there was a small chance we might never come home again.

I will come back to you, Mom. I buried my face in her neck so that no one could see the tears forming in my eyes. *I'll find a way to heal you, and I'll come home to you. I promise.*

Finally it was time to leave. I threw my backpack into the car, waved a final farewell to Tommy, and climbed into the back seat, next to Rita.

It wasn't until Seyer's SUV pulled onto the main road that she formally introduced us to her companion: *Samantha Cassidy, Journeyman of the Domitors.* It didn't take a degree in Latin to figure out the nature of Cassidy's Gift. Suddenly my family's unexpected change in attitude made total sense, as did a few other things, considerably darker in nature. I remembered how many of the other changelings had died because they'd made foolish choices. One had gone surfing in hurricane waters, I recalled, and another had dived into a concrete pool at the wrong angle. And one person with a bee allergy had walked right into an angry hive. Back when we'd first heard about those deaths we couldn't imagine how an outside agency could have caused all that, but if there was a Gift that allowed one to nudge people's thoughts in a particular direction, quieting the inner voice that normally kept them from doing stupid things, maybe it wasn't so great a mystery after all.

I wondered if Samantha had been involved in any of those killings.

Since the Gate in Luray was now buried under tons of rubble, Seyer said she was going to take us north, to something she called an E-Gate. Apparently the 'E' stood for *ephemeral.* Unlike the portal in Luray, this one hadn't been around for centuries, but was a fleeting phenomenon, like the rift Sebastian had run into at the North River. Seyer assured us that the Greys had stabilized it for now, but you didn't have to be a rocket scientist to figure out that something named *ephemeral* was probably temporary in nature. Did that mean that the portal might vanish at any moment? Maybe while we were passing through it?

The Greys are experts at this stuff, I told myself. *Surely they wouldn't let people enter the Gate if it was dangerous.*

We drove for a while without anyone talking. Not

that there weren't a thousand and one questions I
wanted to ask Seyer, but the situation with Devon had
left me badly shaken, and his absence hung like a dank
cloud over our journey. Rita spent most of the trip leaning against the window of Seyer's SUV, staring out at
the passing landscape in silence, so she must have felt it,
too. It was strange for the two of us to be going to Terra
Prime without him. Like leaving part of your own body
behind.

Just before hitting the main highway, Seyer pulled
over for gas. There was a nearby convenience store, and
the Domitor took some money from the glove compartment and headed inside to buy us all drinks. When she
was gone, I turned to Seyer and asked, "How long were
you watching me?"

She raised an eyebrow slightly, said nothing.

"I know that you scoped my house one day, before I
met you. Tommy saw you there. So, was that the first
time you spied on me? Or is this something that's been
going on for a while?"

She didn't say anything. She just looked at me for a
moment longer, smiled slightly, then got out of the car
and went to where the squeegees were stored. A minute
later she was cleaning the windshield. A faint smile
creased her lips, maybe part amusement, maybe something else. Something darker.

She never answered me.

Damn her.

⸻

If you'd asked me a year ago what I thought the portal
to another world would look like, the last thing I would
have said was *The Department of Motor Vehicles*.

Life is full of surprises.

After a couple of hours on the highway, Seyer turned
off onto a narrow dirt road. At the end of it was a large

open field surrounded by a primitive stone wall, and a weathered barn at the far end that had seen better days. The field was full of vehicles, not all of them neatly parked: cars, vans, pickup trucks, even one eighteen wheeler. Some looked brand new, others like they had just come from a demolition derby. Seyer parked at the end of the last row and then told us we would have to leave our cell phones in her glove compartment for safekeeping, as we couldn't bring electronic devices through the Gate. I noted that she took it for granted that we both had our phones with us, which of course we did. I couldn't answer for Rita's motives, but I figured if we wound up returning to Terra Colonna in some unexpected time or place, I wanted my phone with me. With a sigh I checked to make sure my phone was locked, then turned it off and stowed it in the glove compartment alongside Rita's and Seyer's.

I had far worse contraband in my backpack, but of course I wasn't going to tell her that.

It turned out the barn wasn't an old building at all, just a big stage set. What had appeared from a distance to be mildew turned out to be speckled green paint, and a power sander had clearly been used to grind off some of the color in strategic spots, I could see little dents where someone had beaten the wood with a chain to make it look weatherworn. *Shabby chic alien portal.*

Inside was a small foyer, where a pleasant looking woman with nondescript features greeted us politely from behind a cheap Formica counter. "Good afternoon," she said in a quasi-British accent (modified by a Southern twang). "How may I help you?" Wordlessly Seyer removed three small black booklets from her purse and handed them to her; the Domitor apparently had her own. As the woman flipped through the booklets I saw my picture in one of them and Rita's in another. Some kind of passport? The clerk gave each one a cursory glance, compared our names to those on a list on her clipboard, then handed them back to us.

"Departure in twenty-three minutes," she said pleasantly. "Any special dispensations?"

"No," Seyer responded.

"Customs declarations and waivers are over there." She indicated a shelf I hadn't noticed before, also cheap Formica, a narrow ledge running the length of the wall. There were papers stacked neatly in bins and pens in little black cups, the universal symbol for *Hey, you need to fill something out*. "We have lockers for contraband, if you need one."

"Thank you," Seyer said, and she ushered us toward the shelf.

There were two documents there, and Seyer told us to sign them using the names in our passbooks, and date them. The first had a bold heading that read CONTRABAND DECLARATION, and below that a statement in smaller type: *I, _____ verify that I am not carrying on my person, nor will I attempt to bring through the Gate, any of the following items*. Below that was a list of items the folks of Terra Prime didn't want in their world. Some of them we already knew about—*electronic devices of any kind* topped the list—but some were surprising, and a few were just plain weird. Seriously, how much would it threaten their world if someone brought a pack of chewing gum? I reviewed the list, then got to the part where I had to initial a box to verify that I'd read and agreed to it. I glanced at Rita. Did she also have something in her backpack that was less than kosher, or was she playing it straight? Her expression offered me no clue. Finally I sighed, checked the box, and then looked in my passbook to see what alias Seyer had assigned to me. Jennifer Dolan. I signed on the dotted line, thus establishing that my first official act in traveling to Morgana's world was to lie to authorities.

The other document was a legal disclaimer. *I, _____, hereby acknowledge that the portal I am about to enter is a natural phenomenon, neither created for or by, nor controlled by, the Guild of Obfuscates. I acknowledge that while the Guild has established a Gate to help facilitate safe passage, minor temporal disturbances are still possible, which the Guild may not be able to predict or nullify. I verify that I am choosing to enter the Gate fully cognizant of these risks, and will not hold the Guild liable for any temporal disturbance I may suffer, or for any other adverse effect attending my passage.*

It was more than a little chilling, but I figured we were already past the point of no return, so I signed that one, too.

Once we handed in our paperwork we were allowed to proceed to the main room, which was so utterly mundane in appearance that I felt like I'd walked into the DMV. It was a large room with a counter running along one wall, rows of molded plastic chairs in the middle, and a big sign overhead that proclaimed in capital letters, SERVING NEXT: E43. Surely any minute now we would hear an announcement about where to go to get a photograph taken for our portal-crossing license. Thank God Seyer had all our papers in order, so we didn't have to wait in any lines. It was only a short wait before we were ushered through a door at the far end of the room, along with a dozen other people.

Having only seen the Gate in Luray, I'd assumed that the other ones looked much the same: mysterious archways hidden deep underground, flanked by rows of insensate bodies ready to be used as transportation tools. But this arch was a much less imposing structure, smaller and simpler than its Luray counterpart, and without the layered crystals that had lent the other such a fantastic air. Still, I felt my heart flutter with fear as I looked at it.

I still remembered the icy breath of the void that lay beyond that Gate and had no desire to ever experience it again.

Suddenly the space inside the arch began to shimmer. A golden pattern began to take shape line by line, in its center. The design wasn't something I saw with my eyes but rather with my mind. Faint strains of music wafted toward me, as if floating on an unseen breeze. Random chords, haunting and somber, as if an orchestra worlds away was fine-tuning its instruments, and we were hearing their echoes.

Then a Shadowlord stepped through. His sudden presence was like a blast of icy wind, and the hair on the back of my neck pricked upright as I stared at him, mesmerized by the unearthly quality of his appearance. Bloodless skin, empty black eyes, a body whose edges shifted and faded even as I tried to focus on him . . . the sight of him stirred a visceral fear deep within me, and I instinctively stepped back from him. A few of the locals did the same, though more discreetly than I did. Apparently even people who were used to ghosts and shapechangers didn't want to get too close to his kind.

What if this Shadow knows who I am? I thought suddenly. *What if he recognizes me as one of the Colonnans connected to the destruction of the Gate in Luray?* The Shadows might not have considered it worth their time to hunt me down back home, but now I was re-entering their world—their territory—and the rules might change. Every survival instinct in my soul was urging me to turn and run out of here, to get as far away from this unnatural creature as I possibly could. If I could make it outside, into the sunlight, he wouldn't follow me there. Shadowlords hated the sun as much as vampires did.

But the Shadow didn't spare a glance for me, or for any of the tourists; he just spoke briefly to the Grey in charge, then turned back to the arch and addressed . . .

well, empty air. Out of the corner of my eye I thought I
saw a shadow that might or might not be in the shape of
a man, but it disappeared as soon as I tried to look directly at it. A ghost, perhaps? The Shadowlord gestured
toward the Gate, and I saw the wispy shape move
toward the portal. All right, that made sense. Passage
between the worlds required precise coordination, and
since there was no cell phone service spanning the distance, someone had to carry messages back and forth.
And since spirits of the dead were immune to the negative
side effects of crossing, they were the obvious candidates. I
was witnessing the very service that had made Shadowlords the undisputed masters of the multiverse. Without
them, individual worlds like mine were isolated islands in
a vast and angry sea, their wealth—raw materials, slave
species, children with valuable Gifts—hopelessly out of
reach. It was the Gift of the Shadows that allowed Terra
Prime to rape all the other worlds of everything from di-
nosaurs to artwork to infant psychics in their cradles.
Whatever other worlds had that was valuable, the Shadows enabled Terra Prime to claim it.

A gentle prod between my shoulder blades nudged
me forward. Travelers were queuing up to go through
the gate, their order dictated by a Grey reading names
from a clipboard, and when my name—my fake name—
was called, I took my place in line. I tried not to think
about the realm of formless chaos that we were about to
enter. This passage would be different than the others;
the chaos of *between* was no threat to me.

But I remembered the terms of the waiver I had
signed, and I shuddered.

A new pattern was beginning to take shape in the
center of the Gate now, that reminded me of some of
my dream designs, and also of the codex that Sebastian
had given us, the symbolic map that had helped us find
our way home. I concentrated on memorizing its twists

and turns so that I could reproduce the pattern later. Then the line of travelers began to move, person after person stepping through the Gate and disappearing into darkness. As each one crossed the threshold, a different person emerged from the arch to take his place, similar to him in size and shape. The exchange was perfectly synchronized, a dance of almost-twins set to the music of the Gate. I knew enough about how portals worked to understand that these people were here to balance our passage, so that the delicate equilibrium of energy required to keep the Gate stable could be maintained. But given that the last such people I'd seen were wheeled across on morgue gurneys, I was startled to see these walking under their own power. I looked back at Seyer, a question in my eyes, but she just smiled that maddening smile of hers and nodded for me to move me forward.

Into the darkness between the worlds.

Passage lasted no more than a split second this time—apparently it was faster when proper procedures were followed—but that brief moment was almost more than I could handle. I understood the nature of the realm we were passing through in a way these other travelers never would, and even a split-second reminder of that formless chaos, and the visceral terror it inspired, was nearly more than I could handle. By the time I stepped out into Terra Prime my whole body was shaking, and after Rita and Seyer came through, we couldn't get out of the building fast enough for my liking.

Outside there was sunlight: golden-bright, summer-warm, its heat carried to us by fresh mountain breezes. Gradually I relaxed, and my trembling subsided. Seyer arranged for a horse-drawn cab to take us to a nearby train. She'd booked a private cabin for us, she said. The trip to Luray would be long, so it might as well be comfortable. She and Samantha chatted on the way, but it was the kind of small talk that goes in one ear and out the other. Universal custom. I didn't feel like talking to these people, or to anyone.

When we got to the train an attendant in uniform led us to our cabin, and I sank down gratefully onto one of the thickly padded benches. Now that the horror of the Gate was behind us, the exhaustion of the last few days was catching up with me. How long had it been since I'd had a good night's sleep? I was so upset by the attack on Devon that sleep was impossible, and the nights before that had been filled with tossing and turning, as fear of the dream-wraith's return possessed me each time I sank into a dreaming state. Now ... the leather seats were soft and deep, the rhythm of the train was mesmerizing, and though I didn't trust Seyer and her people worth a damn, I suspected the dream-wraith wouldn't visit me while I was in her presence.

I did ask Seyer about the people who'd balanced our crossing. I didn't expect her to answer, but to my surprise she did, explaining that there were many different ways of managing the exchange, and keeping bodies in stasis so they could be sent across was just one of them. It was more expensive to hire an unending stream of people to make the crossing, but this far from a major population center, harvesting local material was difficult. The big cities were full of people no one cared about, but in a small town, people tended to notice when their neighbors went missing.

Harvest. Material. Bodies in stasis. That's all the people of my world were to Seyer and her kind. The un-Gifted had no value save to be used as tools, as commerce, as sport, or as servants. Hell, my world treated dogs better than her world treated people.

With a sigh I leaned back in the seat. My eyes began to slide shut of their own accord, and I lacked the strength—or the desire—to keep them open. I needed to be fresh for my meeting with Morgana, right? Surely it would be far worse to nod off in her presence than to do so now, when I was—in a relative sense, at least—safe.

My last thought as I drifted off to sleep was: *God help me if I ever become as callous as these people.*

9

SEER GUILDHOUSE IN LURAY
VIRGINIA PRIME

JESSE

IT FELT STRANGE entering the Seers' estate through the front entrance, like a legitimate visitor. Strange to be waved in by the guards like a visiting dignitary and helped down from our coach by liveried servants who bowed to us, albeit more deeply to Seyer.

Viewed from the front walk (as opposed to my previous experience of peering through a hedge), the Guildhouse seemed twice as imposing as before. On my first visit I'd taken note of the Egyptian frieze over the doorway and statues of Bast, the cat god, flanking the staircase, but now that I was closer I could see just how pervasive that ancient cultural influence was. Decorative carvings surrounding the base of each column might have looked like simple geometric designs to most people, but I recognized them as stylized lotus blossoms, a common Egyptian motif. The sconces flanking the front doors were in the form of papyrus stalks, and a matching pattern was carved into each door. Was there an actual connection between the Guild of Seers and the ancient Egyptians, or had the architect who designed this place just liked the style?

There was one element that wasn't Egyptian, a geometric symbol etched into a bronze plaque, right over the door. I remembered seeing it on a banner at the fair we'd visited the first time we came to this world. A small circle nestled inside an oblong shape, framed by an equilateral triangle: the sigil of the Guild of Seers. Now that I had a chance to look at it in a calmer setting, without the ruckus of the fair distracting me, it seemed oddly familiar, as if I knew the design from somewhere before. Maybe in my own world? Try though I might, I couldn't place it.

Inside the building, a shadowy entrance foyer with a high vaulted ceiling offered relief from the summer heat. The polished marble floor was inlaid with an intricate mandala-like pattern, at the center of which the Guild sigil was repeated. Our footsteps echoed eerily in the chamber as we crossed it, like footsteps in a tomb, and an abbie stepped forward to meet us. The small slave hominid was dressed in a loose white shift with a gold-and-silver belt, and her hair had been neatly braided and coiled around her head. She was the first abbie I'd ever seen who was nicely dressed. Maybe her species was treated better here.

Seyer told us, "I'll need to brief her Grace before I introduce you. Meanwhile, Sarai will bring you whatever refreshments you would like." She indicated the abbie, who bowed her head submissively and did not look up again until Seyer was gone. In truth I was too distracted to care about eating, but the day was hot and a cold drink would be pleasant, so I asked if she had iced tea. Rita said that any cold drink would do. The abbie bowed again, then left us alone in the echo chamber. I don't think either Rita or I was really thirsty, but I wanted to send the hominid away so we could talk freely.

Suddenly I realized that we'd never heard any of the abbies speak. They'd made animal-like sounds when we spied on them in the woods, but every other time we'd seen them, they were submissively silent. Did they lack the physical capacity for human speech, or had they just decided that silence was the best mode for a slave to operate in? At what point in human evolution did language first appear?

When she was finally gone I looked at Rita. "Does it seem strange to you that Seyer would be briefing Morgana?" I whispered.

She raised an eyebrow. "How so?"

"Well, she knew for a whole day that we would be coming here. Wouldn't you expect her to have contacted Morgana before this? So everything was prepared for our arrival?" I was turning puzzle pieces over in my mind, trying to see how they all fit together. "But that would have required a messenger, either living or dead . . . and the Shadows control the dead."

"She could have just sent a normal person with a message." Rita rolled her eyes slightly. "Assuming anyone could be considered 'normal' here."

"But that messenger would still have to go through a Gate to get to Morgana, and the Shadows control the Gates." I paused. "Maybe Seyer was afraid they would ask too many questions about her business. Or about us."

"Jeez, Jesse." Rita shook her head in mock dismay. "You're seriously overthinking this stuff."

"Says the girl who doesn't have a Gift that people would kill you for," I pointed out. How did the old saying go? *It's not paranoia if people are really out to get you.*

I returned my attention to the pattern at my feet, trying to place where I'd seen it before. I didn't even hear when the abbie came back, and Rita had to nudge my shoulder to get my attention.

The iced tea was good, if a little too sweet for my taste. Sipping it, I suddenly realized why the pattern looked so familiar. Resting my portfolio against my legs, I handed my drink to Rita, then slid my bag from my shoulder and rummaged inside it. My wallet was in a zippered compartment at the bottom, not easy to open without emptying the whole bag. But eventually my questing fingers found the wallet, and I pulled a single bill out of it. One American dollar. I studied it, turned it over, and felt my heart skip a beat as I saw it. Right there. Just like I'd remembered it.

"What?" Rita demanded. "What is it?"

I held it over the symbol on the floor and invited Rita to compare the two. She did, and her eyes went wide. "Holy crap."

On the back of the bill was an unfinished pyramid glowing with light, with a human eye above it. If you reduced that image to a simple line drawing, it would look similar to the design on the floor.

No. Not similar. It would look *exactly* like the design on the floor.

So what did that mean? That the Guild of Seers had designed our currency? My head was spinning from trying to make sense of it all.

Footsteps could be heard now, coming toward us. Probably Seyer returning. I stuffed the bill into my pocket so she wouldn't see it, shouldered my bag again, and took my drink back from Rita.

All my life I'd disdained conspiracy theorists, especially when they talked about secret organizations that manipulated human history for shadowy purposes. But maybe I shouldn't have been so quick to dismiss them. I

remembered how easily the Domitor had convinced my
family to do what she wanted, in a way that no observer
would remark upon. A powerful woman like Morgana,
with all the Gifts of this world at her disposal, could easily nudge human history in whatever direction she
wanted it to go, and no one would be the wiser. Doubt-
less there were Shadows and the Greys who could do
the same. Psychics and undead and aliens, secretly guid-
ing our world. Maybe the conspiracy junkies weren't so
crazy after all.

Seyer looked calm and collected as she rejoined us;
clearly her meeting with Morgana had gone well. She
called for the abbie to take away our glasses, and Rita
took one last sip before handing hers over. This time I
noted that the hominid kept her eyes averted while she
interacted with Seyer, though whether that was from
fear of her, or simply ritual submission, it was impossible to say.

"Come," Seyer told us. "Her Grace will see you now."

||||||||||||

The library where Alia Morgana received us was a tradi-
tional Victorian style study, with dark wooden bookshelves, thickly upholstered chairs, and a polished
mahogany reading table. Positioned between the bookshelves were narrow glass-fronted cabinets that contained mixed assortments of small artifacts, all of which
looked ancient. Music was playing softly in the background—something classical—and Rita and I both
looked around for speakers, wondering what manner of
non-electronic device was broadcasting it. But nothing
was visible.

"Beethoven's Eleventh." The voice came from behind us: smooth, sophisticated, emotionless. I turned
and found myself facing the woman I'd seen with Seyer
at the assessment fair. She was still wearing white, and

the sculpted curls of her golden hair were arranged around her head like a halo. In the midst of all the dark Victorian wood she glowed with light, like an angel. Or perhaps like something darker, that wanted to pass for an angel.

"A bit reminiscent of the Fourth Symphony," she continued. "Although I find his later works more mature."

I had promised myself that no matter what Morgana said or did I wouldn't act surprised. I knew that I needed to exude confidence if I was going to negotiate with her, and gaping like a backwater rube every time she made some reference to Terra Prime technology was not the way to accomplish that. But for all our talk about visiting parallel worlds, I'd never really considered all the artistic implications of that. What masterpieces might Van Gogh have produced if he hadn't died young? Or Mozart? Or John Lennon? Somewhere there were worlds where those people had survived. Where they had continued creating works of genius until they died of old age, resulting in a wealth of art and music that my world would never see. Morgana and her kind harvested those works for their private pleasure, while the rest of us were left in the dark. *They're vultures,* I thought. *Fashionable,* w*ell-spoken vultures, feeding off the carrion of other worlds.*

Speaking of vultures, there was a tall birdcage in one corner of the room, with a creature inside that was both like and unlike a bird. It had colorful feathers arranged in clusters at the ends of its wings and tail, but the body was lizard-like in shape, and when it squawked at me I saw rows of needle-sharp teeth in its mouth.

"Your Grace." Seyer bowed her head respectfully to her mistress. "Allow me to introduce Miss Jessica Drake and Miss Rita Morales, of Terra Colonna."

"Of Terra Prime," Morgana corrected her gently. "They do acknowledge their birthright, do they not?"

Seyer flushed. "Of course, your Grace. My apologies."

The Guildmistress smiled at us. Her expression was polished and perfect, and so clearly rehearsed that it lacked even a hint of sincerity. If she'd been holding a knife behind her back and thinking about how to stab us, she probably wouldn't have looked any different.

"I'm glad to have a chance to finally meet you," she said, "though I admit, the last thing I expected was for you to return to Terra Prime." She looked me over as she spoke, and suddenly I felt very exposed. Was she able to read my thoughts? My emotions? What did a Seer's Gift do, exactly?

She noted the portfolio tucked under my arm. "I understand you have something for me?"

Not trusting myself to speak, I simply nodded.

She gestured toward the reading table. I walked over to it and set the stiff black folder down, but before I could open the zipper Rita put a hand on my arm, stopping me.

"Just so we're clear," she said to Morgana, "the price for this painting includes an audience with her Grace, then safe passage home for both of us. *Safe* passage. You agreed to that, right?"

It was Seyer who responded. "Her Grace is aware of the terms of our bargain," she said acidly. "All the conditions we discussed will be honored."

Rita continued staring at Morgana; clearly Seyer's assurance was not enough for her. After a moment Morgana chuckled softly and said, "All your terms are acceptable, Miss Morales. I shall see you delivered home like royalty."

Rita let go of my arm. I unzipped the portfolio and spread it open on the table so that my painting was exposed. As I stood back and tried to see my work through Morgana's eyes, I realized that the bright colors that had seemed so harmonious at the brightly lit mill looked a bit garish in this dark setting. But that was okay; the goal had been to create a work rich in meaning, not subtlety.

Morgana studied the painting in silence for a minute and then reached out to touch it. When her finger made contact with the canvas I felt a faint cold prickling along my skin, as if she were touching me instead of my work. As she ran her fingers along the ridges of my paint strokes I had to fight the urge to cross my arms in front of my body, to cover myself.

"Not as complex as some of your earlier work," she murmured. Finally her hand fell away from the piece. "The emotional energy is a bit . . . erratic. Had you devoted more time to it, the resonance probably would have been more stable. But the composition is interesting."

"Glad you like it," I muttered.

"I do. Which means you've earned your time with me." Her eyes were an odd mix of blue, green, and grey, I noted, and they shifted color as she moved. Disconcerting. "So what business of yours is so pressing that you think it merits this audience?"

I was pretty sure Seyer had explained to her about my mother's situation, so I just reviewed the highlights. She listened in silence. I couldn't tell from her expression what she was thinking.

When I was done she said, "Mistress Seyer has explained why no Healer can help your mother?"

I nodded. "She has, Your Grace." The title felt strange on my modern American tongue.

"A Fleshcrafter might be able to do something for her, but it would be a chancy operation at best. And they're an insular lot, the Potters. Outside of their work in prepping changelings for adoption they generally keep to themselves, and they don't welcome commissions from outsiders. It would take more than a handful of coin to convince one of them to travel to another world, to help save a woman who, by the measure of our society, is of no consequence."

I bit back on the sharp comment I wanted to make. I knew from our last visit that she considered my little brother expendable, so it came as no surprise to hear that the rest of my family meant nothing to her. But *I* was not nothing to her. I was part of some project she was planning, which meant that someday she might need my cooperation. If she left my mother to suffer now, when she had the ability to save her, she could kiss that cooperation goodbye.

None of which had to be said out loud, I was sure.

In my best negotiating voice I said, "I was hoping that you might be willing to help me cut a deal with them. Maybe there's something I could offer you in return for that?" I glanced pointedly at the painting.

She followed my gaze and chuckled. "You would bargain for my assistance without knowing anything about me, or even why I have such an interest in your art? At least you don't lack for audacity." I blushed slightly but otherwise didn't respond to her; now was not a moment to display weakness. She sighed. "I suppose it's time you understood what's behind that interest. Not that it will be a gentle lesson, I warn you. There is knowledge that has the power to alter a human soul, and once you embrace it, you can't go back." Her lips pursed as she studied me. "Do you want to risk being altered thus? Or go home now, and take comfort in your ignorance?"

The warning was scary (if a bit melodramatic), but I hadn't come here to play it safe. "I want to know what this is all about," I told her.

She nodded solemnly, then walked over to one of the display cabinets, took a key from her pocket, and unlocked it. On the top shelf was a large leather-bound volume, which she handled with extreme care, taking it down and laying it on the table beside my painting. Its surface was stained and worn, and I could see places where the leather had dried and cracked; clearly it was an ancient item. As she opened it, I saw that it wasn't a regular book, but a collection of individual papers of different shapes and sizes, that someone had bound loosely together. She leafed through the pages too quickly for me see what was on any of them, then found what she was looking for, smoothed the book open, and gestured for me to come closer so I could see it.

I did so. And my heart stopped beating for an instant.

On the page was a drawing done in charcoal, clearly rendered hastily by a hand that had little artistic skill. But despite its aesthetic shortcomings, there was no mistaking what the drawing represented, and a shiver ran down my spine as I gazed at it.

It was a fate map.

Each twist and angle represented a choice someone would have to make, a potential future. The sizes and relative position of the elements suggested the possibility that a particular event would take place, while smaller lines splayed off from the main elements like branches of a tree, representing possible consequences. I had no clue who or what had inspired the painting, so I could guess what all the shapes referred to, but not the overall pattern. This was the same symbolic language that I had developed for my own art, which—until this moment—I had believed was uniquely my own.

The paper felt brittle between my fingers as I turned the page, like it might crumble to dust at any moment. The next drawing in the collection was in color, done in a different style than the first one; the quality of the paper suggested it was a more recent work. My hand trembled as I looked at it.

Also a fate map.

I turned more pages, and found more fate maps. Some even had patterns that looked like ones I had trailed behind me when I wandered through my dreamscape. Like someone had been watching me there. I found a few representational works as well, including a watercolor rendering of a mountainous landscape with a disembodied door suspended several feet above the ground. That one really shook me. I glanced up at Morgana to see if she guessed the significance of the image, but she was looking at me, not the book, and I couldn't read her expression at all. I turned another page—and saw something so startling that I backed away reflexively, banging my knee into a chair.

No. No. Not that. Not here.

"Jesse?" Rita sounded alarmed. "What's wrong?"

The drawing was done in ink, and it depicted a ghostly figure reaching out toward a cowering victim. Darkness billowed from the spirit's shoulders like vast wings, and its black body was painted so thickly that the ink had caused the paper to buckle. How did one capture the essence of a soulless void with mere pen and paper? The landscape behind the creature was meticulously detailed near the edges of the page, but the closer you got to the center of the picture the blurrier and more confused the details got . . . as if the ghastly creature was erasing its surroundings.

Or devouring them.

It was the same death-wraith I had seen in my dream. There was no mistaking it. "What . . . what is that thing?" I struggled to keep my voice steady, even as my fear provided its own answers:

It is death incarnate. It eats dreams. It wants to eat you.

"No one knows," Morgana said. "It appears in several of the drawings, and since they were all sketched by different artists, that suggests it isn't just a figment of one person's imagination. Something real probably inspired all these artists, but what it might have been, I haven't yet determined."

It's real, all right. I had to fight the urge to rub my arm where the wraith had clawed me. "Who made these drawings? Where did you get them?"

"They're from young people, mostly. From dozens of different worlds. They have nothing in common save for these images." She paused, and; I could feel her eyes fix on me. "There's no predicting when or where the dreamer's Gift will surface, you know."

My heart skipped a beat. My hand fell back from the page. "You are saying . . . these were drawn by Dreamwalkers?"

"Not exactly. Oh, some of them might have become that, had they lived. But people who are born with the dreamer's Gift these days rarely manifest more than a faint echo of the ancient power. Most likely these artists would have gone through life tormented by strange dreams, and nothing more. However," the grey/green/blue eyes fixed on me with disturbing intensity, "we do need to err on the side of caution."

Was she threatening me? Or warning me? I was suddenly aware of how out of my depth I was. "Is that what you think my art means? That I'm. . . . what . . . one of these Dreamwalkers?" I tried to sound like the idea seemed utterly crazy, rather than something I'd been obsessing about for weeks now.

For a moment she was silent. What if it was her custom to collect Dreamwalker drawings and then kill the artists? That would certainly explain the collection she'd just shown me. If so, I had walked right into the spider's web. A cold sweat was forming on my palms. I fought the urge to wipe them on my jeans.

"I think you're a sensitive young woman," she said at last, "and your dreams are clearly influenced by outside forces. Dreams do occasionally bleed from one world to another, you know; many of humanity's great oracles drew their inspiration from other spheres, without ever knowing it. Are you sensitive to such things, as they were? Clearly so. Does that mean you are a true Dream-walker, capable of altering the dreams of others?" She paused. "If I believed that, I would be honor bound to destroy you. That is the law of the land, and the duty of my Guild in particular." A pause. "You understand me?"

"I do," I said quietly. But in fact I was more confused than ever. It sounded like she had figured out what I was, and was teaching me how to explain it away so that others wouldn't find out. But why would she do that? What was in it for her? From what little I knew about Alia Morgana, I doubted she had an altruistic bone in her body.

"Now, my dear, you see why I've been so interested in your art. And in you." She walked to the other side of the reading table and sat down in a thickly tufted leather chair. Her golden hair glowed against the deep green leather, waves of it rippling like water as she moved. "As for your request . . ." She tapped a polished fingernail on the arm of the chair. "What you've asked for would re-quire me to call in a personal favor from the Potters. That's not the kind of service I'd be willing to provide in return for more artwork, I'm sorry. No matter how in-teresting that artwork might be."

Frustration welled up inside me, and also anger. Had I come all this way for nothing? Was I only standing here so that she could toy with me? "What else can I offer you? There's got to be something."

Her regretful smile was maddeningly insincere. I had a sudden urge to pick up my painting and smash it over her head. "There are few things of value in this world — or any other — that I don't already possess." She nodded back toward the cabinet filled with ancient relics. "What do you have that you think would be of value to me?"

I tried to think of something — anything — but it was

hopeless, and we both knew it. A woman of Morgana's wealth and power, with access to all the human worlds, probably lacked for nothing. What could I possibly offer her?

Then Rita spoke up. "Maybe some kind of service?"

We both looked at her.

"Well, you said Jesse was sensitive to dreams, right? It sounds like that's not a common talent here. Is there something she could do for you, maybe, using that ability?"

Butterflies of dread fluttered in my stomach. Did Rita understand what she was suggesting? If Morgana learned how much of the Dreamwalker Gift I really possessed, she might reconsider her decision to spare my life. But what other option was there, besides just giving up and going home? I held my breath as Morgana considered Rita's suggestion, not sure what outcome I was hoping for.

Finally Morgana got up and walked over to another bookcase. This one was unlocked, and there was a stack of papers on the top shelf, from which she withdrew a large brown envelope. She hesitated a moment, as if considering her next move, then handed it to me. I opened the clasp and peered inside. There was a single piece of paper, folded in half, marked with a webwork of shadowy folds that suggested it had once been stuffed unceremoniously in a pocket or purse. I drew it out and opened it. There was a line drawing, with repetitive geometric forms radiating out from a central point, like a Tibetan mandala. It looked vaguely familiar, but my life was so full of weird, vaguely familiar designs these days, that didn't necessarily mean anything.

I blinked and looked up at her. "Am I supposed to know what this is?"

"One of my Seers drew it while meditating. He believes it is somehow associated with the ancient dreamers.

He also saw a vision of a location nearby, that appears to be connected to it. We believe there may be an artifact of historical significance there."

"That sounds kind of vague," I said doubtfully.

"Our Gift is often cryptic," she agreed.

"So . . . you want to get hold of this thing? But you know where it is, right? Can't you just send your people out there to look for it?"

"I did. Several times. They failed to find it."

"Even the Seer who originally had the vision? Can't he just, like, tune in on it, or something?" As the words left my mouth it occurred to me that a technological metaphor might not be appropriate here, but she seemed to understand what I meant.

"Our Gift doesn't work that way. The images that come to us in our trances arrive without invitation and are beyond our conscious control." She paused. "You may be more sensitive to the influence of such an artifact than my people are."

I drew in a deep breath. "So, let me make sure I'm understanding this right: You're looking for an item that has something to do with Dreamwalkers, and you want me to help you find it? So that you can . . . what? Hunt them better? Why on earth would I help you do that?"

She smiled as she closed the book of drawings. It was a cold expression. "We know very little about their kind, outside of a few dark legends and these cryptic drawings." She tapped the book with a gilded nail. "Perhaps understanding them better would enable us to save them, rather than destroy them."

Yeah. I'm sure that's your real motive, saving lives. "What is it exactly that you want me to do?"

"You're more sensitive to dreams than my Seers are. If you went to the location in question, perhaps your own visions would offer you insight into what this pattern signifies. Locate its source, bring the artifact back to me, and I'll arrange for a Fleshcrafter to tend to your mother."

Before I could respond Rita demanded, "Where is this place? And would you supply transportation? And how long do you expect this to take?"

"It's in a *shallow*, several hours west of here." She raised a hand, forestalling Rita's response. "That's a place where the barrier between worlds is naturally thin, though not physically passable. Native shamans used such locations for meditation, and for ritual purposes. We believe this one may have served as an Indian burial ground at one point. And yes, I'll take care of all the travel arrangements. The last leg of it would have to be managed on foot or by horseback. Your choice. I'll supply you with whatever equipment you need, including a fetter to hold wildlife at bay. It's bear country. And of course Mistress Seyer will accompany you, for security purposes."

"And petty cash?" Rita asked, adding quickly, "Just in case something unexpected comes up."

Morgana's mouth twitched slightly. "And petty cash."

Despite the momentum of the conversation, I still wasn't convinced this was a good idea. "If your Seer picked up on a vision from another world, there might not be any artifact in this world for us to find."

"Then bring me back information on what the pattern represents, and that will satisfy the terms of our bargain."

It was all happening too fast. I needed time to think. God knew, the last thing in the world I wanted was to get more involved with Morgana than I already was. Every instinct in my soul was warning me that the woman was more deadly than a pit viper, and if she was asking me to go somewhere, I should expect that path to be a treacherous one. But there was no denying that her offer tempted me, and not just because it might win me a

Fleshcrafter's service. If there was some secret artifact related to the Dreamwalkers, I wanted to know what it was. And I wanted to see it before Morgana did. Yeah, she would eventually find it with or without me—of that I had little doubt—but if I got to it first, maybe I could do something to minimize the danger it posed to my kind. Or even destroy it, if that was the only way to assure their safety.

I looked at Rita. She hesitated, then nodded, so slightly that Morgana probably didn't see it. Her meaning was clear: She didn't like the situation, but if I chose to go, she would go with me.

"All right," I told Morgana. Sealing my fate. "I'll go there and look for this thing."

"Excellent. I'll have my people gather the necessary supplies for you. Meanwhile, Mistress Seyer will show you to rooms where you can relax until dinner, and afterward get a good night's sleep, so that you can start fresh in the morning."

"We'll share a room," Rita said quickly. Clearly she meant to follow through on her promise of not leaving me alone with these people. God, I was grateful to have her with me. This world was like a mine field, and I couldn't imagine navigating it without her.

"As you wish," Morgana said, smiling slightly. Rita's caution seemed to amuse her.

Seyer moved toward the door, gesturing for us to follow. I nodded respectfully to the Guildmistress and did so, Rita falling in behind me. But as Seyer opened the door, Rita paused, then turned back to face Morgana. "What if the legends are wrong?" she demanded. "What if a Dreamwalker was able to evade your murder squad long enough for his Gift to manifest, and it turned out nothing like what you expected? What if he didn't go crazy—and no one around him went crazy—and all those other assumptions that people have been making about Dreamwalkers being dangerous turned out to be just so much bullshit? So that you've been killing them for no good reason?"

Morgana smiled slightly. If Rita's challenge disturbed her at all, it didn't show. "Then the rules of the game would change, wouldn't they?"

She waved us toward the door in dismissal, and Seyer led us out.

⋕⋕⋕⋕⋕⋕⋕⋕⋕⋕⋕

"We're being played," I muttered.

Rita paused in her perusal of a garnet-and-sterling bracelet. "What makes you think that?"

She was rummaging through jewelry I'd purchased for our trip, trying on bracelets and rings, turning her hand so that one piece after another caught the light. We'd agreed it would be foolish for us to travel without emergency funds, but since the currency of our world was worthless in Terra Prime, we had no choice but to buy things we could sell or pawn once we got here. I'd withdrawn a good chunk of money from my savings account to bankroll that effort; so much for buying a car after graduation. Now that Rita had convinced Morgana to supply us with cash, of course, it seemed a wasted effort. Well, mostly a wasted effort. I still had one thing of value with me, that no local money could buy.

"I don't know," I said. "Maybe the fact that she accepted your suggestion so quickly. Didn't that seem strange to you? It was as if she had that envelope all ready for us." I paused. "Maybe she already knows what this artifact is, and there's some other reason she wants me to go out there. But what? I can't figure it out."

Alia Morgana had made it clear she could kill me with a word. So was I supposed to be afraid of her now, or grateful, or what? I felt like a pawn on a chessboard, surrounded by lethal pieces on every side, trusting a powerful chessmaster to maneuver me safely through all the deathtraps. But what was her end game? My survival might well depend upon figuring that out.

A pawn isn't a piece you protect forever, I reminded myself. *It's something you sacrifice to keep more important pieces on the board.*

Rita put down the jewelry. "Do you want to go home, Jesse? Because we still can do that. Our transportation costs were covered when you gave Morgana the painting, and she hasn't done any other favors for us yet. We don't owe her anything. Do you want to get out of here now, while that's still easy to do?"

Did I? On a purely visceral level, it was tempting. But any hope I had of helping Mom would be shot to hell if I left. And who was to say Morgana would allow me to quit the game? If she'd been planning this deal from the start—as I suspected—she wasn't going to let me just walk away from it. I had no idea why she'd chosen to protect me this long, but if I walked out on her now, I could kiss that protection goodbye.

I had no choice in this. Not really.

"I've come this far to help Mom," I murmured. "I'm not going home empty-handed." Never mind that it wasn't my only reason for staying. Rita didn't need to hear every dark thought that was churning in my head.

With a nod she pulled off the rings one by one and dropped them back into their storage pouch, followed by the bracelets. "Then let's just deal with the task at hand, and not drive ourselves crazy trying to guess at Morgana's motives. Okay? I doubt the devil himself could figure that woman out." She pulled over my backpack to return the pouch to its zippered compartment, but as she did she seemed to discover something. "What's this. . . . ?"

I realized what she must have found. "Don't take it out, Rita—"

But she did, and she held it up in disbelief. "A Kindle?" She blinked. "They told you not to bring any electronic devices with you, and you packed a *Kindle*?"

I tried to grab it away from her, but she held the device high, out of my reach. "Say it a little louder," I muttered. "I don't think people in the next county heard you yet."

"I doubt they'll hear anything over the tussle we're about to have. Or are you going to let me look at this thing without a fight? Because sooner or later I will look at it, you know that."

Exhaling noisily, I gave up and sat back. She opened the cover and activated the device. "Oh look, no Wi-Fi signal available. Who'da thought?"

I sighed. "Can you at least look at it without being snarky?"

I watched her swipe the screen as she went through the index item by item, checking to see what books I had downloaded. Slowly her expression grew more serious. When she was done she looked up at me. "This is for Sebastian," she said softly.

"Very insightful." I took the Kindle from her and shut it off.

"Does this mean you're planning to contact him?"

I sighed. "I'm not *planning* anything. I just thought that if we needed help while we were here, he was the only person outside Morgana's circle that we knew well enough to turn to. And he's a mercenary, so I brought something to pay him with." I pulled my backpack to me and tucked the Kindle deep, deep into it, hiding it beneath folds of clothing. "I wouldn't know how to contact him even if I wanted to."

She was about to respond when we heard someone approach the door. Both of us froze.

A soft knock sounded. "Dinner's being served." It was a woman's voice. "You're welcome to join us in the common room if you'd like, or else we can have something sent up here for you."

Rita and I looked at each other. I suddenly realized that I was clutching my backpack to my chest so tightly that anyone who came in would surely wonder what was in it. I forced my grip to relax.

"We'll eat up here," Rita called out. "Please." After a moment she added, "Thank you."

The footsteps padded away.

"We need to be careful," I whispered.

"I wish you'd told me about the Kindle." Then she sighed. "No, I don't wish you'd told me. In fact, I wish I still didn't know about it."

I closed the pack and padlocked the main zipper shut. Normally I didn't bother with locking it, but I was feeling particularly paranoid at the moment. "How about, 'Don't look in other people's bags if you don't want to know what's in them'?"

She ignored my sarcastic tone. "Are you going to warn Sebastian that he has to read everything in there before the battery runs out? 'Cause he'd have to come back to Terra Colonna to plug in the adapter."

A knowing smile crossed my face. I patted the bottom of the pack. "Portable solar charger. Size of a cell phone."

"Damn!" She shook her head and laughed. "I underestimated you, Jesse."

"Good." I stowed the pack under my bed, wedging it in tightly, so anyone who tried to pull it out would shake the frame and wake me up. "Now let's hope Morgana does the same."

10

"IT'S TIME."

Isaac shut his eyes for a minute, then nodded.

The journeyman who had come for him was a distant relative, someone Isaac barely knew. Giovan Antonin was dressed in formal Guild attire similar to what Isaac was wearing: a long robe the color of smoke, with a silk stola—a long, narrow band of fabric—hanging down both sides of his chest. It was the kind of outfit you had to practice walking in, especially when going up stairs, lest the stola get caught underfoot. Isaac had learned that the hard way. Giovan's stola was gray, a shade lighter than his robe—a journeyman's color—and symbols of his achievements had been embroidered down both sides. By contrast, Isaac's stola was white—the color of a blank page—and the only decoration on it was the crest of House Antonin embroidered on one end. Not until he had earned a journeyman's status would he be allowed to advertise his accomplishments.

Not that he had any accomplishments to advertise. At least not ones the Shadows would celebrate.

"I'm ready," he told his cousin. A half-truth. While part of him was genuinely curious to witness the secret rites of his Guild, another part wished he were miles away from Shadowcrest right now. The fact that his father had pulled strings to get him invited to this event only reinforced the lie that Isaac had been living, and he was sick of pretending that he was interested in following in the man's footsteps. But he'd promised that he would pursue a Shadowlord's education, so sooner or later he would have to attend their rituals. Apprentices were rarely invited to witness a Binding of the Dead, so the fact that he had been invited to this one was a high honor. Or maybe just a measure of how many strings his prestigious father could pull within the Guild. By bringing his son to this ritual, Leonid proclaimed his own power.

Isaac followed Giovan silently through Shadowcrest to the elevator, and together they descended to the Well of Souls. There were so many spirits present this time that the effect was physically claustrophobic, and for a few seconds Isaac found it hard to breathe. What must this place be like for the Shadowlords, to whom the voices of the dead were not muted whispers, but full-volumed cries? He shuddered to think about it.

The chamber Giovan led him to was the one he had passed while walking with his father. Now it was filled with Shadowlords and their ghostly retinues. The black stolas of the *umbrae majae* were embroidered with elaborate heraldic crests, representing dead Shadowlords whose memories the wearers had consumed. Some displayed dozens of such crests, which was a dizzying number when you considered what each one represented.

How someone could absorb the memories of a dozen other people and remain sane was a mystery to Isaac.

Not that anyone had ever accused the *umbrae majae* of being sane.

A few journeymen were standing in a far corner of the room, trying to stay out of the way of their betters, and Giovan led Isaac over to them and quietly made introductions. Several of the younger ones scowled at Isaac, clearly disapproving of his presence. *They'd* had to earn their journeyman rank before being invited to this prestigious ritual, so why should Isaac be exempt from that requirement? Did the same rules not hold for Leonid Antonin's son as for everyone else? They were all polite to him, in a superficial way, but the undercurrent of resentment was unmistakable.

Great way to start out, Isaac thought bitterly.

His father was in the chamber, but he was focused on Shadowlord business and didn't seem to notice that Isaac had entered the room. Just as well. If he paid any special attention to Isaac right now, it would only make things worse.

From where Isaac was standing he had a clear view of the stone table at the center of the room, and he could now see that there were deep channels incised in its surface, as well as the chains and shackles he had noted previously. Several of the *umbrae majae* were arranging the latter so that they lay open and waiting, and Isaac noted that the surface of the table was canted slightly, so that whatever fluid pooled in the channels would flow to the lower end, where a wide brass bowl was waiting to receive it. Isaac felt a knot form in his gut at the sight of it. When his father had invited him to witness the Binding of the Dead, he had assumed that it would be performed on . . . well, the dead. But clearly that was not the case.

The Shadowlords suddenly fell silent, and they began

to move back from the table, forming a wide circle around it. Isaac hadn't heard any kind of signal, but maybe it had been voiced by one of the many wraiths present. The journeymen took their cue from Shadowlords, and Giovan nudged Isaac into position in the circle. Isaac could sense the spirits in the room growing agitated. Though his fledgling Gift allowed him to detect their emotional state, he couldn't make out what they were saying, but it took no great skill to guess what the trouble was. Those for whom death had been a traumatic experience hated to witness the death of others.

A pair of doors at the far end of the room swung open and two *umbrae minae* entered, dragging a young boy between them. He had been stripped to the waist and his skin was slick with sweat. He was obviously drugged, and at one point fell to his knees, so that his escorts had to lift him to his feet again, forcing him to walk toward the gruesome altar. The fact that he appeared to be Isaac's age, or very close to it, made the spectacle doubly disturbing. Where had the Shadows gotten this boy? Had they purchased him from his parents, perhaps, after a Seers' evaluation had declared him unGifted? Or harvested him from the ranks of some orphan gang that was wandering the streets of the city? Or maybe captured him in a raid like the one that had decimated the Warrens? There were a dozen different ways that one might obtain unwanted children for ritual purposes, most of which made Isaac's blood curdle.

Then the boy turned toward him, and Isaac's heart stopped beating in his chest.

He knew this boy.

He *knew* him.

Shaken, he watched as the two *umbrae minae* lifted the boy up onto the stone slab, trying to gather his thoughts enough to remember the boy's name. Jason? No, Jacob. A regular visitor at the Warrens, who often snuck out of the orphanage he lived in for a few hours of secret midnight freedom. Isaac had gone on thieving expeditions with him, and had found him to be a skilled pickpocket, agile in both his hands and his wit.

Now he was here, trussed like a sheep for slaughter.

Isaac felt sick.

As they started to bind the boy down, the full horror of his situation finally broke through his drugged stupor, and he began to struggle wildly. But whatever drug they had given him had sapped all the strength from his limbs, and with practiced efficiency one of the men held him down while the other fastened shackles about his wrists and ankles. Then chains were stretched across his body and hooked in place, binding him down so tightly to the cold stone surface that he could do little more than twitch desperately. Only his head could move freely, and he whipped it back and forth as he searched the room for ... what, exactly? Sympathy? Hope? There was no mercy to be found in this crowd.

Don't look at me, Isaac thought, drawing back into the shadows. *Please, please, don't look at me.*

The *umbrae minae* bowed respectfully to the assembled Shadowlords and took their leave. They might be Masters of the Guild in their own right, but they were not undead, nor planning to become undead, so they had no place here. As soon as the doors shut behind them, two of the Shadowlords stepped forward to take over. One of them, a women robed in deep crimson, took up station on one side of the sacrificial altar. The other, a man in black robes, stood across from her. In his hand was a knife whose long blade appeared to have been carved from obsidian, and the curved facets of its flaked edge glinted in the light as he moved, reflecting fireflies on the walls.

The woman began to chant in a tongue that Isaac did not understand. It sounded ancient. The man in black raised up the knife and presented it to her over the boy's bound body. Seeing the blade, the boy began to struggle even more desperately, looking feverishly around the room, desperate for anything that could save him—

And his eyes met Isaac's.

The boy's sudden recognition of him struck Isaac like a physical blow, and he had to ball his hands into fists in the folds of his robe, struggling to suppress any visible response. Fingernails digging into his palms hard enough to draw blood, he tried to focus on the pain rather than the horrific tableau before him. The one thing he could not afford to do now was display any emotion ... least of all sympathy. But the boy's eyes were pleading with him, and their message pierced Isaac's soul. *Help me,* Jacob begged silently. *You're my only hope. Don't let them kill me!* Isaac's hands trembled in the folds of his robe, and he knew he should look away, but he couldn't. He couldn't bring himself to move. The boy's terror had transfixed him.

Then the crimson Shadowlord took the knife from her assistant and cut deeply into Jacob's arm. He whimpered in pain and jerked against his chains, but his eyes never left Isaac's. It was as though there was a connection between the two of them, an umbilical cord of pain binding their souls together. The woman cut his other arm. Then his chest. Then his thighs. He cried out anew with each cut, but his eyes remained fixed upon Isaac. *Help me,* they begged. *Help me Help me Help me.* Heart pounding, Isaac finally dared to respond, shaking his head from side to side, a gesture so slight that he hoped no one else would notice it. *I can't,* it said. *I'm sorry. I don't have the power to change this.* Even that much sympathy would be condemned as inappropriate passion if anyone noticed it, but everyone else was focused on the ritual, watching with vampiric delight as cut after cut was made, until every inch of the boy's flesh was lacerated, bright scarlet streamers running down from his flesh to the table beneath him, and from there to the brass collection bowl at his feet. Still Jacob's eyes remained fixed on Isaac, as he desperately grasped the one shred of sympathy he'd been offered to keep from drowning in utter madness.

This is why we are taught not to feel, Isaac thought miserably. Maybe if he'd been more attentive to his lessons he would be able to look away. Maybe it wouldn't feel as though every cut was slicing through his own flesh as well as the boy's.

Now the chanting changed to English, and Isaac heard poetic promises about how the boy's soul would find refuge in eternal service, would have this Shadowlord's undying protection, how death was a blessing. Pure bullshit. The Shadowlords didn't give a damn about whether their slave spirits were happy.

Jacob's eyelids began to droop as the last of his life drained out of his veins. The Shadowlord in black retrieved the collection bowl from the end of the table and handed it to the woman. The blood within it contained the spark of the boy's life, Isaac knew, and at the moment of death it could be used to bind his spirit. Isaac was no longer trying to look away from Jacob, but willingly held his gaze for as long as the bloodshot eyes were still open. At least he could give him that much, so that he didn't have to die alone. The contact seemed to steady the boy a bit ... or perhaps he was simply too weak to struggle any more. Then the woman sipped from the bowl of blood, and Isaac could sense a connection being established between the two of them. When the boy's spirit left its body it would discover it was tethered to this woman, unable to leave her side for as long as that blood was in her system. If she could establish mental control over him before it was gone, he would never be able to leave her.

That's what all the torture was about, Isaac realized. To shatter the boy's mind, so that once he died it would be easier for a Shadowlord to take control of him.

Finally Jacob's eyes closed. Isaac's Gift was just strong enough for him to sense the moment of death, which was also the moment of birth: a new wraith coming into existence. It was the first time Isaac had ever witnessed such a thing, and he strained his fledgling senses to witness what was going on. Death was a kind of creation, he'd been taught, and Shadowlords were masters of the process. But when he heard the boy's ghost cry out in terror at its birth pangs, he wondered if anything could justify such practices.

The chamber was silent. The boy's body lay still, relieved at last of its struggles. The new ghost's cries faded in volume as spiritual exhaustion overwhelmed it. It was said that such bound spirits were insane, and now Isaac understood why. Who wouldn't be driven mad by such an experience?

The ritual was over at last. The circle was breaking up, Shadowlords coming up to the woman in red to congratulate her on a successful Binding. With a start, Isaac realized that his father was approaching him. As always, he could hear the moaning of spirits that surrounded the man, just as he could hear the voices of every other Shadowlord's retinue. Now, for the first time in his life, he understood what prompted those sounds, and it sickened him. How many people had his father murdered, tormenting them to the edge of insanity so their ghosts could be dominated more easily? How many of the hundreds of spirits in this room had been initiated into servitude in the same way?

Bile rose up in the back of Isaac's throat as he looked at his father. Surely the Shadowlord had known about him and Jacob. Surely he knew that forcing him to watch the death of someone he knew would be like twisting a knife in his gut. That was why he'd invited him here. To test him. To torment him. To force him to be strong, in the way that only a madman should be strong.

I don't belong here, Isaac thought bitterly. *I never will.*

A cold hand settled on his shoulder. "You did well, my son."

He bit his lip to keep from responding in anger. "I know what's expected of me."

His father's finger touched the underside of his chin, turning his head until their eyes met. Isaac gazed into the black eyes of his undead father—haunted eyes, chilling eyes—and tried not to shudder.

You were human once, he thought. *When did that change? If I continue in this training, will human compassion drain from me slowly, like the blood did from that boy? Or does First Communion cut it out of you suddenly, like a surgeon's scalpel excising a malignant growth?*

"I'd like to go home now," Isaac muttered. "Unless you have more to show me."

His father stepped back, clearing a path between him and the exit. Isaac headed toward it. He walked past the journeymen, who were chattering about how much they looked forward to mastering the mysteries of life and death. Past the Shadowlords and their retinues of wraiths. Whispers of pain surrounded him, soft moaning, an occasional cry of anguish . . . now he understood why the dead sounded like that. Now he knew what it really meant to be a Shadowlord.

He managed to find a private spot, away from all the others, before he threw up.

11

THE LEAVES ON THE TREES were green.

The underbrush was scraggly.

The soil was brown.

It was, on the whole, the most mundane, uninteresting stretch of woodland I'd ever seen.

"So let me make sure I've got this right," Rita said. "Morgana wants you to go to a creepy place and take a nap, and if something creepy happens to you during that nap, you tell her about it. Then we get to go home?"

"Well, except for the fact that this place doesn't seem very creepy ... and we're supposed to bring back whatever is causing the creepiness ... yeah, that's pretty much it."

"Okay. Just so we're clear on the goal here."

I wasn't sure what I'd expected to see at the site of an ancient Indian burial ground. Gravestones? Symbols carved into the ground? Restless spirits haunting the place, half-visible in the forest shadows? Whatever had been here in the past was long gone now, and had left no visible sign for tourists like us to discover.

I sighed and thought, *This isn't going to be easy.*

We'd left Seyer behind at the last small town we'd passed through, a few miles back. She hadn't wanted to split up, but I was resolute. There was no way I was going to test the limits of my dreaming Gift with a Seer watching me. In the end she'd reluctantly agreed, and gave me a fetter that would allow me to signal her when we were ready to leave. Which meant that Morgana had anticipated my request all along.

Damn her.

I had a pretty good sense of how to handle myself in the woods, the result of growing up with a regional forest in my backyard. And Morgana had given us a map of local landmarks, including a long mountain ridge that we could follow back to civilization if we had to, so I wasn't worried about getting lost. Now, after a brisk morning hike, we were here, alone in the woods, able to do whatever we needed to do to search for Morgana's mysterious object without being observed . . . with no clue how to start.

"Let's set up camp," Rita suggested.

So we did that, and since neither of us were experienced woodsmen (woodspeople?), it took a while. Then we searched the *shallow* again, looking for anything out of the ordinary. But there was nothing. Finally we gave up and came back to the camp to light a fire and break out the rations Morgana had given us.

"Too bad Sebastian's not here," Rita said. "I bet he'd know all about shallows."

I bet he wouldn't want to go near one, I thought. *A place where he might hear echoes from his birthworld, near enough to be audible but forever out of reach. It would be torture.*

When it finally got dark I lay down on my bedroll and tried to go to sleep, but it was still too early for that, as far as my body was concerned. Fine by me. The fact that I'd agreed to open my mind to whatever powers were active here didn't mean I was comfortable with the concept. Morgana wouldn't have agreed to our price if she thought this task would be painless. Or safe.

So I watched as stars crept slowly across the heavens and a slender moon appeared in the east, rising up against the black dome of the sky with agonizing reluctance. And I struggled to ignore the feeling of dread that was slowly consuming me, until finally—just when I thought I would go crazy if I had to stay awake one more minute—my body surrendered to the inevitable.

I slept.

‖‖‖‖‖‖‖‖‖‖

The dreamscape is calm tonight, but ominously so. I can sense destructive energy seething behind it, masked by an illusion of peace.

I envision the design that Morgana showed me, forcing my mind's eye to see it in lines of gold against the black ground. I sense that it should connect to something—that it _wants_ to connect to something—but the thing it seeks is not to be found here. The longer I study the pattern, the more I'm sure.

We're in the wrong place.

I let the pattern fade from my mind and look around me, to see if the avatar girl is present. But she's nowhere to be seen. Maybe I frightened her so badly when I took control of her dream that she won't ever come back. Or maybe the dream-wraiths got to her after I left. My blood runs cold at the mere memory of them, and the wound on my arm starts to twitch. Whatever those horrific creatures are, they're not subject to the normal limits of dreaming, and I pray I'll never have to see one of

them again. Especially now, when I'm trapped in a foreign world, with no brother to wake me up if things go bad.

A wave of homesickness suddenly comes over me. The distance between me and my loved ones is so vast it might as well be infinite. My tie to my family, such a strong anchor during my first visit here, has been robbed of its power by my knowledge that in my current reality they don't exist. Yes, somewhere in this vast ocean of probability there is a world where Tommy and Evelyn Drake are going about their daily lives, waiting for me to come home. But in this world, right here, right now, they are unreachable. My heart aches to connect with them, if only for a moment—

Suddenly I'm standing in front of an archway, with no memory of how I got there. I sense that it's meaningful, but I don't know why. I put my hand on the arch, feeling its sharp crystal spines prick my fingertips. The doors in my dreams are usually impassable; only when I tackled the avatar girl was I able to cross through one of them. Could I enter this one, if I wanted to? It would be a dangerous thing to do, when I have no idea how or why I was summoned here, but I have to try, if only to learn more about how my Gift works.

Warily I extend a hand into the arch, bracing myself for the moment when a metaphysical barrier will stop me. But nothing does. Trembling slightly, I extend my arm full length and wiggle my fingers a bit. My hand feels cool and my fingers look misty and insubstantial, as if viewed through frosted glass. Have I reached into another world? Am I now half in one dream, half in another? Or is there some less exotic explanation for what I'm seeing?

There's only one way to find out.

I concentrate long enough to manifest a large hunting knife. The weapon feels comfortable in my hand, reassuring. I manifest a gun as well, modeled on one of Uncle Julian's pistols, but I leave it holstered for now. I'm not that sure I could hit a moving target, but I figure it's good to have it with me just in case.

Looking around one last time to make sure I'm still alone, I step forward.

There's no sense of transition; one moment I'm standing on the black plain, and the next, I'm on a windswept path running along the edge of a deep ravine. The sky overhead is a blue so intense it's unreal, like the cobalt glow of a PC error message. In the distance I can see clouds gathering, and even as I watch lightning flashes suddenly, flooding the entire sky with blinding light. Thunder follows in its wake, rumbling overhead like angry surf. However far away the storm is, it's a powerful one.

As the afterimage of the lightning slowly fades, I can see that there's a figure riding toward me, mounted on a white horse. Nervously, I glance back to make sure the arch is right behind me, just in case I need to make a run for it. It is. I can sense the same otherness in the rider that I did in the avatar girl, and I know instinctively that he is not part of my dreamscape, but from some place outside it. As he comes closer I can see that he's a massive creature, heavily armored, with a sword as tall as a man harnessed across his back and an oversized crossbow clipped to his saddle. His mount isn't a horse at all, but some kind of animal with two spiral horns jutting out of its head and glowing red embers in the place of eyes. If there's a stable in Hell, this is what the Devil's horses surely look like.

As the monster warrior approaches me he draws his greatsword from its sheath, raising it high overhead, preparing to strike. Its edge flares molten white as lightning strikes again, and the long hair that flows out from underneath his helmet is white as well, unnaturally glossy.

I should flee this place. Now. Every cell in my body is screaming for me to do that. But I find myself mesmerized, frozen in place by raw curiosity. In dreams I've looked in on hundreds of different worlds—thousands, perhaps—but all of them were similar to my own universe. Even the avatar's dream-world started off looking normal. This place, on the other hand, is truly alien. I've never seen anything like it before.

I want to understand where I am.

I *need* to understand where I am.

But suddenly he's coming within striking range and my fascination gives way to pure survival instinct. I start back toward the portal—

And he pulls up short. His mount squeals in frustration (definitely not an equine sound) and some gravel that was knocked loose by its hooves plummets down into the ravine. It falls for several long seconds before hitting bottom. Then there's silence. My heart is pounding so hard the knife in my hand shakes, but I stand my ground. Waiting.

One second. Two.

The rider pushes up his visor. His face is pure white, unnaturally translucent, as if carved from alabaster. In the place of his eyes are glowing red embers, like those of his mount. There's no way to read that inhuman expression.

He stares at me for a moment, then says, "Jesse?"

I open my mouth, but find that I'm speechless. Because the voice coming out of that ember-eyed demon is my little brother's. That alabaster hulk is Tommy.

"What's going on?" he asks. "You don't play this game."

Is it possible I'm really in my brother's dream? True, I entered the avatar's dream once—or at least I think I did—but that was different. I'd followed her from the black plain and used her to cross into her world. The concept that I might wind up in someone else's dream without meaning to—and without someone leading me there—is both exhilarating and terrifying.

This may not really be Tommy, I remind myself. *I might just be dreaming that he's in front of me.*

Whatever he is, he's staring at me, waiting for my answer. He thinks this whole scene is real, I realize. I've gotten so used to lucid dreaming that I take it for granted. How do I get him to see that this setting isn't real, and that he can control it? If you tell someone in a dream that he's dreaming, is that enough to make him self-aware? It's worth a try.

"We're in a dream," I tell him.

His eyes widen. "Seriously?"

"Seriously."

"You mean, like, I'm really asleep in bed? Just making crap up in my head?"

I nod. "That's the idea."

"So, did I make you up, too? Or are you really here?"

Isn't that the question? Can Tommy and I really occupy the same dreamscape? Our bodies are in different worlds, and supposedly nothing can cross between the worlds but ghosts and Shadows—

And dreams.

Was it Isaac who talked about that, or Sebastian? Which one of them described to me how dreams can bleed from one world into the next, giving a sleeper access to sounds and images from another universe? Does that mean that in this dream state I can contact people in another world? The concept is dizzying in its implications. But how can you test such a thing? I shut my eyes for a moment, struggling to come up with an idea. Maybe if I share information with Tommy that he couldn't possibly know otherwise, he can confirm it when he wakes up and know that our meeting was real. It won't help me verify things at my end, but it's a start.

"You remember the flowered chair in the front room?" I ask him. "The one with the high back?"

"Yeah. What about it?"

"Go there when you wake up. Reach under the cushion, all the way to the back. There's a crowbar I stashed there. No one else knows about it."

The glowing eyes blink. "Why on earth would you hide a crowbar under the chair?"

"In case we need to break into Uncle Julian's gun cabinet, of course." I shrug, smiling slightly. "I figured something could happen where we might not have time to ask him for the key."

Suddenly I catch sight of something odd in the sky behind him. A small patch of blue is losing its color, turning from a bright shade to muddy grey. Like something is sucking the color right out of the sky.

Panic floods my world. Everything else is forgotten.

"You need to wake up!" Surely he can hear the fear in my voice and will do what I say. "RIGHT NOW! Don't argue, don't question me, just trust me and do it."

How far away is the dream-wraith? How fast can it move? I don't want to stay here long enough to find out, but I can't leave until I know Tommy is safe.

He twists around in his saddle and looks at the grey patch in the sky. "Shit," he mutters. "That's not good."

The patch is getting closer now. The wraith is moving fast.

He turns back to face me. The glowing embers are gone now; my brother's eyes stare out at me, very human and very scared.

"Your first aid kit," he says. "Look in it when you wake up."

And then he's gone.

At which point his dream vanishes.

And so do I.

||||||||||||||||

When I first awoke I was so disoriented I didn't know where I was. I watched the sky in terror for what seemed like an eternity, waiting for the wraith to show up, but it never came. Slowly, very slowly, my heart quieted, and my breathing steadied. I remembered where I was, and I knew that I was awake and safe. At least for the moment.

I got up as quietly as I could, not wanting to wake Rita. Crossing the campsite, I retrieved my backpack and moved off into the woods a bit, so I'd be less likely to wake her when I rummaged through it. When I looked back at her for the last time she was snoring gently, her eyelids twitching as she explored some dream of her own.

The first aid kit was in the bottom of the bag, a small plastic box with a snap lid. My hand trembled as I took it out and popped it open. From fear? From excitement? My emotions were so mixed up at that moment I wasn't sure what I was feeling.

Under the bandages, next to the tube of antibiotic cream, was a flat item in a plastic wrapper. I held my breath as I pulled it out. Even in the near darkness I knew what it was: A toaster strudel.

There was a note fastened to it with a rubber band. I didn't have enough light to read by, so I took out the small flashlight from Dr. Tilford that we had charged earlier and turned my back to Rita so its bright beam wouldn't wake her up. The last thing I wanted to deal with right now was her questions.

I turned on the flashlight, unfolded the note and read it.

I thought if you had to open this kit you might need some cheering up.
Be strong.
Tommy

For a long, long time I just stared at that toaster strudel. Couldn't think clearly. Just stared at it.

I talked to him. I really talked to him. Across the worlds.

The concept was so stunning that I had to reach out to a nearby tree to steady myself. I was shaking like a leaf and had to fumble to turn the flashlight off, so its beam would stop jerking all over the place.

Everything in Terra Prime revolved around the fact that no one could communicate between worlds. Even the spirits of the dead, who crossed freely back and forth to carry messages, couldn't exist in one reality and converse with ghosts in another. It just wasn't possible. And the power of the Guild of Shadows was rooted in that fact, because they controlled the passage of messengers. The power of the Greys derived from theirs. Other Guilds were rooted in that system as well, all of them networking together to exploit that scientific fact for their advantage.

But if it turned out their science was wrong, and messengers weren't needed after all—that the Shadows weren't needed—it would be like yanking the cornerstone out from under a tower. The whole vast construct could come crashing down. That was why they wanted the Dreamwalkers dead, I realized suddenly. All the other reasons I'd been given were bullshit. *This* was why they'd wiped us all out centuries ago, and why they'd established rules about hunting down any new Dreamwalkers who were born. But did the people who were hunting us today know why they were doing it? Or had centuries of propaganda and misdirection obscured the true story, so that even the most fanatical Shadows didn't remember why they wanted us dead? From the few things people had told me about the ancient dreamers—or not told me—it sounded like that might be the case.

I looked back at Rita. Her eyes had stopped twitching, and she was sleeping so soundly now. So peacefully. I couldn't tell her about this yet. I couldn't tell anyone about it.

I needed time to think first.

I looked down at the toaster strudel that was still in my hand—now crushed beyond recognition—and I suddenly started laughing and crying, all at once. This was my symbol of revelation: a ruined breakfast cake. How appropriate.

Thank you, little brother. You have no idea what you gave me tonight. Thank you.

12

Shadowcrest
Virginia Prime

Isaac

THE DEAD WERE RESTLESS.

Lying in his bed in the darkness, Isaac could sense them in his bedroom. Moans and cries and whispers echoed just below the threshold of his hearing, and whenever a spirit drew close he could feel its presence, like prickly pressure on his skin. Sometimes there were so many of them surrounding him that he felt claustrophobic.

He was starting to be able to sense their emotions. Not that the dead were supposed to have real emotions. The Shadowlords taught that ghosts were merely echoes of human souls, that death robbed a man not only of his physical substance but also of his capacity for passion. But Isaac wasn't buying it. Sometimes he could sense the emotions of the spirits that were near him, and they felt totally human. Rage, despair, frustration, resentment . . . it was a dark and disturbing—but utterly human—repertoire.

Besides, if they had no feelings, why did one hear sounds of human suffering whenever they were nearby? His teachers said it was just a reflex, like when you cut the tentacles off an octopus, and they kept on twitching. The wailing of the dead was like that. Postmortem twitching. Yes, it was hard to accept now, when his Gift was still immature, but they assured him that once he underwent First Communion he'd see that it was true. Until then, he would just have to take it on faith.

Tonight the dead were thick as flies in his room, and he pulled the blanket over his head, even though he knew it would do nothing to shut them out. The sounds of the spirit world weren't physical in nature, and merely blocking his ears wouldn't stop him from hearing them. They seemed unusually agitated tonight. Maybe the Shadowlords had committed some new atrocity that upset them. Isaac thought back to the ritual he had witnessed and shuddered. The look in Jacob's eyes as he died was seared into Isaac's brain. He would do anything to forget it.

Suddenly, unexpectedly, the ghostly murmuring ceased. Startled, he came out from under the blanket and looked around. He couldn't see anything, but he could sense that spirits nearest him had drawn back. The space around his bed felt empty now.

Why?

The temperature in the room dropped slightly as a new spirit entered. This one was more substantial than the others, a complete human soul rather than a mere fragment of consciousness. It was rare for that type of spirit to be wandering around Shadowcrest, Isaac knew. The bound servants of the Shadows generally stayed close by their masters, while free spirits avoided this place like the plague.

Isaac stiffened as the spirit approached the bed. In theory it couldn't do him physical harm, but as a mere apprentice he had limited power to banish the dead, so he was wary. But the spirit came to the foot of his bed and just stopped there. Maybe it was making some attempt to communicate, that he couldn't hear. Maybe it was just watching him.

The situation made his skin crawl.

"Who are you?" he demanded. "What do you want?" That's how one was supposed to deal with spirits: firmly and authoritatively. Death robbed a soul of initiative and left it highly suggestible. If you gave it an order in a forceful manner it was likely to obey you.

The spirit made no sound. It didn't move.

"Why are you here?" Isaac pressed.

A cold breeze gusted across his face. He could sense the ghost reaching out to him, as if to make physical contact. Instinctively he drew back from it, until the headboard behind him put a stop to his retreat.

Then the spirit began to speak. Isaac could make out a few scattered words but not enough to figure out what it was saying. That was the curse of his immature Gift: to sense the speech of the dead but not be able to hear it clearly. If he concentrated hard enough, could he do better? It was worth a try. Gathering all his mental energy, he focused his concentration on the spirit. He knew the technique that was required, and tried to envision the spirit standing before him, to give it substance in his mind. He channeled all his strength of will into the effort—

—And suddenly he saw *those* eyes again, the terrified bloodshot eyes of a young boy in the process of being slaughtered. No body was visible—just the eyes—but Isaac could smell Jacob's blood as it flowed across the granite altar, he could smell the stink of sweat and the fear that filled the room, he could hear the chanting of the Shadowlord who held the knife—

Gasping, he jerked backward, slamming into the headboard. The vision dispersed, but the sense of fear in the room remained. He was trembling now, and it was hard for him to force the words out. "You're ... you're ... Why are you here? What do you want?"

But if there was any answer, he lacked the ability to understand it. Maybe Jacob had come to find out why Isaac had done nothing to save him. "I had no power to change anything," he offered. "They just brought me there to watch." Would he have saved the boy if he could have? He'd never asked himself the question before. Until tonight it hadn't seemed to matter.

The chill that had accompanied the spirit's arrival began to fade, and with a start Isaac realized that the boy's ghost was leaving the room. Why? Had Isaac told him what he wanted to know, or was the wraith just giving up in frustration now that it understood the limits of Isaac's Gift? Maybe it had expected him to be able to communicate with it like the Shadowlords did.

He remembered how the boy had locked eyes with him while dying. Was it possible the connection between them had compromised the ritual somehow, so that the bond between this newly created spirit and its mistress wasn't all that it should be? If so, did that mean the boy's spirit was a free agent? Or just poorly bound? Isaac wished he knew enough about how the ritual worked to guess at the answer. Frustrated, he stared into the darkness as the spirit withdrew, cursing the weakness of his Gift. He tried to invoke some kind of vision again, but whatever spark had made that possible the first time was gone.

And then the spirit was gone.

All that remained in the room were questions.

13

Jesse

THE RACCOON SHOWED UP shortly after midnight. At first only its eyes were visible, two tiny spots of reflected moonlight glinting at me from among the trees. They were low to the ground, so at first I just figured they belonged to some small animal, and I wasn't worried. But when it saw me looking back at it, the raccoon turned and scampered into the woodland shadows. Its bushy ringed tail twitched into the moonlight just long enough for me to identify its species. For a moment—one sweet innocent moment—I thought it was a raccoon, and only a raccoon.

Then I realized the truth.

I went over to Rita and nudged her. "Hey. Hey. Get up."

The urgency in my voice must have triggered her innate survival instinct, because as soon as her eyes opened she was sitting upright with knife in hand, looking around the clearing for something to stab. "What? What is it?"

"I saw a raccoon."

She looked at me as if I had just announced I was from Mars. "A raccoon? Seriously?" The hand holding the knife lowered, and she snorted. "Hardly nature's great killing machine, Jess."

I took out the fetter that Seyer had given me and showed it to her. I'd strung it on a cord so I could wear it like a necklace. It was a copper disk with a symbol on one side that looked like a hashtag, only at right angles and with four bars running in each direction. A crudely etched wolf was on the other side.

When she still didn't make the connection I said, "Wards off wildlife, remember?"

Somewhere there was a person whose Gift allowed him to influence the minds of animals. A Weaver had bound a trace of his mental energy to this item, so that for as long as we had it with us, beasts would not approach. Any and all animal brains would be affected.

Animal brains.

"Shit!" Suddenly Rita got it, and from the way she stared intently into the woods I knew that she was thinking the same thing I was. We weren't equipped to deal with Soulriders. "Shit."

"We'll have to sleep in shifts from now on," I said. Not like that would help us much if Hunters attacked in force.

She looked up at me. "Does that mean you want to sleep now? 'Cause I can take a turn at watch if you want."

"No." I sighed. "I'm way too wound up for that. I just wanted you to know what was going on, so if I did have to wake you up to deal with this you'd be prepared." I looked in the direction the raccoon had fled, but there was no motion visible. Even the night breeze was still. "It isn't here," I said quietly.

"What?" Rita looked confused. "Oh ... you mean Morgana's artifact? Did you dream about where it was?"

"I dreamed where it wasn't." I sighed heavily. "We're in the wrong place, Rita."

She exhaled in a hiss. "So what, then? This whole trip was a waste?"

I looked out over the forest. We were high on a hillside, and the moonlight provided a clear view of miles of wooded land, all of it looking pretty much the same. The Seers' Gift allowed them to pick up impressions from people's minds, right? So if something was emanating Dreamwalker energy so strongly that Morgana's people had sensed it from halfway across the state, maybe the source wasn't an artifact. Maybe it was human, and we should search for clues where there was human activity. To the south it was possible to see a faint light in the distance, if you squinted just right. A pale blue glow peeking out between the trees. "What's down there?"

She peered in that direction. "Not sure. Let me get out my tourist guide ... oh, wait, that's right, I don't have one."

Smartass. "I think we should look down there."

"Like, right now?"

"Like, when there's enough light to see by. Duh."

"We'll have to signal Seyer that we're planning to spend another day in the field."

We were supposed to use the fetter Seyer had given me to signal her once a day, to let her know we were still okay, and that we were staying in the forest of our own free will. But we didn't have to tell her why we were staying, or what we planned to do, just let her know we were still all right.

Thank God I told my family I'd be gone for a whole

week. We still had time before anyone back home started worrying.

Seyer was the one who had suggested that, I realized suddenly. She must have known back on Terra Colonna that Morgana was planning to send us on this quest. It was all contrived, from the start. Damn. Was this how a pawn felt when it first realized it was standing on a chessboard? Did it look down at the squares surrounding it and think, *Shit, now I'm really in for it?*

Rita lay back down again. "I'm going to try to get some more sleep, if that's possible." She shut her eyes for a moment, then said, "It could just be that the fetter's not working. In which case, the only thing we need to worry about are bears."

"Yeah," I muttered. "Got that." I'd rather deal with bears than Hunters, any day.

I kept watch till dawn, but the raccoon never came back.

||||||||||||||

Our maps indicated there was a chasm nearby, heading in the right direction, so we decided to follow it by way of a landmark. I marked a few trees as we hiked, as backup, but that turned out not to be necessary. Soon we came across a packed dirt road with a ribbon of scrub down its center; clearly a carriage trail. It was heading toward the area we wanted to explore, probably connecting it to the main road that ran along the ridgetop to our west. We followed it downhill, alert for any sounds of people approaching. But the one time someone came our way, the clopping of hooves and the creaking of carriage springs warned us in plenty of time, and we were able to hide in the brush before they reached us.

Eventually we got to a place where we could see that the road ended a short distance ahead, with an open plain beyond. There seemed to be buildings there, and maybe a fence, but we didn't want to get too close while we were out in the open. So we headed back into the deep woods and crept carefully toward it. When we got to the place where the underbrush gave way to open land we lay full length upon the ground and let the vegetation close over our heads, parting the leaves with our hands just enough to peer between them.

The area ahead of us was large, treeless, and bounded by a tall chain link fence with barbed wire at the top. Short, scraggly grass covered most of the ground, with a small stand of trees in its center. There were a few wooden cabins at one end of the enclosure—including two large ones with barred windows—and a big cinder-block structure at the other. Tables and benches of weathered wood were strewn about the enclosure, more like an afterthought than a decorating feature, and in the far corner was a long building that looked like a stable, with a small carriage parked in front of it.

Inside the fenced enclosure were children. Lots of children. Boys and girls of all ages, wearing loose clothes of unpatterned cotton and simple canvas sandals that made them look interchangeable. All of them had their hair cropped close to their heads, and they looked dazed and listless. Some were sitting on the grass or on the benches, unnaturally still, just staring into space. Others were walking around with no clear purpose or destination, shuffling along with the kind of spiritless resignation I'd once seen in animals in a small zoo, where cramped, featureless cages had sucked the life out of them.

To say that the place made my skin crawl would be an understatement.

"Not exactly high security," Rita whispered.

"Huh?"

"No sentry post. No observation platform. The lock

on the main gate looks pretty basic. Probably easy to jimmy." She pointed to the only guard in sight, a middle-aged man who looked more bored than dangerous. "Rent-a-cop. Token presence."

"There's barbed wire," I pointed out.

"To discourage people from climbing out. Maybe to keep animals from climbing in. It looks more like an animal pen than a prison."

That was uncomfortably close to my own thoughts. "You think maybe they're patients of some kind?"

"Hospitals don't have bars on the windows," she pointed out.

"Some mental hospitals do."

Suddenly I saw a figure I recognized, at the far end of the enclosure. Startled, I squinted to bring her into focus. She'd been a small and wiry child when Rita and I first met her, and she'd worn her blond hair cropped close to her head even then, so she hadn't changed much. As soon as she turned my way I knew who it was.

"Moth," I whispered.

Rita followed my gaze; her eyes grew wide as she spotted the girl. "From the Warrens?"

The last we'd heard about the children living in Luray's sewer system, city officials had been planning to raid the place, and we'd assumed they intended to exterminate them. But this was a world where homeless children had market value, and Moth's presence here suggested that some of the orphans might have been rounded up for sale, rather than killed. Sold to cover the cost of the raid.

So what was Moth doing here? What was this place? She was wandering aimlessly, her eyes downcast, moving slowly toward the fence on the far side of the enclosure. I watched for a minute, then slipped out of the straps of my backpack, "I'm going to talk to her."

It took me forever to scrunch and crawl my way

around the compound without being seen, but Rita had
been right about the security. No one inside the compound was paying attention to anything going on outside. I managed to locate a spot with good cover near
the fence and laid down in it, waiting for Moth to come
close enough that I could risk talking to her. At last,
when she was only a few yards away, I whispered, "Psst!
Moth!"

Startled, she turned in my direction. I raised up my
head just far enough for her to see who I was, then
ducked down into the shrubbery again. "Look away," I
whispered sharply. "Pretend there's no one here."

I could see a tiny spark of life come into her eyes, and
it made my heart ache. I remembered the feisty little
blond who challenged us so boldly when we'd first arrived on Terra Prime. It was hard to imagine what kind
of misery could have turned such a firebrand into the
listless creature I saw now. But hiding from people was
second nature to her, and as she slowly approached the
fence she pretended to be watching the other children.
It was very convincing. Finally she sat crosslegged with
her back to the fence and started playing with the grass,
absently picking one long blade after another to chew
on. It disguised the movement of her lips as she whispered to me. "Jesse? Is that really you?"

"Sure is."

You could sense how much she wanted to turn
around and look at me. "What are you doing here?"

"At the moment, I'm trying to figure out what you're
doing here."

She sighed; a terrible sadness bowed her small body.
"They caught me in the Warrens. They kept me in some
kind of holding cell for a few days, then they brought me
here."

"Are any of the others here?"

She shook her head. "Ethan and Kurt were sent to a

labor camp. I heard a rumor that Maysie wound up in a pleasure house in Front Royal, but I don't know if that's true or not. A lot of kids died in the raid, only a few were taken alive."

"Moth," I asked it gently: "What is this place?"

"Hell," she whispered bitterly.

I lowered my head and waited respectfully for more.

"It's run by the Weavers. There's some kind of laboratory in the brick building over there." She nodded slightly toward the cinderblock structure. "I think they're trying to use us to charge fetters, but you need Gifted people for that, don't you?"

"No one here is Gifted?"

"Just the Weavers. The kids are all deadheads. Like me." She raised up a finger slightly, her hand in her lap, so that only I could see her pointing. "That woman over there is Mistress Tennant. She told me we all had *trace essence*, whatever that means, and that's why we're here. I think she's in charge. She talks about this place like it's some kind of experiment."

The woman she was pointing at looked to be in her forties, a short brunette with an air of concentrated energy about her. I stared at the woman intently, memorizing her appearance so I would recognize her later. "What do they use you for?"

For a moment she didn't speak. Then: "They bring us into the lab one by one and strap us down and do Weaver things to us. Sometimes it hurts. Sometimes it feels like a hand is reaching into you and ripping out your insides. But your body is never damaged." Her voice wavered for a moment. "I heard that they never let anyone leave here, they just drain a kid till he dies and then replace him. There was a boy who died last week, just wasted away after weeks in a coma. Someone told me that while he was still walking around, all he talked about was how much he wanted to die. He said he had someplace to go, a castle that looked different every time he saw it, and once he let go of his body he would be free to go there."

My heart skipped a beat. "Tell me about the castle."

She shrugged. "I don't know any more than that, other than it was something he dreamed about. The others didn't pay much attention to him when he rambled on about his dreams, they just thought he was crazy. Which maybe he was." She drew in a deep breath. "Jesse . . . you came to get me out of here, right?" Her voice was pitiful, like the whine of a wounded puppy.

It was a few seconds before I could speak. "I'll try to figure out a way, Moth."

"Please," she begged. A universe of pain was in that one word.

"I promise."

I reached into my pocket and pulled out the drawing Morgana had given me. Scrunching forward, I slid it along the ground until it reached the fence. Moth looked around to make sure no one was watching, then took it. She opened it in her lap where no one could see. "What is it?" she whispered.

"I was going to ask you the same question. Have you ever seen anything like it?"

She shook her head a tiny bit.

"No designs of this type at all?"

"No. Sorry. Nothing." She looked around again and then slid it back to me. The gesture reminded me of a kid passing notes in class.

"What about dreams?" I asked. "Anyone else here talk about strange dreams?"

"Just that boy and his castle. Otherwise, we dream pretty much what you'd expect in a place like this. Nightmares, mostly." She paused then said softly, "Sometimes I dream how I'll get out of here someday."

I lowered my head to the ground for a moment,

grateful that Moth couldn't see my expression. "Did they try to make a fetter from that boy's energy?" I asked.

"I assume. They try with everybody." She nodded slightly toward the cinderblock building. "There's a safe inside the lab where the experimental stuff is kept. They keep the fetters locked up in a safe because they're dangerous. I heard one of the Weavers talk about how they're not *tempered* yet, whatever that means."

I opened my mouth to ask another question, but just then a loud clanging filled the compound. Moth jumped.

"That's lunch. I have to go. They'll notice if I don't." She dared to look back at me. "I'll see you again, right? You won't just forget about me?" *I helped keep you safe when you first came to this world,* her eyes seemed to be pleading. *You owe me.*

A sudden knot in my throat made it hard to breathe. "I won't forget about you. I promise."

The guard was looking our way now. Moth hurriedly got to her feet. "I'll walk by here every hour or so," she whispered behind her hand. "They won't notice, so long as it isn't meal time."

"I'll get back to you when I can," I whispered.

She headed toward the largest cabin, where all the children were gathering. It seemed to me there was a hint of newfound vivacity in her stride, but maybe that was just my wishful thinking. Once she entered what I assumed was the mess hall I started the long scrunch-crawl back to Rita. By the time I got to her, all the children had disappeared into the building, and most of the adults had disappeared as well. During mealtimes the yard was nearly empty. Something to remember.

"Well?" Rita asked impatiently.

I hesitated. I needed a few minutes to sort things out in my head . . . and to figure out how to talk about the situation without tears coming to my eyes. Was Moth staring out at the woods even now, wondering if we would really come through for her? Or was the concept of abandonment something she just took for granted? "Let's go find a safe place to talk. I'll fill you in then."

We headed back into the woods to find a suitable place to stow our gear, eat, and make plans.

⸻

We found a place that suited our purposes, a small clearing near a stream, far enough from the compound that we could talk safely. As we set out a sparse picnic of bread, cheese, and dried meat, I told Rita most of what Moth had said. I didn't tell her about the castle the boy had described. It sounded like it might be the same building my dream-avatar had fled toward, perched on a black island in the center of a mirrored lake. If so, that was a connection I wasn't ready to share with anyone.

"I'm guessing it was the boy's presence the Seers sensed," I told her. "He's been dead for a week, but Morgana didn't tell us how old her information was, so maybe they gathered it while he was still alive."

"Or it's connected to the fetters somehow."

It seemed the obvious conclusion. But getting to the fetters would require passing through the main gate and into the lab, then breaking into a safe, all without being seen. Rita assured me she could take care of the lock on the gate, no problem, and we could probably dodge the rent-a-cop without too much trouble, but she didn't have any experience with safecracking, and neither did I. So unless we could figure out a time when the safe would be open, there was no point in trying to get to it.

And then there was Moth. It was only a few weeks ago that she and her friends had rescued us from the streets of Luray Prime, and started us on the path that eventually got us home. We owed her. But how were we supposed to get her out of there? And if we came up with a way to rescue her, did that mean we should free all the other children, too? Where would they go, if we did that?

We decided to spend the rest of the day observing the compound, getting a sense of its people and work rhythms. I spent much of my time watching the Weaver who Moth had said was in charge. If I had dreams about this place, I wanted them to include her.

I wondered if I could get into a Weaver's head, the way I had gotten into Tommy's.

14

THE SUN IS JUST BEGINNING TO SET when Master Weaver Marjorie Tennant begins her final rounds. The lights in the compound come on one by one as she walks past them, filling the courtyard with a soft blue glow. It has been a long day, but a rewarding one. The product from one subject is particularly promising, and she suspects that when the girl's fetter is properly tempered it will accept a Gifted imprint.

Project Beta is her creation, her pride and joy, and she loves her work dearly, even if she does not love where the Guild requires her to do it. But their caution is understandable. An untempered fetter is a dangerous thing under the best circumstances, and two dozen wild children producing sparks of energy with no structure or focus is hardly a recipe for stable power. No one has ever tried to collect and store the emanations of the unGifted before, so no one knows exactly where the process might backfire. Which is why her Guild dictated that if she undertook this dangerous experiment, she had to do so in the middle of nowhere.

But imagine if she is successful! No longer will Weavers have to pay exorbitant prices for the other Guilds to empower their fetters. Raw energy can be harvested from the unGifted, and other Guilds will only be needed to imprint that energy with purpose. Which means her Guild will be able to produce ten times as many fetters as they do now—a hundred times as many, a thousand!—and while the market price will inevitably drop, the lesser cost of production will more than make up for it. Net profits will skyrocket in the long run.

And imagine the social implications of it! There can be enough Gifted tech for every household to enjoy, at prices even the lower classes can afford. Imagine what it will be like when every family can have a house full of fetters—even the working classes—without having to go into debt for them. And the new system can provide employment for thousands of unskilled laborers, whose unGifted energy can be bound to empower the new tech. No, she tells herself, Project Beta isn't just about increasing the wealth and influence of the Weavers' Guild—though that is certainly a consideration—but about bettering the entire world.

As she walks the grounds, she notes that everything seems to be in order. The horses sound a little nervous, but they might be responding to the smell of a bear in the distance. Otherwise everything seems peaceful enough. A few of the children are still wandering about, mostly younger ones—they seem to be more resilient than the others—but soon they will retire to the dormitory so they can be locked in for the night. Not because Tennant fears they'll try to break out of the facility, but simply to keep them from disturbing the lab. Some of them are no longer connected to reality as much as they should be, and they often wander where they shouldn't.

A guard nods to her as she passes. What a boring job this must be for him! The closest thing to a threat that Project Beta ever faces is when a forest animal tries to get over the fence. Once a small bear made it halfway up, and the guards and Weavers placed bets on whether it would give up before hitting the barbed wire. And once a large bird got tangled in the wire, and a guard had to climb up to cut it free. They bet on the guard's climb, that time, and later enjoyed owl cutlets for dinner. Which tasted like stringy chicken.

As she heads toward the lab for a final security check, something catches her eye in the distance. Far to the north a faint light can be seen rising from the forest, casting a ruddy glow on the underbellies of the clouds. For a moment she thinks that it's probably just the last few beams of sunlight shining upward from the horizon ... but no, it's in the wrong part of the sky for that. She stares at it for a moment, noting how the clouds seem to pulse slightly, as if the source of the light is unsteady. Suddenly she realizes what is causing it—what must be causing it—and panic sets in.

Wildfire.

The compound has an alarm bell for such events, but it's rusty from disuse, and fallen leaves have jammed the mechanism; she has to yank on the lever a few times before it becomes unstuck. When it finally sounds people come pouring out of the buildings, startled and confused. Her staff has never faced a real fire before, and though they know what's expected of them in theory, they lack any instinctive grasp of the situation. She even sees several of them look at the distant glow in the northern sky and relax, thinking that if the fire is far away they have plenty of time. But she's seen wildfires before, and she knows how fast they can move. And while it's possible that one of the neighboring towns will have an Elemental on call who can turn the flames aside, she can't bet the welfare of her people on that. Besides, few people in the area know Project Beta is out here, so an attempt to divert the fire from nearby towns could wind up sending it their way even faster.

They have to evacuate. Now.

She gives the necessary orders, and people rush to obey. As the horses are led from the stables they whinny nervously, responding to the atmosphere of fear in the compound. Or maybe they can smell the distant fire. But there's something inside the compound that's far more dangerous than any fire, and Tennant knows that if she doesn't secure it properly, more than the compound may be at risk.

"Bring the dolly," she orders her assistant, as she pulls out the keys to the lab and starts running toward the cinderblock building. She fumbles with the lock for a moment, her hands unsteady, then gets the door open and heads inside, several Weavers following.

The lab itself doesn't matter, she knows. Equipment can be replaced. Tennant's lab notes have been copied to Guild headquarters on a regular basis, so even if all her notebooks burn, no important data will be lost. But there's one thing they dare not leave behind, something so unstable that the intense heat of a forest fire might set it off, even if its steel container keeps it from burning.

"Let's get the safe out of here," she orders.

She can hear the jangle of tack outside as a horse-drawn wagon is brought to the front door, and a ramp moved into place. Inside the building, her people are struggling to move the safe onto a reinforced dolly, but it's a heavy piece, and sweat is running down their faces by the time they finally get it settled. As they start to roll it outside, Tennant can see that a carriage and a second wagon are waiting for them, ready to go. There aren't a lot of vehicles in the compound, and she'll be hard pressed to get everyone out of here in time, but all Tennant has to do is get them to the nearest town, and then they will be protected by whatever defense local Elementals provide.

The safe rolls smoothly toward the door and

"Get the safe out of here," she orders.

She can hear the jangle of tack outside as a horse-drawn wagon is brought to the front door, and a ramp moved into place. Inside the building, her people are struggling to move the safe onto a reinforced dolly, but it's a heavy piece, and sweat is running down their faces by the time they finally get it settled. But as soon as they started moving the dolly the Weaver can see that it's damaged. It moves only a few feet before one of the wheels splits off from the base with a sound like the crack of gunfire. A corner of the frame slams down onto the floor, and the safe skids in that direction until part of it slides off the dolly entirely, striking the wooden planks of the floor with enough force to gouge deeply into them.

Frustrated, Tennant stares at the wreckage. Clearly the dolly isn't going anywhere now; the only way they can get the safe out of the building is to push it along the floor, or maybe lift it. She considers the dynamics of the two options, then orders one of her people, "Go get some more help. We'll carry the damn thing out of here if we

As soon as they start moving the dolly Tennant can see that it's damaged. It only goes a few feet before one of the wheels splits off from the base with a sound like the crack of gunfire. A corner of the frame slams down onto the floor and the safe careens in that direction, hitting the wooden planks so hard that two of them split. Now the safe is wedged corner-first into a jagged hole in the floor, with cracks fanning out from it in every direction.

Appalled, Tennant stares at the wreckage. The safe isn't going anywhere. "We'll have to unload it," she says decisively. Her people run to gather the boxes and packing materials she'll need, as she works her way slowly across the floor, easing carefully from one broken plank to the next. Wood creaks beneath her weight, and once she hears an ominous cracking sound, but the floor holds, barely. When she finally reaches the safe she crouches down in front of it and begins to dial the combination. God willing, she'll have time to unload the fetters with the care they require, and then get everyone out of the compound before the fire cuts off their escape route and

||||||||||||||||

I awoke to pain, and an exhaustion so overwhelming I could barely muster the strength to open my eyes. Every muscle in my body burned, as if had just run a twenty-mile marathon and then topped it off by doing a hundred pushups. When I tried to move one arm it spasmed painfully, and my other limbs followed suit, until my entire body was knotted in a shivering ball of agony. I tried to cry out to Rita for help, but my chest muscles had spasmed so tightly it was hard to draw breath, and my voice came out little more than a choked whisper.

After what seemed like an eternity, the pain receded. One by one my muscles began to relax, and I stretched them out as best I could, gasping for breath as I did so. I had a pretty good guess about what had caused all that pain, and it wasn't happy news. Apparently taking control of a stranger's dream was much harder than just chatting with my brother. Getting into the Weaver's head had required herculean effort, and every tiny change I'd made to her dreamscape had required more exertion than the last.

This was the price of my success.

I don't know how long I lay there, so exhausted I could barely muster the strength to draw air into my lungs. I was surprised that Rita didn't come over to see what was wrong. She was supposed to be on watch, wasn't she? When I finally felt I had enough strength to do more than gasp for breath, I lifted myself up on one elbow and looked around for her.

She wasn't anywhere in sight.

Struggling to my feet, I used a nearby tree to steady myself. My legs were still so weak I couldn't stand without support. "Rita?"

She wasn't anywhere to be seen. Not in the camp, not on the nearby hill we'd chosen as a sentry point, not down by the stream. For a moment I wondered if she might have ducked behind some bushes to take care of private business, but if so, she should still be close enough to hear me call her name. I couldn't call out too loudly, for fear that someone in the compound might pick up on it—sound travelled far at night—but if she was anywhere near our camp she should have heard me.

There was no response.

Surely Rita wouldn't have just left me alone, I thought. The whole point of us sleeping in shifts was to make sure no Hunters could sneak up on us, and I couldn't imagine her walking off and leaving me unguarded. But if someone had attacked her, and either killed her or dragged her away, why would that person have left me untouched?

Walking unsteadily to where I'd left my flashlight, I thought I saw a faint light in the woods. It took me a few seconds to be sure it wasn't just moonlight shining down through the canopy, but no, the light was perfectly still, unaffected by the wind-stirred branches overhead the way moonlight would have been. And it didn't look like the color of moonlight, either. I began to make my way toward the light source. The moonlight was barely enough to see by, and my legs were still pretty weak, but I wanted to observe the source of that light, so I kept my flashlight turned off. Once or twice I had to stop to catch my breath, but soon I could hear a voice from up ahead, pitched low to avoid detection. Heart pounding, I crouched low and inched toward it, finally settling behind a fallen tree that was covered in brush. No one looking this way in the darkness would see me there.

The voice was Rita's.

She was standing with her back to me, and at first I thought she was talking to empty air, but as my eyes adjusted I could make out a ghostly image hovering in front of her. A woman's face. I squinted, trying to bring its features into focus, but with Rita in the way I couldn't get a clear view of it. Not until I heard the woman's voice did I realize who she was . . . and when I did the shock was so great I had to grab hold of the tree trunk to steady myself.

"You told me there would be no Hunters," Rita said.

"I said I would do my best to hold them at bay," Alia Morgana responded. "You knew there was risk."

Morgana. She was talking to Morgana. What the hell—?

Rita exhaled in a soft hiss. "Well, they haven't attacked us so far."

"Then they're probably not Virilian's people," Morgana pointed out. "They're certainly not mine. Perhaps some locals are curious about you."

Rita had betrayed me. She was working for Morgana. The revelation was so mortifying that I could barely absorb it. All her friendship, all her support, even her seeming ignorance of the ways of this world, as we traveled side by side ... it had all been a sham. We had guessed that there was a spy among us, and everyone had thought it was Isaac. But of course it wasn't Isaac. A Shadow would have no reason to serve the Seers like that. Rita must have been the one reporting to Morgana all along, informing her of our every move, nudging us in whatever direction the Guildmistress wanted us to go. Thanks to her, we never made a move or had a conversation that Morgana did not know about.

I suddenly felt nauseous.

"Jesse's planning some kind of disruption at the Weaver compound," said the traitor who had once been my friend. "Do you want me to talk her out of it?"

I'd trusted her. In Berkeley Springs she'd been like a sister to me. Hot tears trickled down my cheeks, burning them like acid.

Morgana's eyes narrowed. "I want you to keep your cover. I want you to let her take the lead. Those have been your orders since the day you entered my service, and they will not change. If the Weavers suffer a loss ..." She shrugged. "I will light a candle for them. What about Jesse's dreams? Have you learned anything new?"

Rita shook her head. "She sensed at the shallow that we were in the wrong place, but she said that was just a feeling she got while she was half-asleep. Nothing that a regular Seer might not have picked up on."

"All right. Don't press her for more. It will come when it comes. The single most important thing now is for you to maintain her trust, so that if she does show signs of the Gift we seek, she will want to confide in you."

"I don't think that will be a problem." Rita's smugness was like a knife plunging into my heart.

"For now, no more calls to me. I understand that you were worried about the Hunters, so this time it was justified, but I don't want you contacting me from the field again, unless lives are at stake. It's too risky. Understood?"

It sounded like they were beginning to wrap up their conversation, so I started to edge away from my hiding place, moving off to one side so that if Rita headed back to the camp she wouldn't bump into me. I was shaking so badly that I couldn't take a step without something to hold onto. How long had Rita been working for Morgana? Was she on the Seer's payroll when I first met her, that day in the IHOP with Devon? Before that? Events I hadn't paid much attention to at the time suddenly took on terrible significance. I started remembering comments Rita had made, things she had done; the way Morgana and Seyer had stopped by the fair at exactly the right moment for us to see them ... Rita must have told them we were coming. And she had been the one to suggest that I get in touch with Seyer, which had set this whole trip in motion. Oh my God, it was staged, it was all staged, every minute of it was staged. . . .

Suddenly I remembered how Rita had come to me the night my house burned down, arriving in my bedroom just in time to save me. Her explanation for that had always seemed lame, but what other reason made sense at the time? Seyer had been standing outside the house, watching the fire. Had they been working together all along, trying to get me out of my house in time? That would suggest that they'd known about the arson in advance. My God, what if she'd actually *set* the fire, so that her people could make a show of rescuing me from it?

Tears were pouring freely from my eyes now, and I made no effort to wipe them away. All the pain of my family's suffering was in those tears, all my agony at seeing my mother's spirit wither away, all my rage at the time I had wasted worrying about Rita after our return home, thinking I had killed her, when in fact she was probably just hanging out at Morgana's place having tea and biscuits. It was more than any soul could contain. The best I could do was try to stifle the noise of my sobbing, burying my face in my shirt as my body shook from the force of my sorrow. Was Morgana the one who had orchestrated Devon's sickness? So that the only person traveling with me would be someone who answered to her? Sickness welled up inside me as I realized how thoroughly I had been manipulated. I leaned over and vomited, violently and wretchedly, but the fit offered a perverse cleansing for my soul, so I gave myself over to it. Wave after wave of sickness coursed through me, until my stomach was finally emptied of misery and all that was left was dry heaving.

"Jesse?"

Startled, I looked up. The call had come from the direction of our camp. Rita had gone back and was looking for me. Probably she heard all the noise I just made.

Crap.

With trembling hands I used the front of my shirt to wipe my face dry. There were a few bits of vomit left on my shirt, and on the back of my hand where I'd wiped my mouth, but I left them there. Vomit would be easier to explain to her than tears. "Yeah," I rasped. My throat was so raw I could barely get sound out. "I'm coming."

Thank God I had moved away from my original path when I started back. As I headed back to the camp I circled around even further away from the place where she had betrayed me, and I stumbled noisily through the woods, like someone who didn't know how to move quietly. If she heard me coming from another direction, she wouldn't suspect that I had overheard her treachery.

When she saw me stagger into camp, her eyes went wide. "Holy crap, girl. What happened to you?"

I learned what you are. And I'm so filled with disgust

that I can hardly bear to look at you. "I was sick as hell when I got up," I whispered. "Didn't want to throw up on top of our supplies." I waved vaguely toward the woods. "I think I'm okay now."

"Something you ate?"

I hesitated. We'd eaten the same food, so that story might not stand up to close inspection. My mind raced to come up with another excuse. "I had a nightmare. Really awful one. Left me feeling sick when I woke up."

"What kind of nightmare?"

Instantly I realized my mistake. Morgana had ordered her to report on my dreams, so there was no way Rita was going to let this one pass without explanation. I was going to have to make something up, with enough gruesome detail in it that the Guildmistress would think it was genuine. So I told Rita about a nightmare in which we broke into the Weaver's camp, only to find that Tommy was there, and that he'd been put through the same torture that Moth had talked about, but in a much more literal way. Halfway through my description of my little brother's body turned inside-out on a gurney, organs pulsing outside his skin, Rita decided she's had enough. Looking a little green around the gills, she waved the recitation short. My alibi was credible.

Analyze that one, Morgana.

I did manage to sneak the information about the safe combination into my fiction. There was no way to avoid Rita finding out about that—we couldn't break into the compound without it—but I sure as hell wasn't going to tell her that I'd altered the Weaver's dream to trick her into revealing it. I just told Rita that at the end of my nightmare I had seen three numbers appear, and I thought they might be the combination we needed.

Even a Seer could dream that much, right?

After I finished my story, Rita came over to me and put an arm around my shoulders, gently pulling me close to her. At any other time such a hug would have been comforting, but now that I knew the truth I had to swallow back on my revulsion to let her touch me. Hopefully if she sensed me drawing away from her, she would ascribe it to the aftermath of my nightmare. I had to keep up the illusion of friendship for now, no matter how painful it was. Rita and I were dependent on each other in this wilderness setting, and nothing good would come of our splitting up. As for later . . . I would have to play that by ear. It might be useful to be able to feed false information to Morgana, through her spy, but that would only work if Rita believed we were still best buddies.

I offered to take a turn at sentry duty so Rita could get some sleep, and I changed to a fresh T-shirt while she stretched out on top of her blankets. Then I climbed up the embankment and settled down on the large rock that had become our sentry post. Wrapping my arms around myself, I rocked gently back and forth, trying to comfort myself. If a horde of rabid raccoons had come running by at that moment, I doubt I would have noticed them.

I wanted to go to sleep again. I wanted to visit my brother in his dreams, or maybe Devon. Or maybe even my mother, though she wouldn't understand what was happening. I wanted to hug them so tightly they couldn't breathe, and tell them how friggin' scared I was, and how the one person I'd trusted most had turned out to be a traitor. How everyone around me seemed to be allied to either the Shadows or Morgana, and I was no longer sure which of those I should fear more.

Tears began to trickle down my cheeks again, but they were quiet tears, and Rita slept right through them. Never in all my life had I felt more alone.

15

SHADOWCREST
VIRGINIA PRIME

ISAAC

IF ISAAC HAD BEEN ASKED to name all the things in the world he didn't want to do, meeting with Guild-master Virilian would have been number one on the list.

Yet here I am, he thought unhappily, as he walked the length of the corridor leading to the Shadowlord's audience chamber. The last time he'd come here it was to beg for reinstatement in the Guild. Now all that was done with, but he was being called back, and he could not think of a single good reason why that would happen. Ordinary business would be handled by his father—now that they were speaking again—or perhaps a teacher. A Shadowlord of Master Virilian's rank didn't schedule a private audience with a mere apprentice unless something was very wrong.

Maybe Isaac's father had sensed how repelled his son was by the binding ritual, and was having second thoughts about Isaac's membership in the Guild. Or maybe others had complained about Isaac's attending that ritual, in breach of normal protocol. Or maybe there was some other offense involved. Isaac couldn't begin to guess, so he just braced himself for the worst as he approached the great doors. One of the men standing guard outside cracked a door open and slipped inside, probably to announce him. Wiping the nervous sweat from his palms in that precious moment of privacy, he waited.

The man reappeared. "You may enter."

The doors were opened just wide enough for Isaac to pass through, and they closed behind him as soon as he was inside. The vast audience chamber was filled with an unusual number of ghosts, more moans and screams echoing through the cavernous room than he remembered from his last visit. Or perhaps he was just more sensitive to them. Now that he knew he was hearing the terror of souls that Virilian had murdered, they were harder to ignore.

The Shadowlord was waiting for him at the far end of the chamber, seated on his black throne. The closer Isaac came to him, the louder the voices in the room seemed to become. Within ten paces of the throne he could almost make out words.

His Gift was growing stronger.

When he had come as close as seemed appropriate he stopped and bowed. He held the position for a few seconds, not just out of respect, but because it allowed him to put off the interview a tiny bit longer.

"Apprentice Antonin."

He stood up straight. "Your Lordship summoned me?"

Virilian's black eyes studied Isaac from head to toe. "Your family has taken you back, I see."

Isaac nodded. "My father was most gracious in his acceptance."

"He sees great promise in you."

The concept that Isaac's father might have praised him to the Guildmaster, after all their disagreements, was a startling one. That Virilian would tell him about it was even more so.

But even if my father said good things about me, that doesn't mean they're true. If Leonid Antonin believed that his family interests would be best served by the Guildmaster thinking that he was pleased with his son, then that was the story he would tell. Briefly, Isaac wondered what it was like to be part of a family where relationships were less complicated. Or more honest.

"I hope to serve my family faithfully and well," he said evenly.

The thin, bloodless mouth twitched slightly. "And your Guild, of course."

"Of course, your Grace."

Virilian leaned back in his throne and steepled his hands in front of his chest; It seemed an oddly human gesture for such an inhuman creature. "An apprentice's duty is to serve this Guild without hesitation or reserve. So if I asked you for information regarding your recent . . . adventures . . . you would of course provide it?"

Fear fluttered in his heart. The last thing he wanted to do was talk to Virilian about the details of his two-year walkabout. There were some memories too private to share. But he bowed his head and said, "Of course," because no other response was acceptable.

He wished he were anywhere but here.

"You know what happened to our Gate." It was a question.

"I heard that it was destroyed," he said carefully. "Not much more than that."

The Guildmaster nodded. "The Greys have kept the details of it quiet, at my request. Only a handful of people know the whole story."

Isaac's heart sank. Did Virilian suspect him of having played a part in the Gate's destruction? Or think that maybe Isaac had known the Colonnans were planning it? A thin film of nervous sweat began to gather on his forehead, but he didn't dare wipe it away for fear of drawing the Guildmaster's attention to it.

"It seems," the Shadowlord said, "our visitors had a codex. Presumably one keyed to Terra Colonna, though that has not been officially confirmed. They smashed it against the arch as they passed through, and the resulting explosion was powerful enough to destroy the Gate, along with its counterparts on more than a dozen worlds. The facility on Terra Colonna itself was completely destroyed. Though apparently they made it safely through before that happened."

"But a codex can't—" Isaac began. He bit his tongue and stopped.

"Yes?"

"Forgive me," he murmured. He lowered his eyes in formal humility. "I didn't mean to question you."

"But you should, Apprentice. Because what I just described to you should not be possible. A codex is a recording device, nothing more. It has no special mechanism or power that would enable it to destroy a Gate, much less devastate the surrounding landscape as it did so."

Startled, Isaac looked up at him.

"The Greys believe that some other power was fettered to it," Virilian told him. "They're not sure what, just yet, or who might have done the weaving. Investigation is ongoing." The steepled fingers twitched slightly. "I was hoping you could help shed some light on the matter."

Isaac's mouth was suddenly so dry it was hard to force words out. "I . . . I didn't even know they had a codex. Much less who might have created it."

"No doubt if you had known, you would have told us about it as soon as you returned."

"Of course," he said quickly. If Isaac had known about the codex and not informed his Guild about it, that would have been a mortal offense. He remembered how the boy in the binding ritual had died and he shuddered; with a single word, Virilian could consign him to the same fate.

"You were with the Colonnans while they were here. For how long?"

Suddenly he was very aware of how intently the Guildmaster was watching him. The fact that the Shadowlord had forsworn human emotion in himself didn't mean that he couldn't detect it in others. Isaac needed to choose his words with care. "I met them the week before I returned to Shadowcrest. I believe they had just recently arrived."

"And you taught them about us." The Guildmaster's voice was deathly cold. "Do I have that right?"

Isaac's heart skipped a beat. "Grade school basics, your Grace. The stuff every commoner is taught. Nothing about the Shadows. Certainly nothing about codexes."

The Guildmaster's expression was unreadable. "Go on."

"I travelled with them for a while after that. But they didn't trust me enough to tell me their plans. They didn't trust anyone from this world, to be honest."

The subtle lift of an eyebrow warned Isaac that he might be saying too much. *Don't talk about your relationship with them,* he told himself. *Even if your words reveal nothing, he may sense the emotion behind them.* "We split up as soon as we got back to Luray. They dropped me off at the south docks. I don't know where they went after that." He paused. "They could have gotten the codex from someone in the city."

Or from Sebastian, he thought suddenly.

He suddenly remembered what the Green Man had told them of his history, specifically his past conflict with the Shadowlords. Remembered the look in Sebastian's eyes when Isaac had asked about the death of Guildmaster Durand. Remembered all the fetters on Sebastian's coat, dozens of them, some of which manifested powers Isaac had never seen before. A man who knew how to obtain such fetters would know how to have a codex altered. And he would have the contacts necessary to do it.

"You remember something," Virilian said quietly.

Isaac hesitated. God knows, he owed Sebastian no particular loyalty. The Green Man had made a show of saving his life in the Warrens, but there had never been any real threat to Isaac; all he ever had to do was let the raiders know who and what he was, and they would bend over backward to get him home safely. Sebastian had done nothing more than protect Isaac's masquerade.

A loyal Shadow would tell the Guildmaster everything he knew about the Green Man, right now. A loyal Shadow would be pleased when Hunters brought Sebastian in for questioning, and proud to witness the ritual wherein Sebastian was murdered, his spirit bound to slavery, forced to serve the Guild he despised. A Shadow would be pleased that an enemy of the Shadows had been neutralized. But the man who had tried to save Isaac's life in the Warrens deserved better than that. Hell, *anyone* deserved better than that.

Virilian was waiting. Isaac had to say something.

"I took them to the Assessment Fair." Isaac gazed off into the distance as he spoke, partly so he'd look as if he was trying to access an elusive memory, but mostly so he didn't have to look into Virilian's eyes. "They went off on their own for a while. Someone might have contacted them then. Maybe word of their arrival had gotten out, and someone thought they might serve as a useful tool. I don't know. Why would someone want to destroy the Gate, anyway? Surely they know we could just rebuild it. I mean, I can understand why the Colonnans would have wanted to destroy the Gate behind them, to keep people from following them through it, but why would someone here help them do that? What would they have to gain from it?"

The Guildmaster stared at Isaac for a long moment. "Our Guild has its enemies," he said at last. "As do the Greys, and the Potters, and every other Guild whose livelihood depends upon interworld commerce. What better way to strike at us all than to destroy a Gate we depend upon, then sit back and watch while we blame each other for its loss?" He paused. "Now you understand why it's so important for us to find out where that codex came from."

"Of course," he said evenly. "And I'm sorry I can't help more."

"But you will help in the future, if you can. Yes? You will bring me any new information you find. And bring it directly to me, not entrusting it to servants or messengers?"

"I ... yes, your Grace. If that's what you want."

"It is," he said curtly. He stared at Isaac for another long moment, then gestured toward the exit. "That's all for now, Apprentice Antonin. You may leave."

Heart pounding, Isaac bowed deeply to the Guildmaster, then backed out of the chamber without looking up. It was an apprentice's gesture of humility, a statement of innocence: *Behold, I am nothing but a servant of my Guild, with no higher goal than to serve your will humbly and faithfully.* But inside his mind was churning. Had his answers been good enough to satisfy the Shadowlord? Did the Guildmaster really think he'd been involved in the Gate's destruction, or was he hinting at that just to keep Isaac off balance, so that maybe he would slip up and reveal other secrets?

If the Shadowlord wanted answers badly enough he had ways to get them, Isaac knew that. The binding ritual that he'd witnessed was a nearly perfect interrogation tool; any man the Guild was willing to kill could be forced to reveal all his secrets . . . at least the secrets that survived the mental trauma of the ritual.

My father would never let that happen to me, he thought. *No matter how much I frustrated him—or even angered him—He would never let Virilian do that to a member of his family.*

But the thought was cold comfort as he walked back to his quarters, and it was a long time before his heartbeat settled down to its accustomed pace.

16

Blackwater Mountains
Virginia Prime

Jesse

THE MOON WAS LOW IN THE SKY, half-hidden by the trees, so lighting was minimal, making it hard to see obstacles. More than once we had to work ourselves loose from a particularly aggressive vine or thorn bush, making way too much noise in the process. No one inside the compound seemed to notice—probably they just assumed that local wildlife was making a lot of noise—but it wreaked hell on my nerves.

We had observed three types of people in the compound—Weavers, guards, and experimental subjects—and had decided that it would be best if we looked like members of the first group, in case someone spotted us. Most of the Weavers were dressed casually, so hopefully anyone who saw us from a distance would assume we were members of the staff. Of course that illusion would fall to pieces if someone looked at us too closely—in a facility this small everyone probably knew each other. The three guards were big men whose uniforms wouldn't fit us even if we could get hold of some, and if we dressed like the kids we'd set off alarm bells just being outdoors at night. There really was no other choice. So we brushed the leaves out of our hair, smoothed out the worst of our camping wrinkles and hid our bulkier supplies in deep brush not too far from the compound. None of the Weavers were wearing backpacks.

We knew that whichever guard was on duty could be counted on to make a slow and leisurely round of the compound every couple of hours. Moth had told us that all three guards followed the same routine, and we'd timed the circuit a few times, so we knew when we would have the best window of opportunity to cross the compound. Once we got to the lab building we would climb in through the rear window—Rita assured me she could get us in without breaking any glass—and then search the place for any sign of Morgana's mandala pattern. When that was done, we would set the place on fire. Which—according to the Weaver's dream—would bring everyone running to fight the flames. Hopefully that would clear a path to the kids' dorm, which we would unlock, and then they could flee during the ruckus.

Was it a risky plan? Hell yeah, on at least a dozen counts. But there weren't any guard dogs in the compound, and no one seemed to be carrying firearms, so as long as we kept our exit path open we should be okay. We strung some ropes between trees just outside the fence, to trip up anyone who tried to follow us. I was praying that wouldn't be necessary. Dodging pursuit in the depths of the forest in the middle of the night was a sure recipe for disaster.

As for Moth and the other children . . . maybe it was a questionable mercy to release them into the forest, when we had no way to get them to safety. But Moth had made it clear that she would rather risk death in the woods than spend one more day as a test animal, and she said the others felt the same way. At least they could follow the carriage trail to the main road, which would lead them to nearby towns. And the weather was good, there was water nearby, and Moth was going to organize the children to sneak food out of the mess hall, so they would have supplies to take with them. A few days' hike would bring them to more populated cities, the kind of setting a girl from the Warrens was used to. They would all make it, I told myself. Moth was a plucky kid. She would lead the others to safety.

"You ready?" Rita whispered.

"No."

She grinned. "Good to go, then."

How loyal and brave she looked, as she prepared to follow a friend into danger! I wondered how much hazard pay she was getting for this trip.

From our hiding place we watched as the guard shifted his weight from leg to leg, trying to keep his mind occupied in the absence of emergencies. He looked like he was humming to himself. Every few minutes he checked his watch, and when 3 A.M finally rolled around he looked pleased to have something to do. Slowly he strolled toward the dining hall and checked its front door. Then he walked around the back of the building to check things there. We knew his next stop would be the area behind a row of small cabins, which meant we would be out of his line of sight for several minutes.

"Now," Rita whispered.

We moved through the brush quickly and were soon at the gate. Rita already had a small leather case in her hand, and as soon as we stopped she pulled out two small tools. The handles were mother of pearl, far more ornate lock picks than I would have expected Rita to possess. Probably gifts from Morgana.

She placed an L-shaped tool in the keyhole and pressed it to the side with one finger, then inserted a tool with a curved zigzag shape at the end. She moved the second one around a bit, mostly in a sawing motion, angling the end up or down in response to things she was feeling inside the lock. I heard a few soft clicks, and then the L-shaped lever turned slightly, and the lock snapped open. Just like that. Maybe five seconds from start to finish.

She saw my expression and grinned. "Hey, it's not that hard. I'll teach you sometime."

Jeez. Lessons in breaking and entering from Rita. No comment on that.

She released the bolt, and I took out the wad of glue we had painstakingly scraped from the back of our duct tape and pushed it into the space around it with my fingernail. Then I pushed the bolt back in, released it . . . and it held. No one was going to be locking this gate any time soon.

We slipped inside the compound and Rita quietly shut the gate behind us. The main area was empty right now, but we knew that any minute the guard would come back into view, so we sprinted toward the lab building as fast as we could and managed to slip behind it before he appeared again.

I plastered myself against the wall beside Rita as we took a moment to catch our breath. My heart was pounding wildly, but it was more from exhilaration than fear.

Rita looked at me. "Calm is good," she whispered. "Calm is your friend."

The back of the lab overlooked a drainage ditch, and once we skirted the building and slid down into that, we would no longer be visible from the center of the compound. I looked up at the one window high on the wall overhead and suddenly had my doubts about this phase of our endeavor. The window hadn't looked quite that high when we'd reconned it.

Rita's hand on my shoulder startled me. "It's all good," she whispered.

I nodded and braced myself on the only piece of solid ground, a slab of concrete half-buried in the wall of the ditch. Then I offered Rita my cupped hands and helped vault her up toward the window. It took three tries for her to grab the edge of the frame, and then a few awkward seconds for her to settle her feet on my shoulders. Then I held tightly onto her ankles as she cut through the caulking around a pane of glass. Once the pane was removed she was able to reach in and unlock the window, slide it open, and climb inside. A few seconds later a rope with knotted loops fell down to me, and I was able to climb up to the window and crawl inside.

We'd landed in a washroom, and for a few seconds we both crouched silently, listening for any other activity in the building. But it sounded as empty as it had looked. Rita eased the door open, and we moved into the main area of the building. We didn't want to use our flashlights for fear the light would be seen from outside, but I took out the small glow lamp, which had lost so much power by now that it was hardly brighter than a night light. I cupped it in my hand to direct the beam, and we could see by its light that we were in the lab Moth had told us about.

We were there. We had made it. The sensation of triumph that I felt was so powerful it made me giddy.

Easy, girl, I warned myself. *That was only the first step. Lots to do yet.*

The lab was bigger than I'd expected. A few steel tables with leather straps on them dominated the center of the room, and metal trolleys filled with tools were arranged along the walls. I remembered Moth's gruesome description of the Weavers' experiments, and I shuddered. There were also some filing cabinets, a small desk, shelves filled with tools and boxes, all neatly arranged, and a large industrial sink in the corner. A faint oily smell hung in the air; not unpleasant, but odd.

"Over there," Rita whispered, pointing to an alcove across from us with a small shadowy shape in it. I knew where the safe was located, thanks to the Weaver's dream, but I couldn't reveal that to Rita, so I let her take credit for its discovery. Carefully we moved through the room, trying to avoid all the tables and trays that would make noise if we bumped into them, until we got to the alcove, and yes, that shadowy shape was the safe. Rita grinned and looked at me expectantly.

Suddenly I felt my confidence waver. What if I hadn't really contacted the Weaver, but only dreamed that I had? In that case the combination I had seen her use would be useless. Or what if the dream had been true, but I'd gotten the numbers wrong? By the time the woman had opened the safe in her dream I'd been so exhausted I could barely see straight.

The world won't end even if you screw this up, I told myself sternly. *We'll just sneak back to camp and come up with a new plan. Nothing's happened yet that would keep us from trying again.*

The thought that my input might not matter as much as I'd thought was oddly comforting. Steadier now, I crouched down by the safe door and began to turn the dial, setting the numbers that I'd been repeating to myself ever since I'd woke up. Fourteen right. A whole circuit to the left, then twenty-three. Four right. Drawing in a deep breath, I took hold of the handle and pulled it back.

The door didn't budge.

Shit.

Rita muttered, "It would really suck if you got the combination wrong."

I cursed her silently and shut my eyes, struggling to concentrate. I needed to replay the Weaver's dream in my head, exactly the way I'd seen it, so that I could make sure I had all the numbers right. It turned out to be harder than I expected. The exhaustion I'd experienced while crafting that dream came back to me, as strong as when I'd first felt it; it was as if I was trying to affect the Weaver's mind again, rather than just remember a few details. And the dream itself was hazier this time, like viewing it through a veil of static. I could see the Weaver kneel down by the safe and start turning the dial, but I couldn't get the numbers into clear focus.

Come on, girl. You can do this.

Squinting into the static, I finally managed to bring the dial into focus, and I watched her open the safe again. *Fourteen right. Twenty-three left. Four right.*

So I had remembered the numbers correctly. That was comforting, but not at all helpful. I stared at the safe again, frustrated beyond words. My exhaustion had faded when the dream did, but in its place now was the sharp bite of despair. What if we had come all this way for nothing? Over and over, I replayed the opening of the safe in my mind, over and over. Finally I realized that the Weaver had spun the dial a few times before starting the combination and maybe that mattered.

I turned the dial clockwise a few times, then counterclockwise, then clockwise again—just to make sure—and then I tried the combination. I dialed each number with meticulous care, making sure it was perfectly positioned before moving on to the next. When the whole sequence had been set I took a deep breath, reached for the handle, and tried the safe door.

It opened.

We were in.

"Well, damn." Rita muttered. I could hear awe in her voice.

Inside the safe were three shelves with several wooden boxes on each one. They looked like recipe files, only, instead of printed cards being inside them, there were thin metal plates. Experimental fetters? I pulled one out to inspect and I saw that the surface was inscribed with data, mostly in alpha-numeric codes I didn't recognize.

"Shit," Rita said, looking over my shoulder. "How are we supposed to find the one we need?"

I took Morgana's paper out of my pocket and set it down beside the safe so that I could refer to it easily. "Maybe one of them is marked with this sign."

"Yeah, but there must be hundreds . . ."

I looked up at her. "You have somewhere to be?"

She looked pointedly at her watch. But though it felt like an eternity had passed since we'd snuck through the main gate, apparently, in real time, it wasn't that long. When Rita saw that we still had plenty of time, she sighed and nodded.

I turned back to the fetters. "Why don't I go through these to see if Morgana's symbol matches anything, while you check out the rest of the place? 'Cause we don't know for a fact that what she's looking for is in here." *Anything that keeps you from looming over me like a vulture while I search for Dreamwalker artifacts.* "I'll let you know if I find anything."

Her mouth tightened, but my suggestion was perfectly reasonable, so she moved off to explore the rest of the facility. Which left me alone to flip through the metal plates one by one, looking for any markings that might indicate whose fetters they were. There were several lines of information inscribed on each plate, but aside from a date at the top, it was all rendered in mysterious codes. It soon became clear that nothing like Morgana's mandala design was going to be found here, but that didn't mean there weren't other things I could search for. The fetters were arranged chronologically, so I started looking for ones that had been made while the coma boy was still alive. If I was right about his being the presence the Seers had sensed, then those were the fetters I needed to see.

"Any luck?" Rita whispered loudly from across the room.

I shook my head. "Nothing yet."

I finally found fetters from the right time frame, but they looked no different than any of the others. Clearly this method of searching was not going to help me. With a sigh I leaned back on my heels and tried to think of a new angle. The fetters were supposed to have mental energy bound to them. So if the boy's energy contained a hint of the Dreamwalker Gift, could that be used to identify it? It was worth a try. Risky as hell, since the kid had been a basket case when the fetter was made, but worth a try.

Drawing in a deep breath, I laid my hand on the first fetter and thought: *C'mon, fetter, do your stuff. Let's see what you've got.* Dr. Tilford had said that the glow lamp required both touch and intent to operate, so I offered it both. *Do something.*

Nothing happened.

I tried a few more fetters, and it soon became clear that a general invocation was not going to trigger any of them. Which actually made my search much easier. If each fetter responded to a specific type of command, I wasn't going to set any of them off accidentally.

Drawing in a deep breath, I spread my hands out over the fetters so that my skin would make contact with as many of the fetters as possible. I had to lean forward to use my forearms as well, but once I did that I was able to make contact with the fetters in two of the boxes, all at once.

Give me your dreams, I thought. My command wasn't

in words this time; rather, I was calling to the fettered energy with my own Gift: soul to soul. I was willing it to respond to me, to commune with me, to reveal its true nature to me ... whatever that turned out to be.

Still nothing happened.

Muttering a curse in frustration, I moved into position to test the next batch. Maybe this whole trip was a fool's errand. Maybe experimental fetters couldn't be activated by just anyone. Maybe you needed the Weaver's Gift to do it, otherwise they would just stay inert strips of metal.

Steady, girl. Keep it together.

Carefully I laid my arms and hands across the next two rows of fetters, shut my eyes, and tried to summon whatever residual bit of dream-power one of them might contain.

The castle is tall beyond measure, and shadowy figures can be glimpsed through its windows, each one of which reveals a different time and place. . . .

The tower looms overheard, the signatures of thousands of travelers spiraling around it, leading the eye upward, upward. . . .

The mausoleum is vast, grey and cold. So cold! Tier after tier of stone crypts stack up into the windswept sky, a plaque on each one identifying its occupant. The names are all different, but the same word is carved beneath each name, in identical letters: Dreamwalker. . . .

With a gasp I fell back from the fetters, the image of the Dreamwalker tomb seared into my brain. Was that the same shape-changing structure I had seen in the avatar's dream? If so, it had taken on a pretty dark aspect this time.

"Jesse!" Rita's voice was a hiss. "You okay?"

"Uh ... I cut myself," I muttered. I shook my hand

and sucked at a fingertip, to lend the fiction weight. "These things have sharp edges."

I waited until Rita had turned her attention back to her search before reaching out to touch the fetters again. Slowly I ran my fingers down the first row of plates, touching them one by one, attempting to summon back the vision that I had experienced so briefly. And I tried to lock my body in a rigid position, because I knew that if I moved suddenly or made a suspicious sound when I found the thing, Rita would be on me in a heartbeat. And this time she'd want more than a lame story about a non-existent wound.

Fetter by fetter, my fingertips slowly caressed the stack, and I fixed the position of each one in my mind so that I would not forget which I was in contact with when—

Color bleeds from the sky, from the trees, from the ground. The world is dissolving into thick black muck, and it traps his legs like quicksand so he cannot run, he cannot run! Darkness rushes down from the sky as he struggles to envision the pattern he needs to escape this world, the maps that will open a gateway for him. Desperately he sketches out its shape in his mind's eye, but it's not coming out right, the darkness is skewing his brain, it's not good enough! So he tries another—and another and another and another—and the patterns start overlapping, details running into one another until all he can see is a vast mandala that contains all the patterns he needs, but gives access to none. Then the darkness closes in on him and he hears himself screaming, because he senses what it can do. The taste of death fills his nose and mouth as memories start to rush out of him, every thought and hope and fear and love that he ever knew, sucked out of him into the void and devoured until there is nothing left . . .

*　　*　　*

Suddenly the images were gone. Maybe I banished them. Maybe when you saw a vision so horrifying that your soul begged for it to end, the fetter interpreted that as an "off" switch. Or maybe there was nothing left to be seen. Maybe the boy's emanations ended when the dream-wraith devoured his soul, and that was why he became catatonic. His body had gone on living, but his soul was dead.

Tears threatened to come to my eyes as I removed the dream fetter from the box, keeping my movements as small as possible so that Rita wouldn't notice what I was doing. No one but a Dreamwalker should possess such a fetter. I would take it home with me, and I would explore its mysteries, and maybe learn more about the strange castle which seemed to have such significance to my kind. And I would mourn this boy who had slipped through the Seer's net because they thought his Gift was not strong enough to manifest, who had left me this precious inheritance.

Suddenly my reverie was broken by what was, in our current context, a truly terrifying sound: a key turning in the lock.

"Shit!" Rita muttered.

Desperately we both looked around for cover. The room's interior door was too far away for us to get to it in time, and there were few hiding places nearby. Rita flattened herself against the wall behind a filing cabinet, scrunching down a bit to make sure her head couldn't be seen from the front door, but as soon as someone walked past the filing cabinet she'd be in plain view. I dove for cover under the desk, then realized that I'd left the safe door open, so I nudged it closed with my foot even as the doorknob began to turn. I tried to fit myself completely under the desk, but the space was too shallow for that, and my legs were stuck out the back. Like

Rita, I would be vulnerable to discovery as soon as someone walked past my hiding place.

Things were not looking good.

Heart pounding, I peered under the desk's lower edge to see who entered. My view was limited to six inches above the floor, and all I could see was that the newcomer was wearing black shoes—nicely polished but with mud on them—and blue uniform pants. A guard, most likely. But why was he here? The guards didn't enter this building as part of their regular rounds. Our whole operation centered around that premise. Had someone seen us cross the compound, or heard us moving around inside the lab?

It could be my fault, I realized. I'd spent half the night crafting dreams for the head Weaver, in which her precious lab was threatened with destruction. She might well have felt uneasy when she woke up, and asked her guards to check in here, just to be safe. If so, it was a frightening lesson in the consequences of screwing with someone's dreams. If I survived this, I should learn from it.

The feet had stopped moving, and just in time; two more steps and he would have passed Rita's hiding place. Thank God I'd thought to close the safe. I glanced back at it—and froze. Morgana's mandala drawing was lying on the floor beside it, in plain view. In my panic I'd forgotten about it.

I slid the dream fetter into my back pocket as I waited to see if the guard would come any closer, and I took out my knife, though I wasn't sure I could bring myself to use it on him. This wasn't some creepy servant of the undead, a monster who had helped kidnap my brother, maim my mother, and destroy the house I'd grown up in. This was just some working class guy trying to earn a living, at a low wage job in the middle of nowhere. Maybe Rita could stab somebody like that, but I didn't think that I could.

Maybe he wouldn't notice the paper. Maybe he'd just make a cursory check of the premises and leave without ever seeing us.

A beam of bluish light swept across the floor. It worked its way around the room, then stopped when it hit the safe. And paused there. It was centered on Morgana's drawing.

Shit.

The guard began to move forward—and then suddenly there was a sickening thud and he fell to his knees, stunned. As I scrambled out from under the desk I saw Rita cast aside the metal lamp she'd struck him with, and lunge for the back of his neck. She didn't have her knife out, so I wasn't sure what she meant to do. Tear his throat out with her teeth? My own preference would have been to try to talk our way out of this situation, but that option was off the table now, so I rushed in to help.

Rita was a small girl, no match for the guard's six feet of beefy weight, but she was quick on her feet, and her surprise attack had gained her a few seconds to act. The guard was still struggling to get his bearings when she grabbed him from behind, wrapping her arm around his throat in a chokehold that pressed in on his windpipe, cutting off his air supply. That woke him out of his daze pretty fast. He reached up to try to break her grip, but she was squeezing so tightly he couldn't pry her loose.

Suddenly he lurched backward, slamming Rita into the filing cabinet with a crash. She held on tight, so he tried it again, pounding her back against the thing as hard as he could. But he was rapidly losing strength, and as I ran to help her, he collapsed to his knees. I saw him fumbling for the nightstick he'd dropped when Rita first attacked, and I tried to kick it out of the way. But he was faster than I was and he grabbed it first. The next thing I knew the heavy black rod slammed into my side with stunning force. Pain shot through my ribs, and then I was on the floor, struggling to get my bearings. He resumed his assault on Rita, so I stumbled to my feet and tried to help her, but it was no longer necessary. Lack of blood and air had drained him of strength, and even as I watched, his struggles ceased, and he closed his eyes and slumped down to the floor. Rita still held on.

"It's done," I gasped. "Don't kill him."

She didn't let go. Her expression was cold.

"*Don't kill him,*" I ordered.

Muttering a curse under her breath, she let go of him. I went to shut the front door and set the lock. If someone came to investigate what all the noise was about, it would buy us a moment's time.

"You okay?" I asked Rita.

"Yeah. You?"

The pain in my side was sharp but not unbearable. My ribs were bruised, but probably not broken. "I think so."

She looked around the room, exhaling sharply in exasperation. "What now?"

Our original plan had been to set fire to the place, then exit out the back window and use the drainage ditch to get away. But we couldn't lower the guard's six foot body out that window. And I wasn't going to leave him here to burn to death.

For a moment we just stood there, looking around at the body, the safe, the door, and not saying anything. Time was running out.

"You go out the back," I said. "I'll drag him out the front."

She blinked. "Say *what*?"

There were voices outside now, coming our way. Clearly our struggle had been heard, and people were trying to figure out which building the noise had come from. Any minute now they would test our door.

"I'll make a show of rescuing one of their people," I

said. "My back will be to most of them, and the others will be paying attention to the fire, not me—"

"Jeez, are you *crazy*? You can't just walk out there—"

"So what the hell do you suggest we do?" I demanded. "We can't get his body out through the back window, and I'm certainly not going to leave him here to burn. We need that fire to cover our exit, which means we need to get him out of here. Do you know another way? Because if you do, I'm listening."

She stared at me for a moment. "You've got balls, girl."

"No," I said sharply. "What I've got is no other choice. Now, get the damn fire started while I drag this guy's body over to the door."

I checked his neck first to make sure there was a pulse. There was. Then I started to drag him across the floor, positioning him right in front of the door. It would have been easier if Rita had been helping me, but we needed to get our diversion started, fast. She was grabbing up handfuls of paper from the filing cabinet and cast them across the floor, creating a line of flammable refuse that stretched across the room. If we'd been able to follow our original plan to set the fire in secret, it could have grown to strength before anyone even realized what was going on. But any minute now someone could walk in the door, ready to beat out a small fire. So it had to spread fast.

"Here." I pulled the guard's keys from his belt and threw them to Rita. "Get the kids out of the compound if you can. If not, at least get yourself out."

For a moment she looked like she was about to argue with me, then she just shook her head grimly and pulled out her lighter. Kneeling down, she set fire to the paper in one spot, then another. As the flames began to spread she grabbed up Morgana's drawing and started to back away. It startled me at first that she would save the thing, then I realized she had no clue we had already found what we came for.

The fires spread quickly, joining together to separate us. There was no denying the bone-deep, visceral dread I felt at the sight of it, as memories of my own house in flames flooded my mind. I had to fight to stay focused on the present moment. "Good luck," I heard her say, and then she disappeared into the back of the house.

Muttering a prayer under my breath, I pulled the front door open. There were people right outside, all of whom turned to look at me. Heart pounding, I took hold of the guard's arms and began to drag him through the door, my back to the crowd outside. "He's hurt!" I yelled. "Someone help me!" The panic in my voice wasn't feigned, and within seconds people were at my side, helping me drag the man out of the building. Flames were now visible through the doorway, and I could hear frightened voices coming from every direction. "What's happening?" "Oh my God!" "The lab's burning!" Then the alarm sounded. It was much louder in real life than in the Weaver's dream, and it made my head ring. "The fetters!" someone yelled. "Save the fetters!" To say that nobody was paying attention to me was an understatement.

Once we were clear of the doorway, two sturdy men leaned down to pick up the guard and carry him away. I stayed with the body, pretending to help, using it to shield myself from view. The crowd parted for us, and soon we were past the frightened throng and rushing across open ground. The next few minutes were so wild—and so terrifying—that I lost any sense of where I was in the compound. But then I saw the stand of trees nearby, and I figured that was as good a place as any to make my exit. As we passed by it I broke off from my group, and headed toward the shadows of the tree. No one noticed. No one cared. The men carrying the body were focused on pulling their comrade to safety, and behind us fire was pouring out the doors and windows of the lab, and people were rushing around trying to deal with it. In the chaos that now filled the compound, I was a mere shadow.

I ducked behind the trunk of a massive forked oak and leaned back against it for a moment, trying to catch my breath. People were shouting, water was splashing, and I could hear the spurt of what must be fire extinguishers. Whatever they were doing to fight the fire must not be working very well, because the compound was filled with blazing light, and I could feel the radiant heat of it even from where I stood.

Fetters would melt. Lab notes would burn. Test tubes would shatter. The whole damn place with its history of torture would soon be nothing but ash, like my home was ash. The image was deeply and primitively satisfying.

A hand fell on my shoulder; I nearly jumped out of my skin.

"Easy," Rita whispered. "Just me."

The rush of relief I felt to have her there was undeniable. "Did you get the kids out?"

"Couldn't. Take a look." She pointed toward the center of the compound.

While most of the Weavers were now fighting the fire, a small group of people stood halfway between the lab and the cabins, just watching. I hadn't expected that. In the Weaver's dream everyone had rushed to help out, each person in the compound having a specific role to play. Like cogs in a well-oiled machine. Granted, the dream had depicted an evacuation, not an actual fire, but still, it spoke to how the place was organized—

No, I realized. It spoke to the way the woman in charge *imagined* it was organized.

Damn. Lesson two in how relying on dream knowledge could screw things up.

The spectators were positioned so that no one could leave the compound without being seen. Rita and I could probably have gotten out, since we were dressed like Weavers, but a horde of children in their trademark scrubs could never pull it off.

"There's nothing we can do for Moth now," Rita murmured. "I'm sorry, but that's the truth. We need to get out of here while we can."

"I'm not leaving her," I snapped.

But I had no idea how to get those people to move out of the way. What we needed was a new distraction, something that would jar them out of spectator mode and send them running elsewhere. Anywhere. I tried to think of a way to do that, but I couldn't come up with any ideas, other than an explosion. And we didn't have the materials needed to produce one of those. I inventoried our supplies in my head, hoping that something would spark an insight, but the only things we had with us were stuff we'd packed for the break-in. Nothing useful.

I thought of Moth sitting miserably against the fence during our second secret chat, whispering to me how she would rather die than stay in this place one more day, and my heart clenched in sympathy. I couldn't just abandon her. I couldn't.

Then I remembered something else I had on me. Something that hadn't been stored with our regular supplies. Slowly a plan took shape in my head, and yeah, it was a bit crazy, but it might work. And I wouldn't have to fight with armed guards or stand inside a burning building to pull it off.

"Watch the dorm," I ordered Rita. "As soon as you can break the kids out, do it, and lead them out of here. I'll catch up with you later."

"What—" she began.

But I was already gone, sprinting toward the stables.

The horses were upwind of the fire, and they had no direct view of the lab, so though they'd heard the commotion and smelled the smoke, they hadn't gone into panic mode yet. A few were whinnying nervously, but grooms were working to calm them down, and thus far everything was under control.

As I approached the building I slowed to a walk, dropping behind it so no one would see me. It seemed to me the nervous whinnying increased slightly in volume. Now I could hear the grooms talking, trying their best to instill calm in their charges. "Whoa girl, easy now . . ." "It's okay, don't worry, we won't let anything hurt you. . . ."

I moved a bit closer. The volume of the equine protests increased. There was a loud bang. Someone cursed.

Closer.

The horses started to buck and thrash in their stalls. High pitched squeals split the night. I heard objects crashing loudly to the ground, wood splitting, grooms yelling. A wave of guilt sickened me, but I stood my ground. The horses weren't being hurt, they were just scared. Their fear would fade as soon as its cause left the vicinity.

Or so I hoped.

The ruckus in the stable had become loud enough now to draw attention, and some of the Weavers came running to see what the trouble was. Unlike the fire, this catastrophe wasn't playing out in the open, which meant that anyone who wanted to know what was going on had to head this way. And the spectators came. They came. Not all of them, but enough to clear the way to the gate.

I looked over to the dormitory and saw Rita standing in front of it, keys in hand. *What the fuck?* she mouthed, when she saw that I was looking at her. I lifted the wild-life fetter out of my shirt just far enough for her to see it, then pointed toward the dormitory. As long as I was close to the horses, they would try to get away. She looked at me a moment longer, nodded her approval, then turned her attention to the key ring.

As I started to run toward her, the ground trembled. It only lasted a second, but that was enough to awaken memories of Mystic Caverns collapsing around me. I focused all my attention on Rita, trying to shut the memories out. She tried a few keys, with no success, then decided to kick in the door instead. She struck it right beside the doorknob, with enough force that the frame began to split. Then she kicked again and it gave way, bits of shattered wood flying everywhere as the door slammed open.

Lightning struck nearby with a deafening crack; it was so close that I could feel the electricity prickle my scalp. What the hell was going on? The weather had been calm when we'd entered the compound. Then the ground began to buck and heave, so violently that I lost my footing and fell to my hands and knees. Gasping, I looked at the dormitory, hoping that Rita was doing better than I was. There were children pouring out of the door now, headed toward the gate, many of them clutching food in their arms. Rita herself was staring at something in my direction, unable to move. I followed her gaze to the tops of the trees right behind me, and saw to my wonder—and horror—that they were all sprouting leaves, fresh green leaves, that grew to full size as we watched, then turned red or orange or yellow and fell to the ground, making way for new ones.

She looked at me, then at the mutating treetops, then back at me. There was fear in her eyes.

What the hell was happening?

I struggled back to my feet, and as I started to run toward her, rain began to fall from the cloudless sky. Not normal rain, but a dark, viscous liquid, that looked and smelled like blood. Suddenly I remembered the fetters we'd left behind, now in the heart of the blazing fire. Had the flames somehow triggered them, so that all the energy they contained was pouring into the compound? Lightning cracked again, and I saw a white-hot bolt strike one of the trees, splitting its trunk in two. A massive limb came crashing down right next to me, and I slipped in a puddle of the sticky red rain, almost going down again. As I grabbed at a branch to steady myself I could feel the bark crawling beneath my fingertips, and I let go of it quickly. The whole world had gone mad, and nothing within it was stable or solid any more.

Rita met me at the base of the dormitory stairs. Her face was streaked with red from the unnatural rain, and the terror in her eyes reflected what was in my heart. She grabbed me by the arm and we started to run. By now the ground was muddy—a thick, unnatural mud, that clung to our feet like glue—and the earth heaved repeatedly beneath our feet, as if we were running across the stomach of a living creature.

What had we done?

The gate was standing open when Rita and I reached it. Most of the children had passed through it ahead of us, but a few of the smaller ones were huddled together in fear just inside it. Rita grabbed up the smallest one and yelled for the others to get moving. The plan was for them to follow the road as long as they could, and abandon it only when forced to by pursuit . . . but there would be no pursuit tonight.

Suddenly I heard a horse screaming. I glanced toward the stable and saw that several animals had broken out into the pasture. As I watched, two of them fell to their knees, then collapsed full length upon the ground. I knew in my gut they were dying—they were all dying—and I had caused it. Insects began to swarm into the compound, wasps and bees pouring out of their hives, flying madly through the bloody rain, all sense of direction gone, a whirlwind of wings and buzzing and venom-tipped stings that swept through the compound like a twister.

"Jesse!" Rita grabbed me by the arm. "We have to go!"

Shuddering, I started to turn away from the horror that the compound had become, but out of the corner of my eye I saw something that chilled me to my core, and I turned to look at it. Against a sky seared white by lightning, a single spot of darkness had appeared, a terrible black void that sucked in all light, and it was slowly expanding, taking on the shape of a man—

No! No! Please, God, not that!

There was no mistaking it now: this was the creature from my dreams, the void-wraith, devourer of dreams, whose wound I still bore on my arm. Somehow, the terrible forces we'd unleashed had enabled it to cross into the real world, and now it hovered over the compound, feeding on the chaos. Its presence was an icy wind that sucked all the heat from the world, and I could see a film of frost spreading across the treetops beneath it, the leaves curling and dying as a glistening white shroud enveloped them.

Then the wraith looked at me. I wasn't sure how I knew that, when it had no eyes, but I could feel its scrutiny in every fiber of my being. "Run!" I screamed. But a crack of thunder split the night, drowning out my warning. I could see children strung out along the length of the road, the frontmost ones lost in shadow as they fled for safety. But not fast enough. If I ran in that direction too, following them, the dream-wraith would come after me, and then they would be vulnerable. I thought of the trees behind me, now sheathed in ice, and shuddered. Even if the thing didn't attack the children outright, its mere proximity to them might cause damage. I needed to flee in a different direction, and that meant only one thing: into the woods. I wouldn't be able to run as fast there, but at least I would be running alone, and if the wraith followed me, the children would be safe from it.

So I turned to the north and ran by the side of the fence until I passed the end of the compound, then I dove into the forest and kept running. I had left the fire behind, and the moonlight coming through the trees was minimal, so I ran in near darkness. I tripped and stumbled over various obstacles, struggling to keep on my feet. Lightning struck and for a moment everything was starkly visible, trees looming overhead like hostile aliens—and then that light was gone, too, and in its wake I was left blinded, and had to stumble through the darkness based on the memory of what I had just seen, until my vision cleared.

The wraith was getting closer, its presence a chill wind, each gust colder than the last. I dared to look up when the tree cover thinned, and I saw it looming overhead, its unnatural darkness devouring the stars. Despair gripped me. Where was I running to? What kind of refuge could protect me? This wasn't just a dream, like the last time; I couldn't just wake myself up to make it end. No little brother would hear my screams, shake me by the shoulders, and banish this thing. Sooner or later it *was* going to catch up with me, and not all the running in the world could save me.

Suddenly the trees were gone, and I was sprinting across open ground. I dared another glance overhead; the wraith was so large it looked like it had devoured half the sky, and it was bearing down on me. I turned back just in time to see the ground fall away before me, and I skidded to a stop, desperately trying to save myself. But the earth was too soft, and I couldn't get traction. Dirt crumbled away beneath me and I fell, landing with half my body on solid earth and half of it dangling over a chasm. It was probably the same crevice we'd followed on the way here, but in the darkness it looked ten times as deep. Desperately I grabbed onto an exposed tree root and tried to pull myself back to safety before the wraith fell upon me. Somehow I managed to get back onto solid ground, and as I did so I felt something sharp stab me in the butt. The fetter in my pocket.

The *dream* fetter in my pocket.

The whole world was losing heat now, and frost began to coat the treetops surrounding me. I couldn't see the wraith any more, only a terrible blackness in place of the sky. Why was it coming after me? It had only done that before when I used my dream Gift. It never showed up in my regular dreams. So why was it hunting me now, when I was awake?

I dug the dream fetter out of my pocket. It looked like a piece of inert metal, but I knew the power that was in it. I had seen the wild energies of the other fetters crackling through the air of the compound, warping the very forces of nature. Maybe the wraith was responding to the energy in this one. Maybe it could sense the Dreamwalker's essence in it, the same way Morgana's Seers had.

Twisting around, I tried not to think about all that this fetter could have taught me, all the mysteries it could have revealed, all the powers it might have unlocked. None of that would do me any good if I was dead. With a cry of anguish I threw the thing as far I possibly could, and I watched it arc high over the chasm and then begin to fall. Lightning flashed, turning the smooth piece of metal into blazing fire, just for an instant. Then a dark and terrible presence rushed down into the chasm, passing so close to me that it left a film of frost on my hair. Ice formed along the edges of the crevice as it swept down its length, until it reached the falling fetter and enveloped it. Then the darkness began to draw into itself, blackness folding in upon blackness like some hellish origami. And an instant later it was gone. Half-blinded by the lightning, I couldn't identify the exact moment it vanished from the waking world, but I could feel the frigid weight of its presence lifting from the universe, and overhead the stars returned.

And then there was silence. I waited, breath held, to see what would come next.

Melting icicles tinkled softly overhead. A patch of frost broke from the chasm's rim, crumbling as it fell to the bottom, landing gently.

Nothing else.

Numbly I lowered my head to my arms, and I wept. I wept for the dead horses and the terrified children and even for the Weavers who had just lost all their work, because that was my doing. But most of all I wept for myself, for the loss of that precious hope I had enjoyed so briefly, when the key to knowledge was in my hand, and the future had appeared to be within my control. Now gone.

I was not consciously aware of the moment when this world gave way to the next, nightmares of the solid world morphing into nightmares of an imaginary one. But Rita found me shortly after dawn and woke me up, so sometime during the night that moment must have come.

Sometimes it is merciful not to know.

17

SHADOWCREST
VIRGINIA PRIME

ISAAC

ISAAC WAS ASLEEP when the spirit returned. He sensed it in his dream first: a presence in the shadows that was not quite visible, an unnatural breeze that chilled his skin whenever he looked in a particular direction. By the time he was fully awake, he knew that the event he'd been preparing for was finally at hand.

He squinted as he peered into the corner of the room where the spirit seemed to be. Struggling to see it. His teachers said his Gift was too weak to allow true death vision, but as he was beginning to discover, not everything his teachers taught him was correct. Whether they were deliberately hedging the truth to make him behave in a certain way, or just doing the best they could with the limited information they had, he didn't know, but the end result of both paths was the same: the only sure way for him to discover what his limits were was to test them.

He'd spent the last few days researching the techniques that the *umbrae majae* used to bolster their Gift, and now, as he peered into the darkness, he whispered the spirit's name over and over again, envisioning a ritual design he'd discovered in one of his father's books, something called a *death codex*. Concentrating on it was supposed to help open a window into the world of the dead. *Jacob Dockhart,* he chanted mentally. *Jacob Dockhart. Jacob Dockhart.* He tried to visualize the boy's face, superimposing it over the shifting shadow that was in front of him, but it proved surprisingly difficult. The last time Isaac had seen Jacob, the boy's face had been contorted into a mask of pure horror; it was not the kind of image the mind naturally wanted to recall.

But slowly the darkness in the room seemed to coalesce, until there was a single human-sized shadow. While it lacked any color or detail, and there was only emptiness where its face should have been, it was vaguely human in shape, and Isaac felt a rush of pride at having managed that much. Most apprentices could not conjure a vision of the dead at all.

"Jacob Dockhart." He spoke the spirit's name firmly, because it was important for the dead to know who was in charge. "Why are you here?"

He sensed that the spirit was responding to him, but the ritual that had allowed him to see it did not help him make any sense of its speech. Shutting his eyes for a moment, he envisioned another codex he'd found, which supposedly would open his mind to the voices of the dead. It was a dangerous pattern to invoke, especially for a mere apprentice. If some malevolent spirit decided to take advantage of the fact that he was now opening his mind to the influence of the dead, there was little he could do to stop it. Only a Shadowlord had the power to cast out a possessing spirit.

But no spirit tried to take control of him, and after a few moments of concentration he found that he could make out fragments of the spirit's speech. It wasn't that he heard actual words, so much as he sensed their meaning. The tide of ghostly sounds chilled his skin, it stirred his blood, it made his eyes burn and left a strange taste in his mouth. And in the wake of that came understanding. There was no real sound.

Help me, the spirit seemed to be saying. Isaac's skin prickled as he absorbed the words, not just through his ears but through every cell in his body. Even for a boy who was accustomed to the presence of the dead, the sensation was eerie.

Help me.

"I can't," he said quietly. His voice was pitched low so that no one outside the room would hear him. "You've been bound to a Shadowlord. There's no way I can undo that, I'm sorry."

Again he sensed, rather than heard, the ghost's question. *Forever?*

Isaac hesitated. He knew that such slaves often became free when their masters died, but he also knew that Shadowlords who accepted Communion could claim the bound spirits of their predecessors. He didn't know enough about the process to give the boy's ghost any kind of definitive answer. "Why are you here?" he demanded.

For a moment there was silence. The air around him began to take on weight and substance; he felt as if the darkness were pressing in on him. Fear fluttered in his stomach, and for a moment he was tempted to try to banish his visitor—though God alone knew if he was capable of that. But instead he drew in a deep breath and waited.

After a few seconds the sensation eased a bit. *Unfin-*

ished, came the ghostly flesh-whisper. A bit clearer this time. *Help me.*

"Do you mean, you left something unfinished? From your mortal life? Is that it?"

The spirit's affirmation was a wordless sensation that raised the hairs on the back of his neck. But what sense did that make? The dead couldn't remember their former lives in any meaningful way. Details from that time were just disjointed shards, devoid of the neural connections that were needed to stir living passion. A physical brain was required to make any kind of emotional connection. Wasn't that what they taught in his *Introduction to Necromancy* class? Wasn't the whole point of the Shadows' wretched training program to teach their children how to live without passion, so they could be closer to the dead in their mindset?

Mae. The name was a whisper of ice, of fire. Terrible frostbite yearning.

"You left her behind?" Isaac asked. "Is that it?" He hesitated. "You can't be with her again. I'm sorry, it doesn't work that way."

As the next words were spoken the sensation of pressure returned, twice as suffocating as before. *Three steps from our mark.* A vision of a rising sun flashed in Isaac's mind. Or perhaps a setting sun? The image came and went so quickly he couldn't be sure. *Please,* the ghost begged. *Tell her.*

Then the pressure eased. The spirit fell silent.

Isaac didn't know what to say. This situation was so bizarre that he didn't know how to respond to it. The spirit in his room wasn't just an ordinary ghost, it was a bound spirit, theoretically incapable of independent thought or action. It shouldn't be in his room at all, much less be reminiscing about lost loves and asking him for favors. That was so out of line with everything he'd been taught about spirits that if he told his teachers about Jacob's visitation they would tell him he was imagining things.

But what if his intense concentration on the boy during ritual had screwed things up? Maybe this spirit was not only bound to the Shadowlady in red, but had some kind of connection to Isaac as well. If so, his father would be pretty damn angry when he heard about it.

But his father didn't know about this yet. And neither did anyone else.

Best to keep it that way.

"Where would I find her?" he asked.

The spirit's gratitude rushed over him like hot burning ashes; for a moment he found it hard to breathe. *Where I died*, the ghost said. *Soul death. Not flesh death.*

The death of the boy's flesh had taken place at the ritual, but what did *soul death* mean? Maybe he was referring to the moment when they'd fed him drugs to render him helpless, and he'd lost his last hope of freedom. No, it couldn't be that, because no outsider would have been present. Maybe this Mae was someone he'd known at the orphanage—someone he'd loved—and when he was sold to the Shadows, and separated from her forever, that was a kind of death. The moment at which his former life ended, and he lost control of his fate.

Clearly the trail began at the orphanage. But did Isaac want to follow it? The fact that this spirit retained enough living memory to yearn for closure was all very well and good, but a Shadow was under no obligation to indulge the dead in their last whims. In time—probably very little time—Jacob's final memory of Mae would fade on its own.

But.

Whatever ritual bond had been established between Isaac and the ghost, it seemed to make his Gift stronger.

And that had value to him. So did having a spirit indebted to him. As an *umbra mina* Isaac couldn't bind a spirit to him with one of the normal rituals, but that didn't mean he couldn't control one by other means. If the ghost of Jacob Dockhart was coherent enough to beg for closure, it was coherent enough to owe Isaac a favor. A damned big one.

"Do you think she's still there?" he asked.

But the boy's ghost was no longer in the room. Maybe its mistress had summoned it, to do whatever slave spirits did when they weren't visiting other Shadows. Maybe it had just communicated all that it could and felt no more need to manifest.

Jacob's ghost doesn't belong to me, he reminded himself. *There are rules about this kind of thing. My father would never approve.*

For the first time in his life, he wondered how much that really mattered.

||||||||||||||

The orphanage was a few miles outside of Luray, two train stops south of the place where Jesse and her friends had dropped Isaac off on their way into town. That day he'd had trouble finding a ride, and had wound up tucked between baskets of smelly produce on a cart heading to Luray's central market. Now he was wearing the robes of an apprentice Shadow, and that changed everything. People fought for the honor of transporting him, taxi-drivers jostling each other as they tried to get his attention. Whether that was out of respect for his Guild or fear of a Shadow's displeasure, or simply because they assumed that a member of such a rich and prestigious Guild would tip them well, was anyone's guess.

No one questioned his presence at the orphanage. The minimum-wage security guard standing duty at the gate looked pointedly at the sigil of the Shadows embroidered on his robe and waved him through, then went back to reading his dog-eared novel. Isaac caught sight of the title as he passed: *Seven Guildmasters in Hell.*

He probably could have gone to the main office and asked for help finding Mae, but that would increase the odds of this visit being reported to the Shadows, who would ask why the girl mattered to him. He wouldn't take such a step unless he had to.

He skirted the office complex and headed to where two large, featureless dorms were located. Most of the orphans worked during the day, in factories and workshops elsewhere on the property, so if he found someone to talk to there shouldn't be dozens of other people listening in. After walking around a bit he spotted a couple of skinny boys mowing the grass, and he approached them.

"Your Lordship!" The nearer of the two boys made an awkward gesture that was probably intended as a bow, but he stumbled doing it, and there was no mistaking the edge of fear in his voice. "How can we help you?"

His use of the wrong title wasn't worth the trouble of correcting. "I'm looking for a girl named Mae," he said. "Do you know her?"

The boy looked back at his companion. Whatever silent communication passed between them, it was clear they were both suspicious of the request.

"I just want to talk to her," Isaac said. He shouldn't have to give them any kind of explanation, but their fear was rational, and he respected it.

The younger boy hesitated, then pointed east. In the distance, Isaac saw a low building with smokestacks. "She's working at the mill."

He nodded curtly, thanked them for the information—which seemed to surprise them both—and headed that way. It was a bit of a hike, but long before he got to the building he could smell it. Even diluted by the open air, Its faint chemical odor was enough to make his eyes sting. As he got closer, he could hear the rumbling of machinery inside the building, probably steam driven.

There was no security, only a heavy door with a lock as big as his fist. He raised a hand to knock, then reconsidered and let himself in. There was no antechamber, just a vast workroom with a row of steam-driven looms running down each side. Some of the girls and boys running the machines were so young they had to stretch to reach the controls, while the smallest children of all darted underneath the machines, dodging shifting combs and flying shuttles to retrieve fallen objects and pull gobs of lint out of the machinery. It looked hellishly dangerous.

The overseer spotted Isaac immediately and climbed down from his elevated platform at the far end of the workspace to talk to him. Though his manner was polite, it was hardly welcoming; Isaac guessed he was suspicious about why a young Shadow would show up in his mill. Or maybe the man was just territorial by nature, and the arrival of any stranger in his workspace made his fur bristle. "Your visit honors us, Sir. May I ask what interest the illustrious Shadows have in our facility?"

"I've come to talk to one of the orphans here. Her name is Mae."

The overseer's eyes narrowed suspiciously. "On what business, may I ask?"

"Guild business," Isaac said shortly. He could tell that the overseer wasn't satisfied by that answer, and for a moment the man just stared at Isaac, waiting for him to offer more information. After a moment of silence the man glared resentfully and gestured toward the machines.

"This way." He led Isaac to where a young girl was working, and she was so fixated on her work that when the overseer prodded her she jumped.

"This Shadow wants to talk to you." He nodded toward Isaac. "Ten minutes."

The girl was younger than he was, maybe fourteen, maybe less. The fear in her eyes was unmistakable.

"He just wants to talk," the overseer assured her. He looked at Isaac; his expression was a warning. "That right?"

"That's right."

Isaac turned toward the exit and gestured for her to follow. Another child scurried over to take her place, so that her loom never skipped a beat. Both children were like cogs in a vast machine, perfectly synchronized. Had Jacob worked here too? If so, then he had not been free even when he was alive.

Isaac led the girl out of the mill and a short distance away from the building, until the noise of the machinery was no longer distracting. Then he turned to her. "I bear a message from Jacob Dockhart."

The brown eyes widened in surprise. "Oh my God! Is he okay?" A tentative smile lit her face. "Where is he?"

He'd braced himself for a display of sorrow, but the spark of joy in her eyes was unexpected and surprisingly painful. "I'm a Shadow," he said gently. "Remember what our Gift is."

The smile vanished. The moment of joy faded from her eyes, and fear took its place. "You . . . you speak to the dead," she whispered.

He nodded. What pain there was in her expression now, what raw emotion! No one in Isaac's Guild would ever display their feelings like this, no matter how much they hurt inside. He stared at her in fascination, as if she were some kind of exotic animal.

"So he . . . he's gone?" Her small hands twisted in her skirt, her voice was trembling. "Dead?"

He nodded. "I am sorry."

"Why?" she begged. She started to reach out to him but pulled her hand back quickly. "*Why?*" she pleaded, as tears began to run down her face.

There was no good answer to that, so he didn't try to offer one. Better honest silence than a poorly constructed lie. "I came to bring you a message from his spirit. Do you want to hear it?"

Eyes wide, she nodded. "Yes," she whispered. "Please."

"He said to tell you, *three steps from your mark.*" When she looked confused he pressed, "Does that make sense to you? I believe he was referring to something that belonged to both of you."

Her eyes grew wide. "Oh," she breathed. "Maybe. . . ." The words trailed off into silence.

"You know what he was referring to?" he pressed.

Biting her lip nervously, she nodded. Then, with one last glance at the mill, she started walking. Away from the factory, toward an area dense with trees and underbrush. She gestured for him to follow her. As the trees closed in around him, his long robe caught on a thorned branch, and he had to yank it free. Soon it was no longer possible to see the mill through the trees, or any other part of the orphanage grounds. Then the girl stopped, and she reached out to touch the forked trunk of an aged oak, her fingers gently caressing its bark. At the juncture of its two main limbs a design had been carved. At first glance it looked like some kind of abstract symbol, but then Isaac realized it was in fact two initials intertwined: *M* and *J*.

Unfamiliar emotions stirred deep within him. Sympathy? Compassion? The feelings were exotic, intense, uncomfortable.

"Three paces from this," he said. The meaning of the rest of his vision was now falling into place. "Either due east or due west, directly from this point."

Three paces to the west there was a mass of underbrush with poison ivy woven into it, so thick that it was clear no one had tried to walk through it recently. Three paces to the east was another tree. Its gnarled roots sketched out a V on the ground, its mouth pointed directly at the spot where they were standing. He pointed to it. "Maybe there?"

She went to the tree, hesitated, then knelt in the soil and began to dig at the vertex of the V. The dirt was loose, Isaac noted, as it if had recently been disturbed. Beneath the top layer of soil was a layer of old leaves, easy to move aside. As she brushed them away, a small hole containing a worn wooden box was revealed. She glanced back at Isaac, then pulled out the box and rested it in front of her. From the look on her face it was clear she had no clue what it was.

She opened it and gasped.

Inside the box was money. Not a lot of it by Isaac's measure, but no doubt a fortune to one in her circumstances. There were small coins, large coins, and a thin wad of bills wrapped in string. There were a few pieces of jewelry as well, one of which Isaac thought he recognized from the Warrens stash. A pocket watch, a pendant, a silver brooch . . . the kinds of items one could pinch from a person in passing. Isaac had lived on the streets long enough to know how that worked.

"We were going to run away," she whispered. "He told me . . . Last time I saw him . . . he was almost ready. He said that he had everything we needed, and I could go with him. He said he would take care of both of us. Then the Shadows came, and took him away from me. . . ."

With a sob she lowered her head to her chest. The

sight of her struggling not to cry broke through all the barriers that he had erected to guard himself from human emotion, and made his soul bleed.

We caused this human misery, he thought. *My Guild. For no better purpose than our convenience.*

"You have the power to leave now." Isaac spoke quietly. "I'm guessing that's why it mattered so much for him to make sure you got this. But you shouldn't do so now. The masters of this place know that I came here, and if you disappear right away they'll make the obvious connection. It will help them track you down. You understand?"

"I understand," she whispered hoarsely. The tear-streaked face looked up at him. "He's still around? You can talk to him?"

Isaac shook his head. "An echo of his soul remains, nothing more. Think of it as a recording of his last thoughts, that I managed to hear. Now that their purpose has been satisfied, they, too, will fade. There's no one for you to talk to." At least part of that was the truth.

She lowered her head again and began to weep, this time without trying to stifle the sound. Isaac watched her for a moment, then turned and left. This was not the sort of scene a Shadow had any business being part of.

Love. Fear. Loss. Mourning. There were so many emotional energies swirling about him that it was overwhelming. Isaac wondered what it would be like to live with such emotions every day, like people outside his Guild did. To be at the mercy of those terrible tides each time one suffered a loss. No wonder the boy's identity had survived death, with so much emotion behind it. Maybe when his spirit learned that its final wish had been granted those emotions would fade, until all that would be left was a mindless and purposeless ghost, identical to every other slave spirit.

Or maybe this one would prove to be more than that, and with its help, Isaac could learn more about his own potential.

He looked back at the crying girl one last time, a strange pang of jealousy in his heart, then started down the path toward home.

18

BLACKWATER MOUNTAINS
VIRGINIA PRIME

JESSE

DURING OUR RIDE BACK TO LURAY, I leaned my head against the train window and watched the scenery go by without really seeing it. The vibration of the glass against my forehead might have been soothing, had I been capable of being soothed. I wasn't.

"No one died," Seyer reminded me. "That's a good thing."

"No *people* died," I corrected her.

I was bone-weary, soul-weary, almost too tired to remember my name. I did remember part of a dream I'd had the night before, and it played out again in my mind's eye as I stared out the window. When had I dreamed it? Right after I collapsed, as I lay half-dead at the edge of the chasm? Just before dawn, when Rita found me? All I knew was that I'd escaped the horrors of the night in the only way I knew how, and in my dreams, sought out one of the few people I still trusted.

The field of battle is still. The fallen bodies are gone now, but their imprints remain in the grass, along with their blood. The tang of black powder hangs in the air, mercifully masking whatever human smells might cling to this place. It's lonely here. No, more than that: it is the archetypal embodiment of loneliness.

I see a figure standing atop a hill, a soldier with bands of leather crisscrossing his chest. The fingertips on his right hand are black from gunpowder, his boots are coated in mud up to the calves, and his youthful face is splattered with blood. Not his. He looks young, so young. I never picture him that way.

I start toward him, but my body is so drained from my recent experiences I can barely walk. I stumble in the wet grass and go down on one knee.

"When you talk to Her Grace—" Seyer began.

"I'm not talking to Her Grace." I raised up my head with monumental effort and looked at her. "What's the point? We never found the mandala. We never found anything that even hinted at Dreamwalker activity. All we found were rumors about some boy who slept all the time, and maybe he had something to do with the mandala, or maybe not, but he's dead now, so no one will ever know for sure. I'll tell her all that and then she'll say, I'm sorry, that's not good enough to earn a Potter's service, and I'll say, but what about my mother? And she'll say, it's all very sad, but it's not my problem." I leaned my head back against the glass and stared out at the landscape. "Might as well save myself the trouble."

Did I sound bitter enough for that speech to be convincing? The part about my mom was true enough, though the part about failing in my quest was pure fiction. But I needed Morgana to think I was avoiding her out of despair, not because I feared her ability to sense deception. It was easier to stare out a train window and lie to Seyer—and Rita—than it would be stare into Morgana's eyes and try the same thing. I needed to play my part well enough for Seyer to report to her mistress that the failure of our mission had left me so overcome by despair that there was no point in her meeting with me, so that she wouldn't question why I avoided her.

"Just give us the tickets home," I muttered miserably. "We'll find our own way."

Private Sebastian Hayes is handsome in his youth, his hair still brown, his face still unlined. But his eyes . . . they are ancient, and they will always be ancient, no matter what form his dream body takes. Clearly he's startled to find me here, in this setting from his past. I see him blink as he struggles to make sense of it. "Jessica?"

I try to get back on my feet, but my legs are unsteady—and then he is right there, raising me up, lending me strength, my one certain anchor in a world where everyone and everything else has failed me. "What is it?" he says. "What happened?"

So I tell him the story. All of it. The dreams, the discovery about Rita, the nightmare in the compound, all of it. My delivery is halting and at times not wholly coherent, but he seems to get the gist of it.

When I'm done he's very quiet. I can sense that he's struggling to digest it all, so I wait. Finally he looks out at the blood-soaked battlefield and says, "So this . . . this is something my own mind created for me?" He looks back at me. "But you being here, in the midst of it, my dream . . . is that real? Can you enter other people's dreams?"

I nod. It's unnerving to share that secret with anyone

other than Tommy, but it's also liberating. A weight that has been suffocating me since the night of the toaster strudel eases ever so slightly. "I trust you," I tell him. "I know you would never hurt me."

A shadow passes over his face. "You shouldn't trust anyone on Terra Prime," he says quietly. "Even me."

I put a hand on his arm. "The children need help, Sebastian. They have some food and a general idea of where to go—and Moth has enough courage for a hundred children—but I'm worried for them. Please, can you help them? Bring them some supplies and point them in the right direction? It isn't that far from your own territory. I . . . I have the means to pay for it."

Those ancient eyes fix on me. So much pain in them. So much weariness. "There's no need to pay me," he says quietly. "I can't go myself, right now, but I know someone who might be able to do so. I'll talk to him."

"Thank you," I whisper. Another crushing weight lifts from my soul. "Thank you so much. . . ."

"What will you do about your mother now? Morgana's not likely to help you if you won't do her bidding. And if I were you I would have second thoughts about meeting with her again. It's rumored she can sense when people are lying, and you're keeping a lot of secrets these days."

I draw in a deep breath and look straight into his eyes. "I was hoping you could help me with the Fleshcrafters."

"Me?" He raises an eyebrow. "The Potters owe me no favors. Nothing that I can use on your behalf, anyway."

"No, but you have access to information. You can help me identify something they want, that I can get for them. Or do for them. Or . . . something." He doesn't answer me right away so I press, "Is that too crazy an idea?"

There is a long silence. "It's not crazy," he says at last. His expression is dark. "I do know something they want, and given what you've just told me about your Gift, it might be possible for you to obtain it. Maybe." He sighs. "You go back to Luray. I'll make what arrangements I can for the children and look into the Fleshcrafter issue. Try to get some rest tonight; you'll need your energy tomorrow. I'll meet you at noon, at the pier where we left Isaac. Hopefully I'll have information for you then."

I hesitate. "Sebastian . . . the creature that chased me . . . do you have any idea what it was?"

He shakes his head. "I've heard legends about a wraith that devours dreams, but little more than that. Even if such a creature did exist, none of the legends suggest it would be able to manifest in the real world. The Shadows are the ones who study the dead, so they might know more."

"Yeah. Like they're about to share their knowledge with me." I sighed heavily. "So . . . what? If it shows up again, I just run away?"

A faint smile flickers. "I would."

He leans over and kisses me on the forehead. There is warmth in the gesture but also tremendous sorrow, and I feel a lump rise in my throat. "Be careful, Jessica."

"I can't go home like this," I muttered into the window. My breath frosted the glass. "Going through the Gate brings back such terrible memories . . . I need some time to pull myself together before I have to go through that again." Maybe it was a weak excuse for delaying our return, but I could hardly tell them why I really wanted to stay in Terra Prime. Hopefully Rita would remember the agitated state I'd been in after our first crossing, and buy the excuse.

She looked at Seyer, "Maybe we could spend a night at the Guildhouse—"

"No," I said quickly. "That's not right. We failed in our mission, so we shouldn't be asking Morgana for favors. And I..." I pretended to hesitate. "I really need some time alone, Rita. Just a few hours. I haven't had a minute to myself since we got here. I'm so sorry, it's got nothing to do with you. I just need to pull myself together."

"I understand," she said gently. "I've been feeling a little edgy myself. But where would you go?"

"We've got some cash, right? I guess I could just pay for a hotel room. Like a normal person."

Rita glanced at Seyer—for permission, no doubt—then dug into her backpack. Taking out the wad of petty cash Morgana had given us, she divided it in two and gave me half. The bills were crisp, multi-colored, and had the face of some unknown queen engraved on them. I flipped one over to look on the back and see if the little pyramid was there. It was, but without the eye in it. There were other symbols as well, that I didn't recognize.

Tucking the money into my jeans pocket, I rested my head on the glass again and let the vibrations of the train carry me away.

"The horrors unleashed by your fetters may not be unique," Sebastian says. "I've heard tales of similar things happening out west, in a benighted region called the Badlands. People who try to enter the area generally don't come out, or if they do, they come out mad. Even zeppelins that fly over it are affected, and the last one to make the attempt drifted back into civilized space with nothing but corpses and madmen on board." He pauses. "In the days when travelers still tested themselves against the Badlands' borders, survivors spoke of unnatural rain, trembling earth, sickness that came out of nowhere ... and creatures out of nightmare coming to life."

"You think they meant that literally? The last one?"

"Who knows? All I can tell you is that Gifts don't appear out of nowhere. They require a human source. And while no one ever associated the wild forces of the Badlands with human Gifts, the similarity to what you witnessed at the compound is unmistakable. And that had a human source."

"You think there are people living out there? That no one knows about?"

"It's one possibility."

"Maybe . . . maybe Dreamwalkers? Because that's the only Gift that would manifest nightmares, right?"

The ancient eyes fix on me. So intense, that gaze. So enigmatic.

"Maybe Dreamwalkers," he agrees.

19

MASTER ALASTAIR WELLS took a deep breath before entering Lord Virilian's audience chamber. The fact that the Greys had sent someone of his rank to deliver their report, rather than the usual journeyman, was a sad comment on how they expected that report to be received. Virilian might lash out at a mere apprentice in anger, they'd reasoned, but surely he would exhibit more control with a Master of Obfuscates.

Surely.

Nodding to the guard, Wells reminded himself that not *all* the news he brought was bad. Just the part that would impact Virilian's personal fortune.

The doors opened, and he stepped forward with what he hoped looked like confidence. Virilian, like a wolf, could smell fear. The Shadowlord was seated on his usual throne, with the usual clamor of dead souls surrounding him. Wells had dealt with Shadowlords often enough to regard the latter as background music, albeit of an irritating variety. "Your Grace." He bowed his head respectfully.

The Guildmaster nodded. "Master Wells. You honor this Guild by your presence. I understand you have news for me?"

"Yes, your Lordship. Both good and bad, I'm afraid."

Virilian's eyes narrowed. "In whatever order you like, then."

"We reached the portal, and have evaluated it. I'm pleased to report it's still functional. A bit unstable, but once we restore the Gate we should be able to rectify that."

"That's excellent news. How long before it can return to full service?"

Wells hesitated.

"There's a problem?"

"Not here, your Grace. We cleared out the entrance, and once we put a new Gate in place our people should be able to come and go freely. At this end, at least."

Virilian raised an eyebrow. "But?"

"Our Gate wasn't the only one damaged. Reverberations from the explosion triggered earthquakes throughout our network, destroying the infrastructure on several worlds. Those Gates are still inaccessible."

For a moment there was silence. A spirit moaned softly behind Wells's left ear.

"So what you are saying is, our people can enter the portal safely from this side, and use it to gain access to other worlds, but the points of arrival on those worlds have been blocked, so it is, for all intents and purposes, useless."

"Only on certain worlds," Wells said quickly. "We're cataloging the extent of the damage. Gates outside the Terran Cluster are unaffected, and many of those within the cluster can be restored quickly. Long term, we estimate we can restore eighty to ninety percent of the original network."

"Long term," he mused darkly.

"Yes."

"That does little for us right now."

Wells bridled slightly. "We're working as fast as we can, your Grace. There are still other Gates available. No world has been cut off from contact with ours."

"But commerce must divert to other cities. And merchants may establish such connections there that, even when Luray is restored to full functioning, some will not return."

Wells said nothing. Virilian's personal power was rooted in his control of a major interworld trade hub. Devalue that hub, and his power was diminished. No words from a Grey would change that reality, or make the current situation more palatable.

"I want this addressed as quickly as possible," the Guildmaster said. "Hire whomever you need, Gifted or otherwise. My Guild will cover the cost of it for now ... though your Guildmaster and I will need to have a conversation about that responsibility."

It took all Wells's self-control not to respond sharply. *Don't think you're going to saddle us with the cost of this mess,* he thought. *If you hadn't kidnapped that Colonnan boy, thinking he was a Dreamwalker, none of this would have happened.* "I'm sure our Master will be pleased to receive you." He reached into his frock coat and took out a thick envelope, which he offered to Virilian.

"What is this?"

"A full report on the explosion."

Virilian took the envelope from him. "Have you identified the nature of the Codex?"

He hesitated. "Not yet, Your Grace. We're still working on it."

"Very well. I'll take your report under advisement. Meanwhile, you will keep me informed of your progress on the Gate."

"Of course." He bowed his head respectfully. "And I will communicate to my Guild how important it is that we restore it to full function as quickly as possible."

Like we didn't already know that, he thought acidly. *Like we haven't been overseeing the Gates for centuries, and need you to tell us how to manage them.* But he kept a polite expression on his face, and just in case that wasn't convincing enough, activated his Gift to mask his irritation. Never let a Shadow know how you are really feeling. That was the first rule of Guild etiquette.

If this Shadow wasn't so damn obsessed with hunting Dreamwalkers, the Blue Ridge Gate would still be standing.

He wound up leaving with his head still on his shoulders and his mind intact. Which, given the circumstances, was all anyone could ask for.

20

Jesse

Luray's Long River banks were host to a wide variety of docks—public, private, and commercial—and getting a cab to take me to the one I wanted without my being able to provide its name, or to offer better direction than "it's at the south end of town," wasted a good chunk of my petty cash allotment. By the time we found the right one the sun was setting, and I was hard-pressed to find suitable lodging before it got dark.

The place where I'd booked a room was laid out like a motel, though of course in a world without cars it probably wasn't called that. Two U-shaped floors had small rooms that opened directly onto a central courtyard, allowing guests to come and go without having to pass through a lobby or office. That suited my desire for privacy. It also suited other people who wanted to come and go unseen, who, in this particular neighborhood, were an unsavory lot. I was careful to lock my door once I was inside.

Despite hours of lying on top of the bedspread with my eyes closed, I'd gotten little rest the night before. Maybe sleep deprivation was what drove the ancient Dreamwalkers mad.

It felt strange to spend a night on this world like a normal person. Not hiding in the woods, not cringing in the sewers, and not lying awake at the Seers' headquarters wondering who was spying on my brain emanations. Just me, a rented bed, and enough tired whores and petty drug dealers to give the place atmosphere.

At noon I headed back to the pier, where Sebastian was waiting for me. He wasn't dressed in his usual attire, but in an outfit so mundane that at first I didn't recognize him. Yes, there was a slight period flavor to the collar of his white cotton shirt, and the leather bag slung over his shoulder did have a military air to it, but no stranger seeing him would think to look twice.

I couldn't see his expression as I approached, due to his broad-brimmed hat, but I did see him tense when he spotted me. It took me a moment to realize why he was reacting that way. I'd been living with the concept of visiting other peoples' dreams for long enough that I'd gotten used to the idea. He, on the other hand, had not known up until this moment whether the Jessica who visited him in his dream was real or not. This was his toaster strudel moment.

"It's really you," he breathed, as I approached. Wonder resonated in his voice. "God in Heaven, it's really you. . . ."

Despite my generally somber mood, I couldn't help but smile. "It does take a little getting used to."

He opened his mouth to respond, but just then a couple of people walking along the shore started up the pier. Given the sensitivity of what we needed to discuss, they were getting too close for comfort. "Perhaps we should seek some privacy," he said. He nodded toward where his canoe was moored, a question in his eyes.

I looked across the river, noted that the people on the opposite shore weren't all that far away, and said, "Walls are better. I have a room nearby we can use."

There were only a couple of people hanging around the motel when we arrived, both of them women with smeared makeup and tousled hair, who looked more than a little hung over. They watched with blatant curiosity as I led Sebastian into my room. Probably they were wondering what I would charge a man three times my age for my services. It was not a good neighborhood.

I offered Sebastian the one chair in the room, but he chose to remain standing. I watched as he took stock of the small space, and I was reminded of Rita in IHOP, checking for exits. It was a more wary aspect than I'd seen in him before, and I wondered what had put him on edge.

"You said you had something for me," I prompted.

"So I did." A shadow crossed his face. "You asked me if I knew of a task that you might undertake for the Fleshcrafters. I do, but it would be a dangerous one, with no guarantee of success. Are you sure this is something you want to pursue? It won't be easy."

I shrugged. "Nothing on this world is ever easy." Maybe that sounded impossibly brave, but I had just spent a long and sleepless night resigning myself to the fact that anything the Potters wanted that was safe and easy to obtain, they'd have gotten for themselves long ago. Anything I offered them would have to involve a task so dark, dangerous, or difficult, that they hadn't done it themselves. "Tell me."

With a sigh he sat in the room's one chair; it creaked beneath him. "There's one piece of information that the Fleshcrafters want, and they want it badly. Their Guildmaster approached me about it some time ago, but I wasn't able to help him. Please note, it's rare that a secret is so perfectly guarded that my contacts can't unearth it, but in this case it was true. The commission he offered me is still open. If you were to deliver that information to Guildmaster Alexander, payment of some sort would be guaranteed. I'm sure you could negotiate for what you want."

I looked at him incredulously. "You think I can succeed at something where *you* failed?"

He said it quietly: "You have abilities that I don't, Jessica."

It took me a moment to realize what he meant. "My Gift. . . ."

He nodded.

"Jeez." I didn't know how to respond to that. "All it does is allow me to enter people's dreams. I can't read minds, Sebastian."

"But you *can* alter dreams. You told me how you tricked the Weaver into revealing her safe's combination. That's a formidable power, Jessica."

But the safe combination had been a minor secret, probably known to many within the compound, and the Weaver's mind had invested little energy in guarding it. Sebastian was talking about far more significant information, and a level of secrecy so intense that it would probably affect a dreamer's mind. What would the cost of such an effort be? I remembered the condition I was in after altering the Weaver's dream, and shuddered. Was it possible that I could pour so much energy into dream alterations that my body would be irreparably damaged when I returned? Or that I wouldn't be able to return at all?

I needed to know the details before deciding. "Tell me what the Fleshcrafters asked you for."

"Several years ago a high ranking Master of their

Guild disappeared. His people searched high and low for him, but to no avail. It was as if the earth had swallowed him whole. They asked me to help, but even my resources could provide no clues. If he was murdered—which his Guildmaster suspects—it was flawlessly managed. And whoever knows about it is not talking."

"I'm not seeing how my dreamwalking fits into this. Unless you're suggesting that I use it to look for him, and I don't see how that could possibly work."

"If he was killed, there is at least one person who knows what happened to him."

"You mean his murderer."

He nodded.

"If you're suggesting I invade his killer's dreams, you must have an idea who it is."

"I know whom the Fleshcrafters suspect."

Something about his expression made me shiver. "Who, Sebastian?"

"The missing Potter's last known appointment was with a Shadowlord."

For a moment I was speechless. "You're suggesting I invade the dreams of a *Shadowlord*? Do they even have normal dreams? And do you know which one the Potter met with? Or am I supposed to check them all until I find someone with guilty dreams?" I shook my head. "This is crazy, Sebastian."

"We don't know who he was meeting with. But if any Shadow murdered a ranking member of another Guild, their Guildmaster would surely know about it."

My eyes widened in astonishment. "Virilian? Is that who you're talking about? You want me to go into *his* dreams?"

"I don't 'want' anything," he said evenly. "You asked me if I knew a task you might perform for the Fleshcrafters, of sufficient value for them to heal your mother in exchange. This is the one thing I know of. If you can't do it — or won't do it — then there's your answer. I know of nothing else they need."

I looked away from him, struggling to wrap my brain around the concept. What was it Sebastian had told us about the Shadowlords? *There's madness at the core of them. Dozens of ancestral voices clamoring inside their heads every waking moment, each derived from a Shadow who was himself insane. Madness layered upon madness, all of it trapped within a soul that must walk the borderline between life and death, committed to neither . . . . Never forget what they are. Never forget that no matter how human they may appear to be, they ceased to be human long ago.* That was the kind of person whose dreamscape he was proposing I invade. It was a crazy idea from start to finish. Totally insane.

"I've never met him," I muttered. "Never even seen him. How the hell am I supposed to find his dream? It's not like there's a search engine for that kind of thing."

He reached into his satchel and removed several objects, laying them out one by one on the bed in front of me. The first was a large crescent-shaped brooch with a long pin attached, covered in an intricate knotwork pattern. It looked Viking in design, or maybe Celtic. "This belonged to Augustus Virilian when he walked among the living. He gave it to the Guildmaster of the Potters several years ago, as part of an exchange of gifts that accompanied the latter's appointment. It has never been worn by anyone else." He laid a ring beside it. "This belonged to Travis Bellefort, the missing Fleshcrafter." Beside the two objects he laid out several pictures. "These are photographs of both men. Virilian's was taken when he was alive, of course; the undead don't photograph well."

I looked up at him. "The Potters gave these to you when you were commissioned for this job?"

"The Potters gave them to me yesterday, when I

asked for them." He smiled slightly. "Will they make the task easier?"

I reached out and picked up the brooch; its surface was cool to my touch, but it revealed no special secrets. Morgana had been able to read my essence from my painting; might an item like this have similar emanations attached to it? So that I could use it to focus in on its owner's dream? Even if it did, I wouldn't have a clue how to activate them. "In the past I've needed an emotional connection to my targets." I ran my fingers over the intricate pattern as I spoke. "It was ten times harder to get into the Weaver's head than yours or my brother's, because I lacked a personal connection to her. I had to focus on her relationship with Moth, who I cared about, to make it work. So what would tie me to Virilian? I don't know the man. I've never even seen him."

"But he's the one who ordered the kidnapping of your brother. The one who would have killed Tommy, if you hadn't rescued the boy. Are you telling me you feel no emotion toward Virilian? That there's no connection between the two of you?"

I bit my lip as I considered it. His logic was compelling, but I wasn't sure about the mechanics of it. I was still struggling to figure out how my Gift worked, and everything was guesswork at this point. "So." I drew in a deep breath. "Is that your counsel, then? That I should try to enter Virilian's dreams to gather this information?"

"My counsel?" He laughed. "My *counsel* is that you go back to Terra Colonna, crawl into a warm bed far from any Shadowlords, and try to get a good night's sleep without wandering into other people's dreams. Try to come to terms with your mother's condition and make a new life for yourself, far away from Alia Morgana, Miriam Seyer, and all the other people who care nothing for you except as a pawn. Never think about this world again and never return here. That would be the *intelligent* thing to do." A corner of his mouth twitched. "But it's not what you're going to do, is it? You might be tempted for a while, if you're frightened enough, but in the end that won't make any difference. Dreamwalking will call to you."

His certainty irritated me. "Maybe you don't know me as well as you think."

"I may not know you, but I know the Gifted. I've spent half a lifetime on this God-forsaken world learning how to deal with them, and one thing has become very clear: their Gifts aren't just fancy mental powers. They're a kind of hunger. An obsession. A Seer will instinctively sample the emotions of everyone who walks by him. A Shadow will bind passing spirits to him without conscious thought. A Fleshcrafter will contort his own body into strange and inhuman shapes just because he can. They don't think about doing those things, they don't plan them, it's just part of who they are. So no, Jessica, I don't think you can spend a lifetime denying your Gift, any more than you can spend a lifetime not breathing. And I'm willing to bet that while part of you is terrified by the thought of going into Virilian's head, another part of you is hungry to try it. To find out if it's possible." He paused. "Am I wrong, Jessica?"

I flushed slightly and looked away. For a long time I didn't answer him. "You're not wrong," I muttered.

"Then let's figure out how we can make this as safe as possible. You told me that Tommy woke you up the first time the dream-wraith attacked, and that saved you. So I can stand guard over your body and do the same, if necessary. You need not fear being trapped in a dream. That was one of your biggest concerns, wasn't it?"

I nodded.

He indicated the brooch in my hand. "If these items can't help you establish a connection to Virilian, you'll lose nothing by trying. But if it turns out that you can, indeed, use material objects to invade the dreams of a Guildmaster, and twist his mind to your purpose . . . that would be a useful skill to know about, Jessica."

Something in his tone suddenly made me wary. What was his real interest in this? For decades he'd been a mortal enemy of the Shadows, and now he might have discovered a brand new weapon to use against them. My Gift. Was that why he'd brought me this information? Why he was tempting me to undertake this particular project? Was I just a pawn to him, like I was to so many other people in this damned world? Someone to be tricked and manipulated, so that I served his personal agenda?

Don't trust anyone on Terra Prime, he'd warned me. But I needed a friend on this world. I needed to be able to trust someone. And if the price of Sebastian's friendship was that I allowed him to dream of the day I would help him destroy the Shadows, that was a lot more benign than what others were asking of me.

"I want to try," I said at last. Voicing the words sent a chill down my spine, but he was right; I couldn't turn away from this.

"The Shadowlords generally sleep during the day. So if you need to invoke your Gift while he's in a dream state, that would be the time to try it."

"Tomorrow," I told him. "I have preparations to make first."

I needed to contact Isaac. Yes, that meant I would have to reveal my nature to him, but I needed information on the wraiths that only he could give me, and had no other way to reach him. I could only hope that the fragile bond we'd established would be enough to keep him from betraying me. If not . . . well, I would deal with the consequences of that when I had to. One emergency at a time.

The full magnitude of what I was planning was slowly sinking in. In a quiet voice I said, "Promise that if anything bad happens, you'll get word to my family. You don't have to tell them the truth. Just give them a story that's easier to accept than my disappearing without a trace. Give them some kind of path to closure."

He hesitated. "Jessica, you know I can't go back there—"

"But you can arrange for a message to get to them. Yes?"

"I can do that, yes."

"So promise me."

He said it softly. "I promise, Jessica."

I walked over to the small desk in the corner, took a pen and a piece of paper from the drawer, and wrote down my home address for him. As well as any other instructions I could think of, that he should have if I died.

Tomorrow, I told myself. Tomorrow I would test my Gift. Tomorrow I find out what I was truly capable of.

Or get killed trying.

21

SHADOWCREST
VIRGINIA PRIME

ISAAC

THE WELL OF SOULS is silent and dark, empty of life, empty of unlife, empty even of death. As Isaac walks down the black corridor it echoes his footsteps back at him with the solemnity of a tomb; not even the passing whisper of a wraith breaks the eerie silence. There are doors on both sides of him, and now and then he tries one, but they are all locked. Human bones are scattered along the bases of the walls: skulls, femurs, dislocated vertebrae, random bones bleached white with age. The eye sockets of the skulls are turned toward him, as though their owners are watching. The atmosphere is chilling even by the standards of an apprentice Shadow, and he shivers as he walks down the hall, wishing he were anywhere but here.

Suddenly the corridor divides into two. Confused, he checks each direction, but beyond ten feet it's too dark

to see anything. He doesn't remember this part of the
level having forks in it, but now that he is facing one
he must choose a course. After a moment's hesitation,
he starts down the corridor on the right. It's empty of
life and empty of ghosts, like its predecessor, but there
are many more bones in this hallway. They're stacked
against the walls in no particular order, a junkyard of
bones.

Soon the hall divides again and he must make another choice. He continues on to the right; maybe con-
sistency will help him keep his bearings. But the hall
twists around, skewing his sense of direction, and then it
divides again. And again. There are more bones on the
floor each time, until he has to kick his way through
piles of them just to walk. The entire level has transformed into a maze, he realizes, and he is hopelessly
lost. Is this some kind of test? He calls out his father's
name, but no one answers.

Suddenly he finds himself standing in front of the
great double doors that lead to the Chamber of Souls. A
wave of panic overwhelms him. No, test or no, he won't
go in there again. He turns and starts to walk quickly
back the way he came. The straight corridor leads to a
sharp turn, then to a long curving stretch, then to a fork
where he must choose his direction. . . . and suddenly he
is back in front of the doors. He feels the sharp bite of
fear, and he turns to flee. This time he runs through the
corridors, but that only brings him back to the doors
faster. Either he is circling back to them or they are
transporting themselves in front of him. Try as he might,
he can't get away.

There is nowhere to go but through them.

His heart filled with dread, he reaches out with a
trembling hand to open the door, but it swings open of
its own accord before he can touch it, and a cold breeze
pushes him inside. As he enters the chamber he can see

soul fetters gleaming like malevolent stars on all sides of him. Ghosts begin to appear, grouped around the soul fetters that belong to them, and they call out to him. Some try to cajole him, some threaten him with shame, some deride his lack of courage or loyalty or honor. All are trying to coerce him into submitting to Communion. Their voices merge into a din that fills the chamber and makes his head ring, while soul fetters swirl around him in dizzying patterns. He falls to his knees and instinctively shuts his eyes and covers his ears, even though he knows it won't do him any good. The ghosts are speaking directly to his soul.

Then, suddenly, the voices cease. The ghosts are gone.

Startled, he opens his eyes. There's only one person in the room now besides himself, and she's not a ghost, but flesh and blood. The last person he ever expected to see here.

"Jesse," he whispers.

She's dressed as he last saw her, in a slim tank top and close-fitting jeans. Her face is flushed red with life, her eyes bright with passion. She is warmth. She is energy. He wants to take her face in his hands and feel the heat of her skin against his fingertips, to drink it in like a precious elixir, along with her passion and her strength. After two weeks in Shadowcrest he is starved for humanity, and she is full of it. The desire is so powerful it leaves him breathless.

But what is she doing here? No outsider is permitted in this place.

She looks around the chamber curiously, studying each element in turn as she would artifacts in a museum: the golden fetters, the richly carved doors, the piles of bleached bones. The fetters have stopped their wild motion, and are hanging in mid-air surrounding them. Isaac struggles to think of something intelligent to say, but all he can come up with is, "There aren't usually bones here."

And that's when it hits him: the bones *shouldn't* be here. The corridor shouldn't be twisted into a maze. The doors shouldn't appear in front of him no matter where he runs, and *she* should not be here. So many things are wrong, and while he ignored them before, she is one wrong too many. Only one explanation is possible: He's dreaming.

With the revelation comes awareness. Suddenly he can sense his body lying on a distant bed, and he's aware of just how thin the veil of sleep is that's keeping him here. A single thought could breach that veil and banish everything he's looking at. In fact, he has to concentrate for a moment to hold the dream steady, to remain by the sheer force of his will in a nightmare that ten seconds ago he would have done anything to escape.

But none of that explains Jesse's presence.

How real she looks! He's never dreamed of anyone with this kind of depth and clarity before. Compared to her, the rest of this nightmare is like a cheap stage set, ready to collapse the instant the curtain comes down. But in the same way he knows that he's standing in a dream, and none of this is real, he knows that the Jessica standing in front of him isn't something his mind created. Her existence is independent of him, and when the curtain falls on his nightmare she will continue to exist. But there's only one way that could be possible—

His mind won't complete the thought. He wants to bask in her presence for a moment longer, before speaking the words that will make everything more complicated.

"This is a dark dream," she says. "Do you have it often?"

The casual conversational tone jars him out of his trance. "Every night, pretty much. Sometimes worse than others. I don't get much sleep these days." On impulse he reaches out a hand to touch her—but stops inches short of her skin, not daring to make contact. Part of him is afraid of what he might learn if he did. He remembers how she asked him about dreams the night they first met. How he told her about the Dreamwalkers, that they went insane and infected everyone around them, so they had to be destroyed on sight. That's what his elders had taught him, and at the time he simply accepted it, as he accepted all their teachings. But were they telling him the truth? He's come to question so much of Guild dogma that he's wary of taking anything at face value now. Maybe the Shadows have some other reason to hunt Dreamwalkers, that they wouldn't share with a mere apprentice. Or maybe they're just wrong.

One thing he knows: he could never betray Jesse to his Guild based on those lessons alone. Not when she hasn't done anything wrong, or shown any sign of insanity. He couldn't bear to see them do to her what they did to Jacob.

"Why are you here?" he asks. "Why are you trusting me like this? Yes, I helped you get away before, but this . . . this is . . ."

"So much more?" she asks quietly.

He nods.

A shadow passes over her face. She looks back over her shoulder, as if making sure that they're alone. "I need your help, Isaac. In all of Terra Prime you're the only one who can help me. So I took a chance." Her eyes are fixed on him now, studying his every response. "Was it a mistake?"

He remembers the touch of her lips on his cheek when she kissed him in the dungeon, and the sudden rush of heat to his loins makes him grateful for the loose robe he's wearing, which shields him from any potential embarrassment. "No." His voice is slightly hoarse, no doubt due to the lump rising his throat. "It wasn't a mistake. I don't know that I can help you, though. What is it you need?"

"I've run across something that Sebastian thinks is a ghost, but he can't tell me anything more about it. It keeps showing up in my dreams. The other day it crossed over into the waking world and almost killed me. I have to find out what it is, figure out how to fight it. Or at least how to avoid it."

Again she looks nervously over her shoulder. It's the ghost that she's looking for, he realizes; any minute now she expects it to appear. The thought sends an icy chill down his spine. "Describe it to me."

"It looks like a dark blotch in the sky at first, and then it spreads. Eventually it takes on human form, at least in its outline. It doesn't appear to have any physical substance, it's more like a void where nothing exists. As soon as it shows up in my dream it starts sucking all the color out of the landscape, like it was . . ." She drew in a shaky breath. "Like it was devouring the dream itself. The first time I saw it, it attacked me." She pushed up her sleeve and showed him a jagged gash on her arm, that was just beginning to heal. "I still had the wound when I woke up. That shouldn't be possible, right?"

"Go on," he says quietly.

"When it showed up in the real world it was . . . cold. It didn't just suck the color out of everything, but all the heat as well. All the life. Everything it passed by became coated in ice." Her voice is trembling now, her mask of confidence stressed to the breaking point by memories. "I can't just keep running from it, Isaac. Your Guild knows how to deal with the dead. Tell me what I can do to keep this one from killing me. Please."

He draws in a deep breath, trying to think. A dream-bound spirit that acts like a black hole? He's never been taught anything about that—not officially, anyway—but he's heard legends. Fearful legends, of creatures that even Shadows would be afraid of. "It may be a reaper," he says at last.

"What's that?"

"A type of spirit that's bound to the dream world. I don't know much about it. No one has seen one for ages. Most people think it's only a legend."

"But legends can reflect something real," she reminds him. "You were the one who told me that. Remember?"

He nods solemnly. "I remember."

"So where can I find more information? If I don't, it's just a question of time before this one gets me."

"I don't know, Jesse." He shakes his head. "I've read all the basic primers on spirit types, and nothing like this is described in them. The Masters of my Guild might know—"

"But you can't ask them," she says quickly.

"If you think this thing will hurt you otherwise—"

"I'm a *Dreamwalker*, Isaac. The minute they even suspect that, they'll move heaven and earth to hunt me down. You know they will." She shook her head emphatically. "You can't talk to anyone about this. Not even indirectly. Promise me."

"Okay." The edge of panic that's coming into her voice is unnerving. She seems to fear the Shadows more than she fears the reaper. "I won't talk to anyone. I'll just research it myself. I promise."

Suddenly she looks around the room again. The atmosphere in the chamber has changed subtly, becoming colder by a few degrees. Maybe a bit darker. "I have to go," she says quickly. "I'll get back to you later."

"When do you need this information?"

"Yesterday." She attempts to smile but it's a strained expression, without any humor in it. "There's bad shit going down soon. I need to know how to deal with this thing."

"I'll do what I can—"
But she's already gone.

||||||||||||

There was nothing about reapers in the library.

Of course there was nothing.

He had expected there to be nothing.

That didn't mean the Guild had no information on them. On the contrary, the Masters' archives probably contained the information Isaac was looking for, in a neatly organized format. The only problem was that as a mere apprentice he had no access to that specialized collection. He didn't even know where in Shadowcrest it was located.

A Shadowlord could gather that information for him, and Isaac's father would probably do so if asked, pleased that his wayward son was taking an interest in necromancy. But if the reapers turned out to be connected to Dreamwalkers somehow, then the Shadowlords would know Isaac was interested in that forbidden Gift, and might start asking questions. No, Jesse was right, the risk was just too great.

He would have to research this on his own.

As for Jesse herself, the fact that she had appeared in his dream was no small secret. The Shadows had been at the forefront of the campaign to eradicate the Dreamwalkers, and any sign of the ancient curse reemerging should be reported to them immediately. But the longer he kept Jesse's visit a secret from his elders, the more he realized that it gave him a perverse thrill to defy them. After years of the *umbrae majae* telling him who he must be and what he must become, such an act of defiance was intoxicating. Yes, he'd tasted a bit of independence during his two-year walkabout, but in the end he'd done nothing more rebellious than miss some school and avoid talking to his parents. Even freeing

Jesse and her friends had been little more than a minor offense, since the Shadows were convinced by then that her brother wasn't the person they'd been looking for. This, though . . . this was a whole different magnitude of defiance. It was meaningful. It was dangerous. And it made him feel alive, in a way Shadows weren't supposed to feel alive.

He knew of a place where he might be able to find the information that Jesse wanted, but it would be risky to go there. There was no hard and fast rule forbidding it, but that was only because the Shadowlords didn't think that such rules were necessary. This was a resource that no one but the Shadowlords themselves could access.

Or so they believed.

Now was the time to call in favors, and see just how useful his new ally could be.

⸿⸿⸿⸿⸿⸿

The Well of Souls was black and silent. If Isaac listened hard enough he could hear faint murmurs of the dead, but they sounded distant, as if spirits were passing through the place on their way to somewhere else. The only clear presence was that of Jacob Dockhart, who was staying as close to him as possible. The newly made ghost was clearly terrified of coming down here, but he had agreed to help, and that was all Isaac could ask of him. Without Jacob's assistance this expedition would not be possible.

"Watch out for guardian spirits," Isaac whispered to him. "We'll turn back right away if you see any sign of them."

Jacob's acknowledgement—and relief—prickled his skin.

Slowly they moved down the corridor, retracing the path Isaac had once walked with his father. But as they neared the entrance to the ritual room the ghost grew more and more agitated, and Isaac had to stop several times and whisper assurances to calm him down. It made sense that Jacob would have issues with returning to the place where he was so brutally murdered, and Isaac was annoyed at himself for not anticipating that. For a while it seemed like they would be unable to move past that point. But then Isaac reminded him that they were defying the will of the Shadowlords by coming down here, and that seemed to help.

Once they made it past the ritual room there were no further incidents, and soon they were standing in front of the massive gold doors that led to the Chamber of Souls. Once he crossed this threshold there would be no turning back; he would be in territory reserved for the Shadowlords, and if anyone caught him there, the consequences could be dire.

Assuming he was able to cross the threshold at all.

"I don't know how the lock works," he said in a low voice as he reached for the handle. "I just know you have to do something to help open it." The last time Isaac had been here his father had summoned a spirit to help with the door, but Isaac's Gift had been too primitive back then to observe what the ghost did. Hopefully Jacob would be able to figure it out.

He waited in silence, his heart pounding so hard that he could feel his pulse throb against the door handle. He could sense his ghost ally approaching the door, perhaps touching it, but his spirit sight allowed for no more knowledge than that. The seconds ticked by with agonizing slowness.

Finally the handle turned.

Breath held, Isaac unlatched the right-hand door and pushed it open. He waited a moment to see if Jacob would warn him about anything in the chamber, but all he got from the ghost was a general feeling of dread.

Finally he stepped inside. The place looked the same as when he'd visited it with his father, but since that day he'd returned to it so many times in his dreams, with fresh horrors added, that now it seemed strangely empty, unnaturally peaceful.

It'll be anything but peaceful if I'm caught here, he reminded himself. Quickly he walked to the fetter he'd examined when his father had first brought him here. The collection of biographies that accompanied it opened naturally to the first page, and he read the title underneath the first name again: *Twice-decorated Grand Crusader in the Final War Between the Shadows and the Dreamwalkers*. If there was some kind of spirit that existed only in dreams, he'd reasoned, it might have been active during that time, and hopefully there would be some reference to it. If not, he had no clue how to begin searching in this vast place for a single thread of information.

There was nothing in the Grand Crusader's biography about the reapers, but the names of several other Shadowlords were mentioned who also fought in the Dream Wars, so he located their fetters and started reading their biographies. Not all the entries were in English, but his education had included enough languages that he could pick his way through most of them. By harvesting a few facts from each biography, he was slowly able to piece together a picture of the conflict between the Shadows and the Dreamwalkers, which was far more complex—and confusing—than he'd imagined. Not only had the Shadows played a major role in eradicating the Dreamwalkers, but they had gone to great length to get the other Guilds to join in the slaughter. The biographies never explained why. Maybe the scribes who had assembled these records simply assumed that anyone reading them would understand their context. Certainly some of the *umbra majae*, who had absorbed the memories of Shadowlords from this time period, must know the Guild's early history. So why had Isaac never been taught it?

Hours passed as he worked his way through the fetter records one by one. Jacob disappeared several times, apparently summoned by his mistress to perform one task or another. He always came back, but the brief absences were hell on Isaac's nerves. Without Jacob as lookout he was terribly vulnerable in this place. That, and the effort required to decipher notes faded almost past recognition, written in dialects centuries old, drained Isaac of energy. He wanted nothing more than to quit for a time, to recoup his mental resources.

But he couldn't bring himself to stop reading. This project was about more than Jesse now. He was uncovering a history of the Guild that no apprentice had ever been taught, and he could not turn away.

At last he came to a fetter that made him uneasy, though he didn't know why. The first name on its pedestal was Persian—*Shekarchiyandar*—and the pedigree that followed was shorter than most. It took him a moment to figure out that what disturbed him was not the list of names, but the dates that went with them. Evidently the Shadowlords who first Communed with this fetter had survived only a few years afterward. And the ones who tried later were even less successful; the last person on the list had lasted only a few months. Whoever this Shekarchiyandar was, his memories appeared to be deadly, and no one had attempted to Commune with them in recent centuries. Yet the fetter was still here, displayed among the Guild's active offerings. So it must have great value.

Pulling out the book of notes stored in the pedestal, he looked around to see if Jacob was still standing guard. But the ghost was gone again, leaving him on his own. With a nervous sigh he opened the ancient volume and began to read. The original entry was in Farsi, which was frustrating, as his knowledge of that language was minimal. Slowly he worked his way through the faded and brittle pages, trying to make sense of the ancient script. Some of the words were so faded they were nearly impossible to read, and he had to make educated guesses as to their meaning. But in the end his effort was justified, because he had finally found the records he was searching for.

... created the reapers in order to [bring/begin] battle to walkers of dreams in their [fort/citadel/home]. Originally twelve existed, later [winnowed? destroyed?] to seven during final war. After [exit?] of dream walkers from [awake? Living?] world the reapers were not seen again. [?]

There was a note in English following that, the relative freshness of the ink suggesting that it had been added at a much later date: *Appearance in 1132 A.D. disputed.*

1132. It took him a minute to place the date.

It was the year recorded on the pedestal, of the last attempt to Commune with Shekarchiyandar's fetter.

Heart pounding, Isaac leafed through the book until he came to that entry. It was a short one, no more than a single paragraph, but at least it was in German, a language he could read fluently. Someone named Gunther the Black had attempted Communion with the fetter, but had gone insane in the months following the ritual. In his final moments, just before the other Shadowlords had to forcibly put him down, he screamed something about the reapers returning. Since no one else had seen any reapers around, the chronicler took that as a symptom of his madness. But Isaac wasn't so sure. If the reapers were only active in dreams, wasn't it possible they could appear to Gunther without anyone else seeing them? The same way that Jesse had come to him, without anyone else seeing her?

He was so close to the answers he thought that he could taste it.

He started to turn back to the earlier entries, when suddenly he heard a noise behind him: footsteps, heavy and solid, headed his way. He thought he could hear spirit voices as well, which meant that the visitor was a Shadowlord.

He couldn't afford to be discovered here.

Panicking, he shoved the ancient volume back into its storage slot and looked for somewhere to hide. But as his gaze passed over the entrance he realized to his horror that he'd left the door open. If the Shadowlord saw that, he would know instantly that something was wrong.

Desperately he sprinted across the floor, grabbed the door, and pushed it shut. He tried to hold it back at the last moment to keep it from making too much noise, but the momentum of the heavy panel carried it forward despite him, and he flinched as it slammed loudly shut. Hopefully whoever was coming would be too distracted by the voices of the his ghostly retinue to pay attention to such noise.

Isaac looked around for somewhere to hide, but the pedestals were too narrow for him to fit behind and there was no other furniture in the chamber. If he could climb the stairs to an upper level he might be able to get out of the sightline, but there was no time to do that. So he did the only thing he could think of, flattening himself against the wall beside the door, hoping that when it opened it would shield him from sight. A cold sweat broke out on his face as spirits began to enter the room, not newly made wraiths like Jacob, but the vanguard of a powerful Shadowlord. They didn't notice him right away, and he could always hope that when they did they wouldn't report him. Some of the dead who attended the Shadowlords were slave spirits, like Jacob, but others were independent wraiths caught up in the wake of the undead against their will, who owed the Shadows no love or loyalty.

Isaac held his breath as the door handle turned and the massive doors swung open. He put his hands out in front of his face to keep the heavy wood panel from smashing into him; hopefully the visitor wouldn't notice that the door had stopped short of the wall.

Footsteps entered the room. They passed Isaac's hiding place without pausing. So far so good.

Suddenly a cold wind swept behind the door, raising goosebumps on Isaac's skin. A powerful wraith circled him, prodding him with its essence. Then it moved away, heading back to its master. The game was over.

"What?" he heard a Shadowlord exclaim. "Where?"

There was no point in hiding any longer. Drawing in a deep breath to steady himself, Isaac stepped out from his hiding place.

The Shadowlord standing in the center of the chamber was one he didn't know, but the man's elder rank was immediately apparent, as was his displeasure at discovering that the trespasser his ghost had discovered was a mere apprentice. "Who are you?" the Shadowlord demanded. "How did you get in here?"

"Isaac," he stammered. He couldn't bring himself to state his family name. If news got out that an Antonin had offended against Guild custom, his father's rage would be beyond measure. And causing that kind of emotion in a Shadowlord was a far greater offense than merely trespassing. The other question he couldn't answer without revealing Jacob's role in the break-in, and he refused to do that. If the boy's spirit had been absent when the Shadowlord arrived, then he was safe for now; Isaac would not compromise him, even to save himself.

A spirit whispered something to the Shadowlord, too low for Isaac to hear. The *umbra maja* nodded sharply. "Go. Report it to him." Isaac flinched inside. Report to whom? His father? The Guildmaster? Any hope he might have had that he could keep this situation from getting out of hand had just vanished.

He shouldn't have come here. He knew that now. It had been an act of utter foolishness, sheer youthful arrogance, and the magnitude of the mess he was in was just starting to sink in.

The Shadowlord gestured toward the door. "You will follow me," he commanded.

Isaac nodded weakly and fell in behind the man as he left the room. They walked down the black corridor without speaking, Isaac following the Shadowlord like a whipped puppy, but this time the hallway was not silent. The Shadowlord's ghostly retinue filled it with scorn. *Foolish boy!* they whispered. *Doomed!* Isaac flinched as ghostly fingers prodded at him, mocking his despair.

The Shadowlord entered the elevator. Isaac joined him.

It started to go down.

Not up.

Down.

Isaac felt his heart sink as he realized where they were going. His offense must have been truly dire in the eyes of this elder. After a brief descent the elevator stopped, and the two left the cage and entered the prison level, where Jesse and her friends had once been locked up. As the Shadowlord directed Isaac toward one of the cells, they crossed the very spot where she had kissed him, and a wave of despair suddenly came over him, so powerful that he was forced to stop walking for a moment to pull himself together.

Emotion. He was displaying raw emotion in front of a Shadowlord. The shame of it doubled his misery.

Finally he entered one of the cells, and the *umbra maja* locked the door shut behind him. There was nothing inside the small space—no food, no water, not even a chamber pot. He could lick cave moisture off the stone wall if he got thirsty enough, but that was about it.

"Your father will be informed of this," the Shadowlord said. "He'll deal with you."

There was no point in responding to him. Isaac had gambled everything for the sake of knowledge, and he had lost. Protesting the consequences would only bring more shame upon his family and make his situation worse.

Assuming that it was possible for it to get any worse.

With a sigh he sat down on a stone protrusion and rested his back against the wall. Spiritual exhaustion enveloped his soul like a shroud, the long hours of tension finally taking their toll. Two years ago he had fled from this place to escape a Shadow's destiny, and this was the natural end of that journey. Whatever misery came after this, at least he would no longer have to pretend he was something he was not. In the midst of his despair, it was perversely comforting to know that he would face his final moments being true to himself.

He wondered if Jesse could reach him in this place. He had so much to tell her, but no idea how to establish contact. If he fell asleep, could she come to him again? Or must she wait for him to start dreaming on his own, before she could do that?

He was far too anxious to sleep but too exhausted not to. He lay back and closed his eyes, leaving the choice to destiny.

22

SEER GUILDHOUSE IN LURAY
VIRGINIA PRIME

ALIA MORGANA

THE DAYS WERE GROWING LONGER AND LONGER, Morgana noted, in workload if not in hours. Each one seemed more complicated than the last, and more dangerous. Seeds that had been planted years ago were starting to bear fruit, and a decade of watching and hoping must now give way to a careful—and secretive—harvest. At her level of functioning there was no room for error.

Miriam Seyer knocked and entered. "Rita Morales is here, Your Grace."

A painted eyebrow arched upward. "Send her in."

She had not called Rita to her, but she wasn't surprised that she'd come. Miriam had already reported that Jesse had no intention of talking to the Seers, so there was little left for Rita to do, other than debrief.

Soon a quick, light stride could be heard approaching

the study. The footsteps paused at the door—perhaps uncertain, perhaps just respectful.

"Come in, Rita. Shut the door behind you."

The girl obeyed, taking up a respectful position before Morgana. The Guildmistress noted that she had not seen a Healer yet. Fresh scratches marked her face and arms in a dozen places; combined with the bruises from a week ago, it gave her skin a surreal aspect, like an abstract painting. The scratches were real injuries, of course, unlike the bruises which had been applied as part of her cover story. Not that voluntary bruises hurt any less than the real thing.

Morgana nodded brusquely to her. "I would say you did a good job, but in light of the chaos you left behind you in the Blackwaters, perhaps 'good' isn't an appropriate adjective. Nonetheless, you accomplished the task I set for you."

Rita bristled slightly. "I warned you what Jesse was planning. You told me not to interfere."

"So I did. Though, to be fair, your warning of a 'disruption' was a bit of an understatement. But that was my failing, not yours. You did well, Rita. As always."

The girl bowed her head slightly, a gesture that was respectful but not submissive. Rita was never submissive.

"Tell me more about her dreams," Morgana commanded.

Rita shrugged. "I already sent you a report about her nightmare. It didn't sound particularly significant, save for the appearance of the safe combination at the end. And that just appeared, without any kind of context or story. She seemed to be as mystified by it as I was."

"Do you think that was really the case?"

Rita's eyes narrowed slightly. "Are you asking, would she lie to me? I see no reason why she would. We've been in this together since day one. She told me once that she was coming to think of me like a sister."

"Yet she didn't want you with her today."

She shrugged. "She needs some time alone. I totally get that. And she wants to approach the Fleshcrafters by herself. I get that, too. This is about her mother, her security, her future. I'm just a sidekick."

"You did encourage her to meet with me before the two of you headed home, yes?"

"Yeah. She was pretty adamant about not doing that. You're not on her list of favorite people right now. No offense."

Morgana waved off any concern. "No doubt she wonders how well she can guard her secrets in my presence. A good sign. She's learning the game."

Rita opened her mouth, then appeared to have second thoughts and closed it again.

"You have something to say?"

"It's not important, your Grace."

"You're free to speak your thoughts to me when we're alone together. What is it?"

Rita bit her lip. "Are you planning to tell her who you really are? Because right now she wants nothing to do with you, ever. Maybe if she understood the reason you're so involved with her life . . ." She shrugged. "I don't know, it just seems like if you wait much longer to tell her the truth, you could drive her away for good."

In answer Morgana walked over to one of the bookshelves, pulled down a black leather-bound volume, and placed it on the reading table. "This book explains the process by which Dreamwalkers go mad. It details a five stage process, of which the first two are fairly benign. In the last stage, their madness is broadcast to every sleeping mind within a hundred miles. There's a description of a city that devolved into total chaos because of one Dreamwalker living in it." She pulled down another book and set it beside the first; this one was thinner and bound in faded brown pigskin. "This book explains how they drain strength from other people through their dreams. Perhaps the source of succubus legends." A third book was added. "This one explains how they drain the *life* of others through their dreams—a particularly horrific version." Another book. "This one details how they slowly transform into terrifying creatures, monsters of darkness that hunger to devour human souls."

"Like the thing we saw at the compound?"

"Perhaps." She tapped the top book with her fingertip. "The point is, I can pull a hundred books off my shelves, and each of them will say something different about what the Dreamwalker's Gift is, and how it will change Jessica. We don't lack information. Rather, we have so much information that it's all useless. If the darker predictions turn out to be true, she may wind up being hunted by the Guilds and could fall into the hands of people capable of stripping her mind bare of secrets. In which case, there's one piece of information she can't be allowed to possess." She paused, and a muscle along her jaw tightened briefly. "If that means that when she finally learns who I am she curses my name and walks out on me, so be it. She will still play the role she was destined to. I'll just have to guide her from a distance."

"I don't suppose you'd share with me what that destiny is all about?"

Ignoring the question, Morgana walked back to the leather chair behind the desk and sat down. "You will go back to Terra Colonna, and maintain your friendship with her. Don't press her too hard for information on her dreams; it will only make her suspicious. She'll confide in you when she's ready. As for Devon, I want you to keep that tie close, as well. She may confide things in him that she doesn't tell you, and I want him to trust you enough to share that information."

Rita snorted. "She thinks I'm interested in him."

"Then use that. Use whatever you have to. You are my eyes and ears in that world, Rita. Do what you must to stay informed." She leaned back in her chair, steepling her fingers as she thought. "I want you to keep an eye on the other changelings, also. Report to me immediately if any more of them die suspiciously. The Council of Guilds ordered Virilian to cease killing them and if he persists, proof of it would give me valuable leverage over him."

"I'm surprised the Council is showing so much mercy."

"It isn't mercy, merely expediency. Those murders were sloppy. They revealed the nature of our Gifts too openly, and threatened to draw the wrong kind of attention to us. The Greys are going to work on a short range strategy to distract the locals, while the Council considers more permanent solutions."

"Such as?"

Morgana said nothing.

"It would be nice to know what's coming, if you're going to send me back there."

"Let's just say that right now it's safe for you to return. If that changes, be assured I'll pull you out in time." She paused. "Terra Colonna is an unstable world. It may well destroy itself without our help."

Rita pressed her lips together tightly, but asked nothing further. The girl was a loyal agent, Morgana noted, but that might change if the Council decided to Cleanse a world she had connections to. Stronger alliances than this one had collapsed over such details. Morgana would have to watch her closely.

More and more worlds in the Terran cluster were developing sciences that were capable of revealing the changelings' true nature. Terra Colonna wasn't the first, and it wouldn't be the last. The Council of Guilds couldn't just destroy every world that learned how to decipher the double helix. They needed a better solution.

Rita asked, "Are you going to let her approach the Fleshcrafters on her own?"

"She's welcome to approach them. As for getting what she wants from them without my help, I've set things in motion to see that doesn't happen."

"She's stubborn," Rita warned. "And not likely to give up on something just because you made it difficult."

Morgana smiled faintly. "I'm counting on that." She leaned back in her chair. "You know the proper channels to use to report to me from Terra Colonna. Keep me informed."

Rita bowed her head respectfully. "Of course, Your Grace."

As the door closed behind her, Morgana wondered how long it would be before the existence of a true Dreamwalker became public knowledge. Sooner or later it must; there was no way to avoid it. God willing the pieces of Morgana's plan would have time to fall into place before that happened. If not, a lot of people were going to go down, Morgana first among them.

So many variables. So many unknowns. The game was growing more dangerous by the day.

But that was the kind of game she enjoyed most.

And played best.

23

THE LANDSCAPE IS FRIGID AND LIFELESS, lush forest and majestic mountains draped in a glistening layer of ice that renders everything sterile. In some places the ice is coldly beautiful, like a frozen waterfall, but in most it is simply forbidding. Overhead, carrion birds circle impatiently, their black wings stark against the grey and sullen heavens as they wait for something to die.

They are waiting for him to die.

Shivering, Isaac tries to remember the morning he watched the sun rise over those same mountains, with Jesse by his side. No sun is visible now, and though he tries his best to summon a memory of what that dawn looked like, he can't. His soul is too desolate right now to recall such a moment of happiness.

Suddenly he hears her approaching, her footsteps crunching the surface of the ice. She comes to stand beside him, like she did that morning so long ago, although this time there is no joy in her, only concern. It's his sleeping mind that conjured this setting, and as she watches the vultures circling overhead, she must surely be wondering why it looks like this.

"Jesus," she says. "What happened?"

He shrugs stiffly. "I went somewhere I shouldn't have, and I got caught. In a lesser family that might have been a minor offense, but for an Antonin, who supports the honor of the Guild on his shoulders, like Atlas supports the globe, it was an unforgivable sin." He laughs bitterly. "Right now my body is locked in the same cell your brother was once in. It's a bit warmer than this place, and lacks the vultures, but otherwise it's equally cheery." He looks up at the birds and then adds quietly, "Or maybe we do have vultures there. Just not the kind with wings."

"I'm so sorry." The sympathy in her voice makes him ache with shame. No one should have to feel sorry for him. "Is there anything I can do to help?"

There is more color in her than in the rest of the landscape, he notes. The spark of her life defies the sterility of his dream setting. He longs to reach out and touch her, to connect with that spark. Instead he looks away. "I have the information you want. It's ... it's not good news, Jesse."

"Tell me," she says quietly.

"The reapers are wraiths, bound by their creator to hunt Dreamwalkers. I don't know how he empowered them to enter dreams, as we don't have that kind of ability ourselves, but he did. They haunt the minds of dreamers, and when they find signs of the ancient Gift, then they attack." He pauses. "That's why no one has seen them for centuries. There's been nothing to hunt."

"Now they have me," she mutters. "You weren't kidding about the bad news."

He nods. "There were seven of them originally; I don't know how many are still around. I couldn't find any record of them appearing in the waking world unless their creator summoned them. With him dead, they're probably just running wild." He pushes back a lock of frosted hair from his forehead. "If someone were to Commune with his memories they might be able to take control of the reapers, but he was one crazy sociopathic bastard, even by our standards, so that's not likely to happen." Very quietly he says, "I'm sorry, Jesse. But it sounds like a reaper has your scent, metaphysically speaking, and judging from everything I've read, it won't let up until you're dead."

She bows her head. He waits silently, knowing that she's struggling to process all that he just told her. It's a burden he wouldn't wish on anyone. "So there's no hope?" she murmurs. "Nothing I can do about this?"

"I didn't say that."

Startled, she looks at him.

"They're just wraiths. They may have some fancy powers, but at the core they're still ghosts, subject to the laws that rule the dead. And the universe is full of necromancers. We harvest the most Gifted ones for our Guild, so that's where most of the power is concentrated, but you'll still find echoes of it in other places. Your own world has its share of mediums, and some of those may have traces of legitimate power. If you can find one who does, who knows how to bind and destroy spirits, maybe he can help you."

"I thought the Shadows' Gift was the ability to travel between worlds."

He shook his head. "Our control over the dead gives us the knowledge we need to do that, but it's a learned skill, not inherent in our Gift. All the strange practices that we're known for—transformation into the undead, Communion with the departed—those came late in the game. Near as I can tell, we didn't start doing those things until the end of the Dream Wars. Before that we were simply necromancers." He managed a weak smile. "Or so I've read recently."

"Dream Wars? What were those?"

"Some kind of all-out conflict between Shadows and Dreamwalkers. The other Guilds supported us, but it was really our campaign. Planned genocide." He hesitates. "I have no clue why my Guild wanted the Dreamwalkers dead so badly. That's what I was trying to figure out when I was caught."

She turns away from him. After a moment she says, very softly, "I have an idea of why."

He waits for her to say more, but she doesn't. Finally he offers, "I wish I could be more helpful."

A shadow of pain crosses her face. "You told me what I need to know. If I manage to survive this mess at all, it'll be because of you." She hesitates. "But now you're in danger because of me—"

"No. No. That's not true." He takes her hands in his. How warm they are! How full of life! "No one forced this fate on me. I hungered for a destiny other than the one I was born to, and that hunger betrayed me. But because of it I got to experience life—*real* life—and I'll never regret that."

She is about to respond when the world suddenly begins to shake. Ice shivers on the mountaintops and then begins to crack, shards of it raining down into the valley. The birds overhead screech and then fall from the sky one by one, and as they strike the earth it swallows them. The landscape around them begins to dissolve like smoke.

"It's time," she said, squeezing his hands. "Good luck, Isaac."

‖‖‖‖‖‖‖‖‖‖

"Enough," a voice commanded.

The ghosts who had prodded Isaac to wakefulness withdrew, leaving him half-asleep and disoriented. It took him a moment to focus on the person standing outside the bars of his cell: His father.

"It's time we talked," the Shadowlord said.

Quickly Isaac got up, ran a hand through his hair to bring order to it, and smoothed the worst sleep wrinkles from his robe. The actions were reflexive; even in these dire circumstances he couldn't bear to look disheveled in front of his father.

The Shadowlord watched in silence as Isaac approached the bars. Normally his father's expression was unreadable, but today there was anger in his eyes. The magnitude of emotion that he must be feeling for it to bleed to the surface that way was unnerving. "You have long disdained the sanctity of our customs," he told Isaac. "For two years you denied this Guild and our family, indulging in common passion rather than accepting your duty. Now I'm told you were discovered in the Chamber of Souls, an offense against the authority of the *umbrae majae* and the customs of our Guild. By doing so you bring shame to our family and damage the reputation upon which other Antonin depend. And this time you did it in the heart of Shadowcrest, so that all know the details of your transgression." He paused. "Have you anything to say for yourself?"

Isaac considered apologizing, but he knew his father well enough to realize that they were well past the point when it would do any good. "No, Sir."

"Why did you go to the Chamber of Souls?"

Keep it short, Isaac warned himself. *Keep it simple. The more you say, the more likely it is he will come up with new questions to ask.* "I wanted to learn more about our history, Sir."

"You could have gone to your teachers for that."

"There are things they don't teach us."

"Perhaps there are reasons for that."

Isaac said nothing.

"At least you could have asked a Shadowlord to bring you there, so that your visit was properly sanctioned. You could have asked *me* to bring you there." Now anger was evident in his voice, the fury of wounded pride. The man's own son had been unwilling to come to him for assistance. That was his failing as well as Isaac's.

Isaac felt as if he was standing on a rock surrounded by quicksand; no matter what direction he walked in, the end would be the same. *At least I can keep from betraying Jesse's trust,* he thought. It would be miniscule victory in the face of disaster, but a victory nonetheless.

He said nothing.

The cold eyes fixed on him, taking the measure of his soul. "Is there any reason I shouldn't cast you out from the family, excising you from our ranks to protect those who would embrace their responsibility with more enthusiasm?"

Isaac hesitated. He could launch into a speech about how strong his Gift was likely to become, about all the experience he'd gained in the outside world, and how it would make him a better Shadow in the long run, about the thousand and one things he might do for his family in the future if allowed to stay, that would cast honor upon their House . . . but that was all bullshit, and his father knew it. Isaac didn't belong here. His actions had proven it. No simple words could change that fact.

He said it humbly: "None that I know of, Sir."

"Very well, then." His father's expression was grim. "By the authority of the elders of House Antonin, I sentence you to be cast out of our House, and out of this Guild. All ties of blood and duty will be severed. You will be as one who was born in the outside world, who has no claim to loyalty, assistance, or affection within our ranks. You will no longer be family to us, or to me. Do you understand?"

He had to swallow back the lump in his throat in order to speak. "Yes, Father."

"The possibility that you might share our secrets with the outside world must be addressed. While a Domitor could remove them from your mind, that process would enable him to learn things he shouldn't, and your mind could end up so damaged that death would seem a mercy by comparison. Therefore it has been decided by the elders of the House that a Domitor will be brought in to alter your mind, so that any attempt to divulge Guild secrets, no matter how trivial, will cause you unspeakable agony. In this way your silence will be assured. Do you agree to this course?"

Isaac swallowed thickly. The question was not a rhetorical one; reworking the fabric of someone's mind on that scale required the cooperation—or at least the assent—of the subject. But what choice did he have? Virilian wouldn't allow the Antonin to exile him if there was even a chance Isaac might spill the Guild's secrets to outsiders. It would be far easier just to kill him and secure those secrets forever. Isaac's father was offering him a chance to leave this place alive, as something other than a walking vegetable. Only one answer was possible: "I agree."

"They have decided you will also bear the mark of shame, so that all who see you will know that our Guild cast you out in disgrace. Do you understand what this means?"

Isaac flinched, then nodded.

"Do you have any objections to voice, about any of this? It's your last chance."

None that would matter to you, he thought bitterly. "I do not."

"So be it, then. I'll make the necessary arrangements."

His father turned away and walked out without another word. Isaac stood there in silence, the full magnitude of the elders' judgment slowly sinking in. He had little doubt that he could handle exile—he'd lived on his own for two years already—but the mark of shame that his father had proposed was a brutal punishment, meant to identify those who were unworthy of a Guild's trust. Anyone connected with a Guild would consider it his duty to shun Isaac, while anyone not connected with a Guild would see the mark as the sign of a failed elitist, someone who'd been given opportunities they could only dream of, and pissed on them. Someone who deserved to be taken down a notch.

Or several notches.

At least he was going to live. He hadn't even considered that his Guild might sentence him to death for such a minor offense, but his father was right—the secrets of the Guild mattered more to its masters than a mere apprentice's life. Isaac could be replaced. The secrecy of the Guild could not be.

Shutting his eyes, he leaned back against the dank stone wall and sighed. *You wanted a different destiny,* he told himself. *Now you have it.*

24

SHADOWCREST
VIRGINIA PRIME

JESSE

THE BLACK PLAIN BENEATH MY FEET is unsteady to-night, its surface undulating like ocean waves, barely solid enough to walk on. The blackness laps over my toes, my feet disappearing from sight for a moment, as if blotted out of existence. Will I be able to keep walking, or will the plain give way like quicksand beneath my feet? What will happen to me if I am engulfed in it? The ancient Dreamwalkers were driven mad by their Gift, legends say. Was this what they saw in their final hours? Did the universe buckle and crack on all sides of them, until the primordial chaos broke through and swallowed them whole?

Easy, girl. Easy. I shut my eyes for a moment, trying to steady my nerves. *I'm only projecting my fears onto the landscape. Nothing more. If I can't accept that mechanism and deal with it, I should just wake myself up now and not try to go any further.*

Much as I'd like to turn back, it's not a real option. Yes, I could give up on this insane quest and go crawling back to Morgana to beg for help, choking on humiliation as she fastened her puppet strings firmly to my limbs. Or I could forget about healing Mom, and just go back to Terra Colonna and try to live a normal teenager's life. But then every day I would know that my mother was sick because of my cowardice. And Morgana would know me for easy prey, and it would only be a matter of time before she sent her minions to Terra Colonna to screw with me again.

Granted, she'll probably screw with me even if I succeed tonight; I have no illusions about that. But obtaining a Fleshcrafter's services on my own will at least demonstrate that I'm willing to defy her—that I'm *capable* of defying her—and maybe it will drive home the point that I deserve to be treated as something better than a mindless pawn.

One can only hope.

My efforts to pull myself together emotionally have visible effect; the black plain is merely rippling now, like lake water shimmying in the wind, and as long as I watch my footing I should be safe enough. A feeling of intense relief comes over me. If I can maintain my mental focus and not let my own fears consume me, surely I can manage this journey.

Now I just have to figure out where the hell I'm going.

The doors surrounding me are in the forms of caverns this time, their mouths narrow and ominous, barred like the cell doors in Shadowcrest. The heavy locks look like they've been rusted shut for centuries, and even if I had a key, I'm not sure I could get one open. But how would I even know which door to unlock? I look down at Virilian's brooch in my hand and try to focus my attention on it, my eyes tracing the intricate knotwork pattern, praying it will unlock some secret Dreamwalker knowledge that will enable me to find my target. But though I feel a sharp sense of anticipation, as if something is about to happen, nothing actually does. Frustrated, I think back to Sebastian's suggestion about establishing an emotional link through Tommy, and I close my eyes and picture him as he was when I found him, pale and hollow-eyed and terrified. Virilian is the man who did that to him. Virilian is the man who kidnapped him and starved him and assaulted him with ghosts. Virilian is his Abuser. I remember the anguish that I felt when I first realized my brother was missing, the helplessness I felt later when it seemed like we would never find him, the rage I felt when I learned what had been done to him. All of it Virilian's fault. Everything that was done to Tommy, and to me, was done by this Shadowlord's command.

Suddenly I'm standing in front of a barred door. There's an image engraved on the lock, of a crescent moon with a knotwork design on it. I look at Virilian's brooch in my hand, confirm that it matches, then take in a deep breath and push at the door. It swings open, but reveals only blackness. Whatever lies beyond this point, I won't be able to explore it until I commit myself to the unknown shadows of Lord Virilian's soul.

For a long time I stare into that darkness. Then, very carefully, I alter my dream body. The changes I make to my avatar aren't big ones, but they're enough to function as a disguise, so that if Virilian sees me in his dreamscape, that won't give him the power to recognize me in the waking world.

I take a moment to steady myself, then step across the threshold—

*   *   *

A gust of frigid air blasts me in the face, sucking the heat out of my flesh. Reflexively I try to create a coat for myself, but though that would have been effortless a few seconds ago, it's almost impossible now. A bad omen. Altering small elements wasn't this difficult in anyone else's dream; clearly there's something in the Shadow-lord's psyche that inhibits my Gift.

Concentrating as hard as I can, I manage to create a formless wrap for myself, that keeps out some of the wind. It's the best I can do.

The dreamscape I've entered is white: white snow underfoot, white ice coating the boulders near me, white frost encrusting the mountains in the distance, and a sky so pale one can hardly see where the land ends and the heavens begin. There are no people in sight, nor any kind of house or monument visible. Just snow. I look back to make sure the door is still there—it is—and then move forward cautiously, searching for whatever makes this place meaningful to Virilian.

Soon I come to a place where the ground drops away, giving me a bird's eye view of a narrow valley with steep mountain walls and a ribbon of flowing water at the bottom. A fjord? There's a village on the shore, whose long, windowless houses have holes in their roofs, through which smoke is rising. The people there are all wearing cloaks of fur or wool over primitive garments: tunics, leggings, shoes that look like simple pieces of hide wrapped around their feet. I see a few flashes of metal jewelry, including a pin like the one in my hand. Whatever this place is, it's clearly connected to Virilian's past.

Suddenly there's a scream at the far end of the village, so terrified in pitch that it raises the hackles on my neck. Everyone starts rushing in that direction to see what's happening, and I look around for a way to get closer without having to climb down into the village itself. There's little cover on the snow-covered slopes, and for a moment I'm tempted to alter the color of my clothing to a matching white, but given how much effort it took to create the thing in the first place, I decide against it. God alone knows what challenges still await me, and I need to preserve my energy. Carefully I make my way around the C-shaped escarpment surrounding the village, and yes, if anyone looks in my direction I'll probably be spotted, but I'm figuring I can get back to my door faster than anyone can climb the cliff to reach me. I need to see what kind of narrative Virilian's mind has crafted, so I can figure out how to take control of it.

Two men appear, dragging a third between them. It's the third one who's doing the screaming, as he convulses so wildly they can barely control him. Specks of froth are frozen in his beard, and there is a madness in his eyes so terrible that it makes him seem more demonic than human. The two men, though broad-shouldered and strong in their own right, can barely restrain him.

Then someone yells out a name—or maybe it's a ti-tle—in a language I don't recognize. A moment later a tall blond man comes out of one of the buildings, and as soon as I see him I know he's the creator of this dream, though he looks nothing like Sebastian's description of Virilian. Despite his hollow cheeks and sunken eyes and skin as pale as the snow surrounding him, he's clearly alive. One side of his face is scarred in a zigzag pattern, cutting through his left eye socket, and the eye is miss-ing. The regularity of the wound suggests it was a delib-erate disfigurement. People move out of his way as he approaches, and it's hard to tell if they are doing it out of respect or fear.

The screaming man is convulsing on the ground now, and I can see blood splattered on the snow around him. Another two men have come forward to help, so now there are four burly guys trying to pin the man down, one on each limb. The screamer twists and bites one of them on the cheek, leaving a scarlet gash. I hear what sounds like cursing.

The blond Virilian looms over the group like a vulture, watching the ruckus. I get the sense that it pleases him. Then, raising his hands to the heavens, he begins to speak. The people nearest him back away quickly, and a few men and women at the back of the throng flee from the scene completely, seeking shelter inside one of the longhouses. I can't make out what he's saying, but it seems to be some kind of invocation, and at one point I hear the name of Odin. Suddenly the convulsing man freezes in mid-spasm, his body painfully arched back, and a cold wind rushes outward from him, freezing the blood on the snow to scarlet crystals. Even from this far away I can sense how unnatural that wind is, and for a moment it's all I can do to stand my ground, and not turn and bolt for my dream door. I experienced this kind of cold once before, when the reaper pursued me outside the Weaver's camp, and I have no desire to face such a creature again.

But no color is bleeding from the dreamscape this time, so I wait, breath held, to see what will happen next. An icy fog starts to seep from the screaming man's mouth, nose, and ears, tendrils of white gathering over him. Slowly it takes on the shape of a man, his mouth open wide, frozen in the act of screaming. It's a ghost, I realize suddenly, banished from the man's body by the blond man's ritual. I've been watching an exorcism.

The villagers have all backed far away now, and even the four men who were pinning down the possessed one let go and clear the area. The foggy form is taking on more detail, clarifying bit by bit like a slow-loading graphics file. Suddenly its identity becomes clear, and I take a step back in my surprise, nearly stumbling in the snow.

The spirit's face is that of the necromancer.

Then the features collapse into themselves, the spirit becoming a simple cloud once more—which then explodes, glittering particles of frost rushing outward in every direction, as if blasted from a shotgun. Everyone the frost touches falls to the ground and begins to convulse like the first man did. They're being possessed, I realize, by spirits that wear the face of their exorcist. Who is trying to banish each wraith as it manifests, but there are too many of them. As soon as he gets rid of one, two more appear. I can sense the fear in him as the situation worsens, and I realize that any minute now his mind might prompt him to awaken, to escape this nightmare. If that happens, I'm back to square one. But do I have the ability to change this entire dream, to cut short the gruesome narrative so that he feels less threatened?

No. I don't. I may not understand all the ins and outs of my Gift yet, but that limitation seems clear. I can't change this dreamscape in any major way—

—but Virilian can.

I need to feed him some cue that will set off a chain of associations in his brain, so that his mind switches gears of its own accord, exchanging this narrative for another. But what kind of cue would work? It has to be something small, for me to be able to conjure it; my power here is sorely limited.

Cold wind gusts across my face, sucking the heat from my skin. Down in the valley it must be even colder. Suddenly I realize what I need to do. Summoning all my strength of will, I focus on the concept of *warmth*. The gust of hot air I create down in the valley is only a small one, but it hits Virilian in the face so hard that it's as if some vast, unseen dragon suddenly vomited fire on him. He looks shocked, and for a minute he doesn't move. He's got two conflicting realities now. Will his dreaming mind try to reconcile them by working the blast of heat into its current narrative, creating a fictional source for it? Or will it switch gears instead and change the setting to one where such warmth might exist? I hold my breath as I pray for the latter.

The bonfire blazes high—so high!—sparks filling the night, heat singing the eyebrows of the warriors who are dancing around it. Their skin is ruddy, their hair long and black, and their bodies decorated with streaks of paint: black, white, red, gold. Some of them have fresh wounds on their bodies, but they show no sign of weakness as they dance around the fire, their feet beating out a pounding rhythm on the earth. The dance is a show of strength.

On the other side of the fire is a cage made of tree limbs bound together, with men packed tightly inside. They're all wearing the clothing of an earlier era: 18th century, perhaps? I can't see their faces clearly through the flames, but I can hear them screaming in fear and rage, a chilling concert. They're pale-skinned, and clearly not of the same race as the dancers.

Where is Virilian in all this?

Suddenly two painted warriors appear, dragging between them a man in a bloodstained shirt. He's shorter than the Norse necromancer was, and his black hair is bound back in a ponytail, but there's no mistaking the fact that this, too, is Virilian. He's badly wounded, and is too weak to offer resistance as the men drag him toward the cage.

Suddenly a tall man with a necklace of animal bones blocks the way. The others stop dragging Virilian and wait.

"You are the one who speaks to spirits?" the tall man asks. He has a thick accent.

Virilian nods.

The tall man signals for his release. I'm relieved that he's safe now, as he's less likely to wake himself up to escape this scenario, but I'm also frustrated. I need a

Virilian who knows about Shadows and Guilds and missing Fleshcrafters, a creature of the modern world. What can I change in the dreamscape to make that version appear? It would have to be a small change; already I'm feeling the strain of past alterations, and I remember what a wreck I was after the Weaver's dream. And this is surely not the last alteration I'm going to have to work tonight.

I decide to create a whisper just behind Virilian's ear. Only three words, barely loud enough for him to hear. Hopefully it won't require too much energy.

Inspect the Gate.

He turns around to see who spoke to him, but of course there's no one there. Nor do the words belong in this setting, and his dreaming mind knows that. Suddenly the whole scene around us begins to fragment. I pray that it will give way to something I can use for my purpose.

In the last instant before the dreamscape vanishes, I get a clear view of the men in the cage.

They all have Virilian's face.

We're in the cavern where the Blue Ridge Gate is located, and the arch is intact, though it has no crystals. I can't tell from looking at it if this dream is taking place in the past, before the crystals formed, or after the arch was rebuilt. The whole scene is strangely out of focus, as if I'm looking at multiple versions of the same image layered on top of one another. Only two people are visible — Virilian and a Grey — but the chamber is filled with invisible chatter, voices all around me moaning and weeping and screaming. One is even yelling profanities. The result is deafening, and I put my hands over my ears, but it doesn't help at all; the sounds are in my head. It's a struggle just to think clearly.

Virilian is undead in this dream. That much I can see

clearly, even from behind him. So we're getting close to the time frame I need.

I'm standing in the middle of the chamber, in plain sight, but the two men are talking heatedly and thus far neither has noticed me. I need to find cover before they do. But the closest cave formations are across the chamber, and the few nearby gurneys are covered in sheets whose ends stop short of the ground, making it easy to see under them. I decide the latter is my only viable option, so I dive for the nearest gurney, praying I can duck down behind it before anyone sees me.

But as I move, a sudden wave of dizziness comes over me. I grab for the gurney, then remember at the last minute that it has wheels, and reach out to brace myself against the floor instead. My head is pounding, my mouth feels dry, and the room seems to be swimming around me. Whatever energy I've been drawing on to stay in Virilian's dreams is running out, and the multiple-exposure quality of the current dreamscape isn't helping things. If I collapse in Virilian's dreamscape, will my body disappear, or will he find me lying here, unconscious, still bound by the laws of his mental universe? If he kills me in his dreamscape, will my real body die as well?

The Grey is saying, "We should be operative within the week."

"Excellent." Virilian isn't acting like someone who just escaped a horde of angry ghosts and was beaten bloody by Indians. I wonder if he even remembers those scenes. "And my other request?"

The Grey hesitates. "The Council ordered us not to kill the changelings."

"I haven't asked you to kill them. Simply to encourage Terra Colonna in its natural course. It's an inherently unstable world; encouraging a few key leaders to make ill-advised choices wouldn't even be noticed."

The Grey blinks slowly. "You want Terra Colonna destroyed?"

"I want it to cease to be a problem. If it were to self-destruct, as so many high tech worlds do, that would satisfy my requirements."

There is silence for a moment, at least among the living. Ghosts continue to howl in my ears, but I'm no longer hearing them. Virilian wants my homeworld destroyed. He has the power and the resources to make it happen. And if all he does is hire Greys to tweak the thoughts of key political figures, then no one on Earth—my Earth—will ever suspect the truth.

It's only a dream, I remind myself sternly. *This conversation may not have taken place in the real world.*

But Virilian's dream reflects his desires. If he hasn't given such orders yet, he may well do so in the future.

This is the fate he intends for my world.

"You're talking about a lot of Domitor activity," the Grey is saying. "That isn't cheap."

"Do what you need to do and send me the bill," Virilian says coldly. "I'll pay for it out of my own pocket if necessary."

The ghosts should have noticed me by now, I realize. Why haven't they? There are voices coming from all around me, including behind me, so I know I should be visible to some of them. Why haven't they tipped Virilian off about my presence?

Maybe they have, I think, *and he just hasn't acted on it yet.*

Then another idea occurs to me. A stunning one: *Maybe they can't see me.*

This dream is Virilian's creation, right? Which means that every person in it is conjured by his mind, every event orchestrated by his unconscious. Nothing exists in this dreamscape that is independent of him, other than me. So if he doesn't know I'm here, maybe his creations can't respond to me.

He's turning to walk out of the chamber now. I need to follow him, or shift the dream to another venue, or . . . something. But I'll have to cross in front of the Grey to do that. Will I be invisible to him, as I seem to be invisible to the ghosts? There's only one way to find out. Heart pounding in fear, I force myself to rise up from behind the gurney. My legs are unsteady, though whether from weakness or trepidation, I don't know. At last I'm standing. The Grey is looking straight in my direction. Virilian's pet ghosts swirl around my head, moaning their endless misery. One second passes. Two.

No one sees me.

No one sees me!

Trembling, I cross right in front of the Grey. He just stands there motionless, like a mechanical doll that has wound down. Virilian is heading toward the tunnel that leads up to Shadowcrest, and as he enters it, the cavern I'm standing in begins to dissolve. I have to keep up with him, even though the tunnel will offer me no cover; if for any reason he turns around, he'll see me. And while he may not recognize me, surely he'll sense that I don't belong in his dream, the same way I did when the avatar girl entered mine. That's more knowledge than I want him to have.

I need to transform this setting into something that will serve my purpose. But my strength is fading, and it's getting hard to focus my thoughts. I don't have many alterations left in me.

Small change. I need a small change.

I try a whisper again. With the voices of the dead already filling this place he'll probably assume that one of them is talking to him, which at least will keep my presence here a secret. I form the words in my mind and hold them there for a minute, pouring my fading mental strength into them; then I release them into the dreams-cape. The whisper manifests right beside his ear, and even though I can't hear it myself, I see Virilian stop short when he hears it, startled.

Travis Bellefort, it says. The name of the missing Fleshcrafter.

Suddenly the tunnel is gone. We're in the woods now, in a small clearing with a slender moon overhead. The latter provides just enough light for me to see where the surrounding trees are. Or were. Or will be. Layers and layers of tree-images fill the air, overlapping in mad quantity—young trees, old trees, trees split by lightning and trees hollowed out by birds, all of them occupying the same space. Is this the same multiple-exposure qual-ity of Virilian's dreamscape that I noted in the cavern, only ten times worse? Or is my vision breaking down from the strain of so much dreamwalking?

Virilian's back is to me; I need to get out of sight be-fore he turns my way. I spot a cluster of trees that seems to be holding its shape better than most, and I take shel-ter behind them, flattening myself behind the largest tree in the group, struggling to breathe quietly. For the mo-ment, at least, I'm not visible to the creator of this dream.

"What news?" The Guildmaster demands. His tone is harsh.

The man standing before him is tall, gangly, and has two slender horns growing out of his forehead. I don't need to see the Guild sigil on his ring to guess what his Gift is.

"Bellefort knows," the horned man says.

"You're sure?"

The Potter nods.

"How much?"

"I'm not sure. He started talking to me about a Fleshcrafter who was executed recently in Richmond, for sharing Guild secrets with one of the Seers there.

The message seemed pretty clear. He was warning me against similar indiscretion. Which suggests he has a pretty good idea what's going on."

"You think he knows about our arrangement."

"Given the way he presented his warning, I certainly think he suspects."

"Do you think he would have shared that information with anyone else?"

The Potter hesitates, then shakes his head. "I don't think so. Our Guild is ruthless in matters like this. If anyone else suspected I was spying for you, I doubt I'd be alive to have this conversation."

There is a long silence. The ghostly voices surrounding us have quieted to a murmur, little louder than the chirping of crickets. Finally Virilian says, "You understand what needs to happen."

The horned man shuts his eyes for a moment. "There's no other option?"

"Not if you value your life."

The Potter flinches. "Then at least make it clean," he begs. "Please. For my sake. He's never done anything to harm you or your Guild."

"I have no reason to bind his spirit," Virilian says coldly. "If that's your concern."

"It is," he breathes. "Thank you."

"I'll need someone to take his shape afterward, to establish a false trail. It can't be known that his last act on earth was to meet with me."

"Of course. Of course. Just let me know when and where, I'll take care of it myself."

I've focused so intently on the conversation that it takes me a moment to realize that the color is starting to drain from the Potter's face. His clothes are turning grey as well. I look to the treetops overhead, and see that one by one the dark leaves, barely visible in the moonlight, are losing their color.

Panic grips my heart. I close my eyes and try to re-connect to my sleeping body, to wake myself up, but I can't. Nor can I make my flesh move in its sleep, even a twitch. Which means that I have no way to signal Sebastian that I need help. For as long my body is lying still on that bed, looking peaceful, he'll assume my soul is content.

I'm trapped here.

Clouds are starting to congeal blackly overhead, and something even darker than the night sky is taking shape within them. The spirits of the dead have fallen silent, and the very air is thick with dread. I look around desperately for any sign of the door that brought me here, but of course it's nowhere to be found. I've trav-elled through three different dreamscapes since arriv-ing: God alone knows if the door even exists in this setting.

Virilian suddenly notices the activity overhead. There's no sign of fear in him, and I get the sense from his confident posture that he knows exactly what is hap-pening. He raises his arms to the heavens and begins to chant. Wisps of golden light appear, circling the mass of clouds, and they join together, first in small geometric patterns then in larger ones. Soon a glowing net has been woven around the place where the reaper is mani-festing, a complex web of fine golden lines that is beau-tiful in form, terrifying in its power.

Suddenly the reaper bursts into reality. Wing-like shapes of pure blackness beat at Virilian's golden web, thrashing wildly as the creature fights to break through, like a bird throwing itself against the bars of a cage. The sky trembles with every blow, and streaks of shadow spasm across the clearing as the creature blocks the moon in its struggles. But for now, at least, Virilian's binding pattern is holding it prisoner. The reaper isn't going anywhere.

The Fleshcrafter is staring at the ghastly display in astonishment and fear. "What the hell is that thing?"

Virilian doesn't answer him. He's studying the reaper, as if trying to figure out exactly what it's doing here. Suddenly I see his body stiffen, and with a sinking in my heart I realize he must have put two and two together. Reapers only appear in dreams, so Virilian knows he must be dreaming. And since there is only one reason for such a creature to manifest, he knows there must be a Dreamwalker nearby. I can sense the enlightenment blossoming within him like a putrid flower, and I realize to my horror that by drawing the reaper to this place, I've revealed to Virilian the very thing I most needed to keep secret.

He knows I'm here.

Frozen in dread, I watch as he lowers his hands; the golden patterns overhead begin to dissolve. "Go," he commands the wraith. "Do what you came to do." Suddenly the web breaks apart and dissolves into the night. The wraith howls in triumph, its voice splitting the night like a thousand nails screeching across a blackboard. The leaves on the trees nearest to it freeze, then shatter; brittle fragments fall to the earth like hail. The moon becomes bleached of its bluish hue, the grass in the clearing is sucked dry of color, and even the Potter's face turns completely grey. Only the Shadowlord remains unchanged—not because he is immune to the wraith's power, but because he is eternally colorless. He and the reaper are soul mates.

The wraith turns toward me then, and I know that it can sense me there, standing in the shadows, as easily as a cat can smell its prey hiding in the grass. Desperately I try once more to cast my mind back to my body, to flee to the safety of the waking world, but I can't make the connection necessary. It's as if my body doesn't even exist. Sebastian and I had discussed the risks of this journey before I left, but that had been a rational discussion, performed in a world whose laws we understood and trusted. Now I'm here, trapped in a madman's dream, facing a creature out of my worst nightmares, and it's hard to think clearly, much less remember what we said. *Run!* an inner voice screams, primitive survival instinct drowning out rational thought. *Run! Run! Run!* But running from this thing won't save me. It can move faster than I can, and even if I managed to outrun it, I'd still be stuck in Virilian's dream. No, my only hope is to stand my ground, and so I struggle to do that, even though the primitive part of my soul is howling in terror, my whole body shaking as I fight to control it.

I can't run from this thing. I certainly can't fight it. But there is a third option, that Sebastian and I discussed before I left, and terrifying as it is, I have to try it. Or so I tell myself as Death incarnate bears down on me, its vast wings blotting out the moonlight overhead. The entire world has been drained of color, and my breath turns to fog as it leaves my lips, crystals of ice clinging to my eyelashes, blurring my vision. I draw my knife, bracing myself for the creature's attack. I doubt I can hurt it, but that's not my goal.

I need it to hurt me.

Darkness engulfs me, and with it a cold so intense that it fills my lungs with ice, turning every breath to agony. I stab wildly at the creature, trying to drive it away from my lower body, so that it will strike me where I need it to. It clawed me once in the past, so it must have some kind of physical substance. But there is nothing there—no flesh to slice, no body to bleed. Only Death. Still I keep stabbing at it, my blade angled low, thrusting out again and again and again. Maybe the sheer energy of my assault will convince it to strike a higher target, either my arms or my face ... the only parts of my body that are not clothed in the waking world.

When the blow comes it is not the swipe of talon or claw like I expected, but from a whiplash of pure cold. It cuts across my face like a razor, and blood spurts out in a rain of scarlet crystal. Terror fills my heart, but also elation. Because right now, in that other world, the flesh that I can't see or control is suffering the same wound, and Sebastian will see that. He will know by the gash across my face that I need to wake up, and he will do what is necessary to make that happen.

It's my only hope of escape.

Jesse!

I can hear his voice now. The reaper is striking out at me again, but I focus on Sebastian's voice, using it as a lifeline, as I struggle to reconnect to the waking world. All I need is one moment of awareness, and I'm out of here. But bands of cold are whipping around my body, and wherever they make contact my flesh freezes, leaving behind strips of ice that encase me like mummy wrappings. The vitality is being sucked out of my soul, and my very thoughts are freezing inside my head. I can't connect to my sleeping body yet, but I have to keep trying. I bet my survival on this one crazy gambit, and if it fails now, I'm doomed.

Jesse!

Images begin to flash before my eyes, my brain bleeding out memories as the reaper begins to feast on my soul.

—the thing we're looking for isn't here—

—go over there and kiss, you two—

—you're not Guild, are you?—

Then water engulfs me, and suddenly I can't breathe. Icy liquid is filling my lungs, and I'm drowning, and I'm coughing, and all the memories are gone, and I'm trying to scream for help but I can't get any air into my lungs. Suddenly I can sense my body in the distance, and I reach out to it with my mind, clinging to it so I can shake off this nightmare and escape—

And then I see the changing castle.

It flashes before me as a memory, but it isn't a memory—not my memory, anyway. I never saw it with those turrets, those windows, those pennants flying. Nor did the boy in the Weavers' compound, whose visions I shared, see it that way. Nevertheless, I recognize it. And the shock of having it appear here, now, is so great that for a moment the precious lifeline of Sebastian's voice slips from my grasp. Or perhaps I choose to let go of it, to grasp at knowledge that is even more precious.

It's the reaper's memory.

I can sense the shattered remnants of emotions long forgotten, fragments of an ancient life now dust. I look in the windows of the dream-tower and see images changing there, and I know that the reaper devouring my soul was once in that place, and it understood what those images meant. And I know that it did not come as an invader, or as a destroyer, but as one who belonged there. One for whom that place was built. I see the castle standing in the sunlight—first a red sun, then a golden one, colors flickering across its facade as changing hues swirl overhead—and the reaper's memories are not dark or fearful, but they are buried beneath so much hate and pain I can hardly stand to share them.

Jesse!

How desperately I want to drink in more of this creature's knowledge! I may never have such an opportunity again. But I can feel my bodily organs starting to fail as the life is drained from them, and I know that if my flesh expires in this world I will die in that other one as well. So I force myself to turn away from the landscape of light and wonder, focusing once more on my sleeping body, centering my awareness on the voice that is calling me home—

*   *   *

Pain came first, and with it the awareness that my body was soaking wet, my right cheek burning with pain. Then the sickness hit, wave after wave of it, and I could do little more than gasp for breath between bouts of vomiting. Sebastian held my hair out of the way like a father whose wayward child had got drunk for the first time. Then the convulsions started, and he took me by the shoulders and held me steady until they subsided.

Finally I lay back gasping on the bed, and he went to fetch some towels from the bathroom. I saw a pitcher lying by my side, and realized that he must have dumped its contents onto me to shock me awake. That must have been what all the drowning imagery was about.

He came back with a towel soaked in warm water and handed it to me. I draped it across my eyes for a moment, drinking in its delicious heat, then started to wipe the mixture of tears, blood, and vomit from my face. In my mind's eye I could see the changing castle, and it rotated like a 3-D computer image, its shape shifting as I studied it. Dreamwalkers knew about this place. The avatar girl had sought refuge there. And now it appeared that a reaper had once been welcome there.

The implications of that were staggering.

"Did you get what you need?" he asked.

Startled, I let the vision fade. It took me a moment to remember what the original purpose of my dream journey had been. Yes, I'd invaded the mind of a powerful Shadowlord, and I'd tricked him into dreaming about his secrets without revealing my true identity. The fine details of that dream might have been fictional, but the seeds of truth were surely in it. And I was confident I knew how to interpret them.

"I have it," I whispered.

Had the reaper been a Dreamwalker once? It was a mind-blowing concept, but not an impossible one. Supposedly our Gift turned its users into creatures of nightmare, driving them mad in the process. The reaper I'd seen could certainly fit that description. Did that mean I was fated to turn into the same kind of creature, a specter of Death who haunted the dreams of innocents? That would certainly explain why people had been so anxious to kill all the Dreamwalkers. No grand economic theories were required.

The Shadows had a hand in this, I reminded myself. *Whatever that creature was, it was not wholly natural.*

Perhaps the thought should have brought me some comfort.

But it didn't.

25

FLESHCRAFTER GUILDHOUSE ON THE
OUTSKIRTS OF LURAY
VIRGINIA PRIME

JESSE

WE WERE MET AT THE ENTRANCE of the Potter's en-
clave by twin boys. They were slender and pretty,
with eyes of a shockingly bright violet, and skin so pale
you could see their veins through it. They also had long,
thin horns sprouting from their foreheads, which swept
back over their heads in graceful arcs, circling down and
around to end right in front of their ears. Like a ram's
horns, only more delicate. They were strangely beautiful
things, delicately spiraled with shades of brown and
black and a touch of purple, paler at the base and shad-
ing gradually to dark, almost-black tips.

I wondered if they used them to butt heads during
mating season.

The twins indicated that we should proceed to the
main building. I leaned on Sebastian's arm as we walked,
trying to look more steady than I felt. It was a long hike,

and I wasn't in great shape. If I could afford the luxury of spending a week in bed, that's where I'd be right now.

"It's all right to stare," he told me as we walked. "In this place, it's considered a compliment."

"Then why do they live out in the middle of nowhere?" I looked at the high wall surrounding the estate and the woods that were visible just beyond it; this wasn't the kind of place you chose to live if you wanted people to notice you. "All those twins would have to do is walk down Main Street and they could be stared at to their hearts' content."

"But as curiosities, not artists. Those who like to experiment with self-modification prefer the company of their own kind. And perhaps a few trusted associates." He pushed a hanging branch out of the way. "It's rare that any outsider is allowed to see them. You should regard our invitation here as an honor."

Maybe it was, but I was still too drained from my dreamwalking—and too spiritually sick from the revelation that followed it—to take pleasure in anything. At one point I became so dizzy that we had to pause for a moment, until I could get my bearings again. Was it too soon for me to be up and about? Should I have waited until I had my full strength back—and my spirit—before trekking through the woods to visit shapechangers? Maybe so, but Seyer had told my friends and family on Terra Colonna that we would be back in a week, and that time was almost up. If I didn't return home soon, my aunt and uncle would likely call out the National Guard to look for me. I had no time for a leisurely recovery. Or a leisurely anything.

Was I confident that the news I was bringing to the Potters was correct? Hell, no. And the closer we got to the Potter's headquarters, the more aware I was that all I had to go on was a madman's dream. There was no guarantee that any of its details reflected reality, or that the people and events Virilian had woven into his narrative could rightfully be implicated in Travis Bellefort's disappearance.

But it wasn't the details of the dream that mattered; it was the emotions behind it. Years of interpreting my own dreams had taught me that the mind was a free-association machine that would frequently substitute one person or object for another, so that a nightmare about your dog being hit by a car might really mean that you were worried about your best friend moving away, or filled with guilt over hurting someone. What linked dream and reality together was the emotional charge they had in common. Interpret that correctly, and you could glimpse a dream's true meaning.

Travis Bellefort had discovered something he wasn't supposed to, involving another member of his Guild. Virilian had killed him because of it. That much was likely to be true. Of course, if I turned out to be wrong, and the scene I'd witnessed was simply a meaningless fantasy—or represented something other than what I thought—I was about to bear false witness to one of the most powerful men in the region, accusing an innocent Potter of treachery. That wasn't likely to end well.

Sebastian wouldn't be here if he doubted me, I told myself. *He's too much of a survivor to put himself at risk like that.*

The building that the ram-twins had directed us to was large and ornate, with stylized human and semi-human figures carved into its stone face. As we approached, I saw that the pillars flanking the main door were made up of sculpted figures—human and animal—intricately twisted together. You couldn't tell where one creature began or ended. A slender man with green skin and pointed ears greeted us at the door, and despite Sebastian's reassurance about staring, my childhood training took over, and I did my best to look away as he opened the door for us. The woman who greeted us inside had long peacock feathers trailing behind her, and though at first I thought they were attached to the train of her gown, I could see when she stepped in front of us that they jutted out from the base of her spine. Since she didn't have eyes in the back of her head—that I was aware of—I stared at the feathers swaying behind her with unabashed curiosity. Childhood etiquette be damned.

She ushered us into a large room with golden walls and crystalline chandeliers. It was filled with such a variety of quasi-human creatures that it was hard to know where to look first. I saw a woman with the skin of a crocodile, another with the whiskers and patterned fur of a great cat, and a man with a Medusa-like crown of snakes coiling and uncoiling around his head. There was even a small girl with bat-like wings jutting from her shoulders, the delicate membranes rippling with rainbow colors like oil in the rain. Clothing seemed to be optional here, but eating was not; a vast buffet table stretched the length of one wall, with dishes and bowls and pitchers full of decadent foodstuffs covering every inch of it. Nearly everyone in the room had some kind of dessert item in hand, which they nibbled as they turned to watch us progress down the center of the room. The air was filled with the heady scents of honey and chocolate.

At the far end of the chamber was a large ornate chair, and the figure sitting in it looked more like a Hindu god than a mortal man. His slender body was the color of burnished gold, and each of his six arms rested on a different part of his throne. There were half a dozen people gathered around him, of various shapes and colors, including a naked woman covered in iridescent blue scales. She had a bright scarlet tongue that flicked in and out of her mouth as she watched us approach.

If staring was regarded as a compliment here, then they must have been very pleased by my reaction.

"Well. Green Man." The god-figure nodded to Sebastian. "I hardly expected you back so soon. Does this mean you have information for me?"

"I do, your Grace. But the nature of it would be better suited to a private recitation." He glanced back at the room full of Potters, most of whom were now watching us.

The golden figure looked at him curiously for a moment, then nodded. "Leave us," he commanded loudly. A sweeping gesture of one of his middle arms directed everyone in the room to obey. "All of you. Leave us alone."

Most of them filed out, some Fleshcrafters grabbing a last helping of bonbons or truffles. The ones crowding around the throne seemed reluctant to leave their master's side, but he waved them off as well, until finally only three of his people remained: the woman with the blue scales and two dragon-faced men in matching uniforms. The latter looked like bodyguards and were clearly wary of leaving him alone with outsiders, but the golden Fleshcrafter waved off their concerns. "All is good. You can go." The woman with the scarlet tongue remained by his side.

As the doors shut behind the guards, Sebastian nudged me forward. "Your Grace, permit me to introduce Miss Jennifer Dolan, of Terra Colonna." We'd decided to use the alias that was on my Terra Prime passport. "She has uncovered information pertinent to the matter we discussed." To me he said, "You stand before Master Tristan Alexander, regional Guildmaster of the Fleshcrafters."

The mundane name seemed an odd match to such an exotic creature. "I'm honored to meet you, Your Grace."

I wasn't sure if I should bow or curtsy, so I wound up doing something midway between the two, hoping it didn't look as awkward as it felt.

"I'm pleased to meet anyone who has information for me," the Guildmaster said. He leaned back in his throne. "Tell me what you've discovered."

Sebastian and I had discussed what I should say—and, more importantly, not say—so that I would not have to reveal the source of my information. I chose my words with care. "What I bring you comes from the conversation of two ranking Shadowlords, when they thought they were unobserved. Travis Bellefort was killed by a member of their Guild. Apparently he had discovered that another Fleshcrafter was reporting all your business to the Shadows, and they murdered Bellefort to protect their informant."

For several long seconds there was silence. The golden expression was impossible to read. "Do you know the identity of this informant?" he said at last.

I'd made a sketch of the Potter in Virilian's dream; I took it out now and offered it to him. "I don't know his name, but he was described by the same source who gave me this information. He said this was an accurate portrait." It all sounded suspiciously vague to me, but Sebastian said that everyone would expect me to protect my sources thus.

Alexander unfolded the drawing and studied it. Scowling, he showed it to the blue woman. "This is a serious accusation. How sure are you of your facts?"

Sebastian interjected, "I'll speak for the quality of her sources, your Grace. That said, any report based on hearsay should be verified before it's acted upon."

"That goes without saying." The Guildmaster looked at the blue woman. "Go get the Domitor who worked with us during the Landres affair. Make sure he knows this job is off the books." As she left his side and headed toward the exit, the Guildmaster turned to me again. "Was it a clean death?" he asked.

Sebastian had warned me to expect that question. "They made no attempt to bind his spirit, sir. It seems they just wanted to silence him."

"Good," he murmured, clearly relieved. It was a chilling reminder that I was now in a world where death was not the worst fate a man could suffer.

Sebastian took out the items that I had used to connect to Virilian and placed them on a small table beside the throne. "I thank you for these. They were most helpful."

He nodded. "You've done well, Green Man. Clearly your reputation is not exaggerated. Assuming this information checks out, you've more than earned your reward."

I must have bridled visibly, because Sebastian put a warning hand on my shoulder. "With respect, sir, that should go to the one who was responsible for gathering the information."

A golden eyebrow arched upward. "Indeed?" He looked at me. "Well, Miss Drake. What payment would you like for your services?"

Hearing those words at last, after all I had gone through to get to this point, was nigh on overwhelming. For a moment I couldn't speak. "A member of my family suffered brain damage in an accident, your Grace. I've been told that Healers can't help her, because neurons have to be replaced, but that maybe a Potter could. I don't understand all the technicalities of how that would work, but if one of your people could try, I'd be very grateful."

His eyes narrowed slightly. "That's a small price to ask, given the value of what you just delivered."

Sebastian said quietly, "The work would have to be done on Terra Colonna."

"Ah. Now I understand." He nodded slightly. "We don't like to travel offworld—for reasons that I assume are obvious—but you've done me a considerable service, Miss Drake. Assuming your information is verified, I see no reason why I couldn't assign a Master to such a task."

"Thank you," I whispered. I felt like crying. "Thank you."

"And you." He looked at Sebastian. "Nothing for the man who brought this marvel of investigative talent to me? No finder's fee?"

"To have your favor is sufficient," Sebastian said, bowing his head. He had explained to me some of the ins and outs of Guild negotiation, so I recognized his message for what it was: *I'd rather have you in debt to me.*

"Of course. But surely a small token of favor would be appropriate." He smiled knowingly. "I hear the Hunters are restless these days. Perhaps you would like your scent altered?" When Sebastian didn't respond he offered, "One of my apprentices could do the work."

The value of Guild service was determined by the rank of the person performing it, Sebastian had told me. By specifying an apprentice for his job, Guildmaster was indicating it would be a trivial favor, not sufficient to cancel out the larger debt.

The politics in this place were starting to make my head spin.

"That would be appreciated," Sebastian said graciously. "Thank you."

"Can I get in on that too?" I asked. Maybe I could have asked the question more diplomatically, but if he had a way to keep Hunters from tracking me, it was an opportunity I wasn't going to pass by.

The Guildmaster looked amused. "I see no reason why we can't include that in your payment. That is, assuming that your report checks out. We do need to verify it."

I bowed my head. "Of course, Your Grace."

"We can fix that as well, if you like." He gestured toward the gauze Sebastian had dressed my wound with. I reached up and felt warm wetness where a bit of blood had seeped out.

"Thank you," I said. "I'd like that very much."

Sebastian bowed and urged me to do the same. "Thank you, Your Grace. I look forward to serving you again." With a start, I realized that my first real negotiation with a Guildmaster (as opposed to my scripted sham of a meeting with Morgana) had reached its end. And I had succeeded. I'd wanted to obtain something from this world, and I'd done what was necessary to get it. Without Morgana's help. The sudden realization of that was intoxicating. And my mother was going to be healed! What had seemed an impossible dream a mere week ago was about to become reality. It all seemed unreal.

Easy, I warned myself. *Your information has to check out before he'll pay you anything.* But it would check out. Maybe it was just the intoxication of the moment, but I no longer doubted my conclusions. Virilian's true passions had shaped that dream, and a Domitor would confirm its content.

Hordes of hungry sycophants were allowed back into the throne room as we took our leave. I walked out by Sebastian's side, as an equal. That was how the Guildmaster of the Fleshcrafters had treated me. A fellow information broker.

As we walked past the transformed Potters, I stared at a few of them. They smiled at me, pleased by the attention. One of them offered me a truffle as I walked by. I took it from him and bit into it. The creamy chocolate was delicious, but not nearly as sweet as the taste of victory.

Screw you, Morgana.

26

LURAY
VIRGINIA PRIME

ISAAC

THE WORLD WAS BRIGHT. So bright! Apparently two weeks in Shadowcrest had been enough to dull Isaac's memory of just how colorful the outside universe was. You could get drunk on this much color.

He stayed in the shadows for a while, watching locals go about their business from the entrance of a shuttered store, then finally steeled himself for the inevitable and stepped out into the street. The sheer intensity of the human energy surrounding him was dizzying. Had he felt this overwhelmed two years ago, when he'd left Shadowcrest the first time? Or was he just so exhausted from what he'd been through recently that everything seemed ten times as impactful?

The mark of shame that the Fleshcrafter had etched into his face was livid and unmistakable, a wine-colored streak that ran down the center of his forehead, too perfectly shaped to be natural. Such markings were rare, and Isaac had never seen one before, but apparently everyone in Luray knew what it meant. Crowds parted for him as if he was a plague carrier, and the few people who glanced his way avoided any eye contact. One little girl who clearly didn't know what the mark meant stared at him in frank curiosity, until her mother noticed and jerked her away. As she dragged the girl hurriedly down the street, away from Isaac, he heard her explaining why she should never, *ever* talk to someone whom the Guilds had chosen to shun.

If the mark had a been smaller thing he might have tried to hide it beneath a hat—as far as he knew there was no rule against that—but the bottom of it extended down onto the bridge of his nose, and no hat, bandana, or bandage would cover that. Until the weather was cold enough for him to wear a ski mask, anyone who looked at him would instantly know that his Guild had cast him out and that all civilized folks were encouraged to reject him.

In the sea of color and sound that was Luray, he was a bleak island, lifeless and alone.

He walks through the Antonin home like a ghost, a throbbing ache where his heart should be. His father has given him an hour to collect his belongings, but what does he own that's worth packing? The mementos he collected during his walkabout period, that he'd stored in the Warrens, were all destroyed in the raid. Anything from before that time would reflect a life he is no longer part of, an identity he no longer has a right to. Better to let it all go.

He gathers together some pieces of clothing—the few he has that are not Guild issue—and packs them into a pillowcase. Then he wanders through the house without focus or direction, picking up useful things as he comes

*across them. He finds a few fetters in his father's office
and takes them. Such things have street value, especially
in the poorer districts, and he figures that his father owes
him.*

When he returns to his room, his mother is there.

*How alive she looks! The flush of her cheeks is a pain-
ful reminder of how dead everyone else in this place is,
how lifeless his world is. Is he supposed to respond to her
presence or pretend she isn't here? The moment he was
marked as an exile he became a non-entity to his Guild,
and all Shadows, minae and majae, are expected to shun
him. His father has even sent the servants away so that he
won't cross their path while he packs. Apparently a passing glance from a housemaid is more than an exile is
worthy of. But now here his mother is, standing in front
of him, and he suddenly discovers that he doesn't know
how to ignore her. Sorrow wells up inside him, and he
can see the same emotion reflected in her eyes. It shames
him to inspire such passion in her, when she has spent her
whole life trying to resist strong passions.*

*She gestures toward a canvas backpack lying on his
bed. "I thought you might need this."*

*He has a sudden urge to run to her, to hug her with all
his might, to drink in her living warmth one last time and
take fleeting comfort from it . . . but he can't. She's already
compromised herself by coming here to his room, and
whatever spirits are watching will surely report this scene
to his father. He won't make things worse for her.*

*Slowly he walks over to the backpack and looks inside
it. Fresh underwear. A hair brush. A black leather toiletries case. Items so mundane they make the moment seem
surreal. He's leaving home forever, and this is what she
thinks he needs most? "You'll make it," she says quietly,
as he fingers the items. He doesn't dare meet her eyes. "I
know it doesn't seem that way now, Isaac, but you will."*

"Will you undergo Communion when I'm gone?" He

can't imagine his mother transformed, her eyes black and empty, her skin corpse-cold. But she is an Antonin, raised from birth to seek that terrible half-death. It is inevitable.

She sighs. "I told your father when you were born that I would walk among the living for as long as you needed me."

He feels tears coming to his eyes, and turns away so she won't see them. Technically there's no longer a need for him to hide his emotions—he's not pretending to be a Shadow any more—but the habit is deeply ingrained. "You shouldn't have come here," he mutters.

"I know. But I couldn't let your father's rage be the last thing you saw. Your final memory of us." He hears her come up behind him, and for a moment they both stand still and silent, a stone tableau of misery. "Someday you will understand why this had to happen," she whispers. Her hand touches his shoulder. It's a gentle touch, fleeting, that leaves trails of warmth on his skin even after her fingers are withdrawn. He can hear spirits murmuring in the shadows, probably commenting on the forbidden contact. Will they tell his father that she was here? That she touched him? Must she suffer the wrath of the Guild because she cared enough to say goodbye? "Be careful, my son."

He doesn't trust his ability to speak without breaking down, and that would shame them both, so he says nothing.

A moment later she is gone.

It had been hours since his last meal—most of which wound up on the floor of the Guildmaster's audience chamber—and his stomach was starting to groan from hunger. Fingering the few bills in his pocket, he looked around for some place where he could purchase food with minimal human contact. There wasn't a grocery store within sight, but there was a food cart at the end of the street, so he headed toward that. As he got closer to it, the smells of sausage and cooked onions enveloped him, intensifying his hunger tenfold. Surely he would feel better when there was something in his stomach. And maybe then he'd have the energy to figure out what to do next.

He stopped a short distance from the cart and waited until all its customers dispersed before approaching.

The cart owner did not look up.

Isaac kept his eyes respectfully averted as he told the man what he wanted, hoping that would make the conversation less uncomfortable.

The cart owner did not respond.

A tremor of fear coursed through him. While it was customary for a Guild outcast to be shunned in social affairs, he hadn't expected the custom to extend to necessary, life-sustaining services. Was this man really going to refuse to sell him food? He asked once again, in a tone that he hoped would appeal to the man's better nature, and when that didn't work he tried appealing to the man's greed instead, offering to pay three times the normal price for his wares. But nothing worked. As far as the vendor was concerned, Isaac didn't exist.

The ache of hunger in his stomach was growing stronger by the minute. He needed to find a source of food where the need for human interaction was minimal, so that his presence would be tolerated. A place where he could take what he wanted, put his money down, and leave. Like maybe a grocery store?

He had to search for several blocks to find one. When he did, he observed it from the outside for a few minutes, then entered. The people in the store instinctively moved away from him, and whatever aisle he entered soon became empty. He gathered up a few staples as quickly as he could—a loaf of bread, some inexpensive cheese, a piece of fruit—and then headed to the checkout counter. The people there turned their faces away from him, but they didn't leave. That, at least, was hopeful.

But when it came his turn to pay for his food he found that he was a ghost to everyone here as well. The cashier wouldn't acknowledge him. The customer behind him pushed Isaac's items out of the way and put hers in their place. And when he finally gave up and was about to put some money on the counter and walk out, the cashier swept his items into a container for restocking, out of reach. He stared at her for a moment, then walked out in silence.

Numbed by despair, aching with hunger, he began to walk aimlessly, not caring where his feet took him. The prosperous townhouses and shops of the plaza district gradually gave way to more humble dwellings, and then to run-down shanties. He tried to purchase food at several markets, but no one would take his money, and when he tried putting it down on the counter just walking out with his purchases a pair of store clerks blocked his way until he relented, leaving it all behind. Eventually he gave up trying.

After a while he realized that he had instinctively returned to the territory he'd patrolled while living in the Warrens, where he'd scavenged for food to help feed the small underground community. A whisper of confidence came back to him, then. He knew this place. He knew how to survive here.

He chose a shop whose security he knew was lax, a small grocery with stands full of fruit lined up outside the front window. He waited until no one was looking in his direction, then walked past the store. Instinct took over, and he reached out with minimal motion to claim an orange, letting his hand fall casually back to his side so that the fruit was hidden from view. He knew from experience that if he just kept walking casually by, and acted as if nothing was out of place, people wouldn't notice the sleight-of-hand.

But someone did.

A hand grabbed his shoulder from behind, and he was whipped around to face a burly man with rage in his eyes. The orange went flying from Isaac's hand.

"You stay away from my wares," the man growled. "You got that, boy? Stay away from this whole damn block! We don't need your kind of trouble around here." He shoved Isaac into the street, hard enough that he stumbled and almost fell. As he righted himself, a carriage coming down the block suddenly veered in his direction, and he barely got back to the sidewalk in time.

My skills are just rusty, he thought. But he knew in his heart that wasn't the reason he'd been caught. In the past he'd been part of a nameless, faceless crew of homeless waifs, whose petty thefts were an accepted part of life here. Now, with the Guild's mark of shame blazoned across his face, he was conspicuous. People saw him coming. They watched him out of the corner of their eye even while they pretended that he didn't exist. By becoming socially invisible, he had lost the ability to move unseen.

Exhausted, hungry, and thoroughly disheartened, he wandered into a narrow alley filled with trash, and crouched with his back to the wall, his head bowed. What was he supposed to do now? How was he going to survive? Should he start breaking into houses to steal food? Or go into the woods to play hunter-gatherer? Anger welled up inside him, temporarily drowning out the hunger. How could his parents do this to him? Was there really no fate they could have offered him that was better than this, dying of starvation and neglect on the streets of Luray? All he'd done was break a few goddamn rules! Yes, they were important rules, but surely his father could have come up with a more suitable punishment than this.

I didn't kill anyone, he thought bitterly. *I didn't destroy Guild property, or sell the Shadows' secrets to an enemy. I just hurt the family pride. That's all. Hurt the goddamned family pride!* He wanted to take his father by his undead shoulders and shake him and scream at him at the top of his lungs, *How could you do this to me?*

Suddenly something touched his arm. Startled, he looked up, and saw an abbie standing over him, a small female with a wrinkled face and deeply hooded eyes. She was holding out an apple.

He didn't move.

She nudged him with the fruit, urging him to accept it. Finally he reached up and took it from her. The scent of it made his stomach lurch in hunger. "Thank you," he whispered, ashamed and grateful. "Thank you."

She nodded and went back to her errands, leaving him alone in the alley.

Is this what you want for me, father? That I should sink so low that even the abbies pity me? Do you believe that's a just punishment for my offense?

The flesh of the apple was sweet in his mouth, but the taste of it was bitter.

▭▭▭▭▭

"Tell the Domitor about the ritual you witnessed."

Confused, Isaac looks up at his father. His forehead still burns from the Fleshcrafter's work, and the Domitor's ministrations have left him disoriented; it's hard for him to think clearly. "Sir? I'm not sure I understand."

"You attended a ritual that no outsider should know about." His father gestures toward the Domitor. "Describe it to her."

Isaac slowly turns to face the woman who has just altered his brain. Beside her stands Virilian, the Guildmaster of the Shadows, utterly expressionless. A statue of judgment.

He draws in a deep breath and begins, "It took place on one of the lower levels of Shadowcrest, a place called—"

Nausea wells up inside him suddenly, choking off his voice. It's followed by a wave of pain so intense that he doubles over, then falls to his knees on the stone floor. His flesh feels as if it's being peeled back from his bones, and as he struggles not to cry out in pain, wave after wave of sickness surges through him. Helplessly he vomits, right onto the polished floor of Lord Virilian's audience chamber.

Then, suddenly, both the pain and the sickness are gone. Gasping for breath, Isaac wipes his mouth clean with his sleeve. His whole body is shaking.

The Domitor says, "Any time he tries to share the secrets of your Guild with outsiders, this will be the result. The harder he tries, the worse it will be."

His father looks at Lord Virilian. "Are you satisfied?"

The Guildmaster studies the boy for a moment. Trembling, Isaac can do nothing more than wait on his knees for judgment.

"Very well," Virilian says at last. "You have my permission to exile him."

||||||||||||

The Warrens were empty of life—of human life, anyway—and filled with a fetid odor that was worse than anything Isaac remembered. Maybe some of the bodies from the raid had been left behind to rot. The place also seemed more cramped than he remembered, but it had been a refuge for him when he needed one the most, and there was dark comfort in returning to it, no matter how bad it smelled.

Oil lamp in hand, he walked through the familiar tunnels, reclaiming his memories. He passed the place where he had first talked to Jessica. She had asked him about the dreaming Gift that day. If he'd understood the significance of her question, would it have changed any of the choices he made after that? Eventually he came to the circular meeting room where everyone had stored their mementos, and he discovered that the Lord Governor's men had gone out of their way to wreck the place, crushing or stealing any items that looked particularly valuable. Nothing that Isaac cared about was still intact, but he picked up a few broken fragments that reminded him of particular people, and put them into his backpack. The children here had accepted him despite his aristo origins, and right now, acceptance seemed the most precious thing in the universe.

The Warrens inhabitants had stored their food in metal containers to keep the rats out, and hidden them in the darkest corners of the labyrinth so sewer workers passing through the area wouldn't find them. If those supplies were still intact they might provide Isaac with enough to keep him going for a while. Or so he hoped. But when he reached the first such cache—a rusty locker tucked underneath a maintenance platform—he discovered to his dismay that the raiders had gotten to it already. Packages of food that he'd helped steal from aboveground were all torn open, cans crushed and split, jars shattered. The rats must have had a field day.

Staring at the mess in utter despair, he felt the sharp bite of hunger in his gut. The food stores in the Warrens had been his last hope. If they all failed him, he had no idea what to do next.

The next two caches he visited were as useless to him as the first. Clearly the Lord Governor's men had wanted to send a message to anyone who survived the raid, that they shouldn't even think about coming back here. And the message had clearly been understood. In all his wandering, Isaac saw no sign of another human presence. The Warrens were like a tomb.

Finally, just as his last fragile strand of hope was about to give way, he found a cache where not everything had been destroyed. Maybe the raiders had gotten tired by the time they found it, so they didn't notice when a few cans rolled under a low-slung utility pipe. Trembling with hunger, Isaac squeezed under the pipe to retrieve them, then searched for something in his collection of household items to cut them open. By the time he finally managed to tear half the lid off a can of baked beans, his mouth was so dry he could barely swallow the contents. The cold beans were clammy and dreadful, but they seemed a veritable feast, more delicious than anything he'd ever tasted. In less than a minute the can was empty.

Leaning back against the pipe in exhaustion, he wiped his mouth with his sleeve. Right now he wanted nothing more than to open all the cans and feast—he wanted it desperately—but this was the last food he might find for a while, and he needed to ration it carefully. He reached for his bag so he could pack the unopened cans for later use—

—and suddenly he was aware of another presence in the tunnel. Maybe it had arrived while he was eating, and he just hadn't noticed it, but there was no mistaking it now. A soft, almost inaudible moaning filled the tunnel, rising and falling in volume like the breath of a dying animal. He didn't think the spirit making the noise was a high-order wraith, but it didn't feel like a mere soul shard, a fractured remnant of a human spirit too far gone to think or act on its own. It had a faint aura of volition about it, and Isaac wondered if it had been drawn to him because of his Gift, as the dead so often were, or if it was here for some other reason.

"Who are you?" he asked hoarsely.

The spirit didn't respond.

Probably he should banish the thing. Only the undead

could afford to let unidentified ghosts hang around them, and the ritual used to banish bothersome spirits was one of the first things an apprentice was taught. But Isaac lacked the energy to perform any rituals right now, and perhaps he also lacked the will. This ghost wasn't hurting him. Who was he to decide where it was or was not allowed to go? Maybe it was seeking refuge here, like he was. God knows, enough people had died down here recently; there was probably more than one spirit bound to this place. If the wraith left him in peace, then he would leave it in peace.

That decided, he leaned back against the pipe and shut his eyes, savoring the feeling of fullness in his belly. He was safer here than he was going to be anywhere else. Maybe he should take a few hours and sleep.

Free.

His eyes shot open.

Free.

The primitive thought seeped into his brain without words, but its tenor was jarringly familiar. He knew that spirit's voice.

Free.

"Jacob?" he asked.

Silence.

The presence felt like Jacob; there was no mistaking that. But the murdered boy had been a high-order spirit, capable of complex conversation, repeatedly trying to communicate with Isaac. It made no sense that he would be here now, further from Shadowcrest than any bound spirit was allowed to travel, and barely capable of voicing a single word.

Then suddenly Isaac realized what must have happened, and for one endless, horrified moment he could do nothing more than stare at the place where the ghost was standing, unable to speak. "No," he whispered at last. Forcing the words out. "Please, please, tell me they didn't do that to you . . ."

The Shadows must have discovered that Jacob had helped Isaac break into the Chamber of Souls. Any wraith who was capable of acting against his Mistress's interests was too dangerous to keep around, so they'd condemned him to final death, performing the ritual that was commonly used to destroy malevolent spirits. Normally that would tear an unwanted soul into so many pieces that not a single sentient fragment remained. But Jacob must have survived it somehow. Maybe it was his link to Isaac that enabled an echo of his identity to cling to the living world while his mind was ripped to pieces. Or maybe the boy had simply been stronger than the Shadowlords gave him credit for. Either way, he had paid a terrible price for his freedom. Even Isaac's apprentice-level Gift could sense that the entity standing in front of him was little more than a hollow shell, his mind so fragmented that he probably didn't even know his own name. The best such a ghost could hope for in the wild was to wander endlessly without language or purpose, driven by emotions he could no longer name, mourning the loss of an identity he no longer remembered. Truly, it was a fate worse than death.

The wraith spoke again, this time more strongly. *Free.*

The ritual must have shattered his binding along with his mind, Isaac realized. Whatever fragment of Jacob Dockhart had survived now owed allegiance to no one. Would the boy have chosen such a fate over eternal slavery, had he been given the choice? What mattered more, one's mind or one's freedom? Just asking the question made Isaac queasy. God willing he would never have to make such a choice himself.

"What a pair we make," he muttered. Though the

spirit was too mentally damaged to offer any meaningful companionship, talking to him made Isaac feel less alone. "Hiding in the sewers with no purpose, no future . . . true soul-mates."

The spirit said nothing.

With a sigh Isaac pulled his backpack toward him and untied the top flap. His scavenged items from the Warrens were on top, along with the things he'd taken from home. He took them out and put them aside. After a moment's consideration he also took his clothes out of the pack and the toiletries case, so that the heavy cans could be placed at the bottom of the bag.

But as he picked up the toiletries case he paused. It was smaller than he'd thought, and flatter. Maybe it wasn't what he had assumed. There was a zipper running around three sides of it, and he opened it carefully, not wanting anything to fall out.

Inside was money.

A lot of money.

Spreading the case open like a wallet revealed a thick stack of bills. He stared at them for a moment in disbelief, then took them out and started counting them. Half the bills were of small denominations, the kind of money one might use to buy small items in a shop, but the other half were larger than that. *Much* larger. All told, there must have been at least a thousand pounds in the case. It was a veritable fortune to someone in his circumstances, though God alone knew where he could spend it.

His mother must have put this in the backpack, but why? Money alone couldn't save him now. Surely she would have realized that. Was this merely a ritual gesture, meant to ease his parents' guilt as they cast Isaac to the wolves? Surely if they really cared about him they would have chosen a different punishment and not sent him away forever.

Tears came to his eyes and he blinked them away, not wanting to break down in front of someone. Even a ghost. As he did so, he noticed there was a photo in the case, tucked into a side pocket. Taking it out, he saw it was a family picture, of him and his mother and father standing in some sunlit place, all smiling. It must have been taken years ago, because his father was alive in the picture, and Isaac was just a child. He no longer had any memory of what his father looked like as a living man, so he stared at the image in fascination, startled to discover how much he resembled him.

"Why would they give me this?" he whispered hoarsely. "They threw me out. They cut all ties between us, forever. Why would they think I even wanted something like this? So that I could pretend I still had a family? So that I could remember what I lost and feel even more pain?" There was a murmur of curiosity from Jacob, so he turned the picture so the ghost could look at it—

—and he saw that something was written on the back of it. In his mother's hand.

Startled, he moved the note closer to the lamp so he could read her message.

V wanted you killed.

His hand trembled as he lowered the note.

What? the spirit pressed. *What? What? What?*

Why had Virilian wanted him dead? Because Isaac had broken the rules one too many times? Because he'd corrupted a spirit belonging to a powerful Shadowlord? Or maybe Virilian suspected that Isaac had played a part in the destruction of the Gate. Whatever the reason, if the Guildmaster condemned Isaac to death, no one in the Guild would dare challenge him. Isaac's fate would be sealed.

His father must have protested that judgment. No one of lesser status would have the standing—or motivation—to pull off something like that. Isaac tried to remember what Virilian had said to his father, when the Domitor finished her work. *You have my permission to exile him.* He'd thought at the time that his father wanted to get rid of him, but what if that wasn't the story at all? What if the Antonin patriarch had asked for permission to send Isaac away as an alternative to Virilian killing him? In order to save his son's life?

The Guildmaster would never have allowed that unless the pain of Isaac's banishment was so extreme that the boy would wish for death. Agreeing to anything less might have been viewed as an act of mercy, and a Guildmaster of Shadows was not supposed to be merciful.

"That's what this was all about," Isaac whispered, staring at his mother's note. "The lifetime banishment, the mark of shame . . . he was trying to be harsh enough that Virilian would agree to spare my life. That's what my mother was hinting at when she came to my room. She couldn't tell me outright, not with all the dead watching."

Tears were flowing down his face, and he couldn't stop them. He didn't want to stop them. The dam inside had finally crumbled and emotions were pouring out, all the feelings he'd been struggling to deny since leaving home. Pain, fear, hopelessness, despair . . . but no anger. Not anymore. Shadowlord Antonin had dared to challenge the Guildmaster himself to give his son a chance to survive. Even though the odds of that survival were slim to none. And even though it meant the Shadowlord would never see his son again. Because the alternative to that was death by Virilian's order.

Lowering his face into his hands, Isaac wept.

27

Berkeley Springs
West Virginia

Jesse

HOME. The word felt strange on my tongue, especially in reference to a house I had only lived in for a week. But it was good to be heading back in Berkeley Springs. The people that I loved were there, and I hungered to rejoin them.

Seyer offered to drive us home, and despite my desire to separate myself from everyone and everything connected to Alia Morgana, I did need a way back from Pennsylvania, so I accepted. So did Rita. I would be relieved when we finally parted company; the stress of feigning friendship with her was wearing thin. But the day might yet come when I would need someone with access to Morgana's circle—besides Seyer—so I did the best I could to make her believe that nothing was wrong, even while I fantasized about wringing her neck.

As soon as we got in the car I retrieved my cell phone

and started texting, first to let Tommy know we were on
our way home, then to check up on Devon. Apparently
he had recovered from his strange bout of illness. No big
surprise, if its sole purpose had been to keep him from
travelling with us. Rita was in the seat right behind me
as I texted him, so I had to be careful what I typed, but I
did manage to send a quick warning while she was looking out the window. *Rita was the spy. Details later.* I
wanted to tell him what I suspected about the source of
his illness, including the fact that Rita might have played
a part in arranging it, but this wasn't the time or place
for that discussion.

Is she with u? he texted.

Yeah.

Still friends?

Was he asking if I had decided to overlook the spy
issue, or if I was pretending everything was okay? I
waited until Rita looked out the window again, then
texted, *She thinks so.*

What about ur mom?

Healer coming, I typed. *Family only. No friends allowed.* We hadn't discussed his coming back to witness
the healing, but some things don't have to be said. *Potter
rules,* I added. *Sorry, I tried.*

There was a long pause. *I understand.*

Their call, not mine.

Keep me updated?

K

As soon as Seyer pulled into the driveway, Tommy
burst out of the house and bounded down the front
stairs, yelling my name as if he'd never expected to see
me alive again. When I got out of the car he hugged me
so tightly that he squeezed all the air out of my lungs.
For a long moment I just hugged him back, drinking in
the essence of Terra Colonna through our contact. Then
I saw Mom on the porch, and this time it was me who

did the running. I hugged her like the world was about to end, and since she had no clue what I'd gone through the previous week, she was probably a bit confused by that. I buried my face in her hair so no one would see my face, knowing I could never explain to these people why coming home affected me so deeply. Not until I felt I had control of myself again did I let her go.

Seyer watched our reunion for a few minutes, then said she needed to leave. "It was a pleasure to have you as a guest," she told me, with a faint ironic smile. "If you ever want to visit again, you know how to reach me." I nodded politely and thanked her for the offer, and didn't tell her what I was really thinking, a scenario that involved flying pigs and snowballs in Hell. Then Rita said that she should probably check in with people back home, would Seyer mind giving her a lift to the bus station? And so that final problem was solved.

It was surprisingly hard to say goodbye to Rita. For all my anger about her betrayal, she'd been by my side through some pretty harrowing experiences, and that made for a bond that even rage couldn't banish entirely.

"Good luck with your mom," she whispered. Then she got into Seyer's car, and I watched as it pulled away, feeling a vast weight lift from my chest.

Of course Rose had to feed us all, and over a hearty lunch she made me tell her all sorts of stories about my imaginary week in the mountains. It was hard to make up enough stories to satisfy her, but eventually I was able to turn the conversation to my real business. I said that Seyer had introduced us to a healer who might be able to help Mom, and would they be willing to give that a try? I knew that Rose and Julian were New Age folks at heart, and the Fleshcrafter had coached me on how to present the matter to them. So when I explained that this was a New Age healer specializing in reiki massage, who thought that restoring the proper flow of qi to

Mom's brain might clear out some of her spiritual blockage, I was speaking their language. In truth I think they would have supported any activity that gave Mom a taste of hope, if only for an hour. As for Mom, she wasn't into that kind of stuff, but if everyone else thought this was a good idea, she was willing to give it a shot. What did we have to lose?

After lunch I was finally able to get some time alone with Tommy. I filled him in on what I'd *really* been up to the last week, which was damn refreshing after hours of lies. He listened with wide eyes, surprisingly subdued. "Wow," he said when I was done. "That's just . . . wow."

I sighed. It felt good to unburden myself to someone I trusted, but retelling the story just reminded me of how many things in my life still weren't resolved. Some of which involved people who wanted to kill me. "Yeah. I know."

"They're never gonna let up, are they? Not as long as they think there's a Dreamwalker out there. They may not know it's you, but they're gonna keep looking till they figure it out."

I remembered Virilian's reaction when the reaper appeared in his dream, and I could only imagine his rage once he realized that a Dreamwalker had been messing with his mind. "Yeah," I muttered. "I'm afraid so." Thank God I'd thought to disguise myself in that dream. It wouldn't protect me forever, but hopefully it would buy me time to come up with some kind of plan.

"So," Tommy said, "what can we do about that? I mean . . . there has to be *something* we can do, right?"

I sighed. *Real life isn't like a computer game,* I wanted to tell him. *There's no finite, predictable universe filled with puzzles that have neatly scripted solutions, where all you need to do to defeat a powerful enemy is to assemble the right team and arm them with magical weapons. Real life is messy, and it doesn't always have neat solutions.* "If

I could find other Dreamwalkers, they might be able to help. Maybe they would know how to destroy the reapers." But the only other Dreamwalker I knew about had spent her last moments casting a tsunami at me, and I didn't know if she was alive or dead right now. Even if others of my kind existed, how was I supposed to find them, when their lives depended on hiding their Gift?

The dream tower was the key, I thought. The coma boy had seen it. The avatar girl had run to it for safety. Even the reaper had been there at some point. The tower tied all of us together somehow, and maybe I could use it to find others of my kind. But how did you search for something that, by its very nature, did not exist in the real world? If I searched for it in my dreams I could wind up with all seven reapers coming after me.

It was too much to think about. I closed my eyes for a moment, sighing deeply.

"You okay, Jess?"

"Just tired," I muttered. "It's been one hell of a week."

Was it only a month ago that I'd been struggling to deal with normal teenage angst? Final exam stress, family issues, concern over finding a part-time job for the summer so that I could afford a car next year? It had seemed like so much to deal with, back then. Overwhelming. That was the one upside about being hunted by monsters, I thought dryly. It really put things in perspective.

"Hand me the phone," I told Tommy. "I'll tell the Fleshcrafter we're good to go."

▪▪▪▪▪▪▪▪▪▪▪

The Potter arrived at eight o'clock sharp. Whatever I'd expected our assigned Fleshcrafter to look like, the stocky, ruddy-cheeked senior citizen who showed up at our front door was not it. But apparently Selena Hearst was the perfect person to win my family's trust, and soon Rose was setting out tea for us all and asking about Eastern massage techniques. The Fleshcrafter was surprisingly patient and showed us a collection of river rocks that she used in her work. She said she'd collected them from spiritually significant waterways. Would Rose mind warming them in the oven a bit? They worked better that way. Oh, and Selena would like to brew a special herbal tea for my mother, would it be possible to get some hot water for that? I wasn't sure how much of her performance was real and how much was just cover for her real business, but I suspected it was strongly weighted toward the latter.

Finally we all retired to a back room with Mom, where a table had been laid out with a camping mattress on top of it. I'd asked Rose to get us a couple of boxes of donuts, as per the Potter's request, and they were waiting on the sideboard, their lids folded neatly back. The room smelled of confectioner's sugar.

The Fleshcrafter had Mom drink the tea and then lie down, and she made a show of arranging the newly warmed river stones around her in a pattern designed to channel her vital energies. Or so she explained to Rose and Julian as they watched. Soon Mom's eyes shut, and it looked like she'd fallen asleep. Selena requested politely that everyone but the children leave, as too many people in the room would make it hard for her to channel Mom's qi properly. My aunt and uncle didn't want to go, but clearly they respected Selena's expertise. Soon the four of us were alone.

As Selena reached for a donut I noticed a change in her body language. Gone was the aura of homey warmth that had so charmed my family, and in its place was a sharp and sparing manner, totally at odds with her physical appearance. I must have been staring at her, because when she finished her first donut she looked over at me and said, "No, I'm not really old. Not female, either. That simply seemed like the most effective way to deal with your family."

"It was," I agreed. I looked at Mom. "What did you give her?"

"Something to shut down non-essential mental activity. I can no more fleshcraft an active brain than a surgeon can operate on a moving body. Not safely, anyway."

She (he?) took another donut. "You understand, my goal here is to restore the neural network as it existed before the fire. Any cells which died left their mark on the surrounding tissue, so there are ingrained patterns for reference. I can prompt the body to create new cells exactly where the old ones were." She started inspecting Mom with her free hand as she talked, touching her gently at various points on her face and skull. "Neurotransmitters, on the other hand, are temporary in nature, reabsorbed after every use. I can't judge how effectively they functioned before the fire, so I can't adjust their strength now. The brain will do that naturally once the neural network is restored, seeking its original balance, but that will take time. You should expect a period of confusion, with intense and possibly disturbing dreams. None of which will have any medical significance, save as a sign that she is healing."

Yeah, but it'll be hell to explain to my family, after I gave them a song and dance about how you would make Mom feel better. "For how long?" I asked.

"She seems highly functional, which suggests that repairs will be minimal; I'd be optimistic about the time. A week, perhaps." She looked up at me. "We're in the primary Terran Cluster, correct? Only one moon?"

"Uh ... yeah. One moon."

She nodded. "One month at most, then. If disorientation lasts longer than that, contact me."

"Will there be any pain?" Tommy asked.

"Usually there is. The human body doesn't surrender its birth-form without protest. But since brain tissue has no pain receptors, your mother should be fine."

She finished off the donut and waved us to silence. "No more questions now. I need to concentrate."

Tommy and I watched her fleshcraft. Or more accurately, we stared at a man in an old woman's body while she leaned over our sleeping mother and nothing visible happened. The Potter spread her fingers over Mom's face and skull, lowered her (his?) head until their foreheads nearly touched, then closed her eyes and seemed to go into a trance. Periodically she would awaken from it long enough to get another donut, study Mom as she ate it, then return to her trance. Eight donuts in all. It was a long time to wait for something to happen. At one point I saw Tommy take out his phone and text somebody. Later I took paper from the nearby desk and started sketching the shapechanging castle that I'd seen through the reaper, angling my work so that even if the Potter looked in my direction she wouldn't see it. But the building defied my best attempts to capture it on paper; it was as if it existed only in the world of imagination and couldn't be translated into materials as mundane as pencil and paper. After several tries I gave up, closed the drawing pad, and waited in silence.

Finally the Potter drew back from the table. My mother was beginning to stir now, moving her head from side to side, whispering things that didn't sound like English. I felt a knot form in my stomach. What if this process skewed her brain so badly that she appeared even sicker than before? My aunt and uncle would take her to a hospital for testing, and God alone knew what would come of that. Would tests of her newly restored brain match the ones from before this operation? What would the doctors make of it if they didn't?

Suddenly her eyes opened. I held my breath as she stared at the ceiling for several seconds, then slowly looked around the room. Her eyes were wide. "The colors . . ." she whispered. "So different."

The Potter helped her to a sitting position on the table. Mom seemed very weak, but that might just have been from the drugged tea. "Tell me what you see."

"The colors . . . look brighter. Everything. Brighter. Like I'd been seeing the world through a grey veil before, but didn't know it. Now suddenly it's gone." She laughed softly, a sound of wonder and delight. "My God, I don't know the right words to describe it."

"I understand what you mean," the Potter said softy.

Mom turned to me then, and I went to her and held her, and this time I let the tears come. So did Tommy, I think. He hid his face so we wouldn't see them, but I saw his shoulders tremble.

Finally we disentangled from the three-way hug. Mom looked at the Potter. "Thank you," she whispered. "Whatever you did, it feels like something is better. Thank you so much."

The elderly female face smiled sweetly. "I'm glad to be able to help."

Mom slid her feet down to the floor, tested her weight on them, then pushed herself away from the table. "Even the pressure on my feet feels different," she whispered. "More . . . more detailed."

"The spiritual channels within you are fully open," the Potter said, in her best New Age voice. "Your qi is flowing freely again, and all your senses are coming back to life. It's part of the natural healing process."

Mom looked around the room. "Where are Rose and Julian?"

"In the kitchen, I believe. I asked them to give us privacy. They've been most patient."

Tears glimmering in her eyes, Mom hugged us both

again, then headed off to find the rest of the family. We watched as she walked down the hall, staring at every piece of furniture she passed as though seeing its color for the first time. Soon she was out of sight.

"Was that a normal response?" Tommy whispered.

"Not uncommon. It's a good sign." The Potter looked at her watch, then at me. "We'll give your family some time to absorb the news and express their gratitude, then you and I should retire to somewhere more private for your own alteration. You won't want to be seen right afterward."

I had been so focused on Mom, it took me a moment to realize what she was referring to: my own scent change. "We can use my room," I said. I felt a bit queasy that someone was about to reshape my body, no matter how minimal that change might be.

A few minutes later Rose and Julian and Mom joined us, and the atmosphere was downright festive. Everyone told the Potter how grateful they were for her help, and Julian tried to offer her payment for her services, but she refused, saying that she'd done it as a favor to Miriam Seyer, not to worry about it. So Rose said that if there was ever anything they could do for her, ever, she had but to ask, and Mom said that went double for her. The Potter accepted their gratitude in a friendly old-woman way, and once more I was struck by the ease with which she switched roles depending on circumstances. Finally she said that Tommy and I had asked about her crystal work, and if it was okay with everyone she'd like to go off with us and teach us some things about the energies of semi-precious stones. And of course it was okay, though Rose did make me promise to share the information with her later.

There was a tremor of fear in my stomach as we headed up the stairs to my room, adult laughter fading behind us. But you gotta do what you gotta do.

||||||||||||

My transformation hurt. A lot. When it was finally done
I felt like I'd spent a day on the beach without sunblock,
then rubbed sandpaper into my skin until it was raw,
then taken a bath in lemon juice. And I looked like a
boiled lobster.

But if this was what it took to get my body to exude a
new cocktail of oils and gasses, so that my scent was no
longer recognizable to the Hunters who'd smelled me in
the past, it was worth every minute of the five-donut operation.

Tommy perched by my side during all of it, clearly
wanting to be helpful but not knowing how. At one
point when I was struggling not to cry out in pain he reminded me of the *Mythbusters* episode where they
demonstrated that yelling profanities improved pain
tolerance. The information didn't do me much good—I
couldn't yell anything without my whole family bursting
in to see what was wrong—but it got the Potter's attention, and when she was done turning me into a lobster
she asked Tommy to describe the experiment in detail.
Apparently no one on Terra Prime had ever thought to
ask whether screaming "oh, fuck!" at the top of your
lungs would really make something hurt less. Maybe
you needed an American mindset to come up with that.

The look on Tommy's face during that conversation
was something to see. For a few precious minutes he
wasn't a little kid, or a silent spectator, or even an ignorant Colonnan. He had knowledge that this powerful
alien Fleshcrafter wanted, and she respected him for it.
By the end of the conversation he was glowing so
brightly from pride that you could have used him to
light a room.

I understood just how he felt.

The Potter remained with us until the worst of my

pain had faded then declared the operation a success. As she packed up her crystals and river stones, she told me my unnatural redness should fade within the hour, and recommended I avoid the rest of the family until I looked more normal. She also told me to wash all my clothing and my bedding, and throw out any garments that weren't washable, as they still had my old scent on them. I hadn't thought about that.

I could travel on Terra Prime now, I realized—or any world—and the Hunters who'd tracked me before wouldn't recognize my scent trail. That was a heady concept. The Potter gave me a card with her contact information on it, and told me to get in touch with her if I had any concerns about her work. The name on the card was *Reginald Harrington III, Master of the Guild of Potters,* and the contact point was an office of the Guild of Greys. My hand trembled slightly as I noted that. Yeah, I understood that interworld mail deliveries normally went through the Greys, but servants of the Shadows were the last people I wanted to have knowledge of my business. At least I had the alias that Seyer had given me, so I wouldn't have to give them my real name.

It seemed like all our business was done, but as she turned to leave Tommy suddenly asked her, "What's with the donuts?"

We both turned to look at him—the Potter startled, me aghast.

"You've eaten fourteen of them since you got here," he pressed. "Not like I'm counting or anything. Jesse obviously knew you were going to do that, since she's the one who asked Aunt Rose to get them. So.... are you like, hypoglycemic? Or is it something more interesting than that?"

I was glad that my skin was already red so the Potter wouldn't see me blush. "Tommy, please, don't be rude—"

But she seemed more amused than insulted and

waved off my concern. "It's quite all right." To Tommy she said, "Aside from the energy expenditure required by fleshcrafting—which is considerable—our Gift has certain limits. I can force my flesh to take any shape I please, but I can't create flesh where none exists."

"So you can change your body shape, but not your mass."

"Correct."

"So if you wanted to make your body bigger than it is right now, you'd have to put on weight like a normal person first. Right?" His face had taken on the same solemn expression as when he was reviewing a new game system. I guess, to his mind, he was doing just that.

She smiled. "Precisely."

"So how much weight will you have to put on to go back to your regular shape? The male one, I mean."

She looked down at her stocky form and chuckled. "The bodies are roughly commensurate in mass. Deliberately so."

I suddenly remembered how small the Guildmaster's body had been, independent of his extra arms. And many of the Potters in his grand hall had likewise been slender of build. The girl with the wings had been downright tiny. All of that made perfect sense, if a Potter who wanted to create extra appendages had to reassign existing flesh to do so.

Leave it to my little brother to connect that to their chocolate fetish.

Finally Tommy ran out of questions, and the Potter was allowed to leave. With a weary sigh I fell back on the bed, so tired in body and soul that I felt like I was bleeding into the mattress. Which was a good thing. Any sensation other than pain was a good thing.

For a moment I lay there with my eyes closed, enjoying the silence.

The total silence.

Without the sound of footsteps leaving my room.

I cracked open one eye. Tommy was standing by the bed looking down at me. His expression was solemn.

"What's up?" I asked.

He shook his head and made a tsk-tsk noise.

I opened my other eye. "What? Is something wrong? What is it?"

A spark of amusement glittered in his eyes. "You didn't tell me there was a junk food Gift."

I picked up a pillow and threw it at him. It felt good. Normal, even. I was home.

For now.

28

MORGANA WAS IN HER STUDY when her organizer chimed, alerting her to an incoming call. Taking out the appropriate harmonie, she placed it in the holder on her desk and activated it. The image that took shape before her was of a woman wearing a mask that was half human and half bestial. Morgana nodded a greeting. "Well met on a hot summer day, Lady Fleshcrafter."

"I prefer cool summer nights," the woman responded.

Morgana nodded her acceptance of the coded greeting. One could never be too careful with Fleshcrafters, as any skilled member of that Guild could sculpt his or her flesh to look like any other. Not to mention the caller was wearing her consortium mask, which could transform anyone. An identity check was the first order of business in any such conversation. "You have news for me?"

"You told me to let you know if the Colonnan girl showed up."

A delicate eyebrow lifted slightly. "She approached you?"

"She came to barter information with His Grace. She was spoken for by one whose word he valued, so she was granted an audience."

Morgana's eyebrow rose slightly. "The Green Man?"

"Indeed."

That one is playing a dangerous game, Morgana mused. *I may need to stage another attack on him soon, to remind him of his duty.* "And the information she offered to His Grace?"

"That's Guild business, and it doesn't pertain to the favor you asked of me so, with respect, I would prefer not to discuss it."

"As you wish." Normally the Fleshcrafter wasn't so evasive, which suggested that the information Jessica brought them had been unusually sensitive. Something Morgana would have to look into. "I trust you were diplomatic in turning her down?"

"On the contrary. His Grace approved her petition. A Master Fleshcrafter has been assigned to help her."

Morgana's eyes narrowed. "I asked you to keep her from closing a deal with your people." There was an edge to her voice now, razor-sharp. "Are you telling me you failed?"

"Alexander may value my counsel, but I can't give him orders. Least of all with no explanation. The girl arranged to fulfill an existing commission, for which he'd already promised payment. If I'd tried to convince him not to honor his own contract, he would surely have questioned my motives. Something that would not be good for either of us." A pause. The sculpted mask was impassive, but something about the eyes made Morgana think she was smiling. "I do believe she outplayed you, Alia."

"Apparently so," Morgana muttered.

"Is that going to be a problem?"

She tapped her fingers on the table, a drumbeat of irritation. "I would have preferred to control the exchange. I prefer to control everything around me, you know that. But if she's strong-willed enough to fight for independence, and clever enough to earn it ... well, we'll just have to see where that path leads her."

"You have big plans for her."

"That's hardly a secret."

"Is she part of the experiment you've been hinting about?"

"That part *is* a secret." Morgana chuckled softly. "Have patience, Lady Fleshcrafter. All will be revealed in its proper time."

There was nothing more for them to discuss, so the masked Potter took her leave and deactivated the connection. As her image faded, the Seer leaned back in her chair. A cold smile spread across her face.

Well played, my daughter. Keep this up and you may yet survive what lies ahead of you.

EPILOGUE

CANDLES BURNED ALL ALONG the periphery of the ritual chamber in the Well of Souls, their flames reflected in the polished black stone with such perfection that it was impossible to tell how many there were. Maybe a dozen, maybe a hundred, maybe a thousand. The Shadowlords who filled the room stood silent, and even the ghosts who attended them were unusually still. Tonight's business was somber even by the standards of the undead.

The door to the chamber opened, and the Guildmaster entered followed by a lanky Shadowlord named Caleb Aster. In Aster's hands was a golden box, its surface carved with the images of tormented souls. Reflected candlelight sparked along the edges of the figures as he walked, lending them an illusion of movement.

The Shadowlords gave way before them, forming a

circle three deep around the altar in the center of the room. There were more chains on the altar than usual, and the new ones were padded in leather. Ancient leather, stained with ancient blood. The Guildmaster took up position on the far side of the table, Aster facing him.

"Banish the dead," Virilian commanded.

Whispers filled the room as each Shadowlord present banished the spirits that attended him. Soon only soul shards remained, mindless ghost-fragments that lacked the ability to comprehend such orders. One of the Shadowlords picked up a candle and performed the ritual that would banish those as well, sketching out patterns with the flame. A brief afterimage of each pattern hung in the air for a few seconds before being swallowed by darkness; by the time the last one faded the soul shards were gone.

Virilian parted his robe and let it fall to the ground. Now he wore only a sleeveless linen shirt with ties down the front, and a pair of close-fitting breeches. As a Shadowlord came forward to gather up the robe, Virilian lay down upon the altar, placing his arms and legs into the positions indicated by the waiting shackles. His flesh was as pale as a corpse's, and the indigo blood that coursed visibly just beneath his skin looked more like embalming fluid than a life-giving substance.

Two Shadowlords stepped forward and began to fasten the chains across his body, until every limb was fixed in place, every joint immobilized. The chains were tight, and the leather coverings cut deeply into the pale skin. Movement was all but impossible.

When that was done, Shadowlord Aster took up position by the side of the table. He held the golden box out, over Virilian's heart, presenting it to him. "Augustus Virilian, Master Shadowlord, Guildmaster of Shadows. Do you come here tonight of your own free will?"

"I do," Virilian said.

"Is it your desire to Commune with the soul of a departed Shadowlord?"

"It is."

"Do you acknowledge and accept that if this process fails, the cost will be your true death? That if you cannot make peace with the soul you have chosen to subsume, and all the souls that reside within it, you will not be allowed to leave this chamber alive?"

"I acknowledge and accept it," Virilian said.

"Are you prepared to renounce your worldly ties, human and material, so that there will be nothing to distract you from this union? So that you enter into Communion as an infant enters the world, without title, honor, or obligations?"

"I hereby relinquish my title of Guildmaster and all the duties and honors that go with it. Let the Guild recognize Shadowlord Caleb Aster as its leader, until such time as I am restored to my rank by his word."

A second Shadowlord stepped forward to take the box from Aster, and he held it open for him as the new Guildmaster reached inside and removed a small golden object. Slowly, reverently, he raised it up so that all could see it. The glowing fetter throbbed in his hands like a living thing, and the power that emanated from it filled the room with light, eclipsing the candle flames.

"Behold the essence of Gunther the Black, who ordered the Cleansing of Terra Lorche. Behold the essence of Roland of Acre, who commanded the souls of fallen Crusaders. Behold the essence of Farbjodir, who banished the dead of Lindesfarne. Behold the essence of Shekarchiyandar, he who was called the Lord of Hunters, who slaughtered Dreamwalkers on a thousand worlds, and brought us victory against their kind."

He looked down at Virilian. "These are the souls of warriors, hunters, and destroyers. Their union is dark, even by our standards, and more than one Shadowlord has fallen to madness after Communing with this fetter." He paused. "Is this the union you seek?"

"It is."

"The risk of failure is high. The cost of failure is death. I ask you again: Is this the Communion you seek?"

"It is."

Aster held the fetter over Virilian's heart and addressed the assembly. "Witness, Shadows, that this man seeks Communion of his own free will, naming the fetter of his choice. By my rank as Guildmaster of the Shadows, I hereby grant his petition." He looked at Virilian. "Make ready."

An assistant reached forward and untied the front of Virilian's shirt, spreading it open to bare his chest. Softly changing incantations, Aster lowered the fetter slowly toward Virilian's chest, paused, and then touched it to the flesh above his heart. Virilian shut his eyes for a moment, willing it to activate—and then screamed, more like the wailing of a tormented ghost than a living man. It echoed from the cold stone walls until the whole chamber was filled with it, deafening all who heard it. Virilian's body began to buck against its bonds, struggling wildly to break free, but the iron-and-leather shackles were too strong. The straps cut into his flesh as he strained against them, layering fresh blood over the old, and spasms coursed up and down his limbs, his hands and feet clenching spastically as his body writhed in its bondage. His fingers dug into the stone table so hard that his fingernails split, smearing blood on the table, and he started to moan strange words in an unknown language, biting his tongue after each syllable, until it, too, bled.

The Shadowlords watched in silence.

The unknown words became language, garbled

fragments of different languages cascading from the bleeding tongue in rapid succession, with no clear pattern or purpose. Latin, French, Arabic, Old English, Ancient Norse: the sounds overlapped, producing a torrent of sound whose meaning—if any—was indecipherable.

The Shadowlords watched in silence.

Finally the terrible spasms began to subside. One by one Virilian's arms and legs went limp, as if the muscles within them had dissolved. Slowly his eyes fell shut, and he lay motionless, like one who was truly dead.

The Shadowlords watched in silence.

"Who are you?" The Guildmaster demanded.

For a moment there was no response. Then Virilian's eyes slowly opened. "I am Master Augustus Virilian, former leader of the Guild of Shadows. And I am host to the souls of Gunther, Roland, Farbjodir and Shekarchiyandar, and all the other souls that were in their keeping."

The new Guildmaster studied him for a moment, then finally nodded his approval and placed the fetter back in its box. "I hereby return to you the title that you bestowed upon me, and all the duties and honors of that rank." He nodded to the Shadows who had bound Virilian. "Release the Guildmaster."

One by one they removed the straps, setting him free. He lay still for a minute, gathering his strength, then rose to a sitting position. His body was marked with welts from the leather straps, and blood streaked his flesh and clothing. Brushing aside any offer of assistance, he slid down from the table and stood barefoot on the cold stone floor. The Shadow who had been holding his robe stepped forward and helped him into it. The folds of thick grey fabric hid the blood and injuries of his Communion, restoring him to an aspect of regal dignity.

Guildmaster Augustus Virilian looked around the room. "Allow the dead to return," he commanded.

The ritualist nodded and circled the room once more,

tracing the patterns that would undo their banishment. Spirits began to flow back into the room, their agitated murmurs tainted with fear. Most kept their distance from Virilian.

Raising up his arms, the Guildmaster shut his eyes for a moment, focusing his Gift. Then he cried out, "Come to me, servants of Shekarchiyandar. Your creator walks the earth again, and he has need of you."

A shadow began to shape before him, that was the size and shape of a man, but not a man. It had the aspect of a spirit, but it was not a spirit. Ribbons of emptiness coiled about it like serpents, momentarily obscuring the terrifying Void that was its very core. When the manifestation was complete, a second shadow began to take shape beside it. And then a third. Seven appeared in all, and the force of their combined presence was so compelling that some of the Shadowlords instinctively backed away, sensing in these wraiths something darker than they could ever hope to control.

"Welcome, my reapers." Shekarchiyandar smiled coldly. "We have work to do."

Coming soon from DAW,
the thrilling conclusion to
The Dreamwalker Chronicles:

DREAMWEAVER

Read on for a special preview.

ON THE WORLD THAT HAS NO NAME.

Atop a mountain of black stone.

The skeleton waits.

Its bones are granite and mortar, scoured clean by the wind and sun. Its ribs are tall, vaulted windows, their glass long gone, their peaked arches crumbling. Amidst the ruins a single narrow tower stands, nearly intact, rising from the black earth as if the arm of some long-buried creature is struggling to reach the sun. Its turrets are jagged and broken, and where there are breaches in the walls one can see that the interior is streaked with soot from an ancient fire.

Surrounding the ruins is a field of tall crimson grass, and beyond that a forest of black thorn trees, their branches so intertwined that it is impossible to tell where one tree ends and the next begins. There are animals present: one can hear predators moving through the grass in search of prey, and catch a glimpse of birds amidst the tangled branches, dodging thorns as long as a man's hand. But there is little life on the mountain itself. A few patches of moss cling to the base of the broken walls. A single foolhardy vine has managed to climb halfway up the tower. The leaves of the latter stir in the breeze, giving the tower the illusion of breath. As if the ancient fortress that once stood here is just asleep, rather than dead.

A shadow passes in front of the sun.

A three-headed dog looks up from its hiding place in the tall grass, suddenly alert. A lizard with the wings of a bat crawls out upon a thorned branch so it can see better. A cluster of rats with their tails knotted together peers out from a burrow, its hundred eyes moving in unison as it nervously scans the sky.

The shadow is growing larger now, though there are no clouds in the sky to explain its existence. The leaves of the ivy curl in upon themselves, as if trying to draw away from it. The sky surrounding the shadow begins to lose its color, fading from bright blue to a more muted shade.

One of the dog's three heads whimpers.

The shadow begins to coalesce over the tower, taking on the shape of a man. Its body is not made of flesh, but a darkness so absolute that all light and heat from the surrounding landscape are sucked into it. The sky surrounding it turns grey. The leaves of the ivy begin to fall. Frost forms along the ancient turrets.

The winged lizard hisses in terror and disappears into the hollow of a tree.

The rats dart back into their burrow, tripping over each other in their flight.

Another shadow is beginning to form, identical to the first. It is followed by another. Seven wraiths appear in all, their substance darker than midnight, and the tower grows dim as they circle it restlessly, as if searching for something. Then, suddenly, the first one begins to howl. It is a cry of pure anguish—unbearable fury—and one by one the other shadow wraiths join in. The unnatural sound resonates across the landscape, and it awakens memories of loss in all who hear it. The three-headed dog remembers the mournful night its mate was killed. The lizard relives that terrible day when it returned to its nest to find that its eggs had been devoured. The king rat recalls what it was like to run free in the fields, alone and unencumbered, and whimpers.

And then, as suddenly as it began, the unnatural howling ceases. The shadows circle a few minutes longer in silence, then begin to dissipate. One after another they slowly fade into the greyness of the sky, until they can no longer be seen. The first to arrive is the last to leave.

Not until the last one is completely gone does color return to the world.

C.S. Friedman
The Best in Science Fiction

THIS ALIEN SHORE   978-0-88677-799-9
A *New York Times* Notable Book of the Year
"Breathlessly plotted, emotionally savvy. A potent
metaphor for the toleration of diversity."
—*The New York Times*

THE MADNESS SEASON   978-0-88677-444-8
"Exceptionally imaginative and compelling."
—*Publishers Weekly*

IN CONQUEST BORN   978-0-7564-0043-9
"Space opera in the best sense: high stakes adventure
with a strong focus on ideas, and characters an
intelligent reader can care about."—*Newsday*

THE WILDING   978-0-7564-0202-6
The long-awaited follow-up to *In Conquest Born*.

To Order Call: 1-800-788-6262
www.dawbooks.com

DAW 17

C.S. Friedman
The Coldfire Trilogy

"A feast for those who like their fantasies dark, and as
emotionally heady as a rich red wine." —*Locus*

Centuries after being stranded on the planet Erna,
humans have achieved an uneasy stalemate with the
fae, a terrifying natural force with the power to prey
upon people's minds. Damien Vryce, the warrior
priest, and Gerald Tarrant, the undead sorcerer must
join together in an uneasy alliance confront a power
that threatens the very essence of the human spirit, in
a battle which could cost them not only their lives, but
the soul of all mankind.

BLACK SUN RISING   978-0-88677-527-8
WHEN TRUE NIGHT FALLS 978-0-88677-615-2
CROWN OF SHADOWS   978-0-88677-717-3

To Order Call: 1-800-788-6262
www.dawbooks.com

C.S. Friedman
The *Magister* Trilogy

"Powerful, intricate plotting and gripping characters
distinguish a book in which ethical dilemmas
are essential and engrossing."
—*Booklist*

"Imaginative, deftly plotted fantasy...
Readers will eagerly await the next installment."
—*Publishers Weekly*

FEAST OF SOULS
978-0-7564-0463-5

WINGS OF WRATH
978-0-7564-0594-6

LEGACY OF KINGS
978-0-7564-0748-3

To Order Call: 1-800-788-6262
www.dawbooks.com

DAW 121